THE TALON & THE BLADE

GRACE BLOODS BOOK THREE

JASMINE SILVERA

NO
INSIDE
VOICE

First publication date April 2019

Published by No Inside Voice LLC, Seattle, WA 2018

ISBN: 978-0-9976582-4-8

Cover design by Damonza

Editing Victory Editing

Book Design by No Inside Voice

To Oliver
I'm your huckleberry, Schnuckiputzi

CHAPTER ONE

Having spent the past two hundred years protecting a necromancer named for the angel of death from demons and rivals, little surprised Gregor Schwarz. When the sound of the doorbell interrupted his perusal of the small armory behind his rollaway bookshelf, he decided that the novelty of surprise was overrated.

He kept a residence in Malá Strana south of Prague Castle, close enough to respond swiftly to a summons. The flat, in the narrow building above the winding streets, earned its designation as a penthouse merely by being on the top floor. Aside from impressive views of the red-tiled roofs and the Vltava River, it was an austere clean slate. Unlike his predecessor, Lysippe, he felt no need to fill an entire building with a thousand years of *Schnickschnack* collected while following said necromancer around the world. The building's other residents never saw him coming or going—a cleverly worded geas made sure of that—aware only that a businessman who kept odd hours and traveled often occupied the top floor. The intrusion would not be a neighbor then.

The rest of the Aegis, the necromancer Azrael's oath-bound warriors, would have called first, and even they knew not to bother him when he was packing for an assignment.

The supernatural blade that had been imbedded in his spine in exchange for his soul didn't solidify as it would have if facing a threat.

Still, he palmed his favorite Glock, slid the magazine home, and slipped it into the holster over his pressed dress shirt.

"Enter." With his verbal permission, the wards that reinforced the door lock released.

Isela Vogel rounded the corner, the angle of her chin proud and casually imperious as only a professional dancer could be. Six months ago that's all she had been—a name and a career he followed at a distance, the same as all the others who preceded her.

Now, with her being Azrael's consort, Gregor was doomed to have her as both charge and mistress.

If not for a few fading bruises, he wouldn't have thought her the same woman he'd faced off against in the arena a few hours ago. She'd been in fitted black combat gear then, rather than the baggy cashmere sweater over leggings and ankle boots she wore now, no doubt from a high-end boutique. She still dressed the part of her former career, at least. The simple elegance implied expense, making her seem untouchable and aloof. Though when she'd died helping Azrael, Gregor had seen firsthand how fragile she was. Something stronger than vows bound her to Azrael. And her willingness to sacrifice herself for it had made her more than human. Even resurrected as the chosen vessel of a god, her immortality was fresh enough to leave her vulnerable.

Gregor had almost convinced himself that his concern for Azrael was why he trained her so hard, bent on turning the discipline and muscle memory of dance into a weapon. Losing her once had shattered Azrael. Gregor didn't care to think about the effect on himself.

In the arena she had been more killer than dancer—a blade in each fist and a grin turned into rictus by the blood in her teeth and splatters of red across her cheek. The blood in her mouth was her own. But the spray on her face and blade had come from his jugular. Her training was coming along well.

He fought the urge to touch the now nonexistent mark on his neck. Lysippe would take over in his absence. She could be in no better hands than a 1,500-year-old warrior descended from Amazons.

He needed to focus on his assignment. He knew only that the North American necromancer, having once warned Azrael of an attack, had called in his favor. On obliging, Azrael wanted Gregor to determine the possibility for a more stable accord between them. The responsibility revealed Azrael's confidence in him, and Gregor couldn't afford this distraction. What was she doing *here*?

"Consort." Gregor sketched a bow.

He'd made it clear he wanted nothing to do with her outside the training ring. This had been his sanctuary. Now that she had been in it, he'd have to find another apartment. He was going to miss this view.

Isela paused in the doorway. Tiny flecks of gold shone in her ashen eyes today. He did his best to ignore the way her gaze made the hair on the back of his neck rise.

He should offer her a drink or a place to sit. He didn't. Instead of taking the hint, she roamed the room, clasping her hands behind her back but staring at everything.

He turned back to his armory, considering taking the whole lot of it. It might be overkill, but he liked to be prepared. He had no idea what he would find, but based on his last trip to the Americas, he should count on more surprises. A lot could change in two hundred years, he reminded himself, and Los Angeles was thousands of miles from the ruins of the Eastern Seaboard. Bitterness and relief mingled at the thought that he would not be confronted with his past. At least no more so than by the woman standing in his living room.

A slow anxiety built in him as the soft click of her heels on the floor grew closer. His hands slowed, picking his weapons of choice and sliding them into their assigned places in his travel bag.

She stopped a few feet away. "Lysippe said you like to focus before a mission. Your meditation, she said."

Lysippe talked far too much. Of course, he had the sinking

suspicion that the Amazon was delighted to have another woman in Azrael's inner circle. There had been lovers, but Azrael was discreet and never retained one woman for too long. He'd never taken a consort before Isela.

The two women had taken to having movie nights—"girl time," Isela called it. Consort bonds were rare, but Gregor was certain there should be more formality involved. Particularly with Ito who, as Azrael's head of intelligence, knew far too much about everything that happened in Azrael's retinue.

The Amazon wasn't the only one in Azrael's Aegis to allow their responsibility to protect her grow into something more familiar. Much like her group of cohorts from the Praha Dance Academy, Isela drew people and formed bonds that had nothing to do with vows or blood. Maybe it was the witch in her, or the wolf—after all, both were pack animals. As the leader of Azrael's Aegis, Gregor could stop all this fraternizing. She was a responsibility, no more. He would not allow more.

"Dory called you an ascetic," she mused, taking in the sparse furnishings. "He wasn't wrong."

Dory also talked too much. Of course, Dory was now bound to her, as he and Lysippe were to Azrael. There was nothing she could ask that he would not answer. The start of her own Aegis, on the nascence of her immortality. One more reason Gregor's concern for her training was becoming more obsessive than functional. Perhaps time away would do him good, give him a chance to sort out this mess he was in and gain some distance.

Testing the suspicion that she had been making specific inquiries about him, he asked after the most tight-lipped of Azrael's Aegis. "What did Aleifr say?"

"That you can be a right asshole when you want to be," she chirped. "But Lysippe's still the only one who can beat you in a fight. Pretty amazing, what with you being the youngest member of Azrael's Aegis."

That did it. The six-and-a-half-foot-tall Viking who rarely expressed himself beyond grunts and the odd raised eyebrow was now doling out whole sentences. Gregor was going to have a word with all of them about how to conduct themselves around the consort.

"I also heard you're headed to California." She smiled. "Azrael told me that."

His teeth snugged together so he wouldn't be tempted to reveal his opinion of Azrael's current mental state. Gregor had witnessed the importance of strategy and calculation for surviving in a world full of powerful immortals. Even the consort bond was considered a more tactical alliance than an entanglement of this kind. Gregor feared this thing between Azrael and Isela was the first indication of a creeping madness. She was a twenty-nine-year-old, recently mortal human. Her foolish need to form connections and willingness to sacrifice herself for them was going to get them all killed.

He secured his armory bag and added it to the garment bag by the door. He needed his weekender. If he was lucky, he would be gone a week or less. But in any case, he'd gotten packing light down to a science. He could make do for a month or more if required. He almost swore when he realized he'd left the bag in the bedroom and retrieving it meant passing close to her. She'd showered after their match, and a clean, damp smell drifted from her braided hair. He wondered if he would ever stop seeing her as delicate, childlike, vulnerable.

She called after him. "I have a favor to ask."

He walked faster.

"Won't you just... stop... for a minute," she said on his way back, "and look at me."

He paused, his eyes drawn up obediently.

She realized with horror what she'd done and stepped back. "I forgot you're compelled."

"I accepted my vow, Consort."

She shook her head, her mouth twisting down. Her eyes flickered from gray to gold and back again—a warning sign of the god power within her. The color still fluctuated with her mood until she regained control. Another liability of emotion.

"You never address me by my name," she said, voice tight. "Just a title. Dancer. Consort."

"Should I call you little bird, then?"

Little bird. The shock of recognition still stung him. He called her by her title so that he never forgot. Slipping up just once would be catastrophic. Already these few moments in her presence made him feel anxious and out of breath. He wanted to punch something.

Judging by the way the lights flickered as her eyes went gold again, the feeling was mutual. Isela took a deep breath and regained control. Then she surprised him. Again.

"I wanted to thank you." Earthy gray eyes met his even as gold shot through the irises. "The night after the crash, when Tariq and I were ambushed, it was your voice I heard in the fighting. Everything you've taught me saved my life. It made me capable of holding my own. I thought you were trying to break me down. But you made me stronger."

Gregor exhaled, wanting to look anywhere but into the witch eyes boring into him. The way the gold and silver mixed made them almost hazel. She turned to face the window again. The regality of her bearing, the long line of her nose. Would he ever stop searching for the echo of something familiar in her?

"It was the responsibility I was given." He started for the kitchen, needing to put distance between them. Once he'd reached it, he found nothing to distract him. Not a dish out of place, not a spoon in the sink.

He had been careful to be circumspect. Keep them all safe, keep them at a distance. Not this. Never this. Dryness scored his throat. He contemplated a glass of water, but that would mean he'd have to offer her one. Have to fill it and bear proximity again to bring it to her. Better his tongue dry up and fall out of his mouth. Pain was nothing new. Survival in this world made enduring it necessary.

"It's more than that."

He paused.

"All this time I thought you hated me for being Azrael's weakness, for the way he's willing to protect me even if I'm not worthy of it… But that's not it, is it?"

He registered the flinch in her gaze at the coldness in his. He would never be her confidant. Could never hope that in the light of the truth she would feel anything for him but resentment.

He found his tongue and made a guess as to why she had come to him, unannounced and alone. "You require something of me, Consort?"

She sighed and watched pigeons rise from the cobblestone street to settle in the eaves of a neighboring building. Aha, so this was the crux of it. She wanted him to do something for her. Something she couldn't ask Dory. Perhaps murder a former lover who wanted to use her proximity to Azrael to curry some favor. Or the journalist who kept requesting a follow-up interview. He checked his watch. His flight wasn't until six. He could probably squeeze something in.

"Shoes," she announced. "For my brothers and the kids. Converse, to be exact. I'll provide a list of sizes and colors."

He stopped himself from asking why she didn't just use her considerable pull as the consort of a necromancer to get one pair in every size and every color shipped to her. Cost was no issue. No, she wanted *him* to get them for her.

The gleam of satisfied amusement in her eyes gave it away— this was payback. One he'd earned. He'd only made it worse by being taciturn. Now she *was* enjoying it.

He shrugged on his jacket, head bowed. "From your pen to my hand."

"You're not going to argue?"

"Would it do any good?"

"No, but—"

His phone chimed.

"Then I'll spare myself the trouble," he finished, searching the nearby surfaces for the familiar shape.

She glared at him, arms folded over her chest. But she wasn't angry. Worse. She was smiling at him.

"Where is that infernal device?" He patted his pockets as it chimed again.

He hunted around the apartment. A quick search covered the bedroom, bath, and kitchen in less than a minute.

"I don't get you, Gregor," she said. "But I like you."

For a moment he couldn't draw a breath. Like him? If she knew the truth, she'd never forgive him. But he didn't need her to like him as he did everything in his power to keep her alive. And it was far too late for forgiveness.

When he turned back, she extended one hand, holding a slim black rectangle. It chimed again. She waggled it at him. After a moment's hesitation he snagged it without touching her and glanced at the screen.

"You're growing on me." An inscrutable expression lit her eyes, matching the amused curve of her mouth. "Like a mold."

He grabbed his duffel. "This has been enlightening, but I'm afraid I have a flight to catch."

Before he could reach his garment bag, she grabbed it and folded it over her arm. "I'll walk you to the garage."

"That isn't—"

But she was already moving toward the door. Swearing under his breath, he caught up in a few steps and held it open. She thanked him with a little grin.

"I suspect, this secret mission of yours aside, we're going to be spending a lot of time together," she mused as they headed toward the elevator. "Might as well try to make the best of it, don't you think?"

The thought froze the blood in his veins. He wasn't sure how he would bear it.

CHAPTER TWO

My name is Ana Gozen, but that is a lie.

The mantra circled her head as the familiar repetition of strike drills flowed with her breath. She moved over the solid, burlap-covered training mat, raised slightly from the bare main floor of the training room. She no longer felt the weight of the blades in her hands any more than she would feel her wrists or her fingers. The air passing over edges that had been honed until they sang registered as if on her own skin. Words lied. The blades could not be manipulated, tainted with emotion, or made soft around the edges by the passage of time. They spoke of her true identity, beyond names and history.

When she'd made her vow, she'd assumed one day memories would fade, no longer digging in the spaces between her ribs. Yet the one she wanted most to forget persisted. Before she could stop herself, it swallowed her whole.

The unadorned walls fell away. The sunlight pouring in from the roofed window faded. The racks of practice weaponry, heavy bags, and dummies became a forest in winter.

In the center, the burned-out homestead still steamed in the fresh snowfall. The bones of a few meager structures darkened as moisture hissed and popped against embers. The muddy yard, churned up by hooves and boots around the bodies facedown in the mud. She paced it end to end, grief rising with each step as her mind re-created the pillaging.

When the thieves had come, the man could have holed up inside the cabin and picked them off with a rifle, or let them raid the stock and the garden and then move on. Instead, perhaps thinking himself the gunslinger his bride had taken him for in those early days, he had gone out to meet them. His body lay where they cut him down, clutching at revolvers that had been ripped from his hands after death.

Even without turning the second body over, she recognized the slight figure in the plain calico dress. Takami, the stolen bride, Ana's charge, and the closest thing she'd ever had to a friend, had been dragged out of the cabin. Even in death she clutched their baby to her chest. Had her cowherd-turned-gunslinger still been alive to watch her pleading for their lives? Did he see the pistol whipped across the delicate bones of her full face? Did he hear the two shots that had silenced her and the child forever?

Ana's last meager meal rose in her throat, forcing a path out of her body and into the mess of blood and slush. Her failure to keep Takami safe stained her with shame. Now the stain stretched over her soul. She spat bile and grief. When she could breathe again, she had one purpose left in this world. Vengeance.

A century later, Ana closed her eyes, waiting for the vertigo of memory to pass and leave her in the present. She pressed the breath through her, focusing her attention on the sensation of its passage in and out of her body, letting it draw her from the void of fury and loss. She'd outlived her vengeance by a hundred years and now walked in a whole other world of power and codes beyond what mortals could understand. When she opened her eyes again, the room came back into focus as she sheathed her blades and came to a ready stance, hands fisted at her sides.

She had the training room to herself these days. The only other time it saw action was when two of the other Aegis members had a score to settle. It was the safest place for an all-out grudge match: powerful wards enforced the walls and floor with extra strength. Their master would not have them tearing down the house in their efforts to kill each other.

Ana was first of Raymond's Aegis—for many years it had been just the two of them. The good old days, she mused. These days, they were four including her. Petr and Mitko came after, and it seemed their vow had included some language about keeping her on her toes, because they were determined to make her life miserable every chance they got. Then several whose names she could not remember because they had not survived long enough to be memorable. Finally a young street fighter from Brazil who defected from the Suramérican necromancer's retinue and had enough sense of self-preservation to stay on her good side. The death of the fifth a decade ago still carved a hollow behind her breastbone if she allowed herself to linger on it.

Busy leading the investigation of the attacks, she'd neglected her usual watch of Petr and Mitko. She made a mental note to be on alert for any of their shenanigans. They had designs on being Raymond's first, though she doubted either smart enough to realize only one of them could serve the post even if it hadn't been taken.

Raymond's summons broke her focus. *The garden.*

On my way. She sheathed her blades, reset her topknot, and left the mat.

The necromancer known as Raymond Nightfeather waited beside a pond surrounded by delicate maples and vibrant green bamboo. It had cost Ana a small fortune to construct and keep green in the dry Southern California hills. But after a century and a half as the first of Raymond's Aegis, it was her fortune to spend.

As a member of the Allegiance that had saved the world from the godswar, Raymond had claimed all of North America, more or less, for his territory. Aside from the few universal rules the Allegiance had established for mortals and god-blooded creatures, he handled what went on inside his borders according to his own sense of time and urgency.

He stood on the small wooden walkway over the water, tossing pebbles of food to the gaping maws of koi surfacing beneath him.

The six oldest, in shades of scarlet, yellow gold, emerald, and the great multicolored *bekko* she called Grandmother, gave her more pleasure than she would have ever imagined when she released them, small and timid, decades ago. More recently she'd acquired a few of the metallic scaled "ghosts" that most traditional collectors didn't recognize as true *nishikogoi* because their blood was not pure. Fuck tradition.

She stopped on the bridge beside Raymond, waiting in silence for longer than most mortals would have managed without fidgeting. She'd waited for this summons for days. She told herself she could wait a few more moments. In truth, she resented Raymond's delay as much his refusal to tell her why he waited. They had a situation on their hands. One she would be handling if he hadn't called her away from the investigation and kept her leashed at his side. It was her job, after all. Her purpose.

The final insult—he'd sent out for help. And now, this silence.

No lies, he'd promised long ago when she'd taken her vow, *but there will be secrets.*

She'd taken the bargain anyway, traded her soul for almost-immortality, increased speed, strength, and the ability to see what mortals, and even most grace bloods, would not. She thought her sight, the greatest of the gifts he'd given her, would temper his need to keep secrets. She'd been new to bargaining with immortals, and a fool.

"Our guest arrives in two hours." He checked his watch. "I'd like you to be at the airport."

Necromancers held themselves apart, even from one another. It made the Allegiance so damn fragile and was why she feared it would only be a matter of time before it fell.

As little as Ana liked him calling in the favor, she had to admit the necromancer Azrael had been the logical, best choice. Azrael's adopted daughter, Lysippe, the first member of his Aegis, had history with Raymond. Recent history, as these things went. It had been over a century and Ana didn't know how she felt about seeing the Amazon. If Azrael saw the request for help as an opportunity to gain intel on Raymond's territory, sending a woman who knew him better than most would be wise.

She tested the name out loud. "Lysippe?"

The wind stirred around them, shaking the dark leaves on the trees. "I did not ask."

Ana's fist closed and she kept her eyes on the swirling fish to keep herself from screaming. *He didn't ask.*

She was going straight back to the training room after this.

The edge of Raymond's mouth rose. "Choose to take it as a compliment, Ana. Whomever he sends, I trust you will be able to handle it and the task. Have a little faith."

Faith, she wanted to spit out. Faith was for fools and innocents. And she was neither.

Azrael had the largest Aegis in the Allegiance—Ana hadn't even begun to gather the proper intel on them all. Besides Lysippe, only one other had a reputation that preceded him—the Black Blade of Azrael.

She'd seen Gregor Schwarz in Azrael's great hall. A great lean shadow of man, severe as a honed edge without an ounce of expression on his pale face. She'd hardly believed him capable of the ruthlessness rumored to have been committed at his hands in Azrael's name. And then those eyes had swept her, and the hollow iciness had raised the hairs on her arms.

No way Azrael would part with his favored enforcer to fulfill a debt to Raymond. After all, he faced challenges from all sides of the Allegiance. Having the most powerful of his progeny ascend to take over the Suramérican territory gave him distant relief. There were still six other necromancers, the most powerful in the world, keeping a close eye on him, his god-touched consort, and his unorthodox allies. Azrael could send someone expendable if he wanted to fulfill his debt to Raymond without risk to himself.

That's what she needed: someone who would get in her way and whom she would have to keep alive so that the necromancers could continue to play their delicate game of honor and alliances. Why couldn't Raymond leave this to her?

She made a mental note to put her undead analyst on

collecting as much information about the rest of Azrael's Aegis as was possible in the next two hours.

"He'll send Lysippe," Raymond said. His mouth pulled sideways. "She knows me, after all. He'll think it gives her an advantage."

At least the Amazon would be a known entity. She could handle herself if it came to a fight, and they had been friends, or at least comrades, before the mess with Raymond.

She hoped for Lysippe's sake she'd learned her lesson. Emotional connection was a human failing, one their kind would be wise to shed as necromancers did, as quickly as possible.

CHAPTER THREE

"California, here I come." Gregor adjusted his sunglasses as he stepped off the plane. The sun warmed his shoulders through the dark suit.

In the distance, the main terminals for the international airport where most arrivals and departures were conducted shimmered in waves off the pavement. Perfectly spaced rows of palm trees marked the high fencing around buildings, and armed guards patrolled in the open. More than a few of them were warded, and he counted several minor necromancers among the patrols.

But he wasn't the average commercial passenger. There would be no customs or immigration for him. Come to think of it, forged papers aside, in his travels with Azrael he'd never been issued a passport.

He walked the carpet laid from the base of the charter jet steps to the back door of the waiting limo. The porter moved his bags from the plane's cargo area to the trunk.

The driver held his door. His flat eyes and lack of respiration signaled an undead servant of a necromancer, known on the street as a zombie. This one had been stripped of humanity, leaving little more than an automaton. It didn't even have enough personality left to greet him.

Gregor had expected the limo to be empty and hesitated at the sight of the young Asian woman in artfully torn, loose-fitting jeans, red tennis shoes, and a designer jacket modeled after an old high school letterman. She reclined against the rear-facing seat. The door shut behind him.

Her pale face angled toward him as he settled. Short dark hair swung against her cheeks. Round sunglasses kept her eyes—and gaze—a mystery. Her mouth pursed, full rosy lips shaped like a little bow. Definitely breathing, and he detected the faint pulse of her heartbeat steady at her throat. Within easy reach but not at the ready rested a pair of swords that he recognized by reputation. Not a young woman at all then.

"Mr. Schwarz," she said, a hint of humor in the honey-covered steel of her voice. "This is a surprise. Permit me to greet you in place of my master, who regrets he could not welcome you personally."

He'd spent the flight studying the briefing the head of intelligence had prepared for him. Ana Gozen. The first of Raymond's Aegis, hers was the only consistent face among the North American necromancer's avowed guards over the last hundred or so years. Others appeared and vanished—reports suggested she had killed more than one. The credit for the necromancer's iron grip on the North American territory belonged to the woman known as the Nightfeather's Talons.

Gregor inclined his head. "My apologies. We crossed paths in Prague, but I don't believe we've had the pleasure of an introduction, Ms. Gozen."

The stillness in her body would never be confused with relaxation. He couldn't read her. Not like this. Not without the eyes. The corner of her mouth dimpled, and he wished he could tip those sunglasses toward the edge of her nose without risking his limbs and, most likely, his head.

The pressure between his shoulders increased as the blade began to take physical shape.

Her nails, a sparkling French manicure tipped with black,

danced along the short blade at her side in response. "We expected the Amazon."

"Lysippe was otherwise engaged."

Not that Lysippe hadn't fought to come. But Azrael's sudden flirtation with human emotion included a protective streak. Already chafing at being kept closer than she liked, Lysippe still wasn't speaking to either of them over it. Madness.

He snapped to attention. Did Ana lean toward him? She hadn't moved, but he sensed the sudden engagement in her posture. Losing focus around Ana Gozen would be a mistake. Maybe his last one.

Her lips stretched without showing teeth. "Then Lord Azrael has honored us with the presence of his first."

He leaned back in his seat, letting his smile ease into something more languorous. Us.

Perhaps there was something to the rumor that she was not only the head of Raymond's guard. It would not have been the first time a necromancer took a lover from their Aegis. There could be no betrayal from one who was bound to you for their immortality.

The limo slid out of the airfield and into traffic, picking up speed. The route took them through the eastern edge of the thriving metropolis of downtown Los Angeles. Cities Allegiance necromancers chose for their seats often benefited faster and more from rebuilding after the war.

He hardly recognized it from pictures of the city before the Allegiance had taken over the world and divided it among themselves. The fabled smoggy skies of the old days had been replaced by a robin's-egg blue, thinly glazed with morning clouds. The noise of engines on the highway was replaced by a quiet rush of rubber on pavement and gently whirring electric motors. Like the rest of the Allegiance, Raymond had prohibited the use of fossil fuels for personal transportation. From here it was hard to imagine the ravaging North America had taken during the godswar.

Throughout time, powerful entities often revealed themselves to humans in such a way that they were worshipped and feared as gods. Claiming the bodies of mortals, they mixed with humans and animals, creating all manner of creatures called grace blooded for the power of the gods running through their veins. Necromancers and grace-blooded creatures had lived in the shadows since the dawn of time without revealing their existence.

But mortals weren't content to worship, and learning to communicate with their gods through physical movement led to the godswar. Using dancers to petition the gods, human countries destroyed rival economies, destroyed infrastructure, and brought civilization to the brink of collapse in a matter of weeks.

The eight necromancers emerging from their shadowed existences stopped an apocalypse, but at a steep price—total authority. They left governments standing to administer familiar controls, but the real lines of possession were drawn between the Allegiance, and they settled into their seats and began to restore order.

The images from that time—cites obliterated, forests turned to piles of matchsticks, scorched remains of fleeing humans—were as bad as anything he'd seen done at the hands of a necromancer. Sickened by humanity, Gregor lost any desire to protect it. The mortals had to be put in their place. This was what they did with the power of gods at their disposal. Disgust and rage had fueled him in those days.

Even after decades of rebuilding, parts of the world were barrens created by catastrophic human weapons, godstrikes, or some combination of the two.

"Is it true the East Coast is still in ruins?" Some perverse part of him needed confirmation that returning to the places he remembered would be impossible. *Get it over with and out of your head now. Focus.*

Ana lifted a shoulder. "More or less. Though it's too dangerous to enter some areas even for us. I hear Vanka faced the same."

"Some." Gregor thought of the package Azrael had entrusted him with. "We have more thin places now."

A gift, Azrael had said, something to get Raymond off his guard. *See what it tells you.*

Azrael handed off the warded vial in the secure case. They'd escaped a collapsing mine in disputed territory with a flask full of the liquid in that vial. A liquid only possible due to a place sustaining deep or repeated godstrikes. A thin place.

"I've heard of those," she said. "The West Coast suffered less supernatural damage, though a few god-driven earthquakes and a tsunami took a toll farther north. You'll see some of the damage."

Past Santa Monica and north on 405, the limo wove up into the hills where dense population gave way to sprawling estates. Gregor's senses registered the presence of a powerful necromancer even before they turned off the main road onto the secured driveway of a property that dominated the hill.

He expected something older Hollywood with echoes of European, or at least Spanish, style. But the sprawling compound of timber, glass, and cement had a Pacific Northwest sensibility applied to this sunnier, drier locale. The sharp lines and steep angles of the mansion and surrounding buildings were fresh from a modern architectural magazine.

Raymond and Azrael had different approaches to their status. Azrael lived in the heart of his city with a minimal number of undead staff. In this distant compound, a dozen guards—undead —waited at the gate that rolled aside. Gregor sensed twice as many stationed about the compound.

The limo drew to a stop at the top of the horseshoe drive. He stepped out when the door opened, moving aside as Ana followed him. He disliked having her at his back.

When he angled his body, the corner of her mouth tugged up in response. Of course she knew. Standing, the top of her head barely reached his collar. The sunlight revealed the deep brown of her hair and the freckles across her cheeks and the bridge of her nose.

On the surface, she would have fit in with any of the designer-clad kids burning holes in the credit cards of wealthy parents on business from Tokyo. The whole look should have been garish.

Until she slipped her daishō into the black leather holster with the ease of someone who'd forgotten what it was like to walk around unarmed.

She slid past, leaving the hint of lilacs and steel in her wake. "If you will follow me."

The slim line of her neck disappeared into the collar of the ridiculous jacket. He noted her upper-body strength in the width of her shoulders and the easy, natural swing of her arms. Even the baggy pants couldn't hide the curve of hips. Long legs, in proportion to the rest of her, ate the ground in efficient strides. She moved like a fighter—all soundless grace and economy.

In the cool hall of the compound, she cast a single glance over her shoulder as she removed her sunglasses. Every calculation in him came to an abrupt and reckless halt. Black-framed irises of tawny brown enclosed pupils large as a hawk's and sharp with the intensity of her gaze. The unearthly glare left him flat-footed. Shock raced through him, stirring a distant sensation in his core.

He pocketed his sunglasses, letting his gaze wash over her from top to bottom. Ana Gozen's face did not change, no blush of anger or approval at his frank appraisal. Instead, her mouth twitched again as if marking his gaze for what it was—an attempt to buy himself time. "You are not curious why you've been asked here?"

Marshaling his wits, he shrugged. "Raymond called in his mark."

She spun on her heel. Azrael had left it to him to develop his own strategy for handling the Nightfeather, cautioning only that he would like to have the other necromancer as an ally if it were at all possible. Provoking his counterpart in Raymond's retinue was probably not his best first move. Still, something in him courted a fight with her.

And the curiosity rose again. Within seconds of being in her presence, he knew she hadn't risen to her position due to a necromancer's favor even if she now shared his bed.

Certainly she was capable of a simple hunt.

He caught her in a few long strides, and they both halted before a set of glass doors tinted a smoky opaque. The hall before them expanded into a small waiting area, low-slung furniture designed not to take away from the expansive views on either side.

A matched set of burly men clad in biker's leathers guarded the door. Thick rolls of tattooed skin spilled between every joint of leather and cloth. Like Ana, they were members of Raymond's Aegis, but their matching expressions gave no welcome.

"Little Ana." The one on the left smirked. His thick Eastern European accent added a condescending strand of *e*'s to the title.

"Bringing the borrowed hound?" the other finished, showing identical yellowed teeth.

Gregor's spine stiffened.

The first crossed his arms over his chest. "How does it feel to be replaced?"

"How does it feel to be the glorified doorman, Mitko?" Her voice curled around the name with an edge.

The big man turned red. The second blocked her path.

"Step aside, Petr."

"The master will call for you when he is ready."

Gregor tore his eyes away from the downward twist of Ana's lips in time to catch Mitko's wink. Petr had Ana's focus.

"And what happens when he finds you have kept his guest waiting, you overgrown oxen?" Her hand never moved closer to her blade, but again Gregor registered a shift of attention.

Gregor lunged before he was conscious of the attack. He caught Mitko's thick wrist in one hand, twisting up and around as he planted his foot and yanked the bigger man off-balance.

Behind him, the solid thud of Ana's scabbard making contact with flesh and the grunt of her exhale signaled Petr's attack. Gregor jerked the wrist in his hands until it snapped and flung Mitko backward before realizing he'd gotten the drop because Mitko hadn't been coming at Gregor at all.

They wanted Ana.

CHAPTER FOUR

Ana should have known those two meatheads would start some shit. They were strong, savage, and brainless, all qualities which had served her well over the years. Their vow to Raymond might have put them at her service, but they held no love for her. She figured it a quality she could manage—given the brainlessness. All their attempts to undermine her had failed. At the wink Mitko passed Gregor, the pieces of their plan fell in place a moment before the fight began.

In hindsight, she should have given them more credit.

Inviting Azrael's first to become party in their attempt to usurp her was more clever than she'd given them credit for. The size of Azrael's Aegis was well known. She couldn't imagine managing that many warriors and the constant infighting between them. Staying alive must be a daily battle. Perhaps he was using this assignment as an opportunity to scout for positions in Raymond's Aegis. What better way to prove his value than by taking down the existing leadership? With Gregor on their side, she might have been in trouble.

In this world, she trusted gathered intelligence as far as she could throw it—rumors and nicknames weren't always reliable. Assessing everyone as a potential opponent had been part of her survival strategy long enough to become second nature. She'd known the moment Gregor Schwarz strolled off the plane he would be hell in a fight. In spite of his height and his long limbs, the soundless way he moved indicated absolute control of his body. In combination, his reach would be punishing. If they ever fought, she marked her best chances in staying close to him and striking fast. Giving him time and distance might end her. Especially if he carried soul steel instead of a human-forged sword.

He watched and listened, but he didn't pepper her with questions or try to lull her with chatter. He didn't prod, searching for openings or intel as she would have expected. Even his head-to-toe gaze was not sexual but assessing. It took her a moment to find the word for his expression—curious. Imagine that, after all he must have seen and done, he found *her* curious.

Answering amusement brought softness to places she hadn't even considered in years. Combined with the odd warmth left by the lingering pass of his glacier-blue gaze, she considered her own interior with puzzled confusion.

In the half hour she'd been in his presence, she'd realized Gregor would never be party to a coup. She'd anticipated he would step aside, letting the fight play out without interference.

When he moved toward her, she was surprised to have misjudged the man and switched her focus to deflecting Petr as she turned her bare sword to block Gregor's attack.

The attack never came. Behind Gregor, Mitko crashed over the coffee table, roaring as his wrist flopped at an unnatural angle. Ana's mouth opened in a small *o* of surprise. Gregor flicked a glance over her shoulder. She slammed her mouth shut and spun to face the recovering Petr.

Gregor's tailored suit jacket brushed her back as he slid into her blind spot. The hair on her neck bristled even as confusion kept her from spinning on him. He wasn't sitting it out. He wasn't with them either.

It took all her focus to stay on Petr as she deflected the big man again, kicking his knee out from under him. Ana heaved a breath, willing him to realize his mistake and stay down.

The giants regrouped and attacked, fast and brutal, intending to give them no time to consolidate an effort. Too late. Ana bumped elbows with Gregor. She passed a glance to see his teeth flash as he accommodated her stance before he fixed his attention on Mitko.

He was used to this, she realized. Fighting together. Having allies. He didn't leap to take over the fight in some misplaced attempt at chivalry or in answer to an overblown ego. He *followed* her lead. He had her back.

Her blade's song dulled only as it sliced through Petr's leg at the knee. He hit the floor and she pinned him there with the tip of a blade biting the skin over his jugular. Gregor rested a knee in Mitko's neck, the shiny glint of a knife blade poised below the bigger man's eye. Mitko tensed.

Gregor tapped the blade against Mitko's skin to ensure his attention. "Have you had to regenerate an eye yet? The loss of depth perception is inconvenient. Take it from me."

Ana almost laughed at the clinical disinterest in his voice.

"Petr, Mitko, you're dismissed," Raymond bellowed from within the room. "Ana, show my guest in."

She shoved Petr away, sheathing her blades. When Gregor refused to release Mitko, she snuck a glance. Confusion knit his brows. Fighting he understood. His speed and reach had been every bit as devastating as she'd anticipated, never mind the strength. He hadn't even bared the soul steel. Something about this fight was new to him. New and troubling, judging by the downcast turn of his lips. He stood, hands lifted as if releasing a wild animal. When Mitko ignored him, the blade disappeared into an unseen holster in his suit. Gregor stepped clear of the larger man.

Mitko rose, eyes for his fallen comrade. He fashioned a quick tourniquet.

"You will clean up the mess you've made," Raymond barked from the depths of the office.

"Sire," the unbloodied man said through gritted teeth. He

hauled the wounded man to his good leg and dragged him down the hall.

Gregor tugged his suit and tie back into place as Ana held the door. He paused. "After you."

Smart man.

* * *

"MR. SCHWARZ." The necromancer who controlled North America rose from the recycled-steel desk and stepped around to meet him, hand outstretched.

If he was close to Azrael's two thousand years as intelligence suggested, Raymond Nightfeather had been on the continent centuries before the first Europeans landed. He offered no tribal identification and only the name Raymond Nightfeather when he'd been asked to join the Allegiance. Gregor had never seen him in anything other than battered jeans, a white T-shirt, and motorcycle boots. Raymond smiled without showing teeth and gave a little nod. Waist-long black hair slid over his shoulders as he moved, as straight and heavy as the long, sharp features of his face.

Obsidian eyes with the rainbow metallic sheen of an oil slick pierced Gregor as they shook hands. Waves of power made the contact prickly, but he resisted the urge to flinch. For any necromancer but Azrael, physical contact would range from uncomfortable to painful.

"I apologize for the obstacle course."

Ana exhaled, stalking to the window with arms folded. His awareness of her was a constant thing, tugging at his attention in spite of the fact that the most dangerous person in the room had a firm grip on his sword hand. She muttered something under her breath that must have been familiar to Raymond because his teeth flashed.

"Those two remain somewhat unbiddable, wouldn't you say, Ana?"

Her glance skated over her shoulder before returning to the thin sliver of ocean visible between brown hills. "But predictable."

Raymond knew about the power struggles within his Aegis and did nothing? What fresh hell was this? Serving necromancers was difficult and dangerous enough without constant challenge from within.

Raymond released him, gesturing to one of the modern chairs upholstered in brindle cowhide across from his desk. "It's been a busy morning. Will you take coffee?"

"No, thank you," Gregor said.

One of the walls rolled away to reveal a hidden door from which an undead servant emerged bearing a tray. Her bland, expressionless face was as empty as a corpse. At home, Azrael used the sentence of undead servitude as punishment for humans who violated the laws. He thought of the limo driver. What were Raymond's rules?

Raymond gestured at the desk, and the undead woman deposited the coffee and departed the way she had come. Ana didn't change her position.

Time moved differently for necromancers. In spite of Raymond's assessment of his own schedule, he seemed to have no particular hurry to assign Gregor to a task. Then again, if he had been urgent in any sense, it would have also been a flag. Raymond tended to his coffee, allowing Gregor to prowl the room with his eyes.

Like the rest of the house, it was a testament to modern design. But the sepia-tinged prints hanging on the wall reflected a much older time. He recognized the strongmen first with their neatly trimmed beards and handlebar mustaches twisted to meticulous points. Hands fisted on hips, they stood guard beside a caravan-style wagon hitched to two draft horses. The sign in curlicue scroll declared NIGHTFEATHER'S HALL OF CURIOSITIES. Other photos captured the rest of the curiosities of the traveling village, the wagons and tents and livestock and performers.

Two characters in full costume caught his attention—one in an elaborate if not accurate approximation of Tatami dō armor, and Lysippe wearing a loincloth, breastplate, and a complex arrangement of holsters for blades. The women rode a pair of matched horses. Gregor had known Lysippe long enough to detect the trace of amusement in her stern expression. Motion blurred the other rider's face, but it must have been Ana. Raymond stood between horses with feathers in his hair and wearing buckskin leggings, his chest bare except for a reed vest. Beside him a sandwich board advertised AMAZON VERSUS SAMURAI: WONDERS OF THE ANCIENT WORLD.

Ray's unsmiling expression made Gregor wonder about the fate of the photographer brave enough to capture it. He dragged his attention away. He'd come to do a job and gain what information he could about Raymond as ally or enemy. In that order. Not to be distracted by the past—his or anyone else's. His gaze drifted to the compact, muscular woman at the window.

And he wasn't here to tell her how to run her Aegis. Her bargain with her master was her own.

"There is a creature hunting its way down the Pacific Coast," Raymond said at last.

Gregor's brow slid north at the peculiar choice of phrasing. It would have been ridiculous, for instance, to ask what sort of creature it was. If it were known, Raymond would have announced it. But if it was a grace blood and mortals had been among its kills, his task was clear.

After the godswar and the ascension of the Allegiance, mortals had been at the brink of chaos. The necromancers' first and most important effort was to calm the population, subdue them if necessary. Keeping them ignorant of the greater presence and threat of grace bloods was key to forming one of the few rules all members of the Allegiance enforced without question. A grace-blooded creature revealing itself or its powers to mortals would be subject to death.

It wouldn't be the first time he served as executioner.

This time Raymond did smile. Ana nodded without turning, giving Gregor a distinct indication there had been a telepathic exchange between them.

"You will explain what you know and what you require of me," Gregor said. "Understanding my position in Azrael's retinue, you will not *knowingly* endanger me more than you would your own first. Unknown risks are assumed by the gravity of my presence here. Excess questions at this juncture are superfluous."

He caught the look Ana cast Raymond but couldn't decode it. His words had surprised her in some way. Knowing questions were superfluous didn't mean he didn't have them.

The necromancer's amusement faded, though his smile did not. "Ana, the briefing."

CHAPTER FIVE

Ana reached into her jacket as she returned to the desk. "Juneau, Alaska, eight weeks ago."

She slid a glossy set of photos onto the table. They'd gone through considerable effort to control what information got out about the attacks, which included the inconvenience of going old school with film. Gregor trapped the pile with one long finger.

Raymond leaned back against his chair. With the press of an unseen button on the surface of his desk, the windows dimmed, casting the room in deep shade.

"Impressive for a single creature." Gregor thumbed through the images of the fishing boats found adrift, their nets shredded, their decks coated in the crews' frozen blood and remains that the gulls hadn't feasted on.

Three other vessels had been reported missing and their crew presumed dead.

Raymond sat with ankle crossed over knee, elbows on the armrests of his chair and fingers steepled. He followed the proceedings silently. Some combination of power and the strangeness of necromancer features brought on by age made him beautiful. He could be charming in his way, and there was no accounting for the way mortals were attracted to the edge of danger in the mystery of his power.

Ana provided the next images. "Tsimshian Federation Territories. Near the city you would know as Prince Rupert, Canada."

The creature made land. Buildings smashed, cars ripped apart, mortals torn limb from limb or crushed in the effort to flee. This one had been much harder to contain as word spread among the survivors and into the small town. Stories of a massive beast come out of the sea and destroying everything in its path. Ana declared an epidemic—after godswar-induced biological weapons and the resulting years of unpredictable viruses humans respected quarantine.

But the story spread. In the end, Raymond hadn't hesitated to give the order to wipe the town from the map. The news that there were no survivors and the town had to be destroyed for the sake of containment went over with little protest from the human population.

Ana been Raymond's cat's-paw for almost two centuries. She knew him better than anyone alive. It would be wise to seek an accord with Azrael. Especially now that the Suramérican necromancer had been replaced by one of Azrael's progeny. But in refusing to give up the dancer as his consort, Azrael had fractured the fragile peace in the Allegiance. That also made him a liability.

Ana had her own concerns when it came to an alliance with the European necromancer. Azrael had formed an unheard of emotional bond with this consort. Would he be hard enough to do what must be done to win the war he'd started? Or would he drag them down with him when he fell?

She knew Raymond studied Gregor's every move for insight into his borrowed hound. Flinching at the thought of innocents destroyed for the sake of larger population control might indicate Azrael had softened in the relative postwar peace.

Gregor finished his brief survey. "The next?"

Ana provided images. The third had been shipping yards. No one had survived, but the entire site had been destroyed anyway.

"It's not working alone anymore."

Raymond shifted in his chair, folding his hands so only his index fingers remained steepled. Rearranging the photos, Gregor answered the unasked question.

"The first attacks are crude," he said. "Dismemberments. The scatter indicates the victims made an attempt to flee—that they had a place to flee to. This is organized. There is nowhere to go. And I see bite marks. Large canids."

"Dogs," Raymond said, testing. "Or wolves."

Gregor shook his head. "These are grace blooded. Werewolves."

"Craven beasts." Raymond lifted a lip, betraying his distaste.

Gregor went still, but the latent danger beneath his tailored suit and refined demeanor went active between heartbeats. His mouth set in a thin line, the blue of his eyes dark and cracking with some unspent effort. Anger, she realized. Raymond's words had infuriated him.

Raymond felt it too. His nostrils flared as the air around them danced.

"You are familiar with shifters," Ana said in the taut silence, keeping her voice neutral.

Gregor didn't exactly *move*, but the air around him released its tension as his sardonic mouth tilted northward again. When he spoke, the words were weighted with significance. "Recently?"

Gregor met her eyes with a glimpse of humor in the glacial blue. Azrael's allied coven was guarded by a pack. Both were blood kin of his consort.

"Forgive me," Raymond said, casual and amused. "I didn't realize."

But of course he had. The entire Allegiance had seen the pack of shifters standing among Azrael's own Aegis in the castle. They had been dressed in human finery, the witches and the consort all in matching gowns. A wedding, Ana realized. Intelligence suggested the coven and its pack had bred hybrids. If Azrael's retinue survived this, it would be interesting to see where it would lead.

Raymond wanted to know how deep loyalties ran, how much Gregor cared about his master's new allies. He had his answer.

Ana tapped another recessed button on the desk. A map appeared on the wall.

"Primarily coastal towns." She addressed the map. "None any more than ten miles from the coast. Suggests the creature requires saltwater for survival. It consumed nothing it killed nor took anything of value."

She'd seen individual bodies and mass kills, but there was something especially disturbing about these attacks. Such violence. The bodies had been fouled, left to rot, without even the illusion of predation. Something in this slaughter called to her.

Gregor nodded once, and for a moment she thought he might ask about her experience. What would she say? I know kills like this because I made my own once. Worse.

Instead, his eyes found the map on the wall over her shoulder. Red indicated all the places where the creature—and its allies—had struck. His voice, low and steady, broached the darkness at her back. "How long between kills?"

"A week, more or less, for the first two. The spacing is farther apart once the wolves were involved."

"They're thin blooded," Gregor said.

Raymond exhaled from the shadows, amusement and satisfaction. "Explain."

"They depend on the moon to change. Look at the dates—no more than forty-eight hours before or after a full moon. Stronger blooded weres and true shifters have no such limitations."

Ana called up a calendar, had it cross-reference the dates and overlay the results with moon cycles. She scrambled to recall the night the Allegiance had confronted Azrael in his hall. Some of the members of the pack had already begun to shift, anticipating confrontation. How close had they been to the turning of the moon?

"Why this town, Prince Rupert, or that one?" Gregor asked. "There's a pattern here. Too specific."

"All are sites of historical significance," she said, rattling off settlements and treaties since the first indigenous contact with Europeans and the settling of pre-godswar Canada.

She ended leaning against the front of Raymond's desk, a few feet away from Gregor. Again his sardonic glance, the tell-me-something-I-didn't-know mouth tilt. She wanted to wipe the smug smirk off his striking face.

He was too tall and too formal and too buttoned-up in his tailored suit. She preferred men who inhabited their wildness like wolves, not ones who leashed it like a dog. Still, he didn't seem to fear Raymond, and he seemed to enjoy risking her ire. Something in him hadn't yet been tamed. Curiosity replaced resentment.

"It's personal," Gregor said. "It's settling a score."

The missing piece. His confirmation increased her certainty.

"This continent is rife with old scores to be settled," Ana said archly, quoting Raymond's response when she'd mentioned her suspicions.

"Why it kills may give us a clue of how, and where, to stop it," Gregor said, staring into the shadows where Raymond waited, lips resting against his index fingers.

Ana checked the monitor embedded in Raymond's desk for confirmation. "The system has already begun cross-referencing historical conflicts and locations from Vancouver to LA. We should have a list of potential targets by morning."

Gregor returned his attention to the calendar. "Three days until the next full moon."

"Our best bet is to start in Seattle," she said. "It's got the largest known population of grace bloods on the West Coast."

Gregor shifted in his seat. "Our?"

"You will assist Ana," Raymond said.

Ana gritted her teeth to keep her irritation from showing. The weight of Raymond's gaze settled on her anyway. Gregor kept his own carefully fixed on the screen, ignoring the exchange.

She'd wanted to hate him, this borrowed hound. Ana watched him study the photos again.

Gregor sat back in the chair. When he looked up again, it was not into the shadows but into her face. His gaze searched, through the fine motes drifting along the beam of projected light, shocking in its openness. It took her a moment to realize he sought her approval. It would have been easy enough to look away, knowing he would have left the room and been on a return plane to Prague this afternoon, damned what it might mean for an accord between the necromancers they served. The resentment at his presence, the intrusion into what should have been her task alone, quieted. She lowered her chin once without speaking.

"The charge?" Gregor asked, speaking into the shadows.

Raymond's voice seemed to fill the room, power crackling around the edges. "Hunt and eliminate this creature. If it is beyond your power to kill, you will hold it until it has been captured or contained."

"I accept. The oath?"

Among necromancers and grace-blooded creatures, vows were power. From summoning the dead to binding the warriors of their Aegis, words imbued with the power of obligation or command carried extra importance. To fail to uphold one's word could entail more than censure from their peers. The Code of Raziel laid out the ancient rules of binding and the consequences—a powerful, terminal force called the Retribution—triggered by the breaking of a vow.

After a long pause, Raymond spoke again. "Gregor Schwarz, I charge you with this responsibility. As such, you are under my command in this matter in exchange for my protection. You will ally with no other against me until your contract is complete. Do you submit?"

"I give my loyalty and obedience." The air between them crackled with power. "In this I am your man."

Ana looked away, unable to bear the gaze that rested on her.

* * *

DISMISSED, Gregor stood outside the door of Raymond's office and exhaled a long, low breath as he waited for his escort to appear. The hall outside was immaculate and empty.

In Prague, artwork saved from museums during the godswar lined the halls, the sound of undead servants and his own companions of the Aegis on their way to the training ring, or from patrols and assignments. Since Isela, Azrael had even begun allowing tours in the external buildings of the castle. Gregor would have been drawn and quartered before he admitted to a perverse bit of pleasure in shocking a group of mortals just by crossing their paths on his way across the grounds.

Aside from the faintest smell of blood under disinfectant, this hall might as well have been a tomb. He leaned forward and adjusted the plush cushion on one chair. There. Perfect.

The door opened behind him.

He surveyed the scene again, the sweep of his gaze taking in Ana last. Fixing the out-of-place hair would probably not go over well.

"Something funny?"

"Everything," he said, eyebrow sliding north.

The consort would have been glowering at him by now, her eyes sparking gold. Even Lysippe would have sighed in that centuries-old expression of exasperation. Ana's pale, freckled face did not budge.

"Keep your blade and your tongue sheathed on my behalf. I'll fight my own battles."

He let his smile spread, not bothering to hide his amusement. "I look forward to the next time I can sheathe my blade and tongue on your behalf."

The muscle beneath her cheek jumped a fraction. Without waiting, she stalked down the hall. "Follow me."

Gregor clicked his heels together and gave a little bow at her back. *"Jawohl."*

CHAPTER SIX

A na gave him an abbreviated tour on the way. He showed particular interest in the training room. "You're free to use it whenever you like."

Raymond kept his Aegis close. That still left plenty of room in the interior—Raymond had specified this physical space above match the aedis beneath. Below was the sacred space where he conducted major spell work. He had no love of grimoires or written spells. Raymond's particular brand of power had always favored potions and alchemical brews. He kept his extensive collection under physical guard and wards. She left that off the tour.

She'd approved of Gregor's quarters herself: a small apartment with a stocked kitchen, bedroom, and living room with a peek-aboo ocean view. Close enough to her own to keep an eye on him.

She paused by the door. "Will you require anything else?"

Tall by the standards of the women of her time, she'd lost the advantage over the centuries. She was used to having to look up at men. That didn't stop her from putting the fear of gods in most.

That generous mouth twisted in consideration, the rest of his expression distant. "I had hoped for a sparring partner."

"I'll have one of Raymond's contracts sent up," she said,

thinking of a few of the undead servants that had been combat trained in life.

He strolled to his luggage, keeping her in his peripheral vision, and made a cursory sweep of the room. "An Aegis would be better if one can be spared."

She nodded with a little bow. "At your pleasure."

For the flash of an instant he looked as though he'd seen a ghost.

"Mr. Schwarz?"

Glacial eyes snapped electric against hers. His face shuttered again, impenetrable. He took a step backward. "Ms. Gozen."

She paused on the other side of the closed door. What had he seen—remembered? She shook off the curiosity. It was none of her concern.

Auger, she sent a mental summons on her way to her office. *Spar with our guest. I want a full report.*

* * *

"He kicked my ass. Thoroughly."

Ana looked up from Gregor Schwarz's dossier as a sleek jaguar of a man draped himself in the chair across from her. Emerald eyes much like the big jungle cat fixed on her from beneath a shaggy forelock of curls. Well, one eye at least. He wasn't exaggerating, judging by the bruises shading his brown skin. The worst was the eye—sealed shut and so discolored the skin appeared shades of eggplant all the way from below the eyebrow to the split upper lip.

"Broke my damn cheekbone," Auger muttered, his words muffled. He plucked at the bits of maroon-colored cotton below his nostrils.

Anger flared before she could catch herself, and the pencil in her hand snapped. She swore, flashing on an image of her blades severing Gregor's arms from the shoulders. Wishful thinking.

"Hold on there, boss lady." He raised his palms, the fingers of one hand swollen, pinkie and ring finger taped together. "You asked me to see what he was capable of. I was following orders."

"I did not expect him to—" *Beat you to a fine pulp* sprang to mind first. She had no desire to wound his pride. She changed tack. He was right. His wounds would heal. "What did you learn?"

"Took a bit to get it out of him." Auger shrugged, wincing as one shoulder refused to rise. "I had to push. Even then—"

He shook his head as his words trailed off.

"You think he held back," she finished.

"I think he went just far enough," Auger corrected. "And even then, just so. And you know I can talk shit."

That brought the echo of a smile to her lips. A street-born master of martial arts, Auger knew how to fight dirty.

"I don't think a single word I said got to him. He ended the fight exactly when he was ready. Like an alarm had gone off in his head." He whistled, resting his foot on the edge of her desk and rocking his chair backward until it balanced on two legs. "That's one cold-blooded fuck," Auger swore, and his eyes darkened. "Ana, are you sure—"

She shook her head, cutting him off. "I'm not foolish enough to be sure of anything. He's taken his vow. He's Raymond's now, same as us."

"I don't trust him." Auger frowned.

"And I've lived this long because I don't trust anyone."

"Oh come on, Ana."

"Except you, Auger." He could believe that if he wanted to.

"His vow is to Raymond. But you…" He paused, rocking.

The words had been, she agreed, but Gregor's gaze had never left her. And had she read a request for permission in his eyes before he'd accepted the job. What the hell kind of operation was Azrael running in Prague?

Auger took a breath. "Why don't you take me for backup, just in case?"

"Get your feet off my desk," Ana snapped.

Auger's chair rocked to the floor with a crack as his face fell.

She sighed. "I need you here. With Mitko out of commission, you're running point, on Ray's guard."

He gave her a bloody grimace of a smile. He'd learned once—the hard way—what it meant to buck an order she'd given. He'd never done it again. She had his obedience.

More, if she wanted it. He'd not been shy about that either. She let her eyes roam over him, watching the slow fade of bruises in the silence. He'd have use of the eye by the end of the following day, if not sooner. He was beautiful, as a true warrior, lethal and aware of his own prowess.

Cultivating physical pleasure was like enjoying art or a fine meal. She'd taken lovers often enough to know what she needed at a glance, had even contemplated Auger a half dozen times over the years. In spite of his beauty, his ruthlessness, his irreverence, she had not found a taste for him.

She looked back at the dossier. "The Hessian."

Auger sighed but shifted his attention back to the matter at hand. He never let her rejection get in the way of his work. She suspected he'd come from a warm bed to respond to her summons, and he would have no problem filling it again once his face no longer resembled raw hamburger. Sooner, no doubt.

"Schwarz is quick, and even then… I got in a few hits, and he doesn't register pain. At all. Think he bargained for that? Man, I wish I would have thought of it. Smart guy."

Ana twirled her finger.

Auger sighed. "You were right about his reach. He's not afraid to get his hands dirty." He pointed at his eye. "But I had no luck getting him off-balance, physically or mentally. He's got ice in his veins."

"Good."

"And Ana." Auger sat up in his chair, the smile broken halfway across his face. "He's a gentleman. He apologized for this." He waved his hand at his face. "And I believe he meant it. Said he hoped I got what I needed to know."

Ana's face crashed before she could check herself. Of course Gregor had known this would be a test. Ana cursed herself—she'd exposed them all. Between Petr and Mitko in the hall, and Auger later, she'd given him a complete breakdown of the capabilities of

Raymond's entire guard. Something for him to take back to his boss.

Except her.

She checked her watch. Time to do a little reconnaissance of her own. "You're dismissed, Auger. Watch your back while I'm gone. Mitko's gonna be pissed when his leg grows back."

"Where are you headed?" he asked as she rose, shrugging off her jacket. She didn't miss the brief flash of consideration on Auger's face.

She knew what people thought: that she was not only first of Raymond's Aegis but shared his bed. She'd long ago given up bitterness that accompanied the realization.

Let them think what they liked. She'd held her position against both open rebellions and attempted coups. After she had killed two of her potential usurpers, Raymond joked she was the biggest threat to his Aegis. Still, he trusted her to do what needed to be done. As she would continue to do so, unflinching, unblinking. Those not strong enough would not survive. She wouldn't make the mistake of bringing one unsuited to this life into the fold again.

She smiled. "I have a date."

CHAPTER SEVEN

After showering off sweat and the young street fighter's blood, Gregor booted up his laptop as he dressed. Ana had provided secure network access and relevant passwords, but he hadn't done much before sparring besides surf the internet and test the network security. It had been as he expected: locked tight from the outside world but imbedded with its own tracking programs. He neutralized those while checking the stock markets and installing his own private connection to Azrael's servers. Like the automobile, he found the advancement of communications technology somewhat thrilling. And with nothing but time on his hands, he saw no point in remaining ignorant to such devices.

A humorless smile creased his mouth. Back in the old days, they used scrying glass and spelled bowls of water. Times change.

He snugged his tie, plucking at the knot until it suited him. He was a long way from the forest estate of his childhood. Back then it had been leather and fine cloth tailored for him, as befit a young man of noble—if somewhat inconsequential—birth. He'd never lost the taste for dressing well in any age.

Though time and experience had eroded his sense of the virtues of nobility, he maintained the rigid structures of dress as well as he could. The clothes did not, as they claimed, make the man, but they did maintain order. And a required amount of distance between himself and others.

The phone chimed as the connection was established and the call began. He should have taken Lysippe's offer for a full briefing before he'd left Prague. But he hadn't wanted to have his perception tainted by her experience with Raymond. As always, she'd let him pick his course. He braced himself for an epic *I-told-you-so*.

The black screen resolved to an image of an unfamiliar blonde. He frowned, expecting Lysippe's short curly hair and dark skin.

"You must be the scary one. That was fast—I'll get her." She cupped a hand over her mouth and called out. *"Lys!"*

This one was new. He hadn't known Lysippe had a thing for blondes, but tastes changed.

The view swung past a pair of full breasts to take in a dirt-covered arena ringed in clean white fencing. A copper blur streaked across the screen, resolving to a horse at full gallop. Clinging to its back like a burr, a figure flipped from one side of the animal to the other, her feet touching dirt long enough to send up a few clods before she leaped again. Each side, then a pause over the center of the saddle, balancing on her grip of the pommel and stirrup. Before the horse pounded out of view, she slipped into her seat so subtly the animal scarcely flicked an ear.

They loped across the far side of the arena. No bit, only a rope circling the animal's neck. Lysippe's hips rocked with the horse's movement, her upper body almost motionless.

"Show-off," Gregor muttered.

The blonde laughed and the camera refocused on her face. "I know. I told her the same thing."

Gregor paused, the woman's bone structure hooking him. She was beautiful, almost painful to look at, but alien. Yet he couldn't look away. His nostrils flared in surprise.

Only Lysippe would take a succubus for a lover.

The view swung back.

"That bad, is it?" Lysippe said, breathing a little hard herself as she scissored her legs and dropped to the sand beside the finely bred animal.

"You know I can't divulge—" he began as she took the phone.

"It's a joke." She laughed, then called over her shoulder, "*Habibi*, cool him out for me, would you?"

Well, her preferred endearment never changed.

The blonde hopped over the fence to meet the horse's affectionate nuzzle with her open palms. "Of course. Come, you little sneaker."

The horse blew out and the woman crooned at it. He watched them walk away over Lysippe's shoulder, the woman's fingers light on the horse's cheek.

Lysippe arched a brow. "You were saying?"

"Really?"

"I'll thank you to keep your opinion of my bedmates to yourself."

"Does Azrael—"

"I've broken none of his codes."

As if it would matter. As the oldest member of Azrael's Aegis and his adopted daughter, there would be little he would object to. She'd handpicked and trained each member of his Aegis over hundreds of years. Azrael trusted her. They all did. She'd enforced a code that had made them a unit—they had each other's backs against supernatural creatures and the machinations of necromancers. Having watched Raymond's Aegis try to devour itself just a few paces outside their master's door, Gregor had a new appreciation for Lysippe's strategy.

She wiped sweat from her brow with her forearm and sighed. "I warned you Raymond would hold his cards close. Azrael should have sent me. But tell me what you can, and I'll tell you what I know."

Gregor poured himself a scotch and sat down, pausing to straighten his cuffs. "It's not Raymond I have questions about."

Her brows rose. "You met Ana."

No point in mincing words. "I gave her my vow."

She laughed so hard she had to wipe her eyes before she could speak again. "Rich. And I thought I'd lost a comedian when Dory jumped ship."

He sighed and her face fell.

"You gave a vow to that single-minded homicidal lunatic?"

He gritted his teeth in frustration at the stream of dead and archaic languages that reminded him she was over 1,500 years his senior. She could be such a mother hen sometimes.

She kicked the fence post with enough force the wood cracked and the crossbars buckled. That refreshed her round of swearing. Mostly living languages this time, so at least he understood the bulk of it.

She glared at him. "Letting the little brain make all the decisions, are we?"

"I don't know what you presume…"

Her brow shot north. "How many years has it been? I knew the ascetic thing would be your undoing. Get laid once in a while, wasn't that the first thing I said to you? It will keep you from thinking with your boner."

Gregor recoiled. "My… are you drinking?"

"I will be raising a glass to your memory after this call."

He shoved himself out of his chair, checked the windows, plucked at his tie in the mirror. Energy moved through him, and he had nowhere to put it. He needed a chase, a hunt, a kill.

Lysippe tried again. "Ana Gozen was a trained killer *before* Raymond gave her the gift. She had that bushido bullshit driven into her when she was too young to know any better. She's not a person, she's a weapon, and the only thing she's better at than wholesale slaughter is maintaining her loyalty, and that will *always* be to Raymond."

No bitterness or anger laced her words. She spoke as she always did, with unadorned confidence he'd never questioned until now.

"Then she'll be quite capable of handling herself on this hunt," Gregor muttered. "At least I won't have to worry about that."

She made a little choking noise of disbelief. "Gregor, she will not hesitate to let you hang if it means keeping his house *and* his secrets safe."

"Is that what she did to you?"

It sounded bitter to his own ears, and once the words were spoken, he regretted them. She deserved better than his scorn. Lysippe sighed and shook her head at him.

"The damage done between Raymond and me needed no help." She rubbed her mouth, gazing over the edge of the camera and into her own past.

Then she must have caught a glimpse of one of her animals or the blonde, because the tension in her face eased. She took a deep breath, and when she looked at him, a little smile tugged at her mouth.

"I should have seen it coming. You're alike, you two—you like terrorizing things. And *you* have always enjoyed being in over your head."

Again, Gregor lost his words. Did she really see him as empty loyalty bent to the next kill?

She shrugged, meeting his eyes. "You're a big boy now. I've taught you well enough, or not. Just don't forget what she is and whom she serves. Keep your own countenance, princeling. And watch your blind spot. Everyone has one… Well, except Ana."

The call ended and Gregor poured himself a double. He drank it down with a little laugh, imagining Lysippe on the other end doing the same.

At the knock on the door, Gregor smoothed his lapels and rose to meet his fate. He recognized the undead woman at the door from Raymond's office. Good, his message had been received. He retrieved the package Azrael had prepared. "Take me to him."

She led him to the deck behind Raymond's office. The North American necromancer looked over his shoulder. "You have something for me?"

"My master sends his regards," Gregor said. "And this token of his good will."

Gregor withdrew a small vial. Even packed in unbreakable

glass and sealed with wards, the power from within surged. Not even sunset's glow could dull the shine of the liquid.

Raymond spun, his nostrils flaring. "Ambrosia. Where—"

Gregor gave an apologetic smile. Raymond nodded. He must have known Gregor would be unwilling or even forbidden to reveal the source of such a precious liquid capable of boosting power and increasing the effectiveness of spells. Azrael had anticipated that a few drops of ambrosia taken from deep in the mountains of eastern Europe would be something more precious than Raymond's composure. He'd been right. Raymond took the sphere containing the vial, studying the wards.

"You will thank your master for me and assure him of our future cooperation."

Gregor bowed.

Raymond's fingers curled around the sphere until the light disappeared. "Is there anything else?"

"I understand we will be driving," Gregor said.

"I leave the particulars to Ana's discretion."

"I'd like to request a specific automobile."

Raymond exhaled, facing the hills again and the distant glimpse of the sea. "Is that all?"

According to Lysippe, Raymond came from the Pacific Northwest. Curious that he had chosen to live here, so far from the ocean he seemed unwilling or unable to put his back to for long.

"She's gotten her wish. I'm paying attention now."

Gregor assumed he was talking about Ana. "Sir?"

Raymond lifted his head. "Ana is my right hand. You will not interfere with her in any way. But you will stop this creature, no matter what the cost."

Gregor had survived as Azrael's enforcer for over two hundred years. Necromancers could be cold, making sacrifices with the calculation of a master gamesman. Yet he had never seen one so willing to use a member of his own Aegis as a gambit. And, based on this afternoon's reconnaissance, the most valuable one.

He wondered at what Raymond considered worth the price of losing her.

CHAPTER EIGHT

Ana turned as her door chimed and slid open. Raymond entered without waiting to be invited. She finished buckling the strap of her stiletto and set her foot on the floor. There was no breeze. Whatever irritation Gregor roused in Raymond, he'd mastered it. Good—she didn't have time for any macho bullshit.

He assessed her, folding his arms over his chest as he leaned against the kitchen counter. "You look stunning."

She'd picked a single sheath of cobalt-blue silk, the cowl neckline draping between her breasts, mirroring the backless effect brought on by the draping that exposed her spine to the top of her hips. The dress fell to her ankles but the slits ran well up her thigh. Fight or fuck, she was good to go.

She shrugged one shoulder, sweeping the hair off the back of her neck. "I got a report this afternoon of some trouble with newcomers. I'd like to have it settled before we leave in the morning. I thought I'd take Azrael's hound along for the ride."

"Good," Raymond said. "Get rumors circling in the territory. He's got quite the reputation. Almost as terrifying as yours, I hear."

Her brows rose. "You expect less?"

"He came to see me."

Ana checked her rage. He should have at least done her the courtesy of asking her to arrange the one-on-one. She bit her tongue against the demand for specifics she knew Raymond wouldn't give.

"I get the sense Azrael does many things differently in his court," she mused instead.

"Do you?" The air in the room charged, fine hairs of fabric on the rug and wall hangings beginning to stir.

"Master." Ana palmed her fist and bowed, reminding them both of her place. "I am your servant."

"And he is yours, it appears," Raymond said, mocking now. "Don't bore me with obedience, Ana. I prefer your tongue sharp."

"Do you?" she said, hearing the echo of his words in her own.

"I always have." The necromancer smiled. "He does not trust me."

"Should he?" Ana couldn't check the edge in her tone.

Raymond's voice held a dark timbre when he replied. "It's contagious."

"I *know* you."

"You do," he said, sobering. "We are alike, you and I. We shaped ourselves, birthed ourselves, named ourselves. We survived by our wits until we had the strength and the power to do more than just survive. We don't require the trust of others."

No, she hadn't. At the beginning. But after a century of conflict inside and out, a deep weariness had crept into her bones. The solitary existence of immortality weighed her down. If he would confide in her, just once. Reveal something more than the absolute necessity. Just because.

She took a chance. Maybe this time would be different. Maybe... "What did he want?"

Raymond stared out the window. "He asked for a car."

Her true sight applied to all grace-blooded things. She had been specific when she'd traded her soul for this life. To see the nature they hide. The lie. Ana exhaled, closing her eyes as though it would sharpen her grace-given gift.

Not a lie. But that didn't mean he was telling the truth.

He crossed the room to her and the air moved with him, clattering frames on the walls and buffeting the windows. "I've forwarded the specs to your assistant. It should be delivered before your departure."

The wind swept behind her, cradling her and tugging loose the short hairs at the base of her neck. He stopped a few feet away, hands at his sides, gaze out the window over her shoulder.

Once, he had touched her—tucked hair behind her ear, cupped a palm on the back of her elbow, or some such familiar gesture of an intimate. She could no longer remember. Her reaction, gripping and twisting his wrist away from her as she slipped the blade against his throat, had been swift and unmistakable. She'd done it without thought, forgetting who—and what—he was. Flinging herself away, she folded into a deep bow of submission as shame burned her face, and set her blade at his feet. She would never forget the look in his eyes. He'd never touched her without necessity again.

The irony of the rumors of what lay between them coated her tongue with bitterness. She kept her eyes down.

"I don't care where his true loyalty lies, as long as it is in this house," he said, focused on the spot just past her temple. "And if it is to you, all the better."

"I don't need protection." She glared up at him. "Send him back. I can handle this alone."

Raymond's guarded expression turned more troubled than she had ever seen for the flash of a moment. He held a breath as if weighing his next words.

Then he spun to the door and the crackle of his energy withdrew as the room went still again. "Happy hunting, Ana."

* * *

BY THE THIRD STOP, Gregor was sick of LA and everyone in it. Even his mild curiosity about what this side of the country would look like had died an airless death after ten minutes in a glossy shopping center. Beside him in a body-hugging swathe of blue fabric, Ana Gozen's satiny plum lips rose at the return of the sales clerk. She leaned a hip against the counter beside the stack of shoeboxes piled high, her expression that of one gleefully anticipating a calamity.

"We don't have those in stock," the clerk said after clearing his throat. "But it's no problem ordering them… sir."

Gregor fought the urge to press his fingertips into his temples. The store had emptied of shoppers when they'd come in, but now the window was crowded with gawking mortals. Tourists. Aegises existed in a gray area of the Allegiance code. They were allowed to operate openly as a visible reminder of a ruling necromancer's power. Mortals knew who they were, what they were, and feared them as much as the grace blooded did. Being a prominent member of a necromancer's retinue made him a recognizable public figure. Strangely, the same didn't seem to apply to Ana. Unless she spoke, no one seemed to focus on her. Maybe it was just the novelty of his presence.

He had a reputation to uphold in any case. He sighed and swung his gaze back to the waiting boy.

The boy recoiled at the expression on his face.

Ana laughed, and Gregor's nostrils flared. Against everything, he wanted to hear it again.

When she had appeared at his door after his meeting with Raymond, he expected her to be furious for the breach of protocol. Instead, she gave him a cool smile.

"I am told you have errands in the city. I have some business to attend to. Perhaps we could combine our efforts."

The racing stripes of the white '67 Shelby in the horseshoe drive matched her dress. The V-8 thundered to life as the undead valet climbed out, and Gregor inhaled the sweet perfume of burning gasoline. After Isela had wrecked his coupe, Azrael had insisted he switch to electric. He felt a bit like a recovered smoker getting a whiff of cigarettes outside a crowded bar.

She pulled out of the grounds as Gregor explained his mission.

"Shopping for your master's consort?" Ana said, with a trace of a taunt. "If you provide a list of items you require, I can have them sent to you. Or we can ship them if you'd prefer."

The muttered reply forced its way between his clenched jaws. "She would not make it so easy for me."

"Your mistress has a unique sense of humor."

"Scores to be settled are a universal feature of humanity, it seems," he said, unable to keep the exasperated humor out of his voice.

"Raymond has taken on a few doozies in my time," Ana said. "Is it true Azrael made the dancer his consort *before* she became a vessel?"

"Not one of his best decisions." He wasn't ready to admit his own objections.

"Why?" Ana said, and she seemed puzzled.

He wasn't sure whether she meant a motivation for the consort or Azrael. The word—the answer to both questions—came awkwardly. "Love."

She barked a laugh. "Necromancers can't love. They gave it away with the power of creation when they ascended to master death."

"Even so," Gregor said. "Azrael is changed."

She shook her head. "He's a fool then."

Gregor considered.

"When Azrael was wounded, the consort held off three demons with a blade, so big—" He lifted his hands to demonstrate. "She was safe when he fought the Queen of Diamonds. As consort, she would have had our protection until the end of her days if Azrael fell. Yet she broke her human body to help him stop the angel from manifesting. She may not have mastered death, but she did not let fear of it stop her. What Azrael gave, she earned, a thousand times."

Ana sat back in her seat, focusing on the road. "Enough to send you out to do her shopping then?"

He tapped his fingers on the dashboard, debating. She let the silence stretch.

At last he cleared his throat. "I used her brother as bait for a necromancer trapping shifters to sell on the black market," he admitted. "He ingested a geas that trapped him between forms. Several days passed before he was able to resume either shape. It was payback for a cake the weres made to look like my family's crest, in red velvet."

Ana's laugher set her silver strand earrings tinkling. Her hair had been swept up onto the top of her head, shorter strands flying free around the fringes of the bangs dusting her eyebrows. She hit the turn signal and exited in the shopping district. "Well then. I'd say you'd earned it. Shoes it is."

This was their last stop before whatever errand she had been sent on. Stalking away from the counter, she laid her fingertips on his forearm and smiled at the clerk. "You will have these delivered, and the others expedited. Say, Friday. The compensation will be generous. So also will be the punishment if they are not received."

Back in the car, Gregor glared at her.

One narrow shoulder rose as she steered back onto the road. "We accomplished the letter of your task, didn't we? Enough suffering for one night. What do you say to dinner?"

Dinner at an exclusive restaurant on a bluff overlooking the Pacific Ocean.

The valet met them, bowing as he held the door with a tremulous murmur. "Madame Gozen. The pleasure is ours."

"Our table will need to be arranged," she said, handing off the key.

A subdued urgency swept the staff the moment she stepped inside.

The hostess showed them through the discreetly lit tables. Faces made ghostly by the dim glow of illumination rose to watch as they passed. He recognized a few among them as the most powerful and influential players in the Allegiance's world order, from the reports of Azrael's head of intelligence. Only a few dared follow Ana for more than a glance, though eyes lingered on him with curiosity.

She gave a heavyset balding man a little smile. The man blanched.

He wondered what patron had been moved to accommodate them as they were seated at the best table in the house, overlooking the other diners on one side and the evening-cloaked surf on the other. He instinctively took the side facing the room. It also cast her in the fading glow of sunset.

She toyed with her silverware and cast a sideways look at him. "Soul steel and luxury automobiles. How refined."

"I am a simple man with expensive tastes." Gregor spread his palms. "I didn't figure you for a muscle car aficionado. Is it true your blades have names?"

"American muscle inspires one to rise to the occasion." She grinned at him, lower lip pinched between her small white incisors. "And yes, they do."

She turned her attention to the trembling server presenting a bottle of red wine. She nodded her approval with a cursory glance at the label.

"Mr. Schwarz, will this suffice, or would you prefer something with less body?"

His brows rose with a nod to the waiter. "When in California…"

When the server departed, he leaned in to conspiratorially whisper, "If it comforts you, my last automobile was gasoline powered."

Again that little smile bent her mouth, and she met his glass with her own. "Not a lost cause then after all."

"Not by half."

By the time appetizers arrived, he'd abandoned studying the room in favor of looking at her small ears, her elegant neck leading into muscular shoulders. By the second bottle of wine, her cheeks were pink and her smile came freely. How long had it been since a woman had not feared him? How long since he'd felt drawn to make a woman laugh?

He mourned the artifice of her flirtatiousness, a structured response to his designed seduction. There had been a pleasure in it even then, the parry and thrust of conversation like a round with a fencer whose skill matched his own.

Still, there had been a moment—she'd leaned toward him across the table, her skin set aglow by candlelight and wine—that pure pleasure had sideswiped him. It left him wondering for a heartbeat or two what it would be like if this moment were real.

"This has been a delightful interlude." She sighed, settling her napkin on the table when the dishes had been cleared. "But I have a small matter to attend to. If you will?"

He rose at her side, curious to see how this played out. Every eye in the restaurant rose with them, and silence drew the tension in the room taut in anticipation. Gregor exhaled and fell in step behind her. It wouldn't be the first time he was the last one in the room to know what the hell was going on. He recognized her target within a few steps.

Sweating profusely, the heavyset man gave a tremulous smile, ample jowls trembling. "Madame Gozen. It's a pleasure—"

In full view of the dining room, she drew her sword and sliced a clean line across his throat in a single movement. His mouth kept moving for a few moments before streaks of red appeared below his jaw. Someone in the room choked. More than a few gasps went up. But no one moved. Even the man's companion stayed rooted in her chair, wide eyes taking in the way he paled as the blood soaked into his clothes and pooled beneath him on the floor.

Gregor slipped the button of his suit jacket free as he scanned the room, calculating the quickest way to the exits and how many he'd have to eliminate to get them clear. He settled on Ana last as she calmly cleaned her blade on the tablecloth.

No one in the room reacted beyond wide-eyed stares.

"I'm quite sure it wasn't pleasurable at all," she said, facing the man's companion with a dangerous little smile. "And you, Betta, you knew what risk you ran when you unleashed your pet in my city."

The woman's throat bobbed, her face tightening. "I have no idea…"

Ana cocked her head. "Ah, but you thought perhaps Raymond was too busy to notice."

The woman's pale face flushed and hardened. Something bulged and rippled beneath her skin, snakelike. Not a shifter then. Reptilian grace bloods appeared often in mortal mythology, diluted or misunderstood as they might be. Gregor cycled through those he knew capable of wearing human skin. Kadijah, the necromancer whose territory included much of the Middle East, had taken out the last echidna spawn. Perhaps Tsuchinoko, or the White Serpent.

His trigger finger twitched. In any case, a bullet to the brain would slow down most, if not all, of them. As with most grace bloods, separating the head from the body was the only sure way. Or heads. Hydra were rare, but a nasty surprise.

The woman hissed. "It was just a few... No one missed—"

"Hunting humans for sport is forbidden in this territory." Ana raised her voice loud enough to carry. "No exception. The punishment is death."

The heavyset man was now gray and still, his eyes glassy. Ana lopped off his head, and the scrape of chairs from the neighboring tables chorused as the occupants hurried to get away while the head rolled to a stop.

"There now," Ana said, soothing. "Leave by dawn and you may keep your own head, Betta. If not, well, I cannot be responsible for Raymond's ire. I am, after all, just the messenger."

"Mistress Gozen." The woman bowed her head, the human voice giving way to a sibilant whisper. "Your mercy—"

"Speak nothing of mercy. You tested us and we've answered. Consider this your warning."

"I understand and obey." The woman bowed, and her neck seemed too long for her body as her chin dipped almost to her sternum.

Ana sheathed her sword with one final look around the room. Not a soul dared eye contact.

The Nightfeather's Talons. Judge, jury and executioner. Intelligence got that right at least.

Her gaze crossed Gregor's, and he lifted a brow in question. A little tip of her chin and he holstered his sidearm. He followed her out of the restaurant.

The car was waiting by the time they reached the front door, but there was a mysterious absence of restaurant staff. Gregor caught the door himself, ignoring Ana's scowl. At the sight of her, the valet tumbled out of the car, slinking backward with catlike fluidity.

"Nagas keeping mosquito men as pets." Disgust hardened her voice, but her eyes remained locked to the road as she pushed the muscle car along the winding coastal highway. "One thing you must learn quickly, Mr. Schwarz. Never assume you understand a thing because of where or when it came from. Here, both meet and clash and form new alliances. This place will always surprise you."

Some things never changed.

CHAPTER NINE

The following morning, Ana tossed an electronic key his direction as they stepped out into the full-blown California sunshine. "I presume you'll want to drive."

She didn't pause to watch him catch it, hefting her own bag toward the car without a backward glance.

She'd returned to the standard uniform: baggy jeans, jacket, swinging hair. He spared a moment on the memory of her from the night before. Today the sunglasses were back in place.

Gone also was the Mustang. Instead, the RS 7, so black it seemed to swallow light, waited in the drive. He hadn't yet determined Ana's reason for driving when an airplane would have gotten them there faster, but if she insisted, he'd rather take one variable out of the equation. She slid into the passenger's seat without a word.

The navigation greeted him by name. Good—the techs had managed the remote install of his custom system. It wasn't identical to the model at home, but it would be close enough.

He ignored her smirk. "Seat belt."

Her brow arched over the frame of her movie-star sunglasses.

"What's the speed limit here," he asked as they pulled onto the road.

She laughed. "For us?"

"Good." He began to accelerate and did not stop until the cars around them blurred.

The car estimated a tick under eighteen hours to Seattle. His mental calculation with stops to charge the battery put them at about nine.

"About last night," she began.

Which part? His breech of protocol seemed paltry compared to her carrying out an execution in an exclusive seaside restaurant after dessert. Pausing to dine while their target stewed in his own terror for the better part of two hours seemed gratuitous to say the least. And Lysippe chided *him* for having a "flair for the dramatic."

He decided to stick with his contribution to the evening's adventure. "I overstepped my bounds in approaching Raymond without you. I apologize."

She had turned her face to the passenger window. "I don't blame you for trying to get some sort of advantage. Raymond has never valued transparency in his dealings."

"Yet you trust him," he said, leaving *with your soul* implied.

"He promised me no lies, though there would always be secrets."

"And you don't ask."

"As you said, I trust him."

Gregor returned his focus to the road. He watched another hundred miles breeze by, irritated with America's stubborn resistance to the metric system. What was a mile, anyway? No wonder they all spoke of distances in the time it took to cover them.

Ana removed her sunglasses and spared a glance at him. "This time something feels off. After the third attack he called me off the investigation. And then he called in his favor to Azrael, and now you're here. He knows something he's not telling us. Or he suspects it. I'm not sure yet."

Gregor waited, letting silence be an invitation.

"Ray's been different since we came back from Prague, and now this. Azrael said something to him in the park. He's really stirred things up, your boss."

Azrael's actions might have sent shock waves through the thin peace held by the Allegiance, but he hadn't started the trouble. He'd revealed the conspiracy brewing behind it and stopped a plot by two members of the Allegiance to cut the other six out of power. With one of the conspirators dead and Raymond reaching out to Azrael for an accord, the balance of power in the Allegiance was shifting. The next few hundred years would be full of incalculable risk, and the stability of the mortal world hung in the balance.

"Azrael treats them—mortals—as if they deserve to be here," she said.

Gregor wanted to agree. It was one of his most irritating qualities. But it made him interesting. "You speak as if you were not once one."

"Even then we were different. Unusual. Haven't you figured it out? We didn't come to walk beside necromancers because we fit in."

"True enough."

"Mortals are foolish, impulsive, shortsighted," she said. "They brought the world to the brink with their stupid war—because they learned to call down gods out of greed and hunger for power."

"And necromancers are immune to such lures?"

She stared out the window again, the fixed angle of her jaw indicating her displeasure.

After another hundred miles or so blurred past, he asked, "Any idea what it is he's not telling you?"

Her expression said she wanted to put a sword through him no matter how fast he happened to be driving. It had been a long time since anyone made the hair on the back of his neck stand on end with a look. He found it refreshing.

"You have a death wish."

"I'm not afraid to die," he corrected.

She tossed her sunglasses on the dashboard with an expulsion of Japanese so quick he caught only every third word, give or take. Japanese had been a recent language acquisition and Ito, Azrael's head of intelligence, seemed to delight in seeing him rendered speechless during their lessons. Still, the lessons had served him well: he understood the most salient points.

He tested out a reply. "If you do not enter the tiger's cave, you will not catch its cub."

She swore before trading him idioms in crisp, unaccented German. *"Du gehst mir auf den kekes."*

"Ah, we're informal then." He laughed. "That's progress."

Her hawk eyes narrowed, lips pulled tight. The corner of her mouth rose after a moment. "I can see it, you know, the black blade of yours. When you bait me it flares up, like it realizes exactly what you're about to get yourself into."

Surprised, he sat up a little. Soul steel forged in a necromancer's bargain might be visible to other necromancers, but not their Aegises.

He curled a reckless smile her direction. "And what might that be?"

Her lips caressed the words. "A fight."

His mouth went dry as the blood rushed from his brain.

"It has more sense than you do," she said, sitting back in her seat. "Your sword." She checked the dashboard clock and sat up, all business again. "Perfect timing, I'm starving. Pull off here."

He regained his senses with reflexes honed over two hundred years, dropping out of the fast lane and shedding speed to make the off-ramp. He guided the car toward the large red-and-white sign in a retro fifties motif promising burgers in two directions and frowned. "A drive-through?"

"It seemed your master's consort wanted to give you an authentic American experience," she said lightly as he pulled into the line. "Roll down the window."

Gregor complied, glaring up into the fresh face of a mortal teenager.

"Nice wheels," the boy started before catching sight of Gregor's expression. He jerked half a step backward and squawked a greeting. "What can I get for you…" He swallowed. "Sir?"

Ana leaned across him, and Gregor forgot to be irritated. Her shoulder brushed his chest, the weight of her upper body resting on the hand placed on his thigh as she ordered.

"And for you, sir?" the boy squawked again.

With her hair under his nose, Gregor picked up the faintest trace of lilac. He forgot the question.

Ana sucked her teeth and glanced at the boy. "He'll have the same."

"Will you be eating in the car?"

"Of course," Ana replied, hitting the button for the window as the boy stammered out the price and a request to proceed. She leaned back in her own seat, looking at him. "Informal seems best, given the circumstances. Don't you agree?"

Gregor put the car in gear.

After sliding a greasy, open-topped cardboard box filled with food to Ana, he pulled the car into a space with a charging terminal near an empty cluster of white tables shaded by umbrellas.

"The whole point of the drive-through is to continue driving," Ana protested when he shut off the car.

"I'm not eating *that* in *here*. Also, we should top off the battery."

Under the scant shade of the umbrella, he watched the heat bake waves off the pavement. Away from the ocean, the sun beat down on them. A trickle of sweat rolled between his shoulder blades. Almost-immortality didn't grant him immunity from the basic functions of the body.

Ana shrugged off her jacket to reveal a spaghetti-strap tank top and hopped onto the tabletop. She wasn't wearing a bra, which placed the small mounds of her breasts too close to his face for comfort. He stood up from the bench and joined her.

"Aren't you even going to loosen your tie?" She sighed as he tucked the tail between two buttons in his shirt.

He fastidiously extracted one of the waxed-paper-wrapped arrangements of bread and meat, holding it between his knees to avoid a drip as he found a napkin. "This is ground meat and a pathetic excuse for a salad between two slices of bread."

"Says he of the land of sausage and bread," she said in her best Teutonic accent.

Whatever had happened in the car lay dormant between them, easing some immutable tension of their circumstances.

He shook his head, chewing. "Blegh."

Ana had already wolfed down half of hers and plucked a fried potato from the box with her free hand. "Try the fries, they're incredible."

The potatoes weren't half bad. They had been coated in an incredible layer of salt. Before he could ask, Ana held out a condensation-coated paper cup, the straw of her own between her plump lips.

Whatever her cup contained needed a good deal of persuasion to make it up the straw. Blood, recently returned from its sojourn, decided to go south again and left him glad he was wearing his sunglasses so she wouldn't catch him staring at her mouth like a hungry dog.

"Milkshake," she said between sips.

He forced his attention back to the fries.

"Chocolate," he grumbled after a sip.

She held out her own. "Strawberry?"

Too sweet for his taste, but it went a long way to relieve the salty coating on his tongue.

"How long has it been?" she asked.

Gregor coughed, patting his mouth with the napkin. "Excuse me?"

"Since you've been to the States." She laughed. "The good old US of A."

"Colonies," he said. "They were colonies then."

She guffawed. "A lot's changed."

"The food's still terrible."

She stuck out her tongue, leaving a smudge of milkshake at the corner of her mouth. Taking his life in his hands, he reached up with his thumb and swiped it away.

"Feeling brave with my blades in the car?" Her brow rose.

He took another mouthful of strawberries and cream and wondered if the heat was making him lose his mind.

"They're not part of your bargain your daishō."

She sucked her teeth. "Those are two of the finest blades ever crafted. Not even a necromancer could improve on that."

"Yes, but you have to leave them in the car," he said, gesturing to his back and allowing the air to coalesce just enough to form the hilt between his shoulders.

"You think I can't handle myself without a sword?"

"I have no idea what you're capable of, Ana Gozen."

She went back to chewing for a long moment. He let her have the silence.

"Yet you trust me with your back in this hunt?"

Cornered, he paused. The temptation to retreat, to deflect and pick another angle of attack, rose. Instead, he held his ground.

"You owe me one," he said dryly, and she laughed. Then, with a touch of seriousness, he continued, "I do."

He contented himself sucking the rest of the paper cup dry in her silence. He picked up the carton, plucked a few of the crispiest remaining fries for himself, and offered her the rest.

"Why?" She wasn't talking about the contents of the box.

"Your reputation precedes you."

"Says the Black Blade of Azrael." She snagged the last two fries and grinned at him, sliding off the table.

He rolled his eyes skyward. When they reached the car he paused, bouncing the key fob on his palm a few times as he considered his next words. "You got too close to the answer. That's why he called you back. Which means you're capable of tracking and hunting this thing alone. Raymond called in a favor to ease his own mind. That suggests he knows much more than he's letting on, which troubles me. But *you* don't need me, that's clear."

"Glad you recognized that… Sticks." Something bright lit her voice for the first time.

It had been an honest assessment of her skill. Azrael might not have been effusive in his praise—and he wouldn't hesitate to use force in a reprimand—but Gregor knew he had the necromancer's regard and his trust. It gave him confidence to walk in a world full of mystery. Ana, it seemed, enjoyed neither.

And yet she ventured into the unknown without hesitation.

He brought the car to life again, the throaty rumble attracting the attention of the patrons not already sneaking curious glances. Of course Raymond's workshop had given it an artificial exhaust. What was it with Americans and their penchant for noisy automobiles?

"Sticks."

"Arms, legs," she said. "I'm amazed you can fold yourself into this machine."

On the autobahn—highway, he corrected himself—he eased the car into low flying speeds. He considered possible responses but went with a truth. "My height has always called attention to itself. In the army the quartermaster had a devil of a time finding a uniform that fit."

"Which one?"

He made a questioning noise.

"Army?"

"I was part of a regiment sent to the colonies to quell the sedition."

The memory rose as the air-conditioning cooled his skin, a pale substitute for the feel of wind off the Atlantic. He'd come for the land—for the challenge of exploring new territory, learning new forests and mountains so unlike his home. And to forget. He'd disembarked with the others, startled to find the great resistance to the crown of England little more than a shabby collection of buildings scraped out of the forests and bare earth of this new land.

"I thought Hessians sent to the Revolutionary War had been press-ganged into service."

"True often of the lower classes, those without families. Wanderers often wound up 'enlisted' in the general ranks." He shrugged. "But my father was a contemporary of Frederik. His ideal was a state of young men ready for service. German Sparta."

"That sounds redundant," she quipped. "You were a jäger."

He nodded. "Many were sons of game- and groundskeepers, seeking some sort of name or glory. Each man brought his own weapon, and we had the skills to maintain and use them. My rifle was beautiful—the latest in technology for the day." He paused in memory. "The pay was decent."

"Mercenaries." She made a sound of disapproval.

"That offends you?"

"Your father had the ear of a German prince and you needed money?"

"My parents' union was quite productive in every way. I was the youngest of seven surviving children, too far down the list to be preserved even as a spare. My oldest nephews were my contemporaries, all on their way to land and titles. I had a small but sufficient income, and a generous, if somewhat removed, amount of property settled on me."

"You were bored."

It was easy to give her the unadorned truth. "The young woman I set my sights on was not interested in a life of obscurity on a country estate no matter how impractical and grand. She craved upward mobility, a life of regard. She married one of my nephews. He outranked me."

"You joined a war over a broken heart," she said, but it lacked the bite of her previous words. "It's not the *most* asinine reason I've heard."

His mouth quirked of its own accord.

She looked up at the road signs. "Exit here. We'll be taking a little detour."

"Sight-seeing?"

"Thought you might appreciate the opportunity to get this beast of yours on some curves."

He couldn't hide his pleasure at the thought. Any monkey could jam his foot on a pedal. Real driving required corners. But they were due in Seattle in less than two days, and he still hadn't figured out why she'd wanted to drive and not fly.

"There's someone we should talk to," she said at his hesitation. "An asylum seeker, if you will. Raymond gave him protection because he's old and well-traveled enough to make him a resource. Maybe he can help us narrow down a list of suspects."

"That doesn't sound like a ringing endorsement," Gregor said but took the exit.

"I don't trust him," Ana said. "He's no necromancer, just an old grace blood. But I've always felt like he was biding his time."

Once they'd wound through the tangled sprawl of Redding, the road narrowed to a thin strip of pavement hugging the hills over gorges. He turned off the AC and cracked a window, letting the scent of heat and dust and pine drift into the car. It brought him back to now—a continent away from the snowdrifts and bitter cold of a war tearing an empire apart. He thought he'd known love when he'd wrapped his heart in a uniform and set off to kill or be killed in a new land.

He'd had no idea. The foolish youth who stepped on the boat had been replaced by a young man who'd lost more than the boy could have ever dreamed.

* * *

HE REMEMBERED DYING on the frozen ground in the wilderness —or at least wanting to.

At seventeen, he'd spent much of his life hunting the forest of his home. He could sight, track, or shoot anything that moved. But he hadn't learned the trick of camaraderie.

Gregor's commanding officer had worked his way up through the ranks, and his unit was loyal to him, but he was the son of a groundsman. And Gregor never let the others forget that he himself had been born to privilege. He hunted and read whatever books he could get his hands on and avoided the other men in his unit. Still, the higher-ups took note of him—his height and his bearing and his reputation as the best shot in his unit preceded him. They called for him, deferred to his opinion over his commander's, and Gregor preened under the attention. In short, he was an arrogant prick.

When his commander sent him with two others on a scouting

mission in late December, he should have been wary. It wasn't until they turned on him, deep in the mountains of the Carolinas, that he understood he'd never been meant to go back. He had never excelled in hand-to-hand combat, but desperation proved a powerful motivator. He killed both, but not before one good blow left him bleeding out.

He didn't know he was cold until warm fingers pressed against his brow, lifted his hair, and peeled open his eyelids. He tried and failed to turn his head, speak.

Callused hands made thorough exploration of his uniform coat. Anything of any value was pulled free, tossed aside. He could hear the others turning over the bodies of the two soldiers, the scrape of cold metal and undoing of buckles as the scavengers stripped anything of worth. He tried to muster an objection to their corpses being picked apart, but they had tried to kill him, after all.

"This one's still alive," a woman's voice called out, all honey and whiskey and resonance enough to command attention.

"I can take care of that." A Scottish brogue accompanied the flash of a blade, dull silver in the cold light.

Her hands parted the heavy coat and the woolens beneath. When they plunged into the sticky damp closest to his skin to inspect the wound beneath, she made a contemplative sound.

"Hold on." Fingers pressing against his throat, the touch firm but not rough. She spoke again. "His blood is strong."

"Ah lass, you can't mean?"

"This one won't die today." The hands withdrew and the cold returned, creeping into his bones. "Let's pack the wound and get him ready to move."

Whoever she was, she commanded respect. In spite of initial protests, everyone moved at her order. She kept her word. He didn't die that day. Or the next. Fever set in and snatches of the conversations around him were indistinguishable from dreams of his old life and nightmares of war.

"Let me die," he begged once.

"Not until you've served my purpose, soldier," she said, an order laced with something like humor.

Her voice anchored him to the world when he would have let go. That and a vile series of pastes and bandaging that followed the agony of the needle and thread. Other voices came and went, questions asked that she answered, consultations requested that she gave. Orders and arguments went back and forth, ended by the bark that he recognized as her final word on whatever the matter at hand.

Gradually the blur of lost days and endless waves of pain receded. Awake, weaker than he'd been at the moment of his birth, and feeling more animal than man, he took in the hanging herbs and the ordered items on shelves by the fireplace. His own rifle stood in the corner behind the door. He wore rough home-spun beneath the blankets, his chest bare except for the thick bandages.

Unable to resist, he tugged at the bandages, trying to get a look.

"I wouldn't do that." The door closed behind her.

He started at the first glimpse of her face: narrow and dark, dense brows lowered over eyes hazel with dark brown edges as she peered into his. Searching, intense, unafraid. Backlit by fire, she glowed with light. "Welcome back."

Tutored in English since childhood, his command of the language had improved in months at the colonies, but injury and blood loss robbed him of it. *"Wo bin ich?"*

A voice spoke from beside the door. "Told you he was one of those damned mercenaries."

Her gaze lifted to someone beyond his line of sight. The dark mass of her hair was twisted away from her face in a complex arrangement of plaits save a few curls springing free at her temple and before her ears. "You owe me a bar of that fine French soap you've been hoarding since our last raid, Iain. Get Heinrich."

She assessed Gregor's wound and departed without another word, taking the jäger rifle—his rifle—on her way. He opened his mouth to protest but shut it immediately, realizing the futility of trying to talk her out of it. He imagined she would sell it to cover the cost of his convalescence. He was at their mercy.

A towheaded boy of about nine took charge of him. His small fierce face locked in determination to obey his mandate as interpreter, translator, and guard.

"*Ich bin* Henry." A Palatine, by the accent, the German immigrants lured to the New World with the promise of abundant farmlands.

"Where am I?" he asked again in German.

"This is Haven."

The name meant nothing to Gregor. His unit had been sent south to the Carolinas to scout potential for overland troop movement. They'd taken mountain routes to avoid detection by the militias and chanced on a few hardscrabble settlements in the lower lands. He'd seen what passed for order in the larger towns occupied by the colonists. He'd heard of no place by that name.

Gregor raised his brows. "That… woman."

Henry nodded, firm and quick. "Lark."

"Is she a runaway, a freedwoman?"

"Ask her yourself, sir," Henry said, hesitating for the first time. "Lark abides no gossip."

Not even a common language could endear Gregor to the boy. His loyalty, like everyone Gregor met, belonged to her.

Henry warned him the first night. "Her heart isn't soft. She suffers no liars, no fools or charlatans either. She's part 'risha or spirit-touched or just plain crazy, depending on who you ask. Sees clear through to your soul. Doesn't like what she finds—she may have saved your life, but she'll take it with her own hands."

When Gregor could sit up and care for his own needs, Henry began to take him out for walks in the settlement. He expected a ramshackle collection of lean shelters populated by rowdy, unkempt people. Instead, it was sparse but orderly and clean.

The cabin was one of a dozen or more mixed buildings, each nestled in the trees with cozy trails of smoke emerging from their chimneys. More snow blanketed the ground here than lower in the mountains. And there were many more people about than he expected—women and children as well as men. They were dressed simply but well in clothes clean and warm against the weather. If there had been more buildings, it might have even warranted being called a town.

Lark joined him every supper with questions. She was backed by two of her lieutenants—the Scot, Iain; and Gray Rabbit, a man a few shades darker than she with the long hair kept in the style of the Cheraw.

She asked about his time in the colonies, the places he'd been. Then about his gun and the weapons his unit carried. Troop life and organization—she seemed particularly interested in morale. Every time he thought he would remain vague, she withdrew the line of questioning, pausing to feed him or make sure he got a chance to relieve himself while the other men were present to help him. Eventually she would circle back around, and he found himself telling everything he knew and speculating when he did not. He'd fought his own men for his life; there was no going home after this.

Their interviews lasted longer each day. Sometimes she was shadowed by men from other Native bands he didn't recognize, and their conversations took longer as she translated between multiple tongues. He had begun to regain English, though he often slipped back when the subject grew more complex. One afternoon, Gregor realized they had conducted a conversation in German in which she had understood every word.

"How is it that you...?"

Her mouth canted in one of those sideways smiles and she replied in his native tongue. "You'll have chores to build up your strength."

"She speaks six languages, to my count," Henry told him the following day as he accompanied Gregor on his assigned tasks. Gregor was winded in a matter of steps. "English, French, German, two of the slave languages—and Cheraw. A bit of Cherokee. And the trade language." The boy looked at him sideways. "She just wanted you to be comfortable here. 'In a strange land, people trust their own.'"

"But she's understood me all along?"

"Yes."

He looked at her in a new light when she returned.

"Am I a prisoner?"

Lark's laugh filled the cabin, rough and sweet. "Do we look like jailers to you?"

"Why did you help me?"

"You seemed to want to live."

"Not just because I could give you information about troop movements?"

She laughed again. "Soldier, my people know every tribe from here to New York. We know the troop movements."

This had all been a test. She would ask, listen to his answers, and confirm with her people. What would she have done to him if he had lied? She did not wilt under the understanding in his glare. Instead, she nodded once—admitting, accepting, unconcerned with his judgment. He looked away first. She offered a plate that sent up an intriguing aroma of stewed meat and root vegetables seasoned with local herbs. Like a dog, his mouth watered. It had been the same thing for days but was leagues better than anything he'd been served in the mess tent.

He took the plate. "I can leave anytime?"

"When the weather turns, the boys will walk you down the mountain," she said as she tucked into her own plate. "Blind-folded, of course. Morristown is a week by foot. Sure, you could get back to your people from there."

His belly growled.

"Eat," she said without glancing up. "You look like a scarecrow."

He flushed, unsure of why he cared about how she saw him. Knowing copper eyes glinted on him before sliding away.

"Your bones are good," she said. "Don't worry. This time of year we could all use a bit more meat on them."

CHAPTER TEN

The road opened up from zigzagging hills to low-slung coast much sooner than Ana would have liked. She enjoyed watching the man put his car through its paces. She also dreaded the meeting to come. As soon as they were in cell range she made a call, alerting Rathki to be prepared to see them on short notice.

Her initial decades as the first of Raymond's Aegis had been spent shaking loose her remaining notions of human mortality and coming to grips with the rest of the creatures who occupied the world just outside of human awareness. Few of the grace blooded were powerful enough to create any problem. But occasionally one—like the naga from the restaurant—thought themselves strong or old enough to test the rules. She wondered if Rathki would be the next. She didn't enjoy executions. But she'd learned the hard way that compassion could lead to a knife in the back when she least expected it. Literally.

They wound through one small coastal town after another, the names as optimistic as the hazy bay in the clear autumn sunshine. Ferndale, Fortuna, Eureka. Dreamy names for sleepy towns. Autumn was the nicest time of year here once the inland heat had begun to die down and no longer pulled a marine layer over the coast that gave the towns a soft focus feel.

She directed Gregor into a university campus, through the maze of small streets to a long set of industrial buildings. The aftereffect flicker of the hilt between his shoulder blades faded as they stepped out of the car into the sunlight. He tugged his lapels.

She grabbed a single black-lacquered saya from the seat behind her. In tight places Imouto, the short sword would be better suited. As she led the way between buildings, Gregor slipped into step behind her. He kept far enough back to form an adequate flanking guard but close enough to establish that they were moving together. She might have blended in with the coeds moving between classrooms, but no one would mistake him for a student. Even then, the gazes of everyone they passed slid over her, catching on him before dropping away.

"What do they see," he asked.

She bit back a snarky response when she realized he wasn't referring to himself but the blade she didn't bother to hide.

"Whatever they expect to," she said. "Art portfolio. Or a handbag. Maybe a yoga mat. Who knows. They won't remember the moment they pass me anyway."

"Your gift."

She nodded. To see, but also to avoid being seen. Even the girl had understood what a boon it could be to be overlooked. As Raymond ascended and she gained visibility at his side, it had become a true advantage.

They paused beside a door as a trio of art students piled out, quieting as they passed Ana and Gregor. More than one looked back into the dimness of the studio they'd left behind.

"Campus security," Gregor said.

"Sure, man."

Gregor smiled. All three fled. He held the door, extending his hand. Ana entered.

Her eyes did not so much adjust to the room as switch from the ability to focus in daylight to dimness with a single blink. Another one of her gifts.

Easels filled the open space. Columns of sunlight filtered through dust motes from the skylights above, casting the room in a pleasantly dim glow. A figure-drawing class must have just finished—the remaining students closed their notebooks and slid sketches into oversized portfolios. The model at the base of a platform adjusted his robe.

"It's been a long time since you sat in on one of my classes, Ms. Gozen," the professor said, rising from his stool before the foremost easel. He set down his charcoal.

Most saw a handsome man in his late forties. The trimmed black beard and black-rimmed glasses gave him a studious, distracted air. To her eyes, the disguise lay like a sheen of oil over the truth. Underneath, the real form bulged with fur at the haunches and hocks ending in cloven hooves. Tiny buds of horns rose from his forehead. Raymond had given him the geas to help him blend in as part of his sanctuary.

"I've been busy." She shrugged. "Work. Work. Work."

"That's too bad." He removed his glasses, sliding them into his breast pocket. "I do miss your... interpretations. Would you like to come to my office, you and your companion?"

"That would be good."

Though Gregor didn't have her sight, as with the naga, he seemed content to follow her lead. She appreciated it more than she would have imagined.

The professor put his back to her because she gave him no choice, and all the while her eyes settled in the places near the base of his bony neck where she might insert a blade. He held open the door to a smaller room sectioned off from the main studio, but she used the hilt of her sword to gesture and he scurried inside.

Ana made herself comfortable in the seat across from the desk. Gregor prowled the edges of the room before assuming a watchful post just in her line of sight.

"Tea?" The man looked between them.

"No, thanks," she said flaring her elbows out on the armrests. "How's it been, Rathki?"

"You should know," he said, the distracted amiability falling away to reveal his true nature. "Not enough to keep tabs on me? I've been minding my manners as you… *requested.*"

Raymond overlooked most of Rathki's less desirable traits because he was old and well-traveled. His knowledge of the world and other necromancers made him useful. But she kept an eye on him as more than once his predilections had brought him close to exposure to humans.

"Good," she said, reminding him of their agreement with the flick of her thumb on the blade's guard, allowing the barest glint of steel. "But I'm not here for that. I need your assistance."

An ugly smile creased his face. "Why should I help *you*?"

"Because that was your agreement," she said, as if speaking to a petulant child.

"With Raymond."

"And who do you think brokered the deal? The Nightfeather had other plans for you, you know." She knew Rathki too well to think this would go easily or quickly.

He settled into the office chair behind the desk, folding his hands like a penitent. He didn't fool her for a minute. He eyed Gregor, floor to ears, as if he were a particularly well-roasted piece of meat.

"Oh, I recognize you now," Rathki purred. "The Black Blade of Azrael. From the stories I'd believed you to be something of a monster."

"What makes you think I'm not?" Danger edged Gregor's amusement. Judging by the way Rathki's consuming eyes dropped away, he recognized it. "Some of us are better at controlling our natures, Rathki Demos."

Ana glanced at him, unable to hide her surprise.

Gregor kept his attention on their subject. "There are others who would be interested to know you are, in fact, well."

Rathki swallowed, and his little caprine face paled before he set his jaw. He lowered his head and shook it in Gregor's direction. "I am protected by the Nightfeather."

"Are you?" Gregor leaned forward to meet Ana's gaze, brows raised.

She shrugged and relaxed in her chair. "As long as he's useful."

"All right," Rathki bleated. "All right." He paused, the malevolence in his slitted pupils clear as his gaze swung between them. "How may I assist?"

"There have been a series of attacks up north," she said. "Something from the sea, maybe with an old grudge."

Rathki looked bored. "Would you like it single-spaced and typed?"

Ana planted the heel of her boot on the edge of his desk with a thump, wishing it was his scrawny little neck.

"Someone who may have had Raymond's attention once and wishes to have it again," Gregor said as if to himself.

Her eyes met his, watched him realize something important. She nodded. Rathki's eyes darted between them.

"A friend," Gregor said. "A lover, perhaps?"

Rathki's laugh left a residue on her skin as he fixed his attention back on her. "Is he tiring of you, Ana?"

"You should hope not," she said, smiling. "It doesn't bode well for you if I am replaced."

Gregor folded his arms over his chest and contemplated his fingernails. "I'd be happy to put you in touch with someone who can take him off your hands, Ms. Gozen."

Rathki bleated alarm before returning his attention to Ana. The words tumbled out of him. "There was one once. A woman. But she couldn't let old wounds heal."

"Old wounds?" Ana said.

"Raymond promised her a chance to move on. But she wouldn't forget. Wanted vengeance."

"When?" Ana said, the hair rising on her arms.

Rathki regained his composure. "Before your time, Ana Gozen."

"She'd be long dead then."

"She had a little power, you know." His lips curled in a sly smile. "Not as much as him. But maybe he helped."

"What do you mean?"

"You're not the first to get a gift from the Nightfeather." Now he looked to be gloating.

She stood. Rathki jerked back, but he wasn't as frightened as he should have been.

"What was her name?" Gregor interrupted.

Rathki snorted and lowered his horned head.

Ana's hand went to her sword. "Answer him."

Rathki turned to her, and the look in his eyes was the only sign she needed.

Ana spun to face the coming attack. Gregor started moving before she could warn him. Broken glass and projectiles sliced through the air where he had been standing a moment before. She dropped into a roll and came up with Imouto bared. The first demon charging through the door lost its jaw on the edge of her blade. Black gore spattered as she spun again, using the demon's momentum to propel her out of the path of the second. Now she understood the dimness of the office and the studio. It took a lot of power to summon a demon in daylight—shadows made it much easier.

But even Rathki wasn't powerful enough to do such a thing.

Gregor came to his feet, firing a semiautomatic toward the studio, the blade still an afterimage between his shoulder blades. Two of the undead leaping through the broken window dropped in midair, sliding to a stop at his feet. He had impeccable aim— the only way to end an undead with a gun was a bullet to the brain. He sprang off the chair and through the window, disappearing into the studio.

The second demon managed to hook her bicep with one jagged horn. Ice streaked Ana's arm, numbing it for a moment too long. She hissed, stabbing at an eye. The demon roared in pain, shaking her free. She landed, rolling and sliced up as she passed beneath the twisting demon. Its gut opened in one long line above her.

Back on her feet, she caught the first demon, still gibbering and wailing, on the backswing. The blade sank between its ears and it buckled to the floor. It collapsed into a wet mass of spent flesh, swirling into a mist of vapor.

The second bellowed, thrashing its horned head as it circled out of her reach. Even half blind and trailing its own guts, it could be deadly. She darted around the cloven hooves and avoided the swiping scorpion tail in search of an opening. The tight space of the office limited her options. Gregor shouted.

"Rathki, I am going to gut you myself," she promised, sure he was hiding under the desk, content to let his allies do the dirty work.

His laugh came from somewhere in the larger studio. "I'll take a rain check, dearest Ana."

Then the smell of smoke and burning paint hit her lungs. She coughed. The demon snapped in her direction. She tossed the scabbard, using the clatter of the wood on the desk to draw its attention.

It lashed with tail first and she swerved, severing the stinging tip with the sword before vaulting onto its back. She grabbed a handful of the greasy pelt for purchase with her sword hand, knowing she would leave the skin of her palm behind, and slipped the thin stiletto from the holster at her spine free. With a single thrust, she buried the stiletto to the hilt in the dark mass beneath her where a spinal cord would have been, severing it.

The demon collapsed, spilling her in a pile of guts that evaporated as they fell. The icy vapor burned her hip and leg where she landed in the muck. She staggered to her feet and almost went down again. Rebounding off the desk with a cry, she collected her saya and kept her body low as she fled the office.

Smoke filled the studio, blocking the light and casting everything in an opaque gray cloud. Gregor finished off the last of what appeared to be a dozen undead, though scattered body parts made a count impossible. He looked up, as cool in clouds of billowing chemical smoke as he had been at the fast-food restaurant a few hours ago. If anything, he looked like he was having a good time. The black blade in his hand sent wild curls of power into the air around it; she fancied it too was enjoying itself.

"Rathki?" She coughed, sheathing her sword.

The silk sageo wrapping the top of the scabbard burned her raw palm, but she gripped it even tighter to keep her mind fixed on the present and a quick escape. Healing powers aside, burns were the worst.

"Long gone," he shouted over the smoke alarm.

She dragged the corner of her coat over her mouth but could not stop herself from coughing. Her eyes teared and ran. "Let's go."

He nodded without question, holstering the blade but leaving the semiautomatic at his hip. They met in the center of the room, and he fell into a guard position at her flank as she led the way to the doors. The doors refused to budge. She threw her good shoulder into them, then fell back.

"Locked."

The black blade sent the handle clattering to the floor in pieces. She threw herself at it again. It burst open, sending them both tumbling into sunshine wreathed by billowing gray smoke. She took a knee. Cool coastal air filled her lungs. Then Gregor had her under the arm, lifting her to her feet and half walking, half carrying her toward the car.

He muttered a few words of a geas. She glanced over her shoulder at the surge of power with the spell. Behind them, the studio groaned as the walls collapsed in on themselves and the flames leaped even higher. Sirens grew closer. The firemen wouldn't arrive in time to save anything but the surrounding buildings.

"Nice trick," she said to cover her surprise.

Tension drew the skin tight over his cheekbones, making them even more pronounced. The cold blue of his eyes scanned around them for combatants, and finding none, he slid the blade home even as it vanished in curling trails of power.

He caught her watching, and the corner of his mouth lowered. "That went well."

She coughed a laugh, wiping her cheek with her free hand. It came back coated in a sticky, oily residue. Man, she hated demon ichor. Her jeans were ripped—well more than before—and her shoes ruined.

"You're still bleeding." He sounded surprised, the hand on her elbow tightening to bring her injured arm closer for inspection.

She yanked it free. "Drive."

Whatever wounds he'd sustained sealed before her eyes with astonishing speed. In her experience, bruises vanished quickly, but cuts and breaks took more time. Demon wounds took longest of all. How was it possible that he healed so fast? She slid into the passenger seat as he brought the car to life with a roar and peeled out of the parking spot. She tore a strip of her shirt and wound it around the gash in her bicep. The demon's horn had gone clean through skin and muscle to bone. It ached, a cold, dull throb. Shivers rose beneath goose bumps.

She tried to sit up in the seat, to maintain her composure. She slipped her sunglasses on over her eyes and turned the vents away from her.

"That was an ambush," he said as he pulled onto the highway.

"You don't say," she muttered, keeping her teeth clenched to avoid chattering.

"You took on two demons," he said, changing the AC to heat.

Overwhelming weariness tugged at her. She forced herself to concentrate. "Sorry, didn't mean to deprive you."

"That's not—" He squeezed the steering wheel hard enough to make it groan. "I'd like to get my hands on that satyr."

"That makes two of us." She hissed when a bump in the road jostled her shoulder against the seat. "I didn't think they were grace blooded enough to call demons."

"They're not." He switched hands on the steering wheel to shrug out of his suit jacket.

The highway blurred in front of the car. She didn't realize she'd closed her eyes until the weight of body-warmed fabric settled over her thighs.

"Gozen," Gregor snapped. "Who do you think he was working with?"

She blinked hard, rattling off names of those she kept an eye on. The short list consisted of young necromancers who might crave power, a few powerful grace bloods Raymond had pissed off, and in both categories, an ex-lover or two. None had any known connection to Rathki. Gregor's glare skated over her—no longer ice but fire—and she did shiver.

"Raymond's enemies know they have to go through me to get to him. It's not the first time one has made a run at me. Probably shouldn't have called. Should have just shown up. I was trying to be courteous."

"No good deed," Gregor said as he flipped the car into automatic and reached into the back seat.

It was a curious sensation to feel her own body beginning to shut down as shock threatened. She just needed to close her eyes. *No.* That would be a disaster.

"Raymond has enemies powerful enough to summon demons in daylight and he sends you out—alone—to treat with them?"

"You think Auger or Tweedledee and Tweedledummy could have done better?" she snapped, sick of proving herself capable to arrogant men.

"I think all of them combined wouldn't have stood a chance." He scoffed, surprising her.

"Anyway I wasn't alone this time," she said. "I had you."

A heavy weight settled over her chest and lap. It was soft and smelled of wintergreen and aftershave. Shit, she'd closed her eyes again. She made herself consider his surprise. She wondered if even a demon wound would have slowed him down. Her brain stuttered, thoughts coming together too slowly.

"Tell me about your history with Rathki." His mouth pinched in a frown. "Ana?"

The surprise contact of a hand on hers brought her back to the car, the seat, and the road spooling out before them in an endless ribbon of yellow and black. She glanced at him, the weight of her head almost too much to bear.

"He's a dirty old satyr." She hated the way her voice slurred. "What more do you need to know? This country has collected a lot of refuse. His own people had it in for him."

"They'd have him strung up by his balls if they could get their hooves on him," Gregor said. "Claimed he violated satyr law, which is saying a lot, considering how few a trip of satyrs has to begin with. After today I'm inclined to give him to them."

Her vision stopped spinning and her heart rate eased as her healing ability began to win the fight. "He likes to test the boundaries. Got a little pushy with some of the mortal coeds back in the sixties. Raymond sent me to put the fear of the sword in him."

"No wonder he has a hard-on for you."

"In more ways than one."

Gregor's hand flexed on the wheel. The one on hers remained a solid warmth.

"It was a joke," she said, biting down on a yawn. "How did you know to ask about a lover?"

Gregor's jaw flexed. "Something Raymond said last night, when I met with him. 'She's gotten her wish. I'm paying attention now.' I thought he meant you."

"Me?" Ana snorted.

"But something in his voice..." Gregor's lips pursed in thought for a long moment as his gaze skated sideways toward her. "I've heard it before."

She glared at him. "What?"

"Maybe nothing."

She slipped her hand free, called up the navigation on the dash screen, and entered a destination address.

"That back there was not 'maybe nothing,'" she said, tucking her hand under the warmth of the coat so she wouldn't be tempted to reach for his again. "You heard what Rathki said. Your instinct was right. So tell me."

He flipped on the seat warmers, fingertips drumming on the center console for a long moment. He sighed. "It reminded me of Azrael when he speaks of Isela."

She wanted to laugh. Raymond of all people was incapable of emotion. That a fierce Amazon warrior who had watched civilizations rise and fall in 1,500 years of life had given her heart to him and he'd turned his back on her proved he was incapable of that kind of connection. He may have started the traveling show, but Lysippe's presence among them formed its heart. Her leaving had been the end it. Now only those bound to him—the strong men — remained. And her.

The strain of her body's fight with the demon wound bore her toward the blackness welling behind her vision. But this was the clean weight of exhaustion without the edge of oblivion threatening. Gregor exhaled, his idle hand returning to the wheel.

"I've got it from here," he said. "Rest."

I don't need you, she thought she said before her eyes slid shut.

CHAPTER ELEVEN

When Ana slept, Gregor eased his foot down and focused on the road.

As the highway left the coast and narrowed to a winding mountain road, he shifted down and took the wheel in both hands. Thick trees rose on either side of the two-lane strip of tarmac, dousing the car and the road in shadows. The outside temperature dropped as the sun raced toward the horizon. Steam rose from the road, which had been left damp by an earlier rain shower, joining the soft gray mist clinging to the ferns. He blinked, and for a moment he was in the Great Smoky Mountains again. But the trees were wrong—too big, too red—and the boulders rounded sand and mudstone rather than the knife-edged sedentary rock. That time is gone, he reminded himself. That place is no more.

He pushed the car hard along the road, letting the pressure and release of acceleration be the outlet for the unfamiliar sensations roiling through him. The wheel creaked beneath his grip, and he forced himself to loosen his fingers.

He'd almost believed Ana Gozen's reputation too good to be anything but exaggeration. Now grudging respect gave way to admiration. She had slain two demons single-handedly.

Her heart rate and breathing had returned to normal. Her skin was no longer cold and waxy. The immediate danger of her going into shock subsided, leaving Gregor with unsettling dismay. Demon wounds were pernicious, but this one should not have been enough to have brought her so low. Unlike a necromancer's undead minions who were nominally powered after being animated, Aegis did not succumb to things like shock or bleed out. At least he'd never seen it before.

The basis of a necromancer's gift was an almost-immortality granted by superhuman healing abilities. Gregor would have died a half dozen times in the past two hundred years if not for the strength of Azrael's gift. He'd lost limbs and severed an artery or two and walked away. Even the worst, gored by a demon and tossed off the edge of a cliff into the sea, had not killed him—though the first few hours of pain had made him wish it had.

But that was the bargain he'd made, the gift he'd been given.

Like him, Ana walked into danger each time she stepped to Raymond's side or out in his name. She should be stronger. No. She should be fucking invincible. Raymond owed her that. It appeared Raymond had skimped on this part of the bargain when it came to Ana.

Azrael might see it as a sign Raymond lacked the power to grant that level of strength. It might make him a weaker ally. For Gregor, in this moment, his worry was that Raymond had chosen not to and Ana had no idea what she was missing.

How could she?

He understood that each of the eight Allegiance necromancers ran their territories as they saw fit. Some were more forgiving, others less. Some treated their mortals as labor and resources, others with some level of respect and autonomy. Each Aegis also operated under the unique leadership of their necromancer. Vows of service and exchange of powers did not follow a standard. Ito had served another before Azrael; so had Aleifr. Gregor had never thought to ask them what life had been like under other necromancers. *Everyone has a blind spot*, Lysippe had said. His— thinking every Aegis ran like his own.

Ana stirred in her sleep, turning her body toward the window and giving him a view of her mangled arm. The cloth strip tied around the wound had gone a dull brown. The bleeding had stopped. A good sign.

She shivered in her sleep and a low moan escaped her lips. He thought it carried a name. He turned up the heat. Her hands clenched, fingers curling into balls before she hissed. One hand spasmed open from pain to reveal skin blackened from contact with demons. A few hours' sleep would heal the worst of it, but he adjusted his expectation of what she could withstand.

He tugged the edge of the coat down over her back. Perfect for early fall evenings that turned biting in Prague, the inland California temperatures made it unnecessary. As her shivers eased, he found gratitude for the foresight to pack it anyway. He'd known what it was like to struggle to stay warm, and he'd sworn never to be cold again.

* * *

HE'D COME a long way from the stinking skin coat he'd managed to acquire for his first winter in Haven. Beggars could not be choosy, and until he could do more than a child's chores and earn himself something worth trading up for, it would do. He tugged it closer as he headed to the sounds of celebration around the bonfire in the center of the settlement. Lark's hunting party had returned, loaded with game and supplies after weeks away. Gregor told himself that pleasure at her reappearance came from the sight of his rifle strapped to her back.

Feeling out of place, Gregor sat on the edge of the firelight, watching the others dance. It was a strange moment to be homesick. The reels and jigs of these New Worlders, so different from the organized, staid ballroom scenes of his youth. Gone were the bright colors and elegant fabrics, replaced by genuine smiles and boisterous laughter. Spirits went around, those too a surprising reminder of what he missed. Swallowing the sandpaper burn of hill whiskey, he would have given his soul for a mug of dark beer or even the sweet wine his mother favored.

When he'd left, he hadn't missed any of it. Now it was all he longed for. Well, almost all.

Tales of the hunt came next. Lark demurred in the telling, moving from her place of honor close to the fire as one of the younger men gave a rousing, if slurred, recitation of her taking a mountain lion that had tried to steal their cache in the dead of night.

Weary and heartsick, Gregor traded the comfort of heat for solitude, drifting to the sheep pen at the edge of the settlement. He made a study of the stars streaking across the sky.

"We have the geese for that." Lark's voice came from the shadows as she joined him amid the lowing flock. "You needn't guard."

"Just trying to earn my keep, my lady."

"Lady, eh?"

He was grateful the dark hid his flush. "I've never known anyone like you—"

She shrugged with a little sigh, resting an elbow on the rail. "Maybe I am something of an oddity. But I am what they need me to be."

He longed to know the woman she was alone under the stars, without so many eyes on her. He might never get another chance.

"How did…" He hesitated, uncertain.

"A freedwoman come to lead a band of outlaws?" She laughed. "I use that ignorance to my advantage. At every opportunity. People cannot see coming what they do not expect. I have learned to value that."

He lowered his head, too ashamed to go on. He'd done the same in the first few weeks, repeatedly questioning Henry about how and why she'd come to lead them.

"And you are also something unexpected," she said. "I lost good coin betting you'd make a fuss being assigned to collecting kindling and slopping pigs like an indenture." That she'd noticed warmed him more than a little. "You're a mercenary, but Heinrich says the name von Schwarzberg means something where you come from. Not that either stopped two of your own from trying to kill you. War's hard enough on men, how did you wind up fighting your own for your life?"

"Their orders were to make sure I didn't return," he said, unable to keep the bitterness out of his voice. "I have difficulty making friends, it seems."

She made a soft, thoughtful noise. "Hard to believe. Iain and the others seem to like you well enough. Henry worships the ground you lay foot on. Even the Schmidt's ornery old sow hasn't tried to kill you."

"She likes corn," he said. "I make sure to always bring her a few kernels. Peace offering."

She laughed and her hand went to her shoulder. "I think I need your help, soldier."

He swallowed hard as his mind churned up creative ideas for the possibilities of what she might need him for.

Wordless, he followed her back to the cabin. The fire had banked low. He added logs and stood by the stove, trying not to look eager. In a few moments it crackled, brightening the room once more. She shed layers of outerwear, leaving them on the hooks by the door. She sat on the edge of the skinny bench close to the fire. Her fingers went to the buttons of her jacket.

Lark eschewed proper women's clothing. Even the plain cuts and simple petticoats of the frontier wives would have seemed foreign on her. Instead, she'd assembled a wardrobe of trousers and buckskin leggings, shirts cut down to her size worn under woolen justaucorps that in the distant past had belonged to a slightly built colonial son. She kept her hair braided or pinned under a cap of the kind favored by traders and mountain men. At a glance, she could often be mistaken for someone's son or a young servant.

He'd not thought much about what lay underneath. When he was recovering he hadn't even thought of her in any way other than as his doctor and, perhaps, captor. As she loosened the neck of the plain linen shirt over her collarbones, his body reminded him of his health and his sex.

She looked up. "Bring the box above the shelf beside the fire, would you?"

He paused, dumb. She gestured to the old bandages on her right shoulder beneath her shift.

"It appears my reputation as being untouchable is a bit manufactured." She sighed and admitted, "Mrs. Schmidt will fuss over me like one of the children. She dislikes that I hunt with the men. And that I dress like one. And carry myself as one. But otherwise she's the most sensible one here. I'd hoped it would be a trait you share. Also, you owe me one, I think."

In spite of himself, he chuckled. "This is hardly repayment for a life."

"Well, consider it work toward a debt," she said, exasperated.

How could he be so stupid to think this had been an invitation? Him no more than an invalid, good only for child's labor. She could have any of the men who had already proven their fitness.

But she had asked him. He regained his wits and his tongue over the mixture of shame and disappointment. "Yes, I can do this."

She looked back into the fire, angling her back to him as she slid the outer shirt to her waist and began to work the shift free over her right shoulder. He set the box between them. The scent of pine and bayberry drifted up from beneath the wood smoke and roasting meat smells clinging to her hair. Wide shoulders, muscular from work, did nothing to reduce the femininity of the curve of her neck, the small of her back. The velvety shade of her skin lightened in those hidden places, marked only with freckles.

The movement made her wince. The faintest trace of dried blood showed through the top layer. All evening she had stood with the others with no sign of injury. Now he could see the stiffness as she started to unwind the bandages. He took over and she sighed. At the end, absorbent packing stuck to the wound and he had to work it free.

"Just get it over with." She clenched her teeth on a yelp.

Revealed, the three long scratches looked angry red. The

bleeding had stopped. A sluggish bit of clear and pink fluid bloomed when he pulled the last of the padding free.

She winced. "I cleaned it as best I could without attracting too much attention."

He'd seen enough of wounds that infection could be deadly in the wilderness. "Why didn't you get help?"

"Spirit-touched witch woman," she said with grim humor. "I don't get injured. How does it look?"

"Not infected," he said, his fingers hovering over the scratches and the bare skin above and beneath. "Mostly clean."

"Mostly?" She tried to peer over her own shoulder.

"*Ja*, bits of… here and there." He paused. "Would you like— that is—could I finish cleaning it?"

"I would be grateful."

At the sight of goose bumps on her skin, he threw another log on the fire. Returning with a tin of hot water and a clean cloth, he found himself under her canny gaze.

"You thought I brought you here to seduce you." She turned her back to him again, but she didn't laugh. Wonder edged her voice. Surprise.

"I didn't think." He rested his fingers on the smooth skin above the slashes and focused on cleaning a bit of tree sap and dirt from a spot she hadn't been able to reach. No point dabbing at it. Better to get on with it. She hissed a little but did not pull away or reproach him.

At last he sat back, pleased with his effort. "Which paste?"

"The blue tin," she said. "Smells like sulfur and tar."

He recoiled as he inspected the opaque yellow goo. "Indeed."

While he worked, she began to speak, her voice tight with discomfort at first, then softening. "This was my father's cabin. He fled the highlands after the rebellion to join his brother as a trapper. My mother escaped one of the few farms near Charleston large enough to keep slaves. A band of the Ye Iswa—you call them Cheraw—took her in, and she traveled with them. She also had a bit of sight, and they valued that. Fever took her and my sister when I was twelve. My father never recovered. My brothers and I eked it out here for a while together. Then the eldest, Deacon, went east and married. They own a mercantile. We do a good bit of trade with them."

She exhaled. "War turns desperate men to criminals, wives and families to widows and orphans, preyed on by the ruthless. My other brother and I couldn't stand by and do nothing, so we started bringing them here. The ones who'd been friends with the wrong side and had their homesteads burned out by the other, or were taken advantage of by the lawlessness of unscrupulous men. Ewan died caught up in some skirmish with some loyalists a few years back and that left me."

Forty souls, all looking to her for safety and order. And her, standing alone.

Treated and dressed in clean wrappings, she slid her shirt on and flexed her shoulder experimentally. He meticulously repacked the box, placing the used bandages in the basket he had seen her use many times when she finished checking his wound. She stood, going to the door. She replaced her hat and her scarf, guiding her coat over her injured shoulder before dropping her good arm in the other side. He remained beside the fire.

"Thank you."

"At your pleasure," he said, looking up at her.

He had meant to shutter his gaze. She stared back for a moment and a wondering look formed in the dark-ringed copper eyes. He stared into the fire instead of lingering on her expression. He placed his hand over his chest where the scar burned like a brand. How many times, awake and unconscious, had her healer's fingertips settled there—mending him, willing him back from the edge of death. He'd lain in her bed grasping at life, anchored by her scent, her presence. Bayberry and pine.

Her voice rasped. "Will you go back to the celebration?"

He shook his head, looking around at her cabin. Where did she sleep while he filled her bed? "Still recovering it seems."

The door opened, and he shivered in the gust of night air. The cold startled him, brought him back to himself. He would not long for what he could not have. She paused, closed the door again. When he looked up, she was watching him with those inscrutable eyes.

"I'm something more than human to them," she said again, this time rueful. "It is one reason I'm able to hold the position I do. You're new here, so I should make it clear. I must be above basic things: injury, pain, want."

Her voice caught on the last, but Gregor swallowed hard on the sound of the word in her husky voice. "If you were to feel any of those things, would it be the worst? To want something?"

"I do not *want*," she said. Did he imagine the edge of rawness in her voice, the plea? "Not for myself, in any case. It's just easier that way."

He nodded, but it struck him that her bothering to explain just might mean something he didn't yet understand. He sat up a long time after she left, watching the fire as his own resolve to let her go burned away. He would move in with the other bachelors as soon as possible. He would not be a burden on her or anyone else. In truth, he was not worthy of her. Not yet. But he would be.

* * *

IN THE CAR, two hundred years and thousands of miles away, Gregor slid Ana Gozen's seat into a reclining position and pulled the coat up under her jaw. He warned the part of himself that couldn't stop thinking about what she was owed and what she had done in spite of its absence.

His new mission came into stark relief. Azrael would get his intel. The debt to Raymond would be paid. And Ana Gozen would walk away from this intact.

No matter what it cost him.

CHAPTER TWELVE

The image of Takami's glowing face bathed in moonlight, her tapered fingers twisting around the strands of Ana's hair, which had been so long in those days, and the scent of lilac and sun-drenched dust grew stronger with age. Takami had used her blanket, tying it at the corners to make a small sack that she now tossed over her shoulder like a drifter.

The regret bloomed in shining silver droplets under Takami's dark lashes. *"Forgive me, Onee-san. I'll never forget you."*

In the morning, the open window allowing in the first dusty, sunlit breeze through the curtains convinced Ana it wasn't a dream. And there was the bed, stripped of the outer blanket and the doll Takami had carried across an ocean.

How could she take the doll, Ana wondered, *and leave me behind?*

An older memory, a hot summer afternoon reading and watching the buzz of human activity in the streets of young San Francisco. Takami's eyes, full of unspoken things. *"Would you give everything up for love?"*

Ana had paused reading her tale of pony express riders plagued with villains and wild Indians in their quest to deliver the post. She snorted and heard herself parroting Nanny. *"Love? Duty is love. Obedience is love.*" She looked up from her magazine, assuming the affectionate nickname as her voice softened. "*Takachan, no more romances. Ugh, they make your head mushy.*"

Takami had returned to her own reading, a flush high in her cheeks. Ana wondered if she was thinking of the gaijin cowherd who always seemed to turn up during their visits to the shops. His skin, crisped and browned from the sun, and his pale eyes stood out in stark contrast as they followed Takami. Ana found him horrifying as a specter.

Ana blinked awake as the car slowed to a stop. She couldn't remember being so warm, and every inhale brought the now-familiar scent of evergreen and male. Predawn light came through the window, muted behind a heavy overcast, but still made her squint behind her sunglasses. Her mouth was sticky with a cottony thickness that must have been her tongue.

Gregor drove in his vest, shirtsleeves cuffed to the elbow.

"Is it casual Friday already?" She yawned, sliding her seat into the upright position. She shifted, testing her limbs. The lingering ache of the demon wound would last a day or two. The rest of her body felt stiff. The car stunk of undead. The soft layers of dark jacket and a coat crumpled into her lap.

"Thank you." She smoothed the material with her fingertips.

"Your teeth were chattering," he muttered, lifting one hand from the wheel to rub his upper lip. "It was distracting."

She stared a moment longer than prudent. The faintest prickle of hair shadowed the hollows of his cheekbones and defined his jawline. It didn't seem possible that he could look better than he did when immaculately coifed in his tailored suit. It made her wonder what he would look like completely undone.

"I'm afraid your coat may be ruined," she said to distract herself from what were surely leftover fever-brain thoughts.

She traced her fingertips along the rough spots on the collar where ichor had marked the material. When she looked up, he watched her hands, and the intensity in his face stuck her tongue to the roof of her mouth.

He shrugged and turned his attention back to the road. "I have a closet full of them."

She contemplated a sharp retort, then decided better of it and let her eyes close again.

The Seattle skyline unfolded before them, long and low between hills with an expanse of glittering gray water in the east. The jutting landmark buildings were a recent overlay to her memories of when it was just a ramshackle stop-off for miners on their way to Alaska. She looked back in the rearview mirror for the biggest change since the godswar.

The iconic snowcap of Mount Rainier floating above the horizon like a woodcutting of Fuji had become a jagged, dark crater. Triggered by gods-powered earthquakes, the dormant volcano had erupted and poured ash and lava for days, and the resulting mud and debris slides changed the landscape from the base of the mountain to Puget Sound forever. To this day the lahar zone remained a track of broken trees and sediment being carved by new water flow.

The lit marquees of the remaining sporting stadium stood in stark contrast to the uniform gray of overcast. The glossy black Columbia Center tower reminded her of the man behind the wheel, all reflected planes and sharp edges. Trees framed the city in shades of green capped with gray all the way to snowcapped mountains.

Something in her eased. Home.

Traffic flowed through the city and Gregor exited, following the navigation past the base of the Space Needle and northwest into a hilly neighborhood crowned with Queen Anne-style houses side by side with sleeker modern ones. He wound his way through the narrow streets, up a steep road facing Puget Sound, and paused before a driveway cut into the hill beneath one of the modern houses. The driveway sloped and he tapped the brakes, waiting for the frosted glass-and-metal door to rise.

A row of shining vehicles in identical electric blue lined the garage. Halogen lamps lit, tracking their progress toward the central column of an elevator, reflecting off the polished cement floor.

"Park anywhere," Ana said.

Gregor parked close to the elevator and cut off the engine. Ana opened her door, levering her body out of the seat as best she could before reaching for her swords. Gregor grabbed his own bags and the small duffel she had packed before she could reach the trunk. She did her best not to limp as she led the way to the elevator. Inside, she avoided the mirrors, staring at the instrument panel and watching the lights go up one floor at a time.

At last the doors slid open. She bent down, grabbed the grating, and pulled up. Gregor waited and she stepped inside first, shucking her shoes off into the rack beside the door as she went.

Floor-to-ceiling windows created an expansive panorama of downtown Seattle. A series of masks she'd collected over the years decorated the white walls. She'd been in LA too long; she'd missed this place.

"The guest bedrooms are down the hall on the left," she said, padding across the dark hardwood floor to the open kitchen. "Take your pick. The kitchen is stocked, but if there's anything else you need, let me know. Coffee?"

"Please." Gregor made an unabashed study of the place.

"When the timer goes off, help yourself. If you'll excuse me."

Gregor gave a slight bow. Ana collected her swords and kept her walk steady until she closed her bedroom door behind her. She locked it before letting her body sag with a long sigh.

This was her sanctuary and everything the rest of the house wasn't. The room was awash in colors, the deep gray chaise setting off the vibrant red walls, dashes of cream and peach accenting the rugs and the odd flashes of gold threads in the throw blankets and pillow cases. The wrought iron bed was a re-creation of the one she'd shared in San Francisco, but as authentic as she could find and piled high with pillows and a plush down comforter, framed in netting. Whenever she'd had time to spare, away from Raymond and the machinations of his house, she came here. A pile of paperbacks teetered on the nightstand, begging her to curl up and read as rain slapped the window overlooking the water. When she and Gregor completed the job, she would return for a few days. She'd earned it.

Twin scarlet and-gold vases as tall as she was marked the entrance to the bathroom. She headed to the shower, leaving a trail of ruined clothing in her wake. She flipped the water on hot as she passed on her way to the elevated sink.

Her reflection in the panoramic mirror wasn't as bad as she'd feared. Dark smudges under her eyes and the remnants of fading bruises marked the price of her recovery. She spent a moment working the bandage loose from her arm. Crusted blood flaked away, and with a tug the cloth came free and revealed the puckering white of a scar. Demon wounds seemed to be the only ones capable of scarring an Aegis. She touched one on her thigh, and her fingers found a third on her back, the long whip lash of a barbed tail. That had been her first.

The scar came with a name, Hamish, the last member of the Aegis she had considered an ally, a friend. He'd done knife tricks in the traveling days and she'd never met another who could hone a blade so well. Child of Goibhniu, he claimed with a mischievous grin, blessed metal runs in my blood. Knowing what she did now, it might have been a version of the truth. Most mortals exceptional in some way or another had a god in their bloodline to thank. It was that extra boost, the grace, that made them special.

Grace blooded or no, it was his always-laughing face she remembered most. It had made the years they fought together go so fast. Until that demon. Her opening—the moment her blade had found the beast's heart—had been when it buried its jaws in Hamish's abdomen. Its parting strike had been the lash against her back.

It had bitten him nearly in half—shock and blood loss took him even as his body struggled to heal itself. She'd held his hand as the last light had gone from his eyes. Raymond had dismissed his death as an unfortunate loss.

She counted it another mark against her.

Steam clouded the glass and she shook off the memory,

limping into the shower. Hot water did a world of good, and any pain it inflicted seemed a suitable punishment for the reminder of lives lost due to her shortcomings.

She scrubbed her hair until it squeaked between her fingers. When the water ran clear, she shut off the taps. She wrapped herself in the nubby blue towel and shuffled into the bedroom.

She should talk with Gregor, and check in with Raymond, but right now she just wanted to close her eyes for one more hour and let her gift do the last of its work while the memories battled in her head.

She'd almost reached the bed when she heard a knock at the door.

When she opened it, Gregor had gone. A tray sat just outside her door. A cup of coffee, toast. Beside it, a scrap of red paper had been twisted and folded into the shape of a crane. She peered down the hall into the silent house.

She carried the tray to the bed. The crane's wings flapped at the tug of the beak. She smiled. It was an old trick, one taught to children, but the precision in the folds amused her. Unfolding the bird, she smoothed the paper flat to reveal the small, economic print.

You'll need your strength. Let's go hunting.

* * *

ANA EMERGED, ready to go to war in jeans that hugged her legs and leather boots with a solid sole, daishō at her hip. She'd long ago given up the traditional obi in favor of a custom saya and holster that allowed a quick, single-handed draw of either blade, because fuck tradition. A second low-profile back sheath cradled her shoulders, buckling below her breasts for the stiletto she kept along her spine. She tossed a collarless black leather jacket onto one of the kitchen barstools.

At the other end of the long kitchen bar, Gregor presided over a small armory laid out on a sheet of cloth as he inspected and prepped each weapon. He wore yet another suit, not a hair out of place in the sweep of dark hair. A slate-gray tie was knotted at his throat, the tail buttoned into his shirt to keep it out of his way as he worked.

"I see you found the dry cleaner," she said on her way to the refrigerator.

What his wardrobe lacked in variety, it more than made up for in tailoring. The suits fit him in every way, and she had to admit he wore them well.

He paused, looking up at her for the first time, all business again. A wave of relief washed over her. She could not have borne his pity. Especially when she didn't understand why they healed so differently.

As if reading her mind, his eyes darkened. "Is it that bad when you get injured?"

"Demons are the worst. But a couple of hours of sleep and I'm good as new." She flexed her bare arm with its new white line under the thin merino sweater.

His lips compressed, but he went back to work. "That's inconvenient."

She snorted, retrieving orange juice from the fridge and making a mental note to have her usual complement of groceries delivered during their stay. "I just make sure I don't get hurt. Demon got lucky."

He snorted.

She poured herself a glass of juice and leaned on the counter, watching him. "You heal fast—faster. How is that?"

He met her gaze. "Maybe it's because I'm older."

She rolled her eyes, grabbed the glass, and perched on a stool at the counter, inventorying his armory. Not bad. He favored guns more than she did, but then a jäger would.

"I spoke with a contact who has knowledge of Rathki," he said. "Turns out he's been quiet—here—in his sanctuary until a few months ago."

"A few months ago," she repeated, idly. "He's got to be in on this somehow. Getting info out of him is always a dance, but something was different. Like he was keeping us there until the reinforcements arrived."

Gregor raised a brow but didn't look up from his prep work. "I think someone who's spent a long time planning revenge on Raymond wouldn't be sloppy. Rathki's failure to take you out of the equation might be of particular interest to whomever is running this parade."

"He'll go to ground," she said, admiring the businesslike manner in which he loaded, sheathed, or holstered each of the weapons in his arsenal. To the credit of his tailor, his suit showed nary a hint of a bulge or ripple when he finished assembling himself.

"Maybe," he mused. "Or maybe he'll try to get back into their good graces by sharing information useful to his boss."

"Like that Raymond's brought in the Black Blade of Azrael," she said, sliding from her perch.

His lips pursed. "It does have a nice ring, doesn't it?"

She blew a raspberry and slipped the glass into the dishwasher. She rolled her head on her neck, shaking out her shoulders and hands. Time to go to work.

She looked up to find him watching her. "And the Nightfeather's Talons isn't a tad… dramatic?"

"Takes one to know one." She tugged on her jacket.

Gregor checked his watch and straightened his tie. He met her at the elevator.

"After you." He gestured to the door.

At their approach, the soft sound of the doors unlocking echoed through the silent garage. He paused by the hood as she deviated. She grabbed a helmet and slipped a key into the first of two bikes parked in the row of vehicles.

"We're wired up," she said, tapping the low-profile protrusion on the side of the helmet. "It's the first night of the full moon, and lots of the grace bloods will be feeling it. There are a few clubs we should visit before dawn."

"You realize if the weres *are* involved, there's a good chance we're going into a trap," he said. "Again."

She kicked her heel over the saddle and settled into the seat. "I should hope so. That means we're on the right track."

The lights on the Audi flashed a dull red behind smoked lens covers as the car came to life. The telltale rumbling of an artificial exhaust had been replaced by the silent vibration of the powerful electric motor. The windshield had been dimmed, but even though she couldn't see him, she could feel his eyes on her. Eagerness thrummed in her chest, an unfamiliar sensation. She gave a nod, slid the mirrored face shield into place and led the way into the Seattle dusk.

The city came to life as the fall day gave way to full dark. This far north, daylight would last until as long as it did in the middle of summer farther south. Seattle had always been her favorite city —the crisp, rain-soaked air and abundance of seawater called to her.

She eased the bike into traffic, getting a feel for the engine and her own recovery. Satisfied, she clung to the tank and opened the throttle, letting the bike's motor hit the sweet spot of power and control. He would keep up or he would catch up. Scars fell away, and she exalted in the nimbleness of being astride again.

A memory flashed. She rode the sand-colored pony beside her charge. Takami's face, laughing as her black hair streamed behind her and the shouts of their escort faded in the distance. Ana kept her pony in check, letting Takami pick the path. For as much as she excelled at the sport and gloried in the feel of an unchecked gallop, she never forgot her role. Follow and protect.

Introduced to the household as a distant cousin, she'd been forbidden to acknowledge their connection in any way. Takami was a solitary child raised as the single focus of her household. Ana remembered staring in wonder at the pampered, elegant girl a year her junior but who seemed so much younger.

Even Ana's cover as a country relative could not disguise her poor manners and ignorance in proper behavior. Takami's mother, who disapproved of her husband's decision to bring Ana into her home, mocked her ruthlessly. But they were only words, and Ana had endured much worse.

The intimacies of childhood brought them close. Ana taught Takami to run through the market, dodging vendors and animals. To the bully of a piano teacher, Ana put the fear of the sword in such a personal, delicate way that he could never report it. And Ana proved a good student. She enjoyed all the benefits of her role, singing and dancing lessons, private tutors, and a trunk full of traditional attire and newer Western fashions for a girl her age. With Ana to challenge her, Takami excelled in her studies and the rigorous collection of activities assigned to her.

The only way in which their treatment differed was Ana had a share of household tasks to complete and extra comportment lessons. The labor gave her a chance to continue building strength and discipline as her master had assigned on her departure. It also provided an excuse for her to be absent to continue her sword work.

The voyage to America across the ocean had been a delightful adventure for Ana, though Takami grieved to leave behind friends and the life she'd known in the wealthy district. Ana turned the voyage into a game. How many nights had they spent curled beneath the blankets in the narrow bed while Nanny snored from her pallet of blankets on the cabin floor and Ana whispered stories that turned day's sights extraordinary?

She would never forget her first sight of San Francisco, the low-slung, foggy port city emerging from the hazy sea air, flanked by hills.

"*See the lighthouse there,*" she whispered "*The eye of the ogre watching over his city.*"

"*You are so brave,*" Takami whispered as their nanny hurried them back into their cabin in preparation to disembark.

The entire filthy city teemed with life, reeking of industry. Takami clutched Ana's fingers in sheer terror at so many pale, furry faces and light eyes. Ana listened with one ear to Nanny and the mother complaining about the crudeness and lack of manners. But for Ana, shedding the trappings of an ancient culture that had disdained her was like breathing fresh air for the first time in her life.

Takami withdrew. The only way Ana could reach her was with outlandish tales of the sights she'd taken in on her daily walks with Cook to do the shopping. And riding. They both loved their rides.

A quick check in the side mirror and she smiled in spite of herself at the sight of the familiar headlights sliding behind her rear tire. Of course Gregor could keep up. She tipped her head in acknowledgment of his presence and let go of the reins.

Unlike at the college, she removed the layer of geas that kept her unnoticed the moment they stepped into the first club. Tucked away in the relative quiet of the Pacific Northwest, a vibrant grace blood community thrived with ports connecting populations as far north as Alaska and south to the border.

Rathki's move had been bold, and an example needed to be made for anyone else who thought Raymond's hold on the territory open to challenge. By morning every grace-blooded creature in the city would know that the Nightfeather's Talons and the Black Blade of Azrael hunted together on Raymond's behalf.

She counted on it. Any advantage Rathki would provide by warning his allies would be lost by their open appearance. If Rathki lost his value, he might be cut loose. And then she would have a nice talk with the little horned asshole.

The first two clubs were a bust. They'd certainly ruffled feathers—in the case of the gryphon bartender at Smoky's, literally —striding into Seattle's grace-blooded underground side by side, asking about a rogue satyr.

Most of the lesser creatures would sit this one out. Anyone contemplating aiding the opposition might reconsider. And maybe one or two would see it as an opportunity to curry the necromancer's favor and help them.

On their way out of the second club, Gregor brushed her arm. Ana scanned until her eyes hooked on what had caught his attention. Moving in the shadows of a Pioneer Square alley, a lanky figure darted back toward the exposed brick where her bike was parked. Without slowing, she shifted her helmet to free up her left hand. Gregor's stride shifted to a stalk as he parted from her as if returning to the car, out of the alley's line of sight. She paused at the bike, leaving her back to the alley and fiddling with the ignition for a moment.

The air behind her trembled with movement. She ducked, spinning out and catching the startled figure beneath the chin, shoving him into the shadows of the alley and pinning him to the wall.

Large brown eyes bulged from a round, dark-skinned face. In the low light she made out a full nose and generous lips, tightly curled black hair clipped close to his skull. Beneath, as a double exposure, was a face lupine and furred. He thrashed for a moment, surprisingly strong for one so thin. The thrashing ended when Gregor slipped a semiautomatic to his temple.

"I'd hold still, little wolf," Ana said. "He's got an itchy trigger finger and I'm not in the mood to wet a sword."

"I don't mean to…" He wheezed, eyes flicking from Gregor to Ana with a distinct whine in his voice. "I just wanted to talk. If anyone saw me…"

Ana nodded and Gregor withdrew.

"He's alone," Gregor confirmed, stepping back to keep an eye on the alley opening.

She let the boy's feet return to the pavement. He seemed young, though she estimated him in his early twenties. He was clean, but his clothes had seen better days, and he looked like it had been a while since his last meal. Lone wolves didn't do well in cities.

"Talk."

"I just… I can't get seen." He licked his lips in an expression as submissive in human form as it would be in lupine. "I know something. I mean something you want to know."

Gregor looked doubtful, but Ana sighed. "Get in the car."

The boy looked between her and Gregor, swallowing hard.

"He won't hurt you," she said, addressing Gregor without looking at him. "Will you?"

"Not unless you want me to." Gregor sounded almost optimistic at the prospect.

Ana sighed. She faced the were. "What's your name?"

"Fred," he said. "Smith."

"Okay, Fred Smith," she drawled. "Get in the car and I'll take you someplace where you can get a meal and you won't be seen. If you cooperate, neither of us will hurt you. You have my word."

He swallowed. Gregor unlocked the doors, and Ana opened the rear passenger door.

The boy hesitated. "You want me to go alone, with him…"

She sighed. Riding in a car while wearing her swords was a pain in the ass. She tossed her helmet in, removed her blades, and slid in. "Better?"

Gregor chuckled as he started the car, finding Ana's eyes in the rearview mirror. "Where to?"

"Broadway and Pine."

Gregor groaned as they pulled into the parking lot of a burger stand bustling with mortals. "Not another one of these."

"Go wait in the park." Ana told the young were.

She and Gregor crossed the street to the park five minutes later with four greasy bags loaded with food. She picked an empty bench under a tree where the light of the streetlamp wouldn't reach. This late, the park was quiet except for a game resembling polo on bicycles going on at the tennis courts at the other end.

Fred emerged from the shadows as she handed Gregor a bag of fries and a milkshake. He sidled over, nostrils working overtime. She slid three bags his direction and ignored Gregor's impatience as Fred worked through the contents of two bags full of hamburgers with impressive efficiency. She fancied she could see his stomach beginning to bulge by the end.

After the were had unleashed a thunderous belch, Gregor spoke. "May we begin?"

Fred Smith put down his fries and turned those large, liquid brown eyes to them. "I came down from Idaho a couple of months ago. After I got out of the army. Heard there was a pack taking recruits."

The outline of dog tags pressed against his thin T-shirt. Lone wolves sought discipline and community wherever they could find it.

"They're pretty rough, these guys," he admitted. "Had me running some errands to prove myself."

"But they don't bother to feed or protect you," Gregor said, quiet rage in his voice. "And they collar you."

Fred scratched at his leg. Maybe she'd missed it due to her ability to see beyond his human form, but Gregor's words brought the faint bruising at his neckline into stark relief.

Her teeth clenched. "They did that to you?"

He looked away. "They're testing me. Making sure I'm strong enough."

"So why are you here, talking to us," Gregor asked, "if everything's so good with your new friends?"

The brown eyes looked up with such stark despair she frowned.

"It's not right, the things they do," he said. "I don't want to be part of that just to have a pack."

"Maybe you should just tell us what you know," Ana said, pushing Gregor's abandoned bag of fries back at him.

She didn't like the air of desperation or the way the skin stretched over his bones. If the packs were involved, life wasn't going to get any easier for the young wolf once they got to the bottom of this. Raymond wasn't known for mercy against those who wronged him. And his preference was vengeance served wide as well as deep. If she could get him out of the city...

Fred dragged in a long breath. "About a month ago, Jax— that's the big dog—he starts going up to Canada. The pack has connections up there, his brother's pack. They run weed back and forth and... other things..." His gaze skittered over Ana before falling away. "I heard them talking about something new. Taking advantage of a 'unique opportunity.'"

Ana shook her head. "That could be anything, pup."

"Fred," he said, the flare of pride in his eyes.

She bit back a smile. "Go on."

"They're working with this necro, has a funny accent like your friend here." He jerked his head at Gregor. "Been giving them lots of powers—like 'roids, you know. I only saw him once, but he scared the shit out of me. Don't know his name. He had beef with your boss. Gonna make trouble for him. The Nightfeather."

An old necromancer. Did he think himself strong enough now to make a play for Raymond's territory?

"When do they meet?"

"Just before dawn," he said. "At Murphy's on the water. I'm supposed to work the door."

"Then I guess you'd better be on your way," Gregor growled.

The young man jumped.

Ana slid a few hundreds into the last bag of burgers and fries. "If you breathe a word of this to anyone…"

He shook his head. "They'll kill me if they find out I talked to you."

They watched Fred disappear into the shadows, then rose to return to the car. Gregor tossed the empty paper cup into the nearby wastebasket. "Next time, I pick the restaurant."

CHAPTER THIRTEEN

"What are the wolves like in Prague," Ana asked on the way back to the waterfront.

Gregor inhaled. A damn nuisance. More so since Azrael insisted on including them in patrols. But for all that... "They're pack oriented. They don't dominate. They work together, protect their mates and their children. They are a family."

Ana exhaled. "How is it everything is so different, here and there?"

He shrugged. "They're American, you know, the Prague pack. Parents lived here for a time."

He left off the fact that he'd been the one to help them emigrate, but the brief exchange with Fred made him glad he had intervened.

He didn't like the furrow in her brow or the way she'd turned inward after the young wolf's tip. The darkness in her eyes when she turned them on him didn't feel much better. She looked worried, or as close to it as he had seen her. He found he liked the other Ana better—the one who led the way into traps. Make trouble, her stride suggested. I dare you.

"How did you know Fred was a wolf?" Gregor asked.

"It's part of my bargain," she said. "I see things as they are. Grace bloods disguised as humans, the animal natures in shifters, a lie being told, though not the truth behind it."

"Clever," he said. "What did you miss?"

Her gaze snapped to his face.

"As a human," he elaborated. "You missed something, something you should have seen. And you wanted to make sure you never would again. Aegis always ask for the thing they'd wanted as mortals."

"Is that how you got your soul steel?"

He inclined his head, letting her steer the subject away from herself. "I got what I asked for and more than I deserved."

She studied him a long pause. He wondered what she saw when he spoke. Apparently his words were judged truthful, if not entirely detailed.

"What's the plan?"

She allowed the change of subject. Her smile sharpened. "We wait until they've gathered, go in, ask a few questions."

He dipped his head once, liking the idea there might be some resistance. Just one other thing niggled at him: a necromancer capable of summoning demons in daylight was nothing to be toyed with. That kind of power should have been detected earlier. "And the necromancer?"

"I'll let Raymond know," she said. "We get a name if we can. Our objective doesn't change. We neutralize the creature. Necromancers handle their own business."

Gregor was relieved to hear she wasn't planning to go up against one strong enough to challenge Raymond. "Any necromancers show an increase in power lately?"

Ana shook her head. "By the mid-twentieth century he'd killed or forced an accord out of anyone who would have been a threat. That's part of what the traveling-circus crap was all about. They all work for him now."

"Should I speak with Azrael?"

"You took a vow. It could trigger the Retribution."

"But perhaps he can help identify—"

She shook her head once. "No."

Gregor sighed. "I would enjoy a cup of coffee while you break the news to Raymond."

The American obsession with drive-throughs amazed him. This one delivered hot, gourmet coffee at all hours, served by pleasant baristas. Ana's order sounded like a set of coordinates. But he could get used to her leaning over the console with a hand on his leg as she completed her request.

"Coffee, black," he said after Ana confirmed her order.

In the long silence, the speaker crackled. "Just… a coffee?"

"Black," he repeated.

Ana reached for her wallet, but Gregor held up a hand as he pulled up.

The young person at the counter swallowed when the tinted car window rolled down. Gregor's smile was all charm as they handed him the order. And the consort said he didn't have it in him. Ha. This attendant looked like they would have slid into the car on his lap if he had so much asked for a packet of sugar. The crisp bill he passed was accepted with a sigh.

"You may retain the rest."

"Have a nice day. Night.…"

Gregor tapped the window button and resumed his position behind the wheel, tucking the coffee into the drink holder. Ana lifted the cup to her mouth, pausing at his stern expression.

She snorted but put the cup in the neighboring cup holder. "Out of the driveway make a left, then a right at the light. There's a parking lot by the water."

"Thank you."

She didn't speak again until they were at the stoplight. "Does that work for you?"

He made a questioning sound at the edge in her voice.

"That routine," she said. "The smirk and the bedroom eyes."

"Bedroom eyes?"

She sat back in her seat, drumming her nails on the center console. "I suppose if you like them like that, that's all it takes."

He couldn't keep the amusement out of his voice as he pulled into the parking lot she indicated. "Like that?"

"Young, naive," she said. "Mortal."

He parked at the far end of the lot, closest to the water, and shut off the car before replying. "Ms. Gozen, you have no idea what I like."

He plucked his coffee and left her to her phone call. Before he could talk himself out of it, he put in a quick call to Ito, Azrael's head of security, for a list of necromancers of any known power in the Americas. Ito knew better than to ask why, and Gregor didn't offer. He hung up, then found a scrap of paper, scribbled a name and phone number, and tucked it into his breast pocket.

The overflow parking lot for the ferry terminal was empty at this hour. He walked to the edge, gazing out over the railing. The generous expanse of Puget Sound stretched out before him, blending into the darkness of the mountains on the peninsula across from the city. There were a few lights demarcating buildings close to the waterline. An enormous engine rumbled, and the brightly lit ferry carrying cars and passengers began the slow slide into the dock. Even this late, gulls circled the green-and-white boat, coasting on the gusts of air.

The breeze lifted the hair from his forehead, ruffling it along the back of his neck, and he took simple pleasure in the sensation of the natural world.

* * *

HE THOUGHT he'd known a love of the land in the wild roaming of his youth. But nothing prepared him for the intimacy of knowing a land when his life depended on it. For the settlers in Lark's Haven, the forest was home and larder. They coaxed, cajoled, and occasionally scraped a life from the hillsides by the narrowest of margins.

With little support from the outside, the settlement had to be as self-reliant as possible. Work always needed doing, followed by a meal for everyone who did his share. He lived among a group of bachelors, including Iain and a young Cheraw man his own age who gave his name only as Matthew, though Gregor heard others call him by a Native name.

Gregor took a bit of teasing when his first assigned chores put him among the children—feeding and watering the animals, milking the cows, collecting eggs. Respect came when he set himself to learning them with single-minded focus. A strong set of hands was welcome at every task, and every chore became an opportunity to regain his strength. Before long, he was hauling full milk pails with one or more of the littlest ones hanging off his neck and back like possum kits. He volunteered to clear trees and dig latrines. He learned the simple tools of the carpenter and assisted repairing buildings. One spring morning he peeled off his shirt for his morning ablutions to discover the wound that had almost taken his life nothing more than a pale pink line on his chest over muscle he hadn't possessed the previous fall.

At the stirrings of spring after a long winter, Lark came to the bachelor hut at dinnertime.

"You boys want to have a shoot-off tomorrow?" she asked. "Deacon sent up powder and I've got some young ones I'd like to see sharpening their aim, and it'd be good to have some fun while we do it."

The others nodded.

Gregor remained still, listening to the sound of his own heart thundering in his chest. His fingers itched. For months he'd watched hunters come and go, Lark among them, bearing the rifle the others had called after the German for falcon. Spring made him long to walk among them, but fear of her dismissal made him bite his tongue.

"*Herr Schwarzberg,*" she asked, pinning him in her clear gaze. "Some of the folks would like to see your rifle in action."

In one look she laid his heart bare. He swallowed his mouthful and tried to sound calm. "Imagine they already have on your hunting parties."

She inclined her head in assent. "But not with the jäger who knows her best."

In the morning he came down to the field with the rest. The youngsters were already practicing, picking off targets of rags stuffed with straw and leaves and old utensils and rusted pots. He'd not gone to the cabin first. Gregor wasn't surprised to see several women learning among the youngsters. On the long list of things Lark did not suffer, defenseless people ranked high.

Lark came down at the end of the morning, bearing two rifles. One, a simple but well-maintained hunting rifle in the French style. The second, his. She hefted it. *"Was vergessen?"*

"Ich hab nicht." He shook his head. It was no longer his.

Her brows lowered, but she switched to English and turned her attention to the others. "All right, you littles. Come back here and let the old folk show you a few tricks."

They moved the targets, set the line, and rifles were compared and ranked. A few eyes glanced covetously at the foreign long gun, but no one touched it until Gregor offered it to Matthew, who often led hunting parties. He grunted, pleased. His touch was like a lover—he stroked the barrel, sighted, tested the weight against his shoulder. He nodded and tried to hand it back. Gregor shrugged, dismissing the gesture.

"First round. Forty yards," Lark called, striding up to the start.

Everyone took a turn with the jäger rifle as the distances and the complexity of the targets increased. At one hundred yards only Gregor, Lark, and Iain and remained.

At last he and Lark stood at the line. She deferred, choosing her own rifle. She made the shot. He followed. The penultimate round was the longest. Lark braced the barrel and steadied her aim. Silence descended. The shot clipped the target, wide.

Gregor took his place as their hoots of celebration rose. Lark shushed them. The sun warm between his shoulders and on his hair felt like a caress. A slight breeze tickled his bare neck. For a moment he gloried in the feeling of being free as he had never been in his whole life. He squeezed the trigger.

The cheers startled him. He'd nailed the target square. He stood, surrounded, and flushed with a combination of pride and embarrassment at the flood of attention. When he looked, Lark stood on the edge of the crowd, a smile playing about her mouth. She sketched a little bow.

Blankets had been laid out for a picnic. Matthew clapped a hand on his shoulder in congratulations, dragging him toward the baskets of food. He pronounced a word in Cheraw. Gregor stumbled over it. Matthew grinned and tried again. Gregor managed not to mangle it, again.

The other man squeezed his shoulder. "It means Talking House. My name. And you hunt with us whenever you like."

"Because he never shuts up." Iain laughed. "And when Lark trusts you enough to let you come and go, you're with me."

Iain and Talking House left him behind, bickering at one another over rights to him.

"Wait!" Gregor shouted over the calls to eat. Eyes returned to him faster than he would have expected.

"One more round," he said. "Another go. Perhaps it is the rifle that makes the difference."

Some of the others booed, but most of the men started back up the hill, nodding agreement. Lark planted her hands on her hips. Her wry and defiant glare fixed on him. "I'll thank you not to insult my Lucille."

"And a fine old dame she is," Gregor said, teasing. "But she's past her day. Come. How can it be a fair test if we're not evenly matched?"

Lark stared at him. She knew how to use his rifle. The game slung over her shoulder on return from a hunt spoke to her skill. He wanted to see it. Her narrowed eyes held a mixture of amusement and suspicion. The others called for a last round. Finally she acquiesced.

Gregor shot first. He lowered the rifle, squinting at the target. The weight of her gaze settled on him. He didn't dare look away. She would know if he threw the shot.

He offered the rifle and shot, looking as nonchalant as he could manage.

She checked and loaded the weapon with an efficient ease that took his breath away. Watching her, a strange coiling heat started with desire low in his body and ended close to the scar at his ribs. She was magnificent even before she took aim.

A clear hit. Cheers rose from the crowd. She was their champion after all. His heart tripped at the grin she gave him. Inspection revealed that her shot had gone straight and true. His had just winged the tin.

He knew in that moment he belonged to her. She just didn't know it yet.

* * *

MOVEMENT on the surface of the water drew him out of memory. Gregor held still, keeping his eyes soft and unfocused.

A sleek, tawny head appeared, tiny black eyes shining, and looked up at him. The creature rolled onto its back, and more of it emerged from the water, small paws tucked against the spiky fur of its chest.

"Awfully late for you to be out, isn't it," he murmured.

The otter cocked its head, watching. It disappeared into the waves with a sinuous flip at the sound of boot heels on pavement. Ana rested her elbows on the railing, half-empty cup in one hand, the still illuminated screen of her phone in the other.

"How's Raymond?" he asked, watching the last of the ripples from the disappearing otter.

"Pissed off," she said. The tiny furrow reappeared between her brows. "Concerned. In his way."

"What way is that?"

"The way that makes me think he's known all along what we're chasing, if not why now."

He let the silence linger. He kept his face impassive, looking out over the water. Her eyes fell on him, the weight of her gaze heavy on his skin.

He glanced at her out of the corner of his eye. She still looked troubled, but amusement tugged at her mouth. "What?"

"Azrael must be delighted," she growled. "Raymond asks for help and he gets to send his first into another necromancer's territory. You tested my men, you watch everything, now you know I don't always trust my master. A fine report to make to yours."

Gregor faced her. "Wouldn't you?"

She glared at him, but it lacked any heat.

Gregor sighed. "Raymond helped Azrael once."

"And you're *only* here to return the favor."

"The Allegiance is in crisis." Gregor let his shoulders rise and fall. "It would be wise to determine who our friends are, if we have them."

In the darkness, her eyes were inscrutable. The wind picked up the fine, shorter strands of her hair and sent them flying.

"And you make the decision," she said, the hint of a taunt in her voice.

"My input holds weight," he acknowledged without boasting. He bit his tongue on the question: why don't you have the same, as Raymond's first? It was the most important gift Azrael had given him.

The Aegis served under contracts for lengths of time. Hers must have been centuries. How else had Raymond kept her this long? It had to be the status of their contract. Why else would she not have left him for a necromancer who appreciated her instead of keeping her like a deadly pet on a leash to be loosed at his command? Incomprehensible.

She broke his thoughts with a question. "What *now*?"

It was his turn to be confused.

"Why are you angry?"

He had to look away, this time to hide his surprise. Had he been that transparent?

"You hide it well, but it's my gift."

Something genuine unfurled in her voice without the guard of deference or sarcasm. The words could have been an attack but instead formed the beginning of a bridge. A weight clenched in his chest with the impact of a steel door slamming. Not now. Not again. Never again.

He made a show of checking his watch even though he could feel time in his bones. "Just looking forward to playing catch-up with Rathki. We should go."

CHAPTER FOURTEEN

Murphy's was a biker bar, judging by the parking lot. But scanning the row of shining tanks and glistening chrome, she judged it more upscale than the average motorcycle club joint. She took a quick assessment of Gregor's face. The detachment had returned, but now she was more certain that beneath the mask lay anger.

Gregor was too old and too intelligent to let emotion fuel him. They were alike in that regard. Whatever had made him angry, it had nothing to do with the satyr. If anything, it was connected to the way his face shuttered when he'd admitted how much his words were weighted by his master. She hadn't responded because she didn't want to give him any more reason to think there was a schism between her and Raymond.

At least that was what she told herself. It didn't matter that after a century, she still took orders and was rarely consulted. That was ego talking. Pride had no place in her work.

From the parking lot across the street, they watched the late crowd began to filter out. If Fred was right, the weres would wait until after closing to meet up. If Ana and Gregor were lucky, they would cooperate and share whatever they knew in order to prove loyalty to Raymond and save their own skins.

"How do you want to handle this?"

Ana paused. Was he asking for a plan again? She snorted. "Walk in. Ask some questions. See what happens."

She tapped the center console to get his attention, fixing her gaze on a familiar, lanky figure standing beside a small pile of chain attached to a post used to close off the parking lot after hours. Fred Smith.

A muscled man in leathers emerged from the building. He barked at the club patrons lingering in the parking lot until they scattered. A few more bikes arrived in ones and twos, joining the figures emerging from the shadows and moving to the doors. The last was a van that parked near the doors and shut off, but no one emerged. At some unspoken gesture from the bouncer, Fred picked up the chain and jogged across the open driveway, locking it on the other side. The bouncer conversed with the driver of the van and then stepped back, grinning and rubbing his palms together.

The back doors of the van opened and two men piled out, dragging a third between them. The satyr looked rougher for wear. His glasses were missing, shirt untucked, and slacks dirtied and torn. His human shielding was starting to slip; she imagined even Gregor could see his true form now.

"Rathki." Gregor growled as he recognized the stumbling figure. "Did he run or did they take him?"

The bigger men dragged him, bleating, into the bar. The bouncer followed, leaving Fred outside, stamping in the cold.

"Let's find out."

She climbed out of the car and slipped Imouto and Onee-san into the dual sheath on her hip. An unusual set, both katana and wakizashi were shorter than most, better suited for her reach. She'd had other pairs made for her over the intervening years, but she trusted none more than these.

Gregor lagged as Ana strode toward the driveway. "Front door?"

She showed her teeth. "They'll smell us coming soon enough, I doubt they're smart enough to run."

Fred started at his post when they appeared. His eyes bulged. "Are you crazy?"

"I've been accused of worse, and given what she deals with on a regular basis, I wouldn't blame her if she were." Gregor reached into his jacket. Ana wasn't the only one who thought he was going for a gun.

Fred flung up his hands, desperation drawing his soft baby face taut. Gregor sighed, slowing the motion as he withdrew his hand. He extended a slip of paper and a credit card.

"You'll want to make yourself scarce right now," he said. "Do you know who I am?"

The younger man nodded, swallowing hard.

"Ever been to Europe?"

Fred shook his head.

"Try Prague." Gregor waved the card. "The beer is cheap. The women have legs"—he gestured to his chest level—"to here. When you get to the city, call this number. Ask for Markus. He's a good man. Tell him I said I owe him one."

Fred swallowed. His hand trembled as he took the offering. "Thanks, man."

"Just do me a favor and stay away from witches."

Fred looked between them, hesitating. "These guys, they're no joke."

Gregor tilted his head. "Neither is she."

That didn't seem to soothe Fred. For one horrified moment, she thought he would offer to back them. She couldn't afford to have the liability on her hands.

"Go now," Gregor ordered.

Fred slipped the card and the paper between his teeth. Before their eyes, he shuddered, dropping to all fours. A rangy young red wolf shook off the last of his clothing at their feet. The irony of the dog tags jingling in the ruff at his throat was not lost on her.

"Pup indeed." Gregor chuckled as the wolf scrambled into the darkness.

The club's decor—mechanic's garage meets fifties diner—seemed to mortally offend Gregor. He tapped a battered license plate nailed to the wall, sniffing in distaste. They followed the sound of voices to the stairs in the back of the room.

"…he gonna show or what?"

"We only got three nights…"

"…wasting time. Close the loop now or we're done for—"

"…little shit couldn't do his fucking job, and now the bitch is still loose."

"Quiet. All of you. Someone's coming."

In the darkness, Gregor met Ana's eyes. His brows rose in unmistakable question, one hand sliding beneath his coat.

The corner of her mouth tipped up in answer. She held up a hand. He nodded and released his grip.

The descent led them into a lounge. Vinyl booths around tables lined the walls, broken by the presence of a bar with stools topped with hubcaps as seats.

The conversation stopped as they entered, but no one moved. Ana counted eighteen bodies in the smoky darkness. This wasn't a single pack, based on the clusters around the room. A few females dotted the groups, several dressed in leathers. The rest looked like cocktail servers repurposed for after-hours entertainment. Most were mortal and, beneath heavy layers of makeup, terrified.

Rathki had been seated at the back table. He looked even worse close up. Someone had gone a few rounds on his face, and blood crusted open wounds, blackening around the edges. Bruises covered the rest. Like most grace bloods, he might be long-lived, but he lacked the accelerated healing ability of an Aegis.

The rest of the table must have been the senior members of the packs. They were older, more scarred, than the rest.

"Ana Gozen, I presume," the big male said from the head of the table. He was brawny but had a clever face. "And Gregor Schwarz. The rumors are true."

"You must be Jax," Ana said before addressing their captive. "Nice to see you again so soon, Rathki."

If it was possible, the satyr looked even more miserable now than when they had entered the room. It gave her perverse pleasure knowing whatever he had been through since they last met, he feared her more.

Gregor started for the bar, pulled up a stool, and seated himself. "Scotch neat. A double please."

The bartender sneered, showing inhumanly long teeth. "Don't carry scotch here."

"Whiskey will do then."

The bartender looked about to protest, but the big male in the center of the bosses' table smiled. His ruddy, sunbaked skin broke at the mouth to expose an expansive set of yellow teeth, sharp as knives. "Serve the man. Drinks are on the house. It's not often we have such illustrious company."

Gregor inclined his head.

"For you?" Jax gave Ana her the kind of frank appraisal that would have made her reach for her sword a century ago.

She refused to give him the satisfaction. "No thanks."

Time was littered with men like him—bruisers who came to power through a combination of brute force and sociopathic intelligence who used either when the need struck. She had been wrong about one thing. Jax and his men wouldn't run, not out of stupidity, but because they thought they had nothing to fear. Interesting.

Jax sat back in his seat, considering her. "How can we help you?"

"I have business with Professor Demos," Ana said without changing her tone from mild curiosity. "And some questions for you."

"You can ask your questions," Jax said over the subsonic rumble of the gathered crowd. "But the goat is on his way to an appointment."

Ana shot Gregor a glance. This was the pack they wanted.

Jax misread the look and chuckled. "So now we see who calls the shots, eh, little one? Why don't you come have a seat, Herr Schwarz. Let's talk about your questions."

Gregor stood. The room recoiled at the smooth movement, but he shrugged off his fine wool coat and unbuttoned his suit jacket. She read the question in his eyes and nodded. He settled on the barstool and accepted his drink. "Not my circus, not my monkeys."

The few mortals in the room paled as an audible growl rolled through the room.

"Affirmative action…" Jax smirked. "Is a bitch, ain't it?"

Jax knew how to play to his audience, reminding any of them who might have feared her by reputation that a small female stood before them. Laughter rose as they took their boss's lead. Some things never changed.

She was too old for indignation, too schooled for rage.

The chill of a snowy night in the foothills of the Bitterroot Mountains settled over her. Once, long ago, she had tracked a gang of men more animal than these. When those hard men looked up from their campfire, drunk and satisfied by the spoils of their crime, they laughed at her. A foreign girl, dressed in a man's clothes a size too big for her, carrying a pair of thin metal sticks. A few had even offered her money with the leering gaze she recognized in Jax now. She had not let the laughter touch her then either.

"I'm investigating a series of kills up north," she said, focusing on Jax. "Mortal and blooded slain. Dismembered."

"I missed the question."

"You run the packs from Juneau to the Cascades. Figured you'd have heard something."

She recognized the expectant stillness from the night by the campfire, so many years ago. Back then she had been more vulnerable than she was now, but no more afraid.

Jax's lips curled away, and Ana was struck by how, even in human form, wolves appeared to love baring their teeth. "And if I have heard something?"

"I'll let you walk away intact." She cast her glance sideways. "I'll even throw in Rathki as a gesture of good will and ignore whatever you have going on here."

Rathki bleated and started to babble. She wasn't sure whether he was pleading with her or the weres. A solid thump in the solar plexus from the guard on his left reduced him to a doubled-over, wheezing old goat.

"Are you accusing us of breaking Allegiance law?" Jax sat back in his chair, one massive hand spanning his chest, a look of put-upon dismay on his face.

"I'm inviting you to tell me what you know about the wolves involved, who they're working with, and for," she said, scanning the room to take in the cowering mortals. "As for Allegiance law, you've been breaking that for some time, but I'm happy to over-look it if you cooperate and promise to clean up your act."

He did not move, but the latent violence in the room strained at the tethers of civility. "You consider that an invitation?"

Once, long ago, she had answered another question. "*What do you want here, girl?*"

"*To know… what you did back there to the man and his woman.*" Her heart cried a dead woman's name. *They had nothing. Why?*"

Raucous laughter had drowned out the mourning cries of her heart. His response sealed his fate. "*Because we can.*"

With the answer, she locked her heart away and did what needed to be done. Not a single man had walked away from the campfire.

"All right." She fixed her gaze on Jax. "Tell me about your new ally."

Silence permeated the room for a heartbeat, maybe two. Jax started laughing, the boom of his voice making lesser men all over the room jump in their chairs before they relaxed into the shame-less snickering of cowards behind a big dog.

Gregor shifted on his seat. Ana's brows knit. Would he sit this one out?

He raised his glass. A savage pleasure rose in her. She bared her teeth.

Jax and his cohort howled, laughter turning to something more savage. She could feel the coming break in the calm. *Three. Two. One.*

Four of the closest men leaped toward her at some unspoken

signal. Clumsy and uncoordinated, the attack seemed to rely solely on overwhelming her with size and numbers. How primitive. She sidestepped, drawing Onee-san with a twist of the saya and her hip for two long slashes that sent them sprawling in puddles of their own blood. She spun into the regrouping men, directing each into the singing edge of the blade. When she was finished, two of the four men attempted to drag themselves away. The other two lay still.

"No deal?" she asked Jax, flicking blood from the blade to the table top and spoiling their fresh round.

Maybe he had nothing left to lose. If he had made a pact with this other necromancer, he was dead either way. If the rival succeeded, he'd be hunted down and killed for a lack of loyalty. If Raymond survived, he'd be executed for treason. Maybe he just liked being a thorn in her side. Some people were just like that.

In any case, he didn't look the least bit reluctant as his face elongated before her eyes, his enunciation lost in a canine growl. "No deal."

"All right then, bitches." The corners of her mouth tilted up as she softened her knees and readied her blade. "Let's dance."

* * *

TWICE. Ana tapped the hilt of each blade twice as she and Jax began their parlay. A small, reflexive movement, like a race car driver revving an engine before the start. Her face remained impassive at their laughter and her posture casual under the weight of the pack's stare. Even the growing reek of men beginning to transition didn't warrant so much as a flare of her nostrils. The only tell, Gregor noted, were those quick, repeated motions. Tap-tap. Tap-tap.

Yet when the room exploded around her into snarls and flashes of fur, no one could mistake her for being caught off guard. Between one heartbeat and the next, Ana became a breathing weapon. She fell back, feigned, defended, and when the opponent pressed, she attacked. Nothing extraneous or flashy, simply flowing from one movement into the next.

The bartender went for a gun. Before Gregor could draw, a slim knife flew through the air and pinned the man's forearm to the wall. Gregor's gaze snapped back to her. Ana winked.

Gregor relieved the man of the gun and his consciousness, plucked the knife, and let him slide to the floor. He bounced the knife in his hand, tested the edge on his thumb. Frowned. Not bad. When he caught her eye again she lifted the hilt of the short sword to tip an imaginary cap.

He gave a crisp bow before returning to his seat. He released the magazine and emptied the chamber, then crushed the barrel, grip and trigger in his grip. He dropped the crumpled metal on the bar and slipped the magazine into his jacket pocket, giving the rest of the mortals a long stare. "It's not *your* circus either."

The black blade pressed against his spine, a tangible weight, hungry for blood. He held his seat. He dropped the remaining bullet into the amber liquid in his glass and tilted it at the nearest server. "Another."

After the initial rush and a brief frenzied response to the four downed men, Jax managed to rally his wolves. They moved like a pack now in human and wolf form—worrying, drawing, snipping. Trying to get Ana to let down her guard, to overstep her reach. Ana freed her short sword and things really got interesting.

Every time she opened up, they came, unable to resist an opportunity, and she closed the door behind them, giving them no quarter. She was an elegant killing machine.

In the commotion, Rathki made a run for it. Gregor sighed and tore his eyes away from the sexiest woman he had ever laid eyes on. Time to make himself useful. Finally.

He collared Rathki upstairs, halfway to the door. "I'd hate to miss the end on account of you, Demos."

He dragged the satyr back down the steps, then dumped him on the floor at the foot of the barstool and pinned him with a heel on his neck.

Three wolves remained: Jax—now covered in silver pelt—and

two of his lieutenants. The one on the left, the head of the Seattle pack. The other, a skinny gray male with more cunning than strength. Of the rest, the lucky ones fled. The others would never run under the moon again.

She met the Seattle pack leader's attack easily, but the cunning gray managed to flank her in the distraction. When he went to press his advantage, she moved faster. She hamstrung him in one slash. He crashed to the floor with an agonized howl. She ended it with the short blade, turning to face the remaining wolf.

Jax.

The enormous male circled, head low, ears flat. The thunder of his growl rattled silverware across the room. He was older, wiser, and more patient. He'd spent the battle watching Ana, much as Gregor had.

She drew upright. "Are you ready to behave, dog?"

Jax lost his cool in a furious explosion of snapping jaws and flying spittle. Gregor sucked his teeth in disappointment. He'd expected a real challenge.

Ana stood still, her face a mask. When the wolf struck, she stepped in as if accepting an invitation to an embrace. The wolf hit her shoulder, but she was already rolling away. As he passed, the short blade found the soft opening behind his ribs. She brought the hilt of the katana down like a cudgel at the base of his skull.

He crashed to the floor, sliding to a stop. With a low, tortured whine, he dragged himself to his front paws. The hilt of Ana's short sword quivered in his side as he continued growling and jabbering. Ana took him by the scruff and dragged him to the table. She had to throw all her weight against him, looking like a child with a large stuffed animal. She dropped him, grabbed the chair he had been occupying, and pinned him to the floor with it, straddling the seat. Her blade rested over the big vein on his neck.

"Now we talk."

* * *

ANA LISTENED. Internal bleeding would finish Jax off soon. If not, she would spare him as much pain as possible. The killing cold had left her when she sat down.

On a night long ago in the woods, quiet had also been the only thing left in the end. There hadn't been much of a battle. More than tonight, it had been a slaughter.

"Gonna remember us for a long time, I reckon," the leader of the gang said as she put the blade to his throat, ignoring the tears running through the blood on her cheeks and leaving salt and iron on her tongue. *"Never forget your first kill. Might even regret it someday."*

"You lot weren't my first." She opened his jugular. *"I've forgotten you already."*

Remember, yes? Regret? She hadn't regretted a minute of it, and she never would. Not after the sight of the burned-out cabin, the gutted animals and household possessions strewn around the little clearing like so much flotsam and jetsam. Not after the sight of the body, the clothing charred and torn, and the small bundle of humanity wrapped in cloth that she clutched under one arm even in death. In one night, an entire future vanished.

On the floor beneath her, Jax coughed between bloody teeth. The change came slow—it took a lot of energy to transition, and with every breath his life slid away. He was mostly man again, wolf pelt shading his arms and legs. His hands and feet still narrowed to paws. His laughter died in a wheeze. He spit blood.

She'd killed enough to know the measure of dwindling life by the blood. He had no more than a few dozen breaths now.

"She's coming for him."

"She?" A chill ran up her spine. Across the room, Gregor straightened on his stool, listening.

"Oh, she's got a bone to pick." He chuckled. "A whole burial ground full. And when she catches up with him—I'd be afraid. Whatever she is, ain't right, that's it."

Bones. Burial grounds. Gregor had been right in suspecting someone from Raymond's past. Jax wheezed.

"And the necromancer?"

"Barnabas Huxley." Jax coughed. The name meant nothing to her. "Send my regards. Once you meet him, I suppose I'll see you in hell."

"Save me a seat." She ended it and spent a moment staring at his empty face.

The absence of any emotion in the wake of death no longer troubled her, but she contemplated it anyway. Then she stood up from the chair, sweeping the blood from her blade with a quick chiburui motion. She crouched and drew Imouto from Jax's corpse.

At the bar, Gregor shrugged on his coat and tossed her a bar towel. Rathki sprawled at his feet, bleating.

"Thanks." She nodded at the satyr as she wiped both blades clean.

Gregor raised his still half-full glass. "Feels good to be useful."

"I'll keep that in mind." She slid both blades home and surveyed the mess. "I think we're done here."

Gregor collared Rathki with a shake and dragged the satyr to his feet. "Never have to clean soul steel."

Ana rolled her eyes as she headed for the door. "Noted."

CHAPTER FIFTEEN

A team of official-looking SUVs waited outside the bar. Gregor recognized one of Raymond's men—the one he'd sparred with—in the driver's seat of the lead vehicle. The man had earned a measure of respect for his persistence in the sparring ring, but Gregor found the way he looked at Ana left much to be desired. Auger. The rest were undead.

They must have been on a plane as soon as Ana reported the meeting with Fred.

"Just the one?" Auger met them with a glance at Rathki.

"And a cleanup," Ana said. As in Azrael's territory, the ruling necromancer's Aegis also handled covering up any breeches of the law regarding grace bloods.

He flicked a hand at four brawny-looking undead, sending them into the club. Gregor watched the mortals herded from the bar to the vehicles and wondered what would become of them.

Ana stood, forearm resting on her blade hilt. Gregor imagined it humming with contentment after a job well done. He liked the image of the woman alone on the killing floor, the sword an extension of her body. *She* was the blade.

The black blade pressed into his spine, weighted with unspent energy.

Auger faced Gregor with a smile. He still bore the fading traces of their match. Again Gregor wondered about the healing ability Raymond had granted—or skimped on—his Aegis.

"I'll take that, Gregor." He laughed, reaching for Rathki. Though he stood a head shorter than Gregor, he was broader. He had the casually violent air of a street fighter and a face for movies. Gregor decided he didn't like him much. The muscles in his hand tensed, fingers inches from a fist. Ana looked up, inhaling. In one fluid motion, Gregor lifted the hunched satyr, dumping him at Auger's feet.

Without looking back, he stalked to the Audi.

* * *

"What's with him?" Auger asked as he handed Rathki over.

Ana watched Gregor's back as he moved to the shadows, the purposeful stride giving his silhouette a sinister cast. People like them were weapons first. She recognized the pent-up violence in him. "He sat this one out."

Auger looked offended. "He let you handle it alone?"

"He didn't *let* me do anything," Ana snapped.

Auger held up his palms, but the little smile still stretched his mouth. "I'm just saying, I don't know how they do things in Prague, but I would've had your back."

"He did have my back, Auger."

This time Auger took a step back at the ice in her tone.

Gregor had sat it out because the fight had belonged to her. Her territory. Her reputation. And, most of all, because she'd asked him to.

"Gotcha." Auger didn't look convinced, but he knew better than to keep talking.

Ana focused on Rathki. "Get him back to Raymond. The name Barnabas Huxley mean anything to you?"

Auger shook his head. Ana swore at the thought of a necromancer this powerful managing to stay off their radar for so long.

"Then start looking into him. I want everything. Call in favors. Give them out. Do it fast."

"And you?"

"We're not finished here."

He seemed to want to say something else, but she had already turned her back and headed toward the Audi.

Morning crept over the city. The water was still dark, but strands of light from the east filtered through the buildings to light the pavement.

Gregor waited in the driver's seat. Slipping into the car was like being in a cage with a hungry animal. The hair on her arms rose as the warrior in her turned over in response to the threat.

He started the motor. "Where to?"

She had blood on her jeans and her boots. Unlike demon ichor, it had an organic, salt-and-iron tang. It also stunk like unkempt animal. "Bike. Condo. Could use a shower."

The hand on the wheel flexed so hard the material groaned in response. She bit her lip. Her skin flushed hot and confined against fabric. Maybe he wasn't the only one.

The bike was where they'd left it. While the engine warmed up, she leaned back into the car. "Want to stop somewhere for breakfast on the way?"

Glacial blue eyes settled on her, and the temperature in the car rose a few degrees.

"With your taste in food?" Had he always sounded like liquid sex, or was that just the afterburn of her fight talking? "I think not."

"Race you."

* * *

GREGOR GAVE up trying not to look at her ass one hundred feet out of the parking lot. Ana hit too many of his buttons to resist. So he allowed himself to acknowledge those twin mounds, and when she changed lanes, he followed the sleek line of her waist to her rib cage. The way her lower back arched as she leaned over the tank made him envy the bike.

He pushed the car faster, reveling in the chase.

The sensible thing would be to rein this desire in, finish the job, and go home to make his report to Azrael. There were dozens of women he could slake this thirst with.

But not one in hundreds came close to Ana Gozen.

Maybe Lysippe had been right in seeing their similarities. Crafting and upholding that much distance took the effort of a long-burned heart. Sex and physical contact might be a necessity. But he and Ana were too old—too damaged—for a love story.

Gregor watched the taillights of the bike disappear into the garage ahead of him. He took his time parking, watching her shake her hair into place from the helmet, contemplating his next move.

It wouldn't be prudent, seducing Ana Gozen. But it would be interesting.

He climbed out of the car.

She stood by the elevator, turned into a sleek silhouette by the light of the open doors. "Coming?"

He would be a fool to miss the taunt. "After you."

Hell, no one lived forever.

* * *

THE FREIGHT ELEVATOR capable of fitting a compact sedan felt too small with Gregor beside her. Still, Ana made no move to distance herself from him. So they rode up as they had entered, side by side.

She wondered how it would begin. It wouldn't be the first time she'd made the first move.

On the night she turned twenty, Raymond took her to a bar in a frontier town, pointed at a table full of young cowboys. *"You should pick one. It won't do to go into this bargain with anything resembling innocence."*

She spat on the floor. Cowboys held no interest for her. He'd laughed before the bartender kicked them both out.

In the end she'd chosen the slight boy who did the labor for the mercantile owner. His son, perhaps. He'd had the temerity to smile at her as she walked into town beside Raymond. She left her swords in her bedroll at the camp Raymond set up among the crimson rocks and returned on foot to the outpost. In the back of his father's shop, before dawn, she'd placed the boy's hands where she wanted them, given him permission to go further. In the morning she and Raymond had ridden away. She had not looked back. The next day she traded her soul to become the first of Raymond's Aegis.

The sound of the metal gate sliding open brought her back to the present. Gregor stood aside to let her exit first. Perhaps stepping aside came from the same place as bridling his own hunger for blood to remind everyone in the room who—and what —she was.

He prowled out of the elevator and stood, facing the room in three-quarters profile. He still had the sense not to turn his back to her.

Tension clenched his shoulders beneath the suit jacket as he shrugged out of his coat. Even without seeing his face, she read the lines of energy coiling, unspent, in his long body.

"Would you like a drink?"

Her skin prickled at the invitation. Of all the things she wanted, the numbness of alcohol was not one of them. "I have a better way to take the edge off."

His head whipped around at the words, and she could see the nostrils flare in his profile. Oh, this *was* going to be fun.

CHAPTER SIXTEEN

In the basement sparring room, Gregor checked his watch one last time before laying it on the small table by the door. He walked a circuit of the room, footsteps a susurrus against the sleek floating-wood flooring stained so dark the grain shone in the subtle lighting, and waited.

"I kept you waiting," she said by way of apology.

It was the closest he'd come to being startled in over a century. Reluctantly, his mouth stretched into something resembling a smile. "Not long. Rules of engagement?"

Ana had given up bloodstained designer jeans and leather boots for a simple pair of black cotton pants and a tank top. She set the dual saya in their places and stepped onto the mat in the center of the room, blades bared. She raised an eyebrow.

"Seems only right to ask." Gregor spread his hands and bowed. The blade coalesced on his back. It never weighed so much as it did when he'd been denied a fight. He let his palm find the familiar grip, unsure which came first—the hilt or the touch that sought it. At her pause, he said, "Reconsidering?"

She twirled the short sword in her left hand and grinned. "Nope."

It would have been prudent to strategize, let her come to him, feel out her defense, test her. To hell with that. The blade in his hand was as solid now as any other weapon, but if he'd thought they would meet in a clash of sparks and ringing steel, he was mistaken. Where he struck, she avoided, when he pressed, she slid away. He counted the times they made contact on one hand. His chest heaved with effort, sweat soaking through his shirt when he burned through the first red-soaked rush.

When he withdrew, he left her breathless—with laughter. "You are insane, you know?"

He winked. They crossed the room in the swift dance of feet across the floor. "You expected a courtship?"

Her lips twitched. "I hate a tease."

She moved so quickly she blurred even in his eyes. He reacted on instinct, not waiting for thought. It saved him the loss of his sword. She slipped backward, out of his reach, with a smug little glare.

"You're holding back." She sucked her teeth with a little shake of her head.

"We still have work to do. I'd hate to accidentally kill you." He kept his voice flippant, but he couldn't help thinking of how long it took both her and Auger to heal. Gregor's ability to recover from everything short of beheading owed itself to the speed. Could she bleed out before her body could repair itself?

She snorted. "I'd like to see you try."

This time he let her come to him. Blades kissed with a sweet ring, and he gave himself over to the dance, moving into a space of pure instinct and response. She was waiting for him there. The soft puff of her breath brushed his ear. He didn't think. When she spun, she met him there. He trapped her long sword and twisted it free, sending it spinning. The delight in her eyes surprised him.

Then she lifted the short sword, flicking a bead of red from the blade with a circular sweep of her wrist.

He slid away, his hand finding the open line on his bicep weeping a steady stream of crimson as it sealed before their eyes.

She blew a kiss. "First blood."

He pushed harder. The sweat rolled down her skin in glistening streaks. He knew he had her on the run when her lips parted and a slight wrinkle marred the space between her brows. He pressed until she was on the defense. The moment came and he slipped into the opening, risking a loss of balance for force. He caught her wrist, then the other, dragging her in close and pinching her elbows against his side.

He leered into her face. "What now?"

Her forehead met his nose with a force that made him see stars. Her heel slammed into his foot. He staggered a step, impressed by her ability to shed sophistication for the tactics of a back-alley brawler between one move and the next. She followed it up with a kick to the solar plexus, flinging him backward. Before he could recover, she pressed the advantage, disarming him in three strokes. She hooked his knee, sweeping him to the ground. The woodcuttings on the walls rattled. He snagged her ankle and she slammed into the mat beside him.

On the ground, the elegant dance devolved into bare-knuckle scrabbling. They grappled, hand to hand, in silence punctuated by the odd snarl or sound of tortured cloth ripping under the onslaught of superhuman strength.

"Are you laughing?" She pinned him, their legs twisted together as they wrestled for control of the hold.

He was. "You broke my nose."

"You expected me to be polite?" She got a hand free and punched him in the throat.

He grunted, catching her again before she could break the hold. "I had hoped you wouldn't."

"Good." She sent a knee into the soft spot below his ribs.

He grunted but kept his grip. "Shall we finish this?"

"Please try."

He bucked hard, flipping her onto her back.

She got his wrist, twisted until bones snapped, but pain didn't even distract him. Still, she used the grip to drag him into a roll and she wound up back on top, her legs straddling him, the length of his erection pressed between them. Her breath hitched against her ribs.

She bared bloody teeth and ground herself into him. "Another round?"

The unmistakable heat of her through two layers of cloth almost undid him. His body responded with its own blunt need. He reached for her mouth but she twisted away, preoccupied with shedding the remaining cloth between them. He would have her, but on her terms.

He could live with that.

The sudden shock of skin-to-skin contact drove his breath from his chest. He surrendered to the contrast of cold air and the heat of skin damp with sweat as her fingers plowed the flesh of his shoulders on their way to the source of all the tension burning in him. The air escaped his lungs when she gripped him, guiding him to the fluid center of her body. Then he sank into her. The shock made him rigid, but the sheer rightness made him gasp.

She was muscle and sinew, curve and arch. And for this moment, she was his.

She grunted, fluid strength clasping around him, and her fingers buried in his hair. The combination of tightness, above and below, unleashed something primitive in him.

He shoved himself off the floor, bracing on one arm to get closer to her. Not close enough. The other locked around her waist, forearm molding to her spine, fingertips digging into her hip. A groan escaped him and he drove his hips up until he could go no deeper. Her spine bowed, crushing the last bit of distance between them.

His mouth found the firm mound of a breast as he brushed his stubbled jaw along the soft slope. Fingers tightened in his hair. Ragged breath scraped his ear as she pushed the pace. He slicked a nipple with his tongue before suckling. Her body clenched. Darkness flirted around the edge of his vision. He gripped her hip and for a moment the battle of wills—hers demanding motion, his insisting stillness—clenched them harder than before.

A note of victory rang in his chest when she surrendered.

The slow circular grind, her arms around his shoulders, turned out to be much, much more difficult to withstand.

When his fingers slipped between them, a low growl escaped her chest. He managed to be gentle at first until she pressed herself against his thumb and tugged his hair until he saw stars. He kept it up—damned if he'd stop her from killing him if it gave her pleasure.

He held himself beyond any sense of his own control. When her body began to shudder around him, her breath and heart thundering ahead in release, he let go.

All her fierce strength eased against him between one breath and the next. Without thought, his arms went around her in support. He sucked on the skin of her collarbone as their bodies exchanged residual tremors. The damp weight of her hair, the strands so much finer than he'd imagined, tickled his nose.

The harsh sound of breathing came at a distance. His own. What was left of his pants bunched at his knees. The tattered remains of his shirt hooked around his arm and under his body. It wasn't exactly a defensible position. Or particularly maneuverable.

For the first time in a hundred years or more, he didn't care. Ana shuddered against him. The back of her neck fit in the palm of his hand. He squeezed, and she responded by tilting her head, exposing a long line of pale, perfect neck. He followed the line of her throat to her jaw with his mouth.

The temptation of her mouth, so close, lured him. Lips like satin. What did they taste like? The rough stubble of his cheek against her triggered microshudders of response. Small nips with a lick and light pressure led him to her jawline, her ear, her cheek. He trailed her chin, rising higher. Her breath tickled his mouth.

She slipped out of his grasp in a single graceful evasion and rose to her feet. He knew better than to reach for her.

The rest of her clothes fell away with a few sharp tugs. She blew a lock of hair out of her eyes. Surveyed him. "Better?"

He watched her collect her swords with what he hoped was a nonchalant gaze. "Much."

Her nostrils flared. "I have some leads to follow, and I need to make arrangements to speak with someone who might be helpful."

She stalked away.

* * *

In her own room Ana leaned against the closed door and exhaled. The residual burn of combat combined with the languid ache of release made for a potent mix.

When it came to sex, the body had needs and she could meet them or ignore them with some effort. She stayed in control. Fun. Not essential.

With Gregor, sex was as intense as the sparring had been. She couldn't wait to do it again.

They had a job to finish. They didn't need distractions. Shower, then work.

The woman gazing back from the mirror bore fresh bruises—after all, it had begun as a fight. But these were nothing compared to demon wounds—they faded before her eyes as her body's enhanced ability to heal itself took over. But like the afterimage of the sword between Gregor's shoulder blades, they remained in her vision, catching her attention out of the corners of her eyes as she showered and dried off.

A repeat was out of the question.

She rested her forehead on the door and closed her eyes. Work. She had calls to make, ferry schedules to check.

"Always giri, always working, Onee-san." Takami's voice drifted up from memory, more plea than taunt as Ana went about her chores, leaving her behind.

When Takami struggled to read in the new language, Ana began smuggling dime novels from the gaijin shops. Takami's reading ability grew with the new subject matter. Their tutor took the credit, never knowing the source of the improvement. Ana preferred adventures and Wild West tales. Takami lost herself in tales of chivalry and romances where delicate, helpless girls escaped tyrannical villains to run off with rugged, handsome men. Ana blamed herself for Takami and her cowboy.

The traditional tales from home almost always ended in sacrifice—and the occasional suicide—or at least separation of the lovers for the sake of duty and the inescapable debt one owed to family, liege, or emperor.

It was a new concept, this happily ever after.

And a lie.

Ana had seen that before she swore her vow to Raymond.

After all, what did a cowboy know about homesteading? The little farm Takami and her cowboy had made etched into her memory. Even before it had been ransacked, it had been rough and poor—a far cry from the finery of the girl's childhood. Their clothing had been simple and for this time of year. The only thing of luxury from her old life—warm fur on one side, cheap satin on the other—had been wrapped closest to the skin of the child at her breast. Takami had given up her family, her home, a life of wealth and privilege. In exchange, she had her cowboy and their child. Ana knew what life the child would have in either culture.

The creeping warmth in her belly coiling out to her limbs at the thought of Gregor's body beneath her receded. There was no such thing as happily ever after. Only after. And after, everything ended.

She made her calls, planned the timing of their trip, and sent Raymond a brisk status report. Then she let go of the breath it seemed she'd been holding all day and went in search of her partner.

In the kitchen, Gregor perched on one of the barstools, a half-eaten triangle of toast in one hand, making an intent scrutiny of the newspaper before him. How old-fashioned. And he was wearing another impeccably tailored suit, the tie a satiny crimson. With his hair slicked back and a clean shave, he looked as if he could be on his way to steal some souls for the devil.

"I managed to coax coffee from your apparatus," he said without looking up as she entered the kitchen.

"Thanks." She started for a cup, but one already sat beside the coffee maker. Her favorite—comic book ninja on a street bike.

"Omelet in the oven."

She slid her plate onto the counter, retrieved her coffee, and when she returned, he pushed a plate of toast and the butter dish her direction. "You've already eaten?"

He made a noncommittal sound and lifted his toast. "I am not much for breakfast served after noon. It's the best I could do, given the state of your cupboards."

The perfect, fluffy eggs folded over scallions and ham and little bites of cheese broke apart on her tongue. She battled the urge to moan with delight. Or shovel them into her face. She was starving.

But she must have made a noise, because when she looked up between bites, blue eyes fixed on hers. His mouth stopped moving on the toast.

Carnal knowledge. In all her years, she'd never seen an expression embody those two words as well as his did.

They'd taken the edge off. But even a dull blade could do damage.

Unless she got back in control.

"That was fun," she said, proud she'd managed to sound flippant in the face of his imperious gaze and the intimate knowledge of the savage passion behind it. "But I am not interested in any ongoing—entanglements. Nothing personal, you understand."

"I'm crushed," he said returning to his paper and another bite of toast. "When you've finished, can we get back to work?"

* * *

HE'D MADE WORSE MISTAKES. No, a miscalculation, he thought as they descended to the garage a half hour later. The *sex* hadn't been a mistake.

The mistake—miscalculation—had been thinking it would be easy to blow off a little steam without her becoming a distraction. More of a distraction.

The edge they'd taken off had been honed again the moment she'd come into the kitchen in jeans that had to have been painted on her curvy little ass, her navy sweater cropped at the midriff and revealing a sliver of skin. Now he knew the pliant skin and the hard lines of muscle beneath. The hitch her breath made when she came. The lightness of her spent body on his and the tickle of fine dark strands of her hair. The scent of her, lilacs and steel, and the memory of it mingled with sweat and the sweet salt of her arousal made him rigid.

That, he could have managed.

But the light in her eyes, the spark of surprise when she sat down with coffee and a plate of hot food rattled him. A few eggs and a bit of cheese hastily thrown together didn't warrant that unchecked grin of satisfaction. Or that little purr of delight.

The companionship of his own cohort, the safety and ease it afforded, had always been his constant. For years, Rory had cooked enough food to feed a small army whenever they had the time and facilities. Lysippe joked that she'd recruited the rest of the Aegis just to take care of leftovers. Her first question after they'd survived whatever Azrael had dragged them into: what's for dinner? The responding roll call in the form of favorite foods and outlandish dishes identified each of them. He'd seen the brief flash of relief in her smile enough to know she wasn't worried about the improbability of such a menu.

That Ana tried to distance herself the first chance she got made sense. Surrounding herself with walls may have been a necessity for survival in Raymond's court. But they were in this together. She'd helped him bleed off the tension of the previous night's restraint, never mind fucking him senseless. After a hot shower, he'd gotten better sleep in a few short hours than in the last decade. He wanted to give her the confidence to yield, to be a place safe enough to allow her strength to become softness. He wanted to earn her trust.

Miscalculation? Hell, the sex had been a mistake. One he'd make again the first chance he got.

CHAPTER SEVENTEEN

"Something Jax said," Ana said as they pulled into the ferry terminal, "about a burial ground…"

"You think it's indigenous," Gregor said. "Or was."

She liked how his mind followed her own. There was no questioning or second-guessing. "She."

As they approached the tollbooth, Ana circled her finger to prompt him to roll down the window.

She leaned over his lap, one hand on his thigh. Before, she could have done it without any intention other than to wind him up. Now she was aware of his chest against her shoulder and the lean muscle of his thigh under her palm. His sharp exhale tickled the back of her ear. She fought the temptation to squeeze as she flashed a badge at the clerk and got them on the next ferry to Bainbridge Island.

"There's a Kwih-dich-chuh-ahtx elder who may be able to tell us something," Ana said. "She's agreed to meet with us. Not all stories handed down are put in records or books."

Gregor pulled forward, going around the line of waiting cars to priority boarding. She released the badge into his questioning fingers.

"Badges?" He exhaled, flipping it open to reveal a flattering head shot and her name. "What's NSIU?"

She shrugged, embarrassment creeping up before she could stifle it. "Necromancer Special Investigation Unit or something ridiculous."

Gregor looked almost offended as he echoed her. "Ridiculous."

"It's meant to smooth things over with the mortals," she said, not sure why she was defending it. She'd thought it was idiotic from the moment Raymond suggested it. "They respect badges."

Gregor grimaced and handed it back. "How Hollywood."

Ana sighed. "Rathki said she wouldn't let old wounds heal."

"He gave her a gift. Immortality?"

Ana nodded. Time had a way of working on the hunger for vengeance, twisting and hardening it into something more formidable and less easily assuaged than a single death.

"Why?" Gregor said. "If only to abandon her."

The thought unsettled Ana more than she wanted to admit.

She'd been turned out of the house for her failure to prevent Takami's escape.

"I'll bring her back." She'd knelt at her master's feet, pressing her forehead to the floor in dutiful submission.

"You?" If he had struck her it would have hurt less than the sneer on his face. *"And what would I want her back for? She is disgraced. Worthless."*

He'd kicked Ana out with nothing but the clothes on her back, promising her continued survival would be more fitting punishment than any easy way out.

She contemplated the whorehouse—the madams who often filled her begging bowl had offered her a place among them multiple times, praising her exotic looks. But she never forgot the sneer that carved a hole through her heart and into her soul, spreading a stain of doubt. She stole her swords back under the cover of darkness and set out to find Takami and fulfill her giri.

Her investigation had taken her into the poorest sections of the city. A street gang of young toughs cornered her in the shanty-town after she questioned the keeper of the boarding house where

Takami and her lover had been seen. An old Native man stepped to her defense. She drew her swords when they turned to him instead and ended the confrontation with a pile of bodies.

Her gaze settled hard on him. "*I don't need your help, old man.*"

"*As you say.*" The look in his eyes before he doubled over with coughing held calculating intelligence. He staggered off, spitting a lump of phlegm and blood on the pile of broken bodies.

It had taken her almost two years to track them to the Bitterroot Mountains only to find she was too late and her vow would never be fulfilled. After executing the six men responsible for Takami's death, she'd prepared to take her life and end her wandering.

"*The gods don't care about your duty.*" This time when she saw Raymond, he looked younger and more vital than he had in the shantytown. His proximity and the odd sheen of light in his eyes made the skin on her arms prickle. "*Come with me and I'll show you things beyond this world that don't require your death.*"

By then she was skin and bones and a spent need for vengeance. "*I am nothing.*"

He huffed a laugh. "*Well you could use a bit of flesh. That's truth. But I could use someone at my back. Someone most won't expect. Someone who doesn't flinch when the time comes to settle the bill. The rewards will be multitudinous should you survive.*"

He must have tracked her the whole way, yet he'd waited until she'd gotten her revenge before offering his bargain. Had he learned the hard way how persistent the need for vengeance could be?

Dragging her thoughts away from memory, she watched the arrival of the green-and-white ferry. Wind whipped the sky into a flurry of impressionist clouds and capped the water in sprays of white. Sun glimmered through breaks cast shafts of light against the water. It hadn't rained all day, but by the look of the horizon, it wasn't far off. The pedestrian passengers huddled on the gangway as the ferry pulled into the dock, wind whipping their coats and scarves.

She tossed the badge into the glove compartment. "Once we

cross the water, we're on Native land. Raymond restored the peninsula when he ascended. Tourists are allowed onto Bainbridge, but no farther without express permission from one of the federated tribes."

"Permission you have, I assume," he said, starting the engine as the ferry employee waved them on.

"You saw the badge, didn't you," she deadpanned. "I'm the Nightfeather's *fucking* Talons."

He shocked her by laughing, and the reminder of the night before sent tremors through her. She got the impression Gregor was not a man who laughed often or with genuine humor. It was a shame. He had a beautiful laugh. He parked at the front of the boat.

"Now what?"

Cars loaded onto the boat around them, directed into neat lines by boat crew in reflective vests. "Ever been on one of these?"

"A boat?" His brow rose.

"A ferry." She rolled her eyes, opening the door and snagging her leather jacket from the back seat. "Come on. It's a singular experience. Don't want to waste it sitting in the car."

Gregor seemed prepared to do just that. Ana stepped out, feeling the unusual weight of eyes on her. Before she could activate the geas that would send curious gazes elsewhere, the weight slid away.

Gregor climbed out of the car, the tails of his coat flapping around his legs like the wings of an avenging angel. Scratch that. There'd never been an angel summoned worthy of matching this man. Demon either. His gaze swept the deck like a wolf too sated with his kill to bother with the surrounding sheep.

Ana inhaled.

He rose to his full height, surveying the deck as if unaware that everything living in the immediate vicinity was holding its breath. Eyes that had watched their car with envy as they cut the line, and curiosity as they waited, fell away, skating tentatively back to him in short bursts.

Gregor met Ana's eyes. How could she ever have thought the

blue was cold? The snap of heat lit a flame in her own chest. A joke shared between them, the consideration setting her apart. The expression on his face spoke clearer than words. *Mortals don't need badges to know what we are.*

Ana peeled her tongue off the roof of her mouth and managed a nod toward the stairwells to the upper decks. She started shrugging into her jacket to have the collar lifted. How had he come up beside her so fast, and why did the bells going off in her have nothing to do with alarm? When she reached, the left sleeve was waiting. Gregor let go without touching her as soon as the jacket was settled on her shoulders.

A couple of bikers headed toward the same stairwell veered off at the last minute. Before Ana could reach, Gregor held the door open.

"Be careful. I'm going to forget how to do it myself," she drawled.

He snorted behind her as she jogged up the stairs, aware that the steep staircase put her hips at his chest level. He caught up, slipping past her in the narrow stairwell, so close her hair brushed the lapel of his coat. He opened the door, pacing into the passenger area. By the time she cleared the doorway, a bubble of quiet had formed on the busy ferry as the population endeavored to remain as low profile as possible. Not just humans. She saw a few grace-blooded creatures, though most only strong enough to keep up their human disguises. The ones who recognized her nodded in deference as she passed.

With Gregor lurking at her shoulder and the deferential treatment, the mortals began to let their curiosity win as they snuck longer glances. A pack of teenaged girls hissed envious whispers as their wide eyes took in the pair.

Great gods, she wanted to laugh. Damn Raymond and his obsession with Hollywood and for dragging her into it with his ridiculous—

"Excuse me, miss." One of the bravest of the group stepped just into her path, coming up short as Gregor's eyes settled on her.

She gaped at him, tore her eyes away, and extended something to Ana in shaking hands. "Could I... Could you sign?"

Ana glanced down at the comic book. Gregor's expression was a question she chose to ignore as she snatched the permanent marker, scribbled on the cover, and handed it back. Gregor intercepted the girl's wrist on the return. She jumped as if she couldn't decide whether to swoon or to scream. He didn't seem to notice, pausing to study the book for a moment before letting her go.

Ana kept moving before anyone else could speak. Maybe they should have stayed in the car. The lure of the galley pushed her on. Gregor at her shoulder like a shadow cleared a path.

She acquired two pretzels served with cheese without further incident, then headed up to the empty observation deck. They took up a spot on the railing near the bow. She tried to zip her jacket with one hand as she balanced the food with the other. Gregor freed her hands.

"This is an abomination," he grumbled, gnawing off a chunk.

"It's tradition." She sighed, taking hers back. "Can't ride the ferry without one of these."

"You need some new traditions."

"There is one other one I know of," she said, unable to keep the sly tone out of her voice.

She shouldn't tease. She'd already warned him off. The right thing to do now would be to limit their interaction beyond the hunt.

"Perhaps we should have stayed in the car then." He reached over, thumbed a spot on her cheek, and brought it to his mouth. A ripple of awareness shivered through her.

The wind ripped her hair free of the topknot, sending it swirling around her face. He took her pretzel, staring into the small dipping container. "I believe this substance will glow in the dark."

Still, he took another bite before resting on the railing. His size created a block from the wind. She took the opportunity to attempt to smooth the strands of her hair.

He spoke without looking at her. "It suits you."

A rush of heat rolled up her face. What in the fuck was happening to her? One round of vicious sex and she'd turned into a moony teenager. She grabbed her snack to keep her hands busy.

"Lady Samurai, eh?"

"Fucking necromancers," Ana muttered, ripping off a chunk of bread with her teeth.

"I'm sorry," Gregor said, leaning toward her as if he hadn't heard. "I missed the connection."

She sighed, chewing for a moment. "In my youth, the only samurai left were a pampered class of nobles. They kept their swords as signifiers of their titles. And though some women were trained to defend their homes and themselves, corps like the ones that fought at Aizu were no more. I have never been a samurai."

"And yet." Gregor chuckled. "Should I start at issue one or can I just jump in at issue… what was that, special collector's edition volume twelve?"

He tore off another hunk. How he managed to avoid getting a drop of nacho cheese on his suit in spite of the wind and rocking boat was anyone's guess. Especially when she knew she had his whole attention.

"It's the same bullshit Raymond's been running since the old sideshow days. Give them a good story and they'll overlook the truth."

His brows rose. "Which is?"

"My mother was a whore, American, or maybe Dutch, come to ply her trade when Hakodate opened to outsiders," Ana said, bluntly. "My father, the youngest son of an aristocratic line close to the imperial family. He was enchanted with all things Western. His family threatened to disown him after I was born, but he refused to give her up. Tainted though it was, my blood was still theirs, so I was removed from my unfortunate mother and raised as a servant."

When her father's new wife found out about her husband's bastard, the family sent Ana to a rural village to avoid scandal. There Ana learned early it was fight or be treated worse than the dogs. And she was good at it. She'd beaten up half the boys in the village and was constantly covered in bruises from the other half. She'd been sent farther inland, where she caught the eye of an old warrior woman who had once run a prosperous school before being forced into obscurity for insulting the daimyo.

"The woman who trained me was a hermit in the mountains, kind of old school." Ana laughed. "And probably older than the mountains. Hell, she could have fought at the Battle of Awazu for all I know. But I had an aptitude for brawling and a bad attitude. No one else wanted me."

"A few of the aristocrats were guarded by men who had once been samurai," she said. "When my father received a business contract in America, he fell on the novel idea to bring me as a guard and companion for his daughter."

"Your half sister."

She made a wordless noise. "I was forbidden to speak of it. They told her I was a distant relation. Low enough birth to be treated a step above the servants, but raised alongside her, a handmaid."

"Onee-san, hurry," Takami called as they raced down the hall to watch the traveling Noh troupe arrive from the balcony. Even with only a year between them, Ana seemed decades more mature.

Somehow their father found out about the nickname. He had Ana beaten until she convinced him that she had not revealed her parentage. When Ana limped into their bedroom, Takami had sobbed at the sight of her bruises. Ana snapped and sent her to bed before limping to her own pallet on the floor.

"You must never call me sister again," Ana whispered over the soft sound of Takami's weeping in the dark. *"It is an insult to your family."*

Ana fixed her eyes on the horizon. "We came to the US when she was fourteen. Two years later, she eloped with a cowboy. I tracked them down but not before they got themselves killed by robbers. Raymond found me. We've been traveling together ever since. That Lady Samurai bit came from the old traveling show. For a time, Lysippe and I had an act—you saw the photo. Wonders of the lost world."

Spoken aloud, the words prodded at emotions older than the ache of failure. They recalled happiness and a time of contentment that she had buried in an effort to subdue all the rest.

"Lady Samurai and the Last of the Amazons made a good story," he said.

She hesitated. "How is she?"

Gregor studied her for a moment, and Ana recalled the expression on Azrael's face when Raymond had asked after Lysippe. Ana wondered what it would have been like to have such powerful males as protective of her well-being.

A hundred years ago, around a campfire, Lysippe passed the sack of sweet biscuits she'd liberated from the provisions locker. *"My mothers put the bow and the knife in my hands and the horse beneath me when I was old enough to walk. These men. They are like old people. Always worrying."* The dying light from the cook's fire lit her smile. *"Why do you think I'm here?"*

"Lys will always be fine," Gregor said. "It's who she is. She doesn't speak much of that time."

After the takeover, Raymond had taken the "bread and circus" approach to controlling the mortal population. Feed them, amuse them, keep them complacent. But to be turned into a sideshow for their entertainment rankled Ana. It had been the first time she voiced disagreement with any of his decisions. Not that it had done anything but make her resent him for the first time in a hundred years.

"I agreed to the comic book and the novels," she admitted, pretending it was forgiveness. "But I fought the television show, as much good as it did. The royalties... Well, I have acquired a taste for expensive motorcycles."

He laughed. Oh, she could get used to that sound. That was not a good thing.

"Usually people don't..." She plucked the end of the bread and stuck it between her teeth. She wasn't ready to explain why they didn't recognize her unless she wanted them to.

She wore the obfuscation geas Raymond had given her as part of her gift most days, with the couture and the attitude. Like the one impressed on her daishō, the low-level shielding kept people from seeing her when she wanted to move among mortals more easily. That morning she just hadn't bothered. She liked the way Gregor fought her, the way he treated her—with the doors and the deference. After a hundred years of blending in, being over-looked and underestimated, maybe she liked feeling seen.

They watched the gulls surf the air beside the ferry in silence. After a long moment she pointed a finger at the distant whitecaps. "There."

One hundred yards off the side, the sleek black dorsal fin of a male orca broke the surface, the saddle of white visible at its base. A plume of spray rose above the waves. Two others surfaced behind, smaller dorsals but similar saddle markings. Sunlight shone off their obsidian skin before it slipped between the waves again. A flick of a broad, black tail sent water spraying in all directions.

She couldn't help the delight rising in her, childlike and unbidden, at the sight of the unearthly beauty. The male with the tall dorsal disappeared for a long moment, and she thought he'd gone. Then he broke the surface closer to the boat. He rolled onto his side for a moment, his great dark eye staring back at her. She grinned in spite of herself. She could not take her eyes off the small family, and when they parted from the ferry, she turned to see Gregor watching, not the waves but her face.

"I see you, Ana Gozen."

CHAPTER EIGHTEEN

Bainbridge Island was a quaint town, full of tiny boutiques and shops. Most seemed aimed at tourists. Gregor recognized the bold colors and stylized, arching designs of orcas and ravens on store signs and sandwich boards, indicating places where tourists might acquire "authentic Native art." Ana drove through without stopping. Beyond the town, houses clung to the water's edge along the sound, and the bobbing sailboat masts in the harbor below gave the whole view a timeless appearance.

Ana drove inland, and the wall of trees rose around the road on either side. They passed a casino before reaching a guardhouse beside the gated road. Two armed and uniformed men approached the car. One wore his shoulder-length hair loose, the other in a ponytail at the base of his skull. As the tinted window slid down, revealing Ana's face, the nearest one broke into a smile. Gregor inclined his head, listening to the music of the language the guard greeted Ana in. She returned the greeting, switching to English for his benefit.

"This is Gregor Schwarz," she said. "He is here to assist me in my hunt."

"You're joking, right?" The young man looked incredulous, his round face and cheery eyes full of humor and, Gregor noted, a distinct lack of fear. Ana's stern expression made him clear his throat. He leaned in the window, offered his hand. "Welcome to the Federation of the Northwest People, Mr. Schwarz. I'm Jamie. This is my brother Atlas. Any friend of Ana's is a friend of the Kwih-dich-chuh-ahtx."

Gregor took the offered hand. The man had a good grip. Jamie rested his elbows on the open window, cocking one hip with a grin at Ana. Gregor fought the urge to sigh. They didn't have time for a palaver. Ana put the car in park for an update on the school performance of Jamie's youngest sibling and the progress of his suit for his girlfriend's hand. From the sound of things, he was optimistic.

"Her family, man." Jamie shook his head. "They're so old school."

"She is an Elwha woman." Ana shrugged. "One of the Strong People. You aim high, Shoestring. Good thing you're so handsome."

Atl crowed laughter from the other side of the car as Jamie's fair skin flushed with embarrassment.

"Good thing, yeah." Jamie grinned, then his voice lowered. "What brings you up north? I heard you got a meeting with Grandma."

"Raymond's business," she said, chiding him a little. "You know I'm not always at liberty—"

"I know," he said, still laughing as he pulled away from the car and tapped the roof. "Will you stay for a couple of days?"

Ana's smile slid a little. "Not this trip. Be good, Shoestring."

"Good hunting, Auntie."

The gate rose and Ana put the car in gear. Her smile came easy here and didn't fade as she eased the car to speed.

"When Jamie was little, the other kids teased him they could use him to tie their shoes."

"You turned it into a cherished nickname."

"That's what aunties do." She shrugged. "I also taught him a few moves that would help a little guy get the better of bigger guys."

"Of course you did."

Her gaze settled on him. "Wow, I thought you'd filled your quota of smiles for the day."

By the time he looked over, her eyes were on the road again.

Oddly content, he returned his attention to the path ahead. The forest beyond covered the land on either side of the continuing road in green. The canopies cast the trunks and brush below in textured shadow. The light changed, diffusing and softening contrasts between the clusters of green and the break in the trees carved by the road. The air grew heavy enough with moisture to leave damp streaks on the windshield.

The wipers came on. She didn't slow.

He leaned forward against the seat belt, peering up through the verdant canopy. This was nothing like he remembered from his time in the colonies. He stared, aware of Ana's eyes tracking him in regular glances away from the road.

"It's the largest temperate rainforest in North America." She waved her hand at the haze. "The trees hold in the water and keep it circulating. And with so many of them, they're able to create their own rain."

If anything, it brought to mind the brief summer he'd spent near Hornisgrinde Mountain as a child. Even in June the rain had been heavy and constant, leaving the air in a shrouded haze between bursts of precipitation. He'd spent afternoons roaming the edges of the tree line, half expecting to see creatures from his nurse's Schwarzwald tales step out to take him on a terrifying adventure.

In hindsight, he'd always been looking for the gateway into somewhere *else*. Perhaps that's why he'd embraced Azrael's world.

"There are some parts of the forest in the mountains so thick you can hardly tell day from night." Her voice drifted to him.

"It's magnificent."

"Yes," Ana said, the softness in her voice filling the car. "It is."

He'd forgotten wonder. How each new turn this life among necromancers took, each new creature he'd once thought a myth or legend, filled him with awe. Before the godswar had left a bitter taste in his mouth, he'd lived in a world of wonder and discovery. She was right. They were always meant for this life. But not because they were born to fight. Because they felt wonder where others knew fear.

He brought himself back to the present to keep the memories from filling up his chest and leaving him senseless. He couldn't afford to lose himself at the moment he needed to be in control the most. "All of it belongs to the federation now?"

"Raymond assembled the federations after the war." She flipped on the headlights. "Part of the bargain he struck was that they must steward the land, bring it back to its natural state, or as close as possible."

"Kills two birds with one stone," Gregor said.

Her mouth quirked. "You understand him better than I did."

"I've known a lot of necromancers," he said, as much a reminder for himself as an explanation. "They are nothing if not efficient. And they're not afraid to use whatever fulcrum and lever is at hand."

"It's a nice bit of symmetry anyway."

"Most of the population lives on the coast, but the nine nations manage the entire peninsula, from Neah Bay to the harbor, and the nearby islands. And they're loyal to Raymond. He's closer to this federation than any of the others."

"They're his own people?"

"I suspect as much. Klallam maybe, from what I've been able to pick up of the language. But he's never said."

It no longer surprised him how much Raymond kept from her. But it didn't bother him any less.

"We spent a lot of time up here," she said. "Before the Allegiance. I knew Atl and Jamie's grandparents when they were small. After, I got up here as much as I could, as much for myself as for him."

"They knew about us, before the Allegiance," he said, surprised.

"I think they'll know *something* about what we're hunting," she agreed. The knowledge didn't seem to give her pleasure. "Raymond has never hidden what we are from them."

"They keep his secrets—ones he's hidden even from you. And you think this elder will reveal them to us."

"Me," she said. "I think she'll tell me what she can. And I hope it will be enough."

She gave a half smile, and he wondered at her secrets. The rote recitation of her past on the boat had been designed to shock him out of asking more questions, the delivery meant to convince him of her indifference. It covered all the salient points, to be sure. His thoughts kept returning to the gaps. What must it have been like to undertake the journey to find her sister, only to arrive too late?

He admired the single-minded focus of a girl who had been no older than the mortals clamoring for an autograph on the ferry. In a strange new country, without a friend or an ally, she'd carved out a life. He'd been not much older when he arrived on the continent the first time. And though his start had been rocky, he'd had Iain and Talking House, Gray Rabbit and Lark. They'd given him a home and a purpose, forgiven his faults and his arrogance. They kept him human enough that when he'd met the wretched, dirty prisoner held in the hold of a pirate ship, his first instinct was to make an ally, a friend.

Different roads, same destination.

The road wound out of the impenetrable forest to thinner trees before a long coast. Sunlight and cloud shadow broke together on the choppy waves. The water stretched out for what seemed like an eternity, curving into the horizon.

"To the Makah, this is the place where the world began," she said.

He slid his sunglasses on. The road descended into a series of small coastal towns. Each tidy, neat row of modern buildings painted bright colors looked like something out of a touring magazine. People bustled in and out of buildings, some in jeans and canvas workmanlike jackets, others with traditional blankets thrown over their shoulders. For a moment he saw another village two hundred years ago.

* * *

LARK TOOK him on the next hunting trip.

It felt good to have his rifle in hand again. The nerves were something else entirely. He had something he wanted to prove, even if he couldn't name it yet. He fell in behind Talking House and Gray Rabbit. Jocular Iain joined them. Lark rounded out the party, her stride long and able.

They spotted a flock of geese taking refuge in a shaded spring. Iain gave him a nudge, letting him set up for a shot. At the last moment, a sound startled the flock and they took flight. Gregor had already sighted his prey, anticipating its motion, and the bird fell like a stone. The others clapped him on the back. Envious looks at the rifle made him proud.

It was easy, returning to this role. He was pleased he could keep the pace, even on the new terrain. His regiment had been mostly scouts and sharpshooters. But the thought of sighting down the long barrel to human form had not sat easy on him. He had not seen much of the battlefield. To hunt, to kill, was done for many reasons. He had not yet been able to reconcile war as one of them.

Gregor noted they weren't headed back the way they came as the day lengthened into sunset. He fell in stride with Lark. She read the question on his face.

"We'll overnight with some friends, the Ye Iswa," she said, jerking her chin toward Talking House's stout back. "Hunt our way back to Haven in the morning." She lifted the brace of ptarmigan off her shoulder. "Do a bit of trade."

A small, prosperous band greeted the hunting party with cries of welcome, a few of the young women eyeing him with unconcealed interest. Gray Rabbit nudged him with a big grin in case he hadn't noticed.

Lark matched his stride as they made their way to the meal. She pitched her voice low for his ear. "Only engage with the ones who come to you first."

She quickened her step, meeting their hosts. Gregor's eyes

followed Lark, the way she greeted a distinguished older member of the band with both hands and her rare unchecked smile. He returned the gesture, and they conversed as he led her to a seat close to his at the fire.

The birds made a fine meal, though Gregor spent most of it avoiding the attentions of the female members of their host. Mumbling what little of the common trade tongue he knew, he retired early, going to the shelter set aside for the guests and curling up in the bed he'd been provided. The others returned in various states of drunkenness. Lark's pallet lay empty. A spark of jealousy raged in him before he forced it down. He drifted into an uneasy sleep.

When he woke, Lark and the others slept in their blankets. After goodbyes were said and they had shouldered their packs and set off, Gregor found himself at the back of the party. Lark dropped behind to keep pace with him after a while.

"You're too serious, soldier. I hear that's a fatal flaw in your people."

He fixed his gaze on the ground to hide his glare. She hooked his bicep in her hand.

"Don't judge what you don't understand. Things are different here: the women choose their own partners and relations are flexible. Their affections are given freely. No one expects you to be a monk."

"Just them?" he muttered, unable to keep the accusation out of his voice.

"You wait one blasted minute," she said, jerking back hard on his arm and drawing him up fast.

The others paused. At the look on Lark's face, they dropped their gazes and trudged ahead.

"Is that what you meant by trade," Gregor hissed, glancing at the pack on her back.

Her hand snaked out so fast it took him by surprise. The shock of it—the slap, the pain—brought ringing clarity to his head.

"You spoiled, arrogant prick."

He took a step back, surprised at his own jealousy. Lark had made her position known. He'd never been one to sulk. But the feeling in his chest blinded him. He'd lost her and he'd never had a chance to try.

"Henry told me about you," she went on, fixing him with a withering look. "Little German prince, running away from home to have an adventure in the colonies. Looking down your nose at us savages the whole time."

"I'm not a prince," he said, surly now.

She guffawed, stamping a few feet away before turning to him. "I should have left you to bleed out."

He gritted his teeth and stared back at her. "Why didn't you? The rifle and whatever else you picked from my pockets would have been yours."

She flushed a deep crimson, her mouth set in a tight line. "I don't scavenge corpses."

"Your boys do. You taught them everything else they know. Scavenging and God knows what else." He scoffed. "Witch woman."

Rage transformed her face. She closed the distance between them, and for the sheerest instant he knew she would strike him again. And not a slap this time either. "Is this the first time a woman hasn't fallen at your feet because you've taken to mooning after her like a lovestruck yearling?"

The air left his lungs along with any pseudo-righteous reply he might have made.

"My bed is my business," she said. "If you return with us, you'll remember that. If you can't, you can walk out of this valley now. Turn your back to the sun and keep walking. You'll find a trail in half a day. A road, tomorrow."

She spun, stalking into the bush after the others. He walked the opposite direction until the heat had burned out of his chest. Shame and recrimination remained. The words he'd spoken, the insinuation he'd made, had been unforgivable. He'd deserved the slap, and more.

He swore in three languages. Then he turned back and started walking. He could track them, he hoped. They would be hunting during the day, slowing them down some. All he had to do was keep a steady pace.

He picked up a jog, feeling the comfortable burn of effort in his lungs. The rifle weighed nothing. Muscles rebuilt in simple tasks of labor warmed to work. It wasn't long before he found the place where she'd left him. Following the trail tested his skill, but months in the wild had strengthened it. He paused to feel the raw edge of a broken twig, explore the divot of mud turned up against rock. Boot, not hoof or paw. Content, he kept moving. They were following a deer trail, making their tracks easier to follow. Hopeful, he climbed the ridge above the track for a better vantage. When he got to the top he paused, scanning the gully below. At the flash of buckskin and a bit of red from Iain's neckerchief, he whooped. The movement paused. Eager, he quickened his step, jog sliding down the slope to rejoin the trail.

He almost ran into the bearded stranger on the trail leading a mule loaded with skins. A second man on horseback rode behind him. Even in his flat moccasins, the man with the mule towered over Gregor. His beard was long and unkempt, thick with gray and tangled with greasy bits of his previous meals.

Gregor took a step back.

"Have a look, Davy," the man said, appraising Gregor with an eye sharp enough to make him tense.

The second man nudged his horse around. Gregor was flanked. The man took him in. A bit cleaner than the first, his face bore the crags of pox scars under lines of a life lived outdoors. Watery eyes lingered a bit too long on the rifle before returning to Gregor's face.

"Big one, he is," the blond said, "for a Hessian."

"Look familiar to you?"

Davy leaned his forearm on the pommel of his saddle as he pinned Gregor with his eyes. "I never forgets me a face."

"You must have me mistaken for another," Gregor said.

"Nope." The bearded man shook his head. "Don't suppose we

do. I don't forget a face either, especially when it's attached to a reward for murder and desertion."

Murder. Desertion. The words struck the air from his chest. Wanted. Deserters were lashed and imprisoned. Murder? And the shame to his family. Knowing his father's head would hang at the mention of his name. His mother unable to grieve because instead of just dying in war, he'd been executed for crimes committed against his own. Lark had more than saved his life. She'd kept him safe, hidden among her folk. There were punishments for that as well. Harboring a fugitive. Instead, she'd given him a bed and a full belly for whatever labor he could provide. No questions asked.

Although it might have helped if she had warned him.

Davy aimed the gun at him. "You just put down your rifle easy there."

Gregor was profoundly glad he'd been caught alone. He hoped the others kept going, Lark's anger at him driving them home. When he didn't catch up, she might wonder, but she wouldn't go back. Not for him. Not after what he'd said.

He set down the rifle, sliding the bird off his other shoulder as he kept an eye on the barrel pointed his direction. Before he could rise, the bearded man's rifle butt caught him in the solar plexus. The air left his lungs, and the stunned muscles refused to draw more. He staggered, going to one knee. At the corner of his eye, the rifle butt rose for his face.

"Stop right there, Andrew Fell." A familiar voice rang through the trees. Lark.

Gregor, voiceless, lifted a hand to warn her off. His jaw worked as his throat closed.

Lark stepped into the clearing alone, gun trained on the horseman. "Davy. Didn't plan on seeing you again so soon."

"*Miz* McAvoy." Davy brought his free hand up in a mocking salute but spit on the ground her direction.

Gregor wanted to punch the remainder of his teeth out as the craggy blond looked her up and down. His senses returned as his lung function did.

Iain came from the other direction, rifle trained on the

bearded giant making a slow move for the gun tucked into his waistband. "Hold right there, Andy, my boy."

The bearded man lifted his hands. He smiled, gaping black holes where teeth should have been. He stepped back toward the mule, Gregor's rifle in one hand.

"Sheltering outlaws and worn-out slaves is one thing," Andrew Fell said. "But this one's got crown money on his head."

"Way I see it, the redcoats are far too busy with the war to worry about one lost Hessian," she said, flexing her finger on the trigger. "Now be on your way and we'll be on ours."

"Don't stand about, you great gilly gaupus," Iain barked at Gregor, tension thickening his brogue. "Up, man."

Gregor moved, but not toward the others. He stepped right up to Andrew. The reek of onions and rotted teeth made him hold his breath. He gripped the barrel of his rifle over the man's hand. Andrew resisted.

"Now, soldier," Lark ordered.

Andrew released the gun so suddenly Gregor lost his balance. The big man lunged after him, reaching for the knife in his belt. They wrestled, the shouts of the others a frantic chorus. The horseman's gun went off, then an answering crack of a rifle from the trees.

Gregor got control of the knife and struck upward, burying it to the hilt under the giant's rib cage. Andrew's weight crushed him. The reek almost undid him. He went down, cracking his head on the soil so hard he bit his own tongue. He heaved Andrew off, retching as he rolled to his hands and knees, his only thought of Lark, exposed in the clearing, and the shots. Davy slumped over his saddle, a blossom of red growing from his chest. His horse shied, dumping the body on the ground. Talking House caught the animal before it could run or slip off the narrow track to its death.

"Are you all right?" Lark crouched beside Gregor, dropping her smoking rifle to pat him down. She rocked back on her heels with an exhale. "Iain?"

"Still breathing," Iain called, yelping. "Provided this damned mule don't kick me to death."

He looked down at his hands, covered in blood where the knife had opened up Andrew as they fell. There was so much of it, stinking of iron and salt and shit. He nodded. Or he thought he did. The blood held him rapt. He tried to rise and tangled in his own limbs.

"Just sit still a minute," Lark murmured at Gregor, surveying the scene. "You arrogant fool, don't go whooping and calling in these woods. We're on trapper trade routes. We're all wanted for something."

"My soul and my reputation is lily-white," Iain objected, securing the mule.

"Like his ass," Talking House said. He dumped Davy's body from the horse.

Coming out of the trees with the barrel of his rifle still smoking, Gray Rabbit wheezed a laugh. Lark took them all in with her legendary glare, but a smile tugged the corner of her mouth.

"I have no idea how to be an outlaw," Gregor admitted, teetering on hysteria as he again contemplated the wetness growing sticky on his hands.

"Lesson number one." Iain held up a finger. "Assume everyone is out to catch you."

Talking House rummaged through the horse's pack.

Gregor's vision spun again as the words tumbled out of him. "I was just excited I caught up to you. I understand if you don't forgive me, but I hope… then I hoped you wouldn't come to my aid and endanger yourselves. But here it looks like I owe you my life. Again. I have no idea how to repay two lives."

"Not a bad likeness," Iain said when Talking House handed him a tattered page. "Rule number two. Acquire a disguise. Lark dresses like a man. You… you're too tall and ugly to make a passable woman. Gonna need to cut all that hair. Maybe break that fine aristocratic nose of yours." He reached for his dagger. "A scar. That'll throw them off."

"Be quiet, Iain," Lark ordered.

She took Gregor's chin in her hand and dragged his gaze into her eyes. "You've never killed a man up close before, have you?"

"The two in the woods."

"Suppose those were different," she said. "Half dead yourself. Instinct takes over."

"It seems," he said, feeling as if she were speaking to him from far away.

"Soldier," she snapped. "This was a mistake. Andrew and Davy were bad men but probably didn't deserve to die today."

Iain snorted. Talking House grunted. "Had it coming."

"Done is done." Lark settled an iron grip on Gregor's shoulder. "No going back. You have to decide right now if you're going to live with it or not. Want to go turn yourself in and add to your body count? The redcoats will be happy to help you find the end of a hanging rope. But come with us—you leave this behind and keep living. Understand?"

"That's two ultimatums in one day," he said, dazed.

She almost smiled. "That kind of day, I suppose. Now get up, help us clean up this mess, and walk on, or stay here and God help you whatever comes next."

CHAPTER NINETEEN

The car chimed with an incoming call. Ana glanced at him but he shrugged, so she tapped the screen to accept.

"Auntie," Jamie shouted. "It's Granny—"

Between the broken connection and the man's agitation, Gregor caught every third or fourth word.

Ana did no better. "Slow down, James."

"We just got the report on the comm," he said. "There's been an attack at the old village. Something come up out of the sea. Federation police are en route, but I can't get ahold of Mom or anyone—"

"I'm almost there," Ana said. "I'll call you as soon as I can. Mind your post, Jamie."

Ana whipped the car into a higher gear when the call disconnected. The car clung to the wet pavement, leaving the towns behind in a blur.

"This place didn't come up as one of the potential targets," Gregor said, scrolling through his tablet. "Should it have?"

She hit the steering wheel with the heel of one hand. The car shuddered but kept to the road. It was the first time he'd seen her control crack.

"It came out of the sea," he repeated. "And the wolves in the bar, they were getting testy waiting for orders."

"I expected it to hit Seattle."

Now she told him.

"So why out here?" he asked. "Why go from large, obvious targets to this smaller, isolated place? Even the town we passed would have made a better choice."

Her hands flexed on the wheel. "We're to meet Jamie's grandmother here. Amelia's an elder in the nation."

"The one who might have our answers."

"The same." She frowned. "How did it know we were coming."

"The other night, before the bar, in the parking lot by the water." He sighed, feeling absurd for even saying it aloud. "There was this otter. It was curious and unafraid to get close."

She held her silence as a burst of rain pelted the car, triggering the wipers for a few long strokes before it cleared and the crisp, wet sunlight lit the interior. The realization settled on her face. "Orcas never come that far into the sound. I thought we were just lucky, seeing them."

"It's been tracking us."

She jerked the car into a slide off the highway and along a narrow track winding down to the water. It ended in a cove framed by tree-lined cliffs. The parking lot opened to a driftwood- and sea-boulder-littered beach. She pulled in overlooking what had been a traditional longhouse. The front half of the overlapping-board structure had been smashed and splintered. A long track of churned-up wet sand and rocks led from the surf to the destruction.

In the flashing lights of the local law enforcement, he spotted armed civilians closing in on the wreckage. On a nasty piece of driftwood, a man's body hung impaled on a branch.

Gregor leaped out as the Audi skidded to a stop. The sword on his back grew heavy with anticipation. At the sight of Ana, the faces of the mortals took on a look of universal relief. Everyone spoke at once. Something had come up out of the sea, with many arms and a terrible beak and the face of a woman. Ana froze at the sound coming from inside the wreckage of the once-beautiful building.

"Still in there," Gregor said as Ana drew her long blade.

"Old Amelia's in there," one of the badged men cried.

Ana started down the beach, and Gregor fell in step. "I'll draw her, you flank her."

He considered arguing, but Ana's face hardened to something almost feral. The wolves had gotten off easy. This was personal.

They moved together, past the wary ring of armed men. He slipped down the beach. She headed for the longhouse doors. Beach sand crunched under his feet, the grains big enough to give a slippery, pebbly feel. He adjusted to the terrain. Running would be shit in this, and whatever it was still managed to maneuver fast up the strand.

A crash came from inside. Ana yelled. Gregor charged. He'd seen a lot in two hundred years, but the thing shifting from a murky gray to anemone red in the smoky darkness of the wreckage defied classification. The vast turgid body was coated in a textured skin like an octopus, but it was the wrong shape and far too large to be anything natural.

He tried to make sense of it, looking for a head or feet. And then one of the long tentacles snaked out and slapped him across the room. It spun on him, revealing the face and the beak. The remnants of its humanity lay in the vague semblance of features surrounded by tentacles as thick as his torso. It had no interest in him now, focused on the small cluster of humanity behind Ana. Even with two walls reduced to timber and rubble, the building stank of rotten seaweed and a drowned fire.

Ana stood guard, her blades making quick work of one rope of muscled flesh that snaked her direction. It screamed in pain and thwarted rage. The enormous body shone with sea water and a slime of its own, sliding left and right. Ana couldn't hold it off forever, and not on her own. And she wasn't going to leave the people under her protection.

Time to play bait.

Gregor's sword became a halberd with the thought. He thrust in and sliced, demanding the creature's attention. It struck out with tentacles, grabbing for the blade, but he moved fast, darting away from the attempts catch him. When one locked around the shaft of his weapon, he changed intention and length disappeared from the grip to become a sword again. He drew his gun, firing into the thick, pulpy hide. The creature turned to him with a roar.

"Go!" he called to Ana as he headed for the doors with the creature in pursuit.

It moved faster than he expected. The big tentacles worked in concert: those not attacking propelled the creature. He tumbled out the doors and slipped in the sand. When he emptied a magazine, he reached for the second gun and kept firing.

One tentacle hooked his ankle and he went down. Instead of away, he rolled into it, changing the sword into two and thrusting up. His blade sank into hide surprisingly tough for its liquid appearance. The creature shrieked and retreated, whipping tentacles in its wake.

A metallic weight attached to one snapped the bones in his forearm when it hit him. He rolled to his feet, switching his sword hand. The tentacle slipped away, but not before he spied a thick band of rusted iron inscribed with characters he couldn't make out.

He stepped back, drawing her nearer, careful to keep his balance in the sand. Two of the tentacles looked eerily like arms, ending in long, misshapen hands and fingers. He kept a few steps out of reach, moving away from the building, down the sand, and contemplating his next move now that he had its full attention.

"Get down!" Ana's voice.

He dove and the air filled with the thunder of firing guns. The creature screamed, her face a contorted mask of rage and pain. She howled into the line of fire even as bullets tore through chunks of flesh. With a liquid flip, she galloped down the beach and disappeared into the surf. For the first time he considered maybe it wasn't a bad thing Raymond hadn't hidden this world from his people. A lot of firepower came in handy sometimes.

"What the fuck was that?" Gregor scrambled onto his back. The surface of the water was still again except for gentle waves.

Ana crouched beside him, eyes on the waves. "Our quarry, I'd guess. Come on, let's stay on her."

Just how the hell did she propose to do that? He strode up the beach after Ana, shaking off slime and sand. He'd torn the sleeve of his suit jacket. Bruises healed beneath as his shoulder relocated and the bones of his forearm knit together. The usual.

The sheriff, an old man with a face like leather framed by cropped silver and black hair, joined them. His thick mustache bounced as he spoke. "We've got a boat for you."

A small elderly woman wrapped in blankets caught Ana's arm, babbling about—of all things—helping the creature as the women around her struggled to steady her. "You don't understand, Ana. You can't do this thing!"

Ana detached the older woman, easing her into the hands of her companions. She brushed a kiss on her cheek. "We'll take care of it, Granny. Call Jamie. Let him know you're okay." Ana jerked her chin at Gregor. "Let's go."

A Zodiac bearing official lettering and the seal of a stylized sun pulled right up to the shoreline, engine thrumming.

Gregor hung back, shaking his head. "A boat?"

"The Makah have been hunting the sea since the beginning of time." She smiled, jumping aboard. "One of those rounds had a tracker. The boats will run relay to keep her in sight as best they can. The satellites will do the rest."

He'd never been good with boats. The ferry was one thing. The size made it stable enough for him to almost forget it was a boat. This... The water outside pitched and rolled.

She frowned. "What?"

"I hate boats."

As soon as he was aboard, the pilot pulled away from the shore. Ana swiveled the screen beside the steering wheel in her direction. A flickering symbol moved fast, headed toward the protected waters of Puget Sound. Within minutes they sped into the fast-moving Strait of Juan de Fuca. With the sun at their backs, the waters grew choppy under a strong evening wind. Gregor gripped the boat rail and did his best not to be sick.

"Not a fan of the water, eh?" the infuriatingly calm mortal shouted over the wind and the constant roar of the motor as it surged over the chop.

"If men were meant for water, they'd have been born with fins," he said between clenched teeth.

Ana laughed, joining him at the rail. She caught his wrist. He tensed but didn't withdraw.

The wind rose, drowning her words, but he followed her gaze. She led him to a long bench behind the windscreen, keeping his wrist in her grip. The hand she slipped up to his ear made a good distraction. Before he could comment, she began to applying pressure along the outer edge of his ear.

Her hand on his wrist had also settled into a pressure point. Miraculously, the waves of sickness subsided.

"I can tolerate the calm just fine," he said. "It's unpleasant, but this is unbearable."

The ghost of a smile touched her face, lit by the artificial lights of the instrument panel. "Has it always been this way?"

"On the way back from the war, the ship was caught in a storm," he explained. "We survived, only to be set on by pirates. They kept me in the hold with no daylight for weeks. I thought I would never see land again."

When he looked away from the horizon, her eyes waited.

"My cellmate," he said, forcing a smile. "A nobleman who appeared young but turned out only to have aged well."

"Azrael," she said. The boat bounced, sending her shoulder rocking into his.

"The captain was also a necromancer," he said. Perhaps she had found the pressure point for his tongue. He couldn't seem to keep it from wagging. "Which explained the state of his crew. I'd never seen an undead before. He and Azrael had been feuding for centuries. They'd reached a stalemate. The captain had captured Azrael by luck, but since he was not strong enough to kill Azrael, he kept him out at sea where Azrael could not use his powers without risking burning down the ship and drowning himself."

"How lucky for you," she murmured. She'd leaned in, and he could smell lilacs, even surrounded by sea. The sound of the engine dropped away.

The quirk of her mouth was an appealing wrinkle so close. His voice lowered, faltering a little. Her ear was just a breath away now. "We became friends."

Her face tightened, and the curious warmth in her eyes guttered out like a candle flame. She sat up a little straighter. "Feeling better?"

"Much." His free hand slid over hers on his wrist. "Thank you."

Her eyes, hawk bright, slid over his shoulder to take in the sweep of coastline off the starboard side. "Keep your eyes up, on the horizon. Should help."

Ana reclaimed her hands and stood, navigating the rocking vessel to return to the copilot's chair. He'd said something wrong.

The boat dropped speed well after dark. The creature was slowing. Maybe they'd scored a damaging hit after all.

"We've got her," the pilot said as the radio crackled. "She—it's —stopped near Fort Warden. Just sitting there."

"What's there?" Gregor asked.

"The fort is at the northern end of Port Townsend," she said. "There's nothing…"

"But what?" Gregor urged at her pause.

"Are they still running a ferry to Whidbey Island?" she asked the pilot.

He nodded. "Just restarted this year after the Snohomish finally signed the agreement to participate in federation governance."

"Go," Ana barked as her eyes met Gregor's. "Go!"

They arrived as tentacles writhed out of the churning white-caps and wrapped around the bow of the ferry.

The boat might have been smaller than their earlier vessel, but there could be no mistaking that the creature had gotten larger since they'd seen it on the beach. It was as long as the boat, not counting the length of those two hand-like tentacles. Its engines screamed against the new mass. The ship let out a creaking groan. A deeper rending noise underlaid the screams of passengers and the cacophony of car alarms. As the ship tilted, vehicles slid across the wet deck, adding to the general chaos.

Now this was the kind of target he'd expected. A packed boat in the middle of a highly traveled waterway. It wouldn't be so easy to cover this up—Raymond would have his hands full with the mortal population when the news spread. Unless they stopped her here.

Gregor lurched to his feet, shelving those loose threads as the ferry lights began to flicker. His irritation with this creature had already reached a new height, driven by hours on the small speed-boat. He'd take it on solo, barehanded if it meant he could get out of this small, rocking craft. Not even the threat of dark open water and a sinking ferry could dissuade him.

"Get us close," Ana said to the captain, slinging her swords onto her back before leaping onto the bow before the windscreen. "Then get as many people out of the water as you can and get clear. We have to stop her here."

Gregor tapped the sheriff, pointing. "The stern."

The creature pulled the ferry apart, flinging people and cars and pieces of the boat into the dark, churning water. The stern rose under the weight, but the captain steered in closer than Gregor would have dared. Ana sprang, using her free hand to hook a slim ledge in the boat's hull and sling herself onto the deck. Gregor landed beside her.

"My turn to take point." He grinned. "I'll hold her, get the people clear, then we get to work."

CHAPTER TWENTY

He's suicidal, Ana thought, watching him race down the deck, bounding across the hoods of sliding cars and leaping parts of the fractured deck toward the maw of the creature. That massive shape blotted out the once open end of the ferry's car deck.

The word *maniac* came thereafter at the glimpse of his grin. They might have had the same almost-immortality, but even she knew when to pace herself. She supposed when one healed as fast as he did—and seemed to not register pain—it unlocked a new layer of fearlessness. She envied it a little bit. Okay, more than a little.

Smoke softened everything, turning the scene before her to gray and black shades of hell. She raced to the opposite end where the crew labored to free the emergency inflatables.

She pushed them aside, moving faster and with greater strength.

She got two boats off before the ferry began to sink. The creature roared in pain, so Gregor must be having some success. But there wasn't going to be enough time.

"Take as many as you can, then get clear," she told the first mate.

"What about you, miss?"

She drew Imouto from the saya at her back. "I'll figure something out."

She arrived as the creature flung Gregor into a crumpled pile of cars. He landed with a dulled crunch of plastic body panels and fracturing glass. A breath later, he leaped at the tentacle. She hacked, drawing the slimy ichor before severing the limb. She spun away from the response and went after another tentacle. For every one she severed, it seemed two more struck back.

Across from her, Gregor yanked a broken pipe from the wall of the ferry. The next tentacle whipped toward him. In a smooth punch, he pinned it to the wall, kicking a VW Bus against the pipe to hold it there. The creature screamed and writhed, but attempting to free the tentacle only succeeded in wedging the bus against the boat railing.

Ana sheathed her sword and broke off a nearby pipe. New plan.

She drove the ragged end into the meaty tentacle and the deck beneath. She met Gregor's eyes across the smoky distance. He saluted, and she leaped cars and wreckage, drawing the attack toward him.

Gregor speared a tentacle with one hand. He tossed her a length of sheared-off metal railing with the other. She snatched it out of the air. When the second tentacle snapped toward her, she stabbed it backward and into the roof of a compact car before bending the exposed railing and trapping it. Another yanked the car from beneath her feet. Ana tucked her body in midair, preparing herself to land hard. She hated breaking ribs.

Gregor hooked her elbow in one hand, sending her into the cushion of life vests. She bounded to her feet and back into the fray as the creature slapped Gregor to the deck by the throat, pinning him. His improvised spear clattered free. She snatched it up and sprang, driving the metal spike through the tentacle and into the deck six inches from Gregor's neck.

He rolled free with a laugh. A lunatic, she decided, and it

brought out the madness in her. What else could they be, having taken this bargain from necromancers?

The urge to laugh bubbled up in her chest. In spite of everything, or maybe because of it, she was having fun.

The ferry gave up the battle to stay afloat and dragged the creature with it. The deck tilted away from their feet. Gregor caught her by the shoulder when she lost her footing, flinging her toward the rising stern of the boat. They scrambled back the way they had come.

Gregor skidded to a stop before a trailer wedged into the portal between car decks and tore open a cage containing propane tanks. She paused just a moment to follow this new development before leaping past him to the fire station and yanking the hose from the wall.

Not a bad idea—a good explosion took care of most everything. Even a sworn Aegis rarely survived being blown to bits. And it might be a big enough diversion to quell the rumors of a rogue grace blood.

She tossed him the nozzle end and went rummaging through the emergency kit in the trailer. When she returned, clutching three white-capped red tubes, he tied off the last of the tanks.

She lifted her hand. "Thought these might come in handy."

His teeth flashed red in the emergency lighting, a savage grin. "Quite."

The ferry went vertical, yanking the deck from beneath them. Ana caught herself on the trailer, but Gregor slipped, weighted down with the clanking pile of canisters. Ana let go of the flares to snag him by the back of his coat, feeling fabric tear as she gripped the trailer with her free hand.

Gregor grunted with effort, managing to catch two.

"Got them." He wedged the flares in the tank handles and sparked them, then let the tanks fall. He scaled the cage with inhuman agility, grabbing her by the waist on his way up and slinging her onto his chest like a rucksack. "How good of a shot are you?"

"Good enough." She hooked her legs around his waist as he clambered hand over foot up the walls through cars and wreckage.

The lights from the ferry surrendered, casting them in intermittent darkness. The tanks bobbed in dark water beneath them, lit an eerie red by flares and surrounded by tentacles pinned to the boat like the petals of some bizarre flower. Her hand slid beneath his coat, along the muscular plane of a chest straining with the effort of the climb, and she drew the semiautomatic.

"Did you just cop a feel?" he grunted.

She took the gun in both hands around his back. Guns bored her, but it was hard to make an argument against efficiency in a pinch. "Ready."

Without waiting for an answer, she emptied the magazine into the propane tanks as Gregor launched them from the ship. He twisted in the air, and the heat and flames cut off as his body shielded her from the blast. The explosion boomed, echoing against the remains of the boat. An inhuman scream chased them into the water. When her grip slipped, his arms tightened around her.

They surfaced, coughing, nose to nose.

One dark brow arched upward. "Should we stick around for calamari?"

"You *are* nuts, Sticks." She chortled, disentangling their limbs and pushing off his chest. She started swimming for the boats holding a safe distance away.

Gregor caught up in a few long strokes. The pilot spotted them in the sweep of light off his bow. Ana took the hand he offered, levering herself onto the deck before reaching back for Gregor.

"Back on this fucking boat again," Gregor groaned when the engine roared and the boat swung toward the distant shoreline. He extended his wrist in silent request. Ana took it.

* * *

BENEATH THE THICK layer of clouds, dawn crept in muted

pastels before Gregor steered the Audi into the garage beneath her house. By the time they'd set into the dock, Raymond's cover-up team had already begun to work. Auger was missing, perhaps transferring Rathki back to Raymond, but several of the undead could almost pass for mortals working their way among the media outlets as the necromancer's spokespeople.

The cover story—a freak engine malfunction—was as flimsy as it came. But the survivors had been sequestered in a secure area for "medical treatment" and relieved of all their devices. The tribal federation closed ranks, backing the official story and refusing outside investigative assistance. Again, Gregor considered that Raymond having some mortals on his side wasn't a bad idea.

Ana stepped into the role of the necromancer's official liaison to the people who mattered—government and law enforcement. Even soaked and wearing only one boot, she made an impenetrable barrier to any who questioned the official story. The hand she kept resting on the hilt of her long sword helped. Human governments were a necessary evil—most necromancers had no interest in the day-to-day running of their territories—but damned if they didn't decide once in a while to *demand some answers*. Usually once a camera had been pointed their direction. Watching Ana stare into the face of the blustering, red-faced police chief until the man clamped his mouth shut and backed down was a supremely satisfying moment. Still, it made for a long night, coupled with lingering seasickness and a growing hunger.

Jamie delivered the Audi to the ferry terminal. Ignoring the condition of Gregor's clothes and his expression, the younger man threw his arms around him, thanking Gregor for saving his grandmother with tears in his eyes. Blame it on his own bleary-eyed exhaustion, Gregor fished out a soggy handkerchief and sent him on his way.

Now the car interior reeked of dried seaweed and burned squid. Gregor's clothes couldn't seem to decide if they were crusty with salt or slick with oily water. Everything itched.

Ana scraped the stiff, tacky hair from her cheek to join the rest of the tangled mass and giggled. She'd started laughing in the water and amusement had spilled from her in intermittent bursts the entire ride. It had been strained at first, as if her body didn't quite know what to make of it.

Each fit of laughter grew rounder, longer, deeper. He smiled.

In the apartment he slumped onto the little bench beside the door to shuck off his ruined shoes.

Her jacket hit the floor with a soggy thump. Her remaining boot joined it. The hopping on one leg like a demented crane with her ichor-stained jeans dangling from her ankle got his attention. The cheeky layer of wet red satin clinging to her backside didn't hurt either. After brief consideration, she tore the remains of her shirt free and dropped it too.

His shoelace tangled as he struggled to free his foot without taking his eyes off her. He gave up. He sat back, resting his elbows on the railing behind him, and stared.

"I'm going to take a shower," she said, shaking free of her jeans and plucking a tendril of kelp out of her hair.

Ana Gozen wanted things on her own terms. But it was hard to focus on the appeal of a can-you-scrub-my-back-and-fuck-me-while-you're-at-it rounds with his stomach preparing to gnaw holes in the surrounding organs. Had the last thing he'd eaten been that abysmal pretzel?

She stared back, eyes narrowing. "Well?"

He bent to resume removing his shoes. "Don't take too long. Breakfast is in forty minutes."

She snorted. He focused on the knot. He waited until her footsteps retreated down the hall before he gave up resisting the urge. His gaze rose in time to catch the quick look she threw over her shoulder. She bit her lip.

He slid into his own shower a moment after her door closed and finished cleaning himself up in record time. The robe was too short. When he finished collecting tattered clothes in a plastic bag and tossing them back in the elevator, he headed to the kitchen, pleased to see the groceries he'd ordered while waiting on the dock had been delivered. Time to get to work.

CHAPTER TWENTY-ONE

Pink about the edges from a vigorous scrubbing and wearing her fluffiest bathrobe, Ana followed the scent of cooking meat to the kitchen.

Her brain came to an abrupt, scrambling halt.

She'd admired Gregor's reach as they fought. His grace in spite of his height and the length of his limbs made him dangerous. This close to naked and moving expertly about her kitchen made him deadly. Loose limbs bound with lean, rigid muscles and dusted in fine dark hair, he was flawless except for a single scar on his chest. It stood out against the unblemished rest of him. His lean torso narrowed into the crisp white towel just below jutting hipbones. Bare feet slapped against the floor. She tugged her gaze north to find him offering a mug of coffee with a smug expression.

It had been a hundred years since she'd gone all blushing, stammering innocent at the sight of a half-naked man. If he wanted to prance around the kitchen in a towel, she damn sure wasn't going to miss out on the show.

Damp hair slicked away from his face made his cheekbones and full mouth stand out, and he smelled divine. Which said a lot considering there must have been bacon in the oven.

He took a sip from his own mug, gesturing to the table. "Good thing you're on time. I'd hate to start without you."

"All out of clean clothes?"

"The cleaners will be making a pickup later this morning," he said. "The robe was too short."

"Don't you have pajamas?" She ruminated over how little force it would take to undo the tight tuck of the towel.

"I do not own… pajamas."

Her brain stuttered as that towel turned into messy sheets and the mental image of him sprawled in a bed after sex. She choked on her swallow of coffee and retreated to the table. His laugh followed in her wake.

Point, Gregor.

The coffee tasted like heaven. She picked the seat where she could watch him and also the city waking before the enormous windows. He'd ordered the paper. She'd left her tablet in her room after updating Raymond, and though she wasn't interested in doing anything other than watching Gregor, it wouldn't do his ego any good to know it. She thumbed through for the entertainment section.

Bacon came out of the oven, and she winced at the sight of grease popping onto his arm as he drained the strips, but he didn't even flinch. The mark had healed by the time brought the plate to the table.

"Can I help with anything?"

"I'd prefer you stay out of my way," he said, arriving with a bowl of fruit and more coffee.

She snorted. Trust Gregor to make it sound like a mild insult.

He slipped a grape from the bowl with two long fingers and popped it into his mouth before returning to the kitchen. The parade of items appearing on her table was as intriguing as the deliverer. Creamy spreads and fruit jams, slices of cheese and cold meats, a basket of fresh-baked rolls. Eggs in their shells clustered in another basket, butter, pickles, tomatoes. And then the more familiar breakfast items appeared: scrambled eggs, bacon, toast.

When he sat down, he looked thoroughly pleased with himself, if a little smug.

She surveyed enough food for a small army. "What is all this?"

"A real breakfast."

He snagged a roll, sliced it open, and dug into a spread loaded with herbs. She watched him stack meat and cheese and then bite into it, open faced. Strong white teeth, the flex of his jaw as he chewed, and the smile. All bare chested and relaxed.

He lifted his gaze on his way to the second roll. "Aren't you going to eat?"

She made her own plate with familiar items. Greasy fried meats, eggs prepared a hundred different ways, loads of carbs. She'd had a lot of time to consider, and American breakfasts were her favorite.

She watched him crack the shell of a soft-boiled egg with the dull edge of his knife, pop the top, apply salt, then obliterate the soft material within. He must have eaten half a loaf of bread, never mind plowing through enough meat and cheese to fill a deli case.

"I feel like I'm watching a sporting match," she said, gnawing on a slice of bacon. "I feel bad for the rolls. They don't stand a chance."

His brow rose. "Breakfast is important. One should eat heartily." He topped off her coffee. "Who knows how the day will turn out."

She hadn't realized the depth of her own hunger until she scanned her empty plate. She looked at his basket of soft-boiled eggs smothered in a kitchen towel to keep them warm. "May I?"

He slid the bowl toward her, reached for another roll, and went to work loading it up. That one looked as if it'd been trapped in a battle between seeds and spices. The spicy scent of pale yellow spread disappeared under layers of ham and cheese and tomato.

She must have been staring at his latest creation too hard because he offered it up. "Would you like one?"

Pride took a distant second to a healthy appetite. "Please. But without the pickle."

He had the grace not to look pleased with himself as he assembled a second roll.

When he'd cleared meat and cheese, he attacked jam over butter on sweeter breads. With the urgency gone, he unfolded the paper and sat back in his chair.

Restless, Ana considered getting up. They'd killed the creature. Raymond was busy tracking Barnabas and would let her know when he needed her. And what did she want?

She spied Gregor, attention fixed on the business section as he methodically chewed bread buckling under a tractor-trailer-load of Nutella. He popped the last piece between his teeth and, without looking up, slid the plate containing the second slice her direction.

"Try it." He didn't even look over the edge of the page.

Feeling a bit like a feral animal, she snuck the bread off the plate and took a bite. A joyous moan escaped her before she could check herself.

His brows rose, blue eyes flickering up to meet hers. "Exactly."

She grimaced and sat back in her chair, picking up her section of the paper. She hadn't realized she'd kicked her foot up onto his thigh until his hand closed over her arch. Just cradling. She held her breath, torn by the urge to stay and the desire to flee. They'd completed the job. This was as much a victory meal as a last one. Raymond would release him, Azrael would call him back to Prague, and it would be done.

The sun chose that moment to break through and cast the dining room and kitchen in broad strokes of warm gold contrasting against the billowing waves of gray clouds. She closed her eyes, rested in her chair, and exhaled. Long, dexterous fingers began to knead her arch.

She turned her attention back to the paper and finished her bread.

* * *

ANA LAUGHED at something on the page, and her toes curled a

little against his fingers. They were small and round like little pearls and painted like a punk rock unicorn threw up a glitter bomb. He pushed his thumb under the ball of her foot with a little more pressure.

It took all his composure not to crow victory when her other foot joined the first. There was no doubt he'd won this little battle of wills. She probably didn't realize she was smiling, engrossed in whatever article had caught her attention. The robe parted above her knees, and through the glass tabletop he caught a glimpse of pale, freckled thighs.

His thumb stroked down toward her heel, keeping the pressure firm and steady. She wasn't ticklish, but she had squirmed a bit at first, like someone not used to being touched. She fought, she fucked, but when had she last been stroked, petted, held? He knew the feeling. When she'd first reached for his wrist on the boat the night before, he'd tensed for a fight. The moment her fingers had left him, he'd longed for more.

Contact.

Now he had it, and he would be damned if he moved his leg or drew her attention to the fact that he'd been working his way toward her ankle and the long line of her calves. The stock section gave him the chance to appear fixed on the same page for much longer than was necessary. He should check in with Azrael, attend to his weapons, and arrange his flight home.

As she read, a little furrow grew between her brows and the corner of her mouth twisted. Her eyes moved fast over the words. He didn't withdraw his gaze before she looked up and caught him staring. Her nostrils flared and a little smile creased her lips. She lifted her heels and slid her feet to the floor.

It couldn't last. He'd known it from the beginning, and yet part of him still mourned.

"Well, this has been…" She surveyed the wreckage of the table.

He rose before she could finish, emptying the last of the coffee into her mug. He cleared his throat. "I'll see to the kitchen."

She sat back in her chair, reaching for the comics. "If it pleases you." She eased back into her seat with a frown and kicked her heels up onto his empty seat.

Wait.

He'd miscalculated again. Maybe she was just adjusting her position, getting more comfortable. Maybe she hadn't been pulling away. Now his fantasy of clearing the table and laying her out like dessert went down the drain with the soapy water. He'd finished loading the dishwasher and set to work on the pans and knives when her hands settled on his shoulder blades. He almost cut his index finger off.

"Sorry." Her little chuckle hummed through his rib cage as her arms slid around his waist. "I thought you heard me coming."

He should have. That didn't bode well. She could have stuck a knife in his back. He hated not being able to see her face. He craned his gaze over his shoulder, but with her cheek tucked against his spine, all he could make out was the top of her head.

"They say when a wild animal trusts you, it gives you its back." Her breath brushed the thin skin covering his vertebrae. "You haven't turned your back to me since you got off the plane." Palms splayed on his ribs, fingertips sliding down. "I thought we were making progress."

Progress? She skittered away from his touch and bounced from flirting to keeping him at arm's length. He'd been polite, deferential... cold. Oh.

He was up to his forearms in soapy water when the towel puddled at his feet. His brain stuttered. "What are you—"

"While I enjoyed breakfast, you forgot dessert." A moment later, her hands made it clear what she was after.

The breath left him in a sharp exhale. "Dessert is not typically served with breakfast."

"Don't be such a stick in the mud." She slid her fingers around the partial erection he'd been nursing since the sight of those cheeky red panties. "So rigid. Live a little. 'Who knows how the day may turn out.'"

He scanned for the dishcloth to dry his hands. Spotted it on the other side of the stove. Wished for longer arms.

"Relax, Sticks," she crooned. "Unless you want me to stop."

Stop? He'd just caught up with what had started.

Ana slipped between him and the sink, something wicked and calculating in her gaze. When she slid down against the counter, he realized what she intended a moment before her mouth settled on him.

Her name escaped his lips on a low breath, more plea than protest.

When her hands joined her mouth, her grip strong but attentive, his protest died a strangled death in his throat. He braced his hands against the backsplash to resist the temptation to grasp her by the head, but he couldn't stop his hips from twitching of their own accord. It only served to encourage her. Her low hum in response sent him to the edge.

"Dear gods," he groaned. "I want—"

She cupped him in her hand, all long strokes and wet tongue.

Desperate, he scrabbled at the fetters of his control, but every thin strand blew away from him, leaving him at her mercy. He teetered there, unable to resist jerking his hips toward her. Knowing she wouldn't kiss him made this more arousing than it already was.

The hoarse exclamation came out like a plea. "Fuck me."

"Later." She laughed and then enveloped him in heat.

Point, Ana.

* * *

If there was anything sexier than Gregor Schwarz trying not to lose himself in her mouth, she didn't know it.

He muttered a combination of swearing and inarticulate vocalizations. Hungry for his release, she braced her hands on his hips, angling her head to take him deeper.

Tension wracked his body. He drove his free hand into the wall until a tile cracked. She revised her previous preference for less buttoned-up men—driving a man so self-possessed to such senselessness intoxicated her with power. She could bring him to pieces without a single blade.

A groan rumbled through him all the way to his core as his body gave up the fight and shattered under her touch.

In the aftermath, he leaned over the sink, hands braced on the countertop. His eyes clenched shut, and his chest heaved in ragged breaths.

She rocked back, unable to keep the victorious grin off her face. When he opened one eye, the corner of his mouth quivered once before his face went hard as marble. He found the dishrag and dried his hands with a measured inhale.

Watching him reassemble his control was a thing of wonder, but like the sword at his back, she couldn't not see a hazy after-image below what lay over the surface.

She gasped when he dragged her up and set her on the counter next to the sink. He undid her robe and pushed his way between her thighs. His gaze swept her full of warning and possession. He gripped her hips. Dragged her to the edge of the counter. She drew him, threading her fingers through waves of damp hair. His teeth found her neck and sank in until she shuddered. Her body throbbed in anticipation of what would come next—the sudden fullness, the motion, the climb, the inevitable release.

"That was incredible." His breath on her neck sparked goose bumps over her arms and an electric tingle between her thighs. "But you still seem to think you're in control."

She shivered when he cupped her breast, plucking at a nipple. She forced the words out. "Aren't I?"

One hand traveled the center line of her body, fingers sliding between her legs. He smiled at the slippery wetness he found, dipping two fingers deep inside her before removing them. She gasped, biting her lips to avoid begging him for more.

His head cocked, thoughtful as he inhaled the scent of her. "You'd like to think so, wouldn't you?"

He flattened the length of his body against her and she shivered. Hot breath rushed her ear. "Now let me finish without further disruption. And don't move until I tell you to."

"Or what?"

"Or I won't give you what you want." He returned to the dishes with methodical focus and a smile on his face.

She gaped. Was he going to just leave her like this while he—naked and sated—did the damn dishes? She pressed her thighs together, trying to stifle the heat as the sight of his bare back curving into the slope of a tight little ass and muscular thighs delivered a rather vivid fantasy of how it would look driving between her thighs.

The sword flickered against her gaze. She'd half expected to feel it when she first approached him, but there'd been nothing more than the tingling connection of his skin against her own.

He looked up from a frying pan as if she'd telegraphed the thought. Without pausing, he leaned over and took her nipple in his mouth. She moaned as the jolt rocketed down to her core.

"Don't touch yourself." He resumed scrubbing. She wanted to throw something—preferably bladed—at him. Now it was all she could think about. What kind of fool…

The same kind of fool that sat on the counter obediently because he was right. She wanted him—long arms and muscular grace and the piercing softness that seemed to enter his gaze when it settled on her. *I see you, Ana Gozen.*

She reached to turn off the water, ready to fuck away the unexpected tenderness. He knocked her hand aside, a threat and a promise, and went right back to work. She wanted to scream with frustration, but she wouldn't give him the satisfaction of knowing he'd undone her, without a word or a weapon.

She watched him chase the droplets of water from the last dish with the same intensity of focus as the first. He settled the plate in the rack beside the others. She didn't need this kind of game—whatever game he was playing.

In one swift motion he swept her off the counter and pinned her back to the wall. He went to his knees, dragging her thighs over his shoulders.

When his mouth covered her, she lost the ability to finish a thought. The ache moved lower, spreading through her hips and thighs all the way to her curling toes. Her fingers found his hair, and when she tugged the thick, wavy strands, he grunted and drove his tongue against her. She barely heard the "more" muttered against her swollen flesh, but she complied until the deep, steady throb became waves of release leaving her boneless and trembling.

He rose, letting her slide down his body until he could hook her thighs around his waist. His lips hovered over hers, but before she could evade him, they settled at her ear. "Your bed or mine?"

CHAPTER TWENTY-TWO

Her bedroom proved as unexpected as the rest of her—a rich splash of color and texture at the heart of her modern sanctuary. The scarlet walls made a warm contrast against the view of blue-tinged gray water and green shore dominating the floor-to-ceiling window. On the far wall, soft overhead lighting fell on the matched pair of swords mounted over the simple altar. The only other thing on the altar, an antique shakudō bracelet worth a small fortune, looked just large enough to fit the wrist of a child.

His toes dragged through the deep sheepskin rugs in cream and beige, over the charcoal cement floors on the way to the wrought iron bed. Threads of gold streaked through the darker shades covering the pillows.

He knocked aside pillows and the comforter, making a nest for her on the bed. She wouldn't kiss him. He would solve that mystery another time. For now he would cover the rest of her and show her lips what they were missing.

Cheeks, chin, the curl of her ear, the round, firm spot behind each.

The freckles led over her shoulders. He followed them with long, wet kisses to her breasts, the ridges of her rib cage, the spot in her belly that hollowed when his tongue slid against it. By the time he followed the line of the scar to the small of her back, the mounds of her ass, the thin skin behind her knees, the breath left her in long, low moans. Kneading muscle below scars brought the long lines of her thighs to his mouth, sucking pressure flushing the skin with blood.

"Ana," he murmured registering the way she pressed back against him as each kiss found a home. "My Ana. My Ana."

The last of the hard breaths wrung from her chest gave way to the telltale hitching of sobs. He slowed and let the long strokes of his palms on skin soothe when words wouldn't do. He waited for her to push him away, to assume the safety distance provided. He followed the line of her calves to her heels, curling a finger under each of the small round toes.

"Strong Ana," he said in that same reflective tone. "Precious Ana. Fierce Ana. Beautiful Ana. My Ana."

On the way up, he took the measure of her body with his hands. He could circle her foot with a palm, close his fingers around her calf. Bracketing her thighs, his forearms ran the length from knee to hip. Her ass fit in his palms. He bridged the small of her back in one hand. Both didn't quite span her back from shoulder to shoulder until he fanned out his fingers. The length between his index finger and thumb cradled the back of her neck. Up close, the difference in their size struck him for the first time. Even knowing how inadequate her healing ability was, the word fragile never crossed his mind.

She buried her fingers in his hair again, gripping hard enough to hurt. "I want…"

He rose over her, the curve of her hips bringing them in intimate contact. In the dim light filtered between the curtains, her skin flushed dewy soft beneath him.

His thumbs swept the skin below her jaw, the pulse pounding back against the contact. "Tell me what you want."

"Gregor, please."

"Tell. Me." He nipped her earlobe after each word.

"This," she gasped, rolling her hips to rub herself against him.

He dipped against her, withdrew. "Just this?"

A low moan escaped her. "You. I want you."

Swollen and tender flesh yielded to his intrusion, leaving them both gasping. Her fingers dragged long furrows in his shoulder, hips curling in an unmistakable invitation. He guided her leg over his thigh, rocking until he was buried inside her. Thought slid away, leaving instinct and pressure and the drive to release. He buckled in the end when the sound of her surrender robbed him of the scraps of control.

Afterward, her head fit comfortably on his chest. Her fingers tapped the echo of his heartbeat on the skin of his belly. No longer an edged creature, sharp and biting, desire gave way to exhaustion. She slept for a while as he stroked the line of her spine, from the downy soft hair at the base of her neck to the sweeping curve above the cleft of her ass. He didn't notice he'd dozed until she woke him with the brush of her mouth on his scar. They tangled in the sheets and pillows, no longer as urgent but still insatiable.

Who started talking first? Unbidden the stories came between them: old war stories of tight scrapes with the necromancers with whom they'd bargained their souls, comedic misunderstandings as they learned about the new world they'd entered, the deaths they'd witnessed, both noble and ordinary.

"You don't feel pain," she said, tracing the lines on his shoulder. She'd drawn blood during the last round. He'd sucked it off her fingertips as she came.

"I do," he said, settling back in the pillows.

Her spine curved against his chest. He rested a palm over her navel and let his thumb slip back and forth over the soft skin. Her gaze found him over her shoulder, skeptical.

"I thought it was your gift?"

"In a manner of speaking," he said. "But maybe not the one he intended."

When Azrael offered him a place in his Aegis, Gregor considered what he would ask of his new master. Time as the rare mortal in a necromancer's retinue had taught him that while guns were effective, they were prone to fail around supernatural creatures. Bladed weapons could always be trusted.

He spoke. *"Steel that will come to my hand whenever needed."*

"Soul steel," Azrael pronounced after a considering silence. *"It will manifest in response to your need, in the form you desire. It will never fail you. But there is no way I can find to give this gift to you without a price."*

Gregor accepted.

Azrael had sketched a geas between his shoulders. It burned into Gregor like a brand. He did not flinch or cry out as the spell etched itself along his spine, threading into his chest and the base of his skull. The first time he drew felt like pulling a jagged bone from his own body. He knelt, gasping at the sight of the obsidian blade in his hand. His vision blurred.

Lysippe watched, a concerned eye on him, but her words for Azrael. *"What good will it do us if it leaves him broken?"*

"He will learn to bear the pain." Azrael's response tattooed itself on Gregor's soul. *"He must, to survive in this life."* He'd rested a hand on Gregor's shoulder and crouched to meet his eyes. *"This is the sign of our covenant. But I suggest using mortal blades for a while."*

Gregor found Ana's face in the darkness. "Sometimes I wonder if an inhuman tolerance for pain was Azrael's true gift. It's true, the sword never breaks, never dulls. It can be a broadsword or an assassin's blade, a machete or a rapier with a thought. I learned to anticipate the pain, to master it, and finally to ignore it altogether. It comes in handy."

She made a small, thoughtful sound.

"Ana," he said as a memory of the previous day caught up with him. The expression on Ana's face as she stood between the creature and the elderly women, as if she was searching for something but unable to find it. It wasn't until much later that he recalled her gift. "What did you see, when you looked at…"

"The giant squid woman-thing?" She shrugged. "Nothing. It's like that with some grace bloods. What you see is what you get."

"But you expected to see something else?"

She rolled onto her back, glaring up at the patterned ceiling as if the repeating squares held her answer. Tin, or something that had been made to look like pressed metal, a feature that would not have been out of place in a building around the turn of the century in San Francisco. He looked around the room with a new understanding: the antique bed, the furnishings. She had recreated something, modernized and updated perhaps, but familiar.

She sighed. "After all the talk about Raymond's past and an old bargain, I expected—"

"Something that had once been human."

She nodded once, mouth working over unspoken words before sinking into a frown. "Anyway, it's done. Doesn't matter."

Dipping his nose to her small curved ear, he breathed her in. His marks followed the slope of her neck to her collarbones. With each nip she had arched into him, squeezing him so tight he'd shuddered. But she was not immune to pain as he was. He thumbed the livid, bruised flesh, dismayed by how slow the marks healed. He pushed himself onto one elbow to stare into her face, alarm growing.

She stopped the question before he could form the words. "I liked it. It grounds me. Reminds me I'm alive."

The irony of an immortal life among necromancers was to be surrounded by death but untouched by it. Though not always. In low, halting tones, she spoke of the guardsman who had been her second-in-command, and a rare ally, until a demon had bitten him in half.

"I picked him." She whispered the confession in the darkness. "I convinced Raymond to make him. I trained him and protected him until he could survive in this world. He went in alone, unprepared for demons. He died screaming."

She no longer tensed when his mouth drew close to hers. He thrilled a little when their breath mingled and they were nose to nose and she didn't pull away. She had given him her boundary. Now she trusted him to respect it. Instead, he tasted the dampness at the corner of her eyes and drew her into the curve of his chest.

His index finger rode the long scars left by demons, reveling in the shivered response of her body.

When her fingers played over the scar on his chest, he went so still she raised her head to look into his eyes. The sight of her face, raw with emotion and crowned with a tousled mess of hair, robbed him of his breath for a moment.

The steadiness of her gaze verged on tenderness. "Tell me about your demon."

Had he thought to reach her without revealing himself? The locks he'd placed on his heart closed one by one and left his mouth dry and silent.

"Not a demon," he said at last.

She frowned. "Nothing else marks a guard."

That wasn't true. He knew she would press. He would have.

Before she could, he rolled her on top of him and filled his palms with her breasts, pinched the pebbled nibbles between his fingertips until her gaze grew soft with want. A wicked smile curved her mouth, but it did not meet her eyes. She knew. Of course she knew.

And yet she let him distract her with this, rolling her head back and sliding her eyes shut with a long sigh as their bodies joined again.

They lost themselves and the conversation. Afterward she fell asleep on top of him. He held her for a long time, listening to her breath and feeling the beat of her heart against his own. It served as a reminder—this could not be a love story. That's not who they were. He drifted into unconsciousness. It was the deepest sleep he'd had in years.

He woke alone.

The steady gray overcast lit the city in a dull, even light. It was impossible to make out the time of day. He contemplated the passage of time. Had they lost an entire day? It felt like a dream now, the scraps fading as he opened his eyes, alone in bed. Except this was her bed her scent was all over him. His hands, his mouth, his body.

His fingers traced the outline of her place in the rumpled

sheets beside him. He rested for a moment, pondering the strange, hollow sensation in his chest at her absence.

"It's too late for that now," he chastised himself, dragging himself out of bed and heading for his own suite. "You had your chance."

The house was empty. He emerged from a shower cleaned and shaved, a fresh towel around his hips. His bed, unused, served to remind him of the future he'd made for himself.

His phone screen flashed—a message from Azrael. He booted up his laptop, leaving it on the dresser. While he waited until he had a secure connection, he laid out a suit for the day. He plucked a cobalt tie from his dwindling selection. It was a good thing their assignment had been completed.

His fingers stilled on the silk. The creature, whatever it had been, was at the bottom of the sound. Azrael's debt had been repaid. He had more than enough information about Raymond's territory to satisfy both Azrael and Ito. Raymond might request a postmortem, but more than likely Ana could deliver it alone. He wasn't needed here any longer. He could be on a flight to Prague in a few hours. His time in Ana's bed came into stark relief. It had been a goodbye.

His hand clenched the silk. He snarled, tossing the tie back into the bag. He was a fool. The biggest kind. She had gotten what she needed. She was done with him.

He slid a black tie with subtle crimson pinstripes around his collar. The laptop chimed, alerting him to an open connection.

"Master."

Azrael's face appeared on the screen. "Good morning to you too."

He was at the estate. Gregor recognized the new kitchen from having the dubious pleasure of overseeing its reconstruction and ensuring the placement of the consort's belongings. Feminine laughter and an eager yipping filled the background. The dog. How had he forgotten? The latest sign of Azrael's madness. A cautionary tale about what happened when you stopped thinking like an immortal and started being more like *them*. Human.

Dogs. Foot massages while reading the Sunday paper. A whole day in bed, fucking like rabbits. How did anyone in love get anything done?

Love.

"It's not morning there," Gregor snapped.

"But it is *there*."

Gregor grunted, trying to make sense of the lost time. At some point they'd drifted to the kitchen for more food. Once. Twice? He'd lost track. Take-out boxes and a bottle of wine next to the bed.

"Is there something you needed, master," Gregor said, shrugging his weapons harness over the dress shirt.

Even after a shower, a shave, and fresh clothes, she lingered on his skin. She had gotten to him. He had laughed away the darkness with her. He touched her scars and listened to the way her voice cracked as she remembered losses. He curled his body around her as she slept, as if to protect her. As if *they* meant something to one another.

Azrael sat back, wary. "Isela spoke to Nix about your seafood problem—he seemed surprised that you were successful."

"And the necromancer?"

Azrael frowned, shaking his head. "Barnabas emigrated before the godswar. I've got nothing of use. But I don't like this at all."

At the click of the knob, Gregor turned. The door opened.

"The best waffles in Seattle, but they don't deliver." Ana backed in, carrying a greasy paper bag and a beverage tray with two cups of coffee.

She looked fresh out of bed after a night of wild sex.

The strap of an oversized tank top slipped off her shoulder, revealing a lacy hot-pink bra beneath. Her hair had been hastily swept on top of her head, short strands floating loose around her small, love-bitten ears and neck. A pair of sweatpants made from the kind of material that should have been shapeless clung to the curve of her hips and tapered at the ankles.

His chest throbbed at the sight of her.

"I can't compete with your skills in the kitchen." Ana huffed, turning as she balanced the load. "But I thought if it was breakfast *in bed* you'd overlook my failure to—"

She looked up, taking in the open laptop and Gregor on opposite sides of the room. Her eyes darted to the face on the monitor. For a second she froze with the sheer desperation of a cornered animal. Her deep flush met the cups of the flimsy little bra. Ana dropped the coffee on the nightstand table, and her eyes darted back to Gregor.

Then the meticulously constructed mask returned. He saw it for what it was now, the effort, and how little it suited her. Composed, she bowed stiffly. "Lord Azrael."

"Forgive me for interrupting." Azrael coughed.

Gregor blocked Azrael's view with his body, snarling. "We're done."

He realized he'd been misunderstood when she drew up sharply. The flush went from a beguiling rose to deep red, and her mouth settled into an angry line. If she'd been armed, she would have run him through. But for the first time since they'd set out, her swords were nowhere in sight. She'd let her guard down.

"Please excuse me," she said with a glance around him at the screen.

She spun on her heel and stalked out of the room.

Gregor's fists bunched at his sides. "Ana, wait—"

The image on the laptop swung so quickly it blurred. Isela's face appeared, her eyes wide. "Go after her, you idiot."

Gregor slammed the laptop closed, cutting off Azrael's entreaty to call him back. He'd broken through Ana's network security. It was a violation, to be sure. But more worrying was the vulnerability in her eyes, the embarrassment. He had done with intimacy what he could not have with a sword: disarmed her. And then exposed her.

By the time he reached Ana's room, the door blocked him. He took a deep breath and knocked. No answer. He tried the handle. Locked. For a moment he considered breaking the thing down.

He splayed his palm on the door instead. "I must speak with you."

In twelve hours or less he would be on a plane bound for Prague. This was not a love story. The pragmatic thing to do would be to take the opportunity to walk away.

She came back. She hadn't left him alone in bed with the intention of not returning. She'd come home with breakfast and coffee and the intention to climb back into bed and enjoy both, with him. The little huff of her voice in her explanation betrayed her impatience, eagerness. She was vulnerable and deadly and sexy with her messy hair and incongruously delicate underwear. The shower turned on and he swore, even as his cock jumped again at the thought of her under the cascade of water. No matter how much he tried to release the sensation of connection to her, he could not fully sever it.

"Ana," he tried again, an edge of desperation sitting tight in his throat. "Please."

Silence.

CHAPTER TWENTY-THREE

Ana strained to catch the last of Gregor's footsteps retreating down the hall and released the breath she'd held. The shower ran on, pillows of steam drifting out into the bedroom. She tore off a bite of a cooling waffle between her teeth and attacked the sex-soaked bedding with the ferocity reserved for a horde of undead.

She'd ask the decorating service to order everything new. Even the bed would have to go. She had needed something more in keeping with the rest of the apartment for years. This room had always been a silly notion, out of step with everything she'd become since she left her mortal life behind.

She swept the empty boxes of takeout into the delivery bag with the bottle of wine, closed the book he'd plucked from the pile to read until she'd tempted him back to more mutually rewarding activities. How could she have been so stupid?

She eyed her daishō hung in their places of honor. When she'd left them there before joining him for breakfast, the flutter of anxiety in her belly had begun almost instantly. Then she'd laid eyes on him, and the glacial blue gazed back at her with naked desire driving every restless worry beyond the edge of her consciousness. Stupid.

When she woke up to him sleeping like a corpse beside her, his lax face woke a fierce tenderness in her chest. They had done nothing but eat, sleep, and fuck on repeat for a span of time stretching impossibly long in her memory, and still she had not had her fill of him. His long-limbed body molded itself to her so well.

So what, he wouldn't explain a scar to her? He had not pressed, or even asked once, why she wouldn't kiss him. He accepted it, and her, anyway. They had lived many lives in their time, not all made for amusing anecdotes. Some memories filled up vast portions of their chests with ache. There were stories it would take her time to reveal.

One day she might kiss him, and one day he might tell her the story of the only scar that marked him.

This was not a love story. But it might be more than just swords and sex.

Her network should have notified her of a breach and traced the receiver with an alert. He must have been able to encrypt his call out, to fool the system. Another time she might have admired the ingenuity of his setup. But in addition to compromising her security, the object of his conversation was another necromancer.

Respect and formality formed the pillars of her relationship with Raymond. Respect for the power the necromancer possessed. Formality to preserve the distance between them. It gave it clear perimeters and limits. It had kept peace between them for centuries.

One did not appear before a necromancer unarmed, in one's underwear, and bearing takeout. Gregor had compromised her. She'd appeared weak, vulnerable, *used* before the most powerful necromancer of the Allegiance. A cold thought gripped her— what better way to display his ability to undermine Raymond's Aegis.

Gregor's dismissal, curt and merciless, convinced her. His words had not come shrouded by the misty haze of a lie as her gift would have detected. Whatever had passed between them was over and she meant nothing. She needed to hate him. She would once she got over feeling as though someone had thrust a dull blade between her ribs.

Stupid, stupid, stupid. She stripped off her tank top. Might as well take advantage of the running water.

She would put him on the next plane to Prague. Auger's latest report said Rathki had given them a long list of places to look for Barnabas. She could afford a few more days in Seattle. She would not be licking her wounds.

Her phone buzzed. She snapped, "Gozen."

"Auntie, you're not going to believe it," Jamie said. "You know the thing you killed two nights ago?"

Ana's brain stumbled. Two nights. Had she lost track of twenty-four hours? No wonder every time they came up for food they had been starving.

"Auntie?"

"Go on."

"I was going to dump the tracking data," he said, "but I turned on the receiver one more time. I just had a feeling."

The hair rose on the back of her neck. "It's not dead, is it?"

"It hung around for twelve hours, then it started moving down the coast."

"Send me the tracking link," Ana ordered.

She disconnected the call and autodialed a new one, flinging open the bedroom door. Her jaw opened.

Gregor stood on the other side, looking like a thundercloud interrupted in unleashing its storm. "Ana Gozen, you don't get to brush me off that easily."

The flare of lightning in his eyes made her aware of the fact that she wore thin sweatpants and a bra. His hand flexed on the doorframe. The wood creaked with pressure.

She wanted to throttle him. Or wrap her legs around his neck and ride his face to the floor.

Where had that come from? She listened to the unanswered ringing with one ear. "Like you just did? 'We are done.'"

She must have done a passable impersonation of his sexy, lightly accented voice because his lips twitched.

"I was *talking* to Azrael," he said. "Since he took up with the dancer, he's been a meddlesome old man."

She hesitated. She would have seen a lie if he had spoken it. Maybe she had misinterpreted the delivery and the dismissal was a truth not aimed at her. He *had* blocked the camera with admirable speed.

She ignored the release of pressure in her chest and waved the ringing phone at him. "We have bigger problems."

Raymond wasn't answering. She spun out of the doorway and hurtled the phone into the wreckage of the bed.

"It's alive." Gregor followed a pace or two behind, pausing to take in the stripped room. "Redecorating?"

Ignoring him, she stepped out of the sweatpants on her way to the closet.

"You haven't yet showered?" His voice held something that sounded like wonder.

She turned to him, jeans in one hand and heat rising in her face. "Why do you care? And why does everyone know about this fucking sea monster before I do?"

He crossed his arms, leaning against the doorway, and stuck out his thumb. "One, I don't think an hour is going to make a difference in us catching up to this thing." His index finger rose. "Two, you'll feel much better after a shower. Three." He ticked off his middle finger. "Azrael spoke with the consort's pet phoenix. And it's going to take much more than an improvised bomb to kill your mythical beastie."

She paused, astounded. "Azrael's consort has a phoenix. For a *pet.*"

"He's more man than a bird now." Gregor waved his hand. "It's a long story."

Ana faltered.

Necromancers didn't forge alliances with other grace bloods. Until Azrael made a god vessel his consort and allied with wolves and witches. Now she kept a phoenix, rumored extinct after the godswar. No other grace-blooded creature possessed the kind of knowledge a phoenix did.

Raymond would need to know that Azrael was involved. The thought made her pause again. Did he?

Doubt churned in the pit of her stomach. The cold waffle she'd gnawed on earlier didn't help the sensation.

It was all Gregor's fault: his easy camaraderie with Azrael hinted at the possibility for a different sort of bond. She suspected Azrael kept little from his Aegis. She'd bet he never sent Gregor on missions with as little information about what he hunted.

And yet he hadn't refused. Instead, he'd met her eyes, seeking permission, laying his vow not at Raymond's feet but hers. And it wasn't just his word. She had traveled with him, fought beside him. He'd covered her back enough times to reveal how normal he found it, expected it even.

Whatever Gregor had done, he'd been the one thing she could trust in all this. Tension fled on a long exhale. Without looking back, she stepped out of her underwear.

"Maybe I will catch that shower."

* * *

"Have you reached out to him?" Gregor said when his wits returned. "Raymond."

Focusing with her standing around in the scraps of lace sold as women's underwear in this age proved challenging. Bright fucking pink. As if the peekaboo provided by lace and the strategic cut wasn't attention grabbing enough. He should to take it as his opportunity to go back to his room. He should pack his things, or clean his guns, or jerk off to clear his head.

But whatever she had been thinking before she'd turned her back to him left a haunted, uneasy look on her face.

He had enough sense to know this mess hadn't distracted her from being furious with him. But they still had a job to do. He gave one last thought to making an excuse and leaving. If she was going to put on a show, he'd be damned if he missed it.

He rummaged through the open bag of takeout and plucked a waffle from the cardboard container before trailing her into the bathroom. It wouldn't have been half bad under better circum-stances. Maybe her taste in food was redeemable after all.

"He's not answering," she admitted, stepping under the water. "What did the consort's pet phoenix have to say?"

"That it must be destroyed by that which created it," he said, shaking his head. "Which, I take it, in this instance was not a cobbled-together propane-tank bomb."

"A lovely stroke of creativity, by the way," she called.

"I do my best."

When she stepped out, he had a towel waiting. She dried her hair. "It needs to swan dive back into the fires of whatever Mordor spawned it."

"Exactly." He leaned back against the counter sink, wondering who or what was a Mordor.

She marched past, leaving a trace of lilac in her wake and his brain shuttered. He closed his eyes. He paused. They might still have a job to complete, but first he needed to make this right between them.

Whatever *this* was. Whatever *right* meant.

"Ana, this morning," he said, filling his lungs for an explana-tion or an apology.

"You broke protocol and my network," she said from the bedroom. "Which might have been considered a violation of your vow to Raymond, but since you haven't been struck down, I'm assuming whatever you said was indirect enough not to trigger the Retribution. Lucky you."

He shoved off the counter, stalking after her. She wasn't going to make this about his vow or their work. Not now. Not when a few hours ago they'd been… The wreckage of the bed made sense now. A flicker of something resembling hope leaped in his chest before he could squelch it.

"I said nothing to compromise my vow to Raymond." Gregor started, dodging a pair of pants flung past him.

"Ah, just a personal call," she said. "Showing off your bedmate."

He came around the corner to find her buttoning up black jeans before disappearing back into the closet. "Ana, that is the most ridiculous—"

"Is it?" She emerged, bearing a pair of chunky ankle boots and a thin black top.

A flush rose in her breasts above a lacy black bra with crimson satin cups. The small voice in him, probably the one that made everyone think he was halfway insane, noted her underwear matched his tie.

Shut up, he snarled at it.

She threw down the boots and fought her way into the shirt one sleeve at a time. Her tousled, damp head emerged as the stretchy material molded itself to her chest. The wide neck fell off one shoulder.

He took a breath. "When I woke up and you were gone, I assumed—"

"Ass. U. Me."

He threw up his hands. "Raymond sent us into this thing blind. We needed help. Information. Azrael has resources—"

Her phone rang.

Gregor sighed and swiped it off the bed, tossing it her direction. He folded his arms and paced across the room to the big window.

"Where is he?" she said, pausing for the response. "And you accepted that?"

Ana switched to Japanese to reveal her dismay. Sometimes only one's mother tongue would do. He caught every third or fifth swear word, but he liked the sound of it coming from her small, lush mouth. The same mouth that had been like warm honey on his cock.

He slammed the door on the thought. He prided himself on his ability to compartmentalize. This whole situation was *en die Hose gegangen,* and all he could think about was the next time he could get Ana Gozen between those creamy sheets. Or bent over a chair. Or riding his face to the floor.

"You are to stay by his side." Ana's voice reached a toneless fury he'd never heard before. "When you hear from him, I need to know. Am I understood?"

She sighed once but he kept his back turned, giving her a moment to compose herself. He tested the waters. "Raymond is gone?"

"Did your pet phoenix happen to know anything about Barnabas Huxley?" Deceptive calm softened her tone. He had a brief flash of her interrogating Jax in the bar as the were's lifeblood stained the floorboards.

Gregor turned, brows raised. "No, but after you... left... I spoke with Dante, Azrael's progeny. I figured since Barnabas wasn't a known entity when I took the vow, it wouldn't trigger Retribution to ask a few more questions."

Ana paused. "You'd risk Retribution..."

Gregor shrugged. He didn't care to linger on how carefully he'd worded his request, aware that the wrong ones would end his almost-immortal adventure quite painfully. "He's been categorizing necromancers by power. Barnabas is a water and licensed in Azrael's territories to perform exorcisms and release trapped ghosts. He got into some trouble with the Sevillan satrap, and then he disappeared. I'm assuming he worked his way here."

The powers of necromancers were not as defined as they liked to lead humans to believe. Raising and communicating with the dead was energy work, pure and simple. All had some affinity with a classical element: water, wind, fire, earth. More indistinct were the skills that, like control of their element, strengthened with time, practice, and power. Barnabas was an unknown factor.

He had several theories about Huxley's sudden appearance in Raymond's territory. All led to an uncomfortable conversation about Raymond's strength, which he did not want to have while she was already the iciest version of apoplectic he'd seen in almost two centuries. He resisted the urge to glance at the swords in their place of honor above the small altar. In close quarters he made an awfully big target. There was probably some fault in his wiring for why he found that thought as arousing as foreplay.

The chime of the house security system saved him from answering. "Intruder?"

She shook her head, reaching for the longer of the two swords as she started for the front door. "We have company."

CHAPTER TWENTY-FOUR

Gregor recognized the elderly woman from the wreckage of the longhouse. Amelia. Accompanying her, a cluster of women not much younger, the sheriff, and the two young men, Jamie and Atl. They all wore jeans and flannel under puffy vests, in service to the damp chill of the Seattle air, except Amelia, resplendent in her wool cape of black and white geometric patterns over a denim dress, skin leggings, and moccasins. The men removed their hats as one when they stepped inside, casting him a few wary glances. He retreated to the edge of the room, trying to make himself as unobtrusive as possible.

Ana situated Amelia in the most comfortable chair and went about making coffee with an air of ritual that filled the silent room while her visitors surveyed her quarters with open interest. Once the coffee had been served, Ana knelt at the woman's feet.

She bowed her head. "Grandmother."

Amelia's face, an assemblage of deep creases and soft speckled skin drew itself into a look of great regret. A single tear rolled down her cheeks. "I come to beg your forgiveness, Auntie."

"There's no need, Ame," Ana said, rising to catch the tear. She stroked the old woman's graying hair away from her face like she would a child's.

Before the Allegiance assumed world leadership, necromancers had lived among humans, in the shadows. Whenever Azrael settled in a place, it would be for no more than twenty years, just long enough for people to begin to question why they did not change. Then they would move on. Gregor had relied on it to keep him distant from any mortals they engaged for any length of time.

But for this family it seemed normal that Ana should remain unchanged while they were born, aged, and died. She slotted herself into their hierarchy of respect for day-to-day purposes, but no one forgot it was she who did not change. He wondered what acceptance might have felt like if he'd made different choices.

"I am an old woman," Granny said, eyes shining with emotion. "But I remember being a girl. You have been my Auntie since those days. You held my hands when I took my first steps. My children, my grandchildren, all look to you. Thunderbird's Son, we honor as our protector. Our loyalty must be to him first. But you we love. You are our family."

Ana sat back on her heels, her empty hands resting on her lap and bowed shoulders making her look small and fragile for the first time since Gregor had known her.

"I can no longer keep his secrets," the old woman said. "No matter what the punishment might be."

Her escort clearly disagreed based on their subtle, restless shifting and the taut lines of their mouths and frustrated, clenched hands. A few more glances went his direction, and Gregor realized they were assessing the likelihood that *he* would be their undoing.

Ana caught his gaze.

"Amelia, I have been lax in my introductions," she said. "This is Gregor Schwarz. He is the first of his master as I am of mine. He has come to help me track the creature. He is my ally, and I trust him with my life. Amelia, she carries the old stories."

Gregor kept his face even under Amelia's solemn, assessing stare. He stepped forward and made his bow. Amelia reached up imperiously, and he placed his hand in hers. She gave him the kind of shake he expected from a man half her age and twice her size.

"I may be old," she said, dragging him closer for an inspection. "But my eyes are as good as ever. This is a fine man you have taken, Ana."

Gregor couldn't remember the last time a human had dared to touch him, never mind jerk him around like a puppet.

"Ame," Ana cautioned, ready to intercept.

Gregor crouched before the matriarch. He cupped her small, wrinkled hand in his, and it disappeared in his larger palms. "Our focus must be on the creature now."

"Forgive me then." The old eyes danced. She dropped her voice, her eyes sliding to Ana. "I reckon he could be yours if you wanted him."

"The creature," Ana repeated dryly.

"Not a *creature*," the matriarch said. "A *woman*. She's trapped... same as you. This is what I tried to tell you, but you were too bent on the kill to listen to an old woman."

Mute, Ana flattened her mouth to a hard line.

"Raymond charged us with killing it. You might understand our confusion," Gregor suggested.

Amelia shook her head as he looked between them. "There must be a mistake. *You* cannot kill her. What she is must be undone by what was the creation of her."

Mordor again. Ana's gaze flickered to his. Did confirmation of the phoenix's words surprise her?

"We thought she meant you harm, Ame," Ana said. "The longhouse and the dead man."

"Poor boy." Amelia shook her head, then her voice hardened. "But I told him not to run from her. She knew you wouldn't listen to her, but the orcas told her you were coming, and she hoped I could intercede on her behalf. Which I intended to do until all the damn shooting started."

The men in her escort all busied themselves staring at various points in the room.

Gregor sighed. "Maybe you should start from the beginning."

Amelia nodded at him. She tapped her half-empty coffee cup, her brows raised.

"Mama," the sheriff said. "Too much caffeine. Doc said—"

"I am an old woman." She interrupted him with thunder in her voice. "And my throat is dry."

Gregor took the hint. She beamed at him before taking a sip. The matriarch began to speak.

"In the time of this story, Thunderbird's Son had wandered far from his home and his people for more years than a natural man's life held. When he returned, he looked as young as before.

"At a great potlatch to celebrate a successful whale hunt, he met a beautiful young woman called Laughing Girl of the Quilotes. She was born with great power, believed brought forth from a great whale spirit, because her mother had gone into the sea and returned swollen with child. She would sing and fish would fly into the nets of the fishermen. Many fine men made suit for her. But she had eyes for Thunderbird's Son.

"Thunderbird's Son surrendered his heart to this woman. He too had been touched by something not of this world, and he saw himself in her, though she did not command death, as he did, but living things."

"A witch," Gregor whispered. "She—"

Amelia silenced him with a hard look. "When the first great boats of the Europeans began to contact the villages, there was much trade and celebration. Raymond had witnessed the decimation of the People of the east in his long travels and spoke caution. But his words were dismissed by the young. The trouble began soon after. The young men took to stealing items of little value from the newcomers, trying to top each other. For sailors, these small acts were seen as a threat. They grew wary, anxious, so far from home.

"A party of canoes met a Spanish ship to do trade, but the ship fired on canoes, and the warriors struck back. In retaliation, the soldiers destroyed the village. Laughing Girl's heart broke.

"Thunderbird's Son urged her to look to those left behind. He promised her safety and love and long life if she would stay with him. But she could not rest. She begged for help to avenge her people. Thunderbird's Son could not deny her. In those days he was still human enough to love. And love makes fools of us all."

Point, Gregor acknowledged.

"What they did together was anathema. The spell corrupted, and she became something unnatural. Unable to survive on land, she fled to the depths. Thunderbird's Son called to her, tried to restore her to what she had been. But the spell had diminished him, withered his body with age and left him hollow. The transformation hardened her heart to his cries.

"Rumors of a many-armed monster they named Whale Eater traveled with every band. It is believed that she mated with the creatures below, and many of the stories of giant squid seen by men are her children."

"You were forbidden to tell this story to anyone," Gregor said, trying to make Ana see the truth of how much Raymond had hidden from her.

Amelia nodded without answering, but Gregor registered the plea in her eyes.

"Why is she back now?" Gregor asked.

"She's been caught up in something." Amelia sighed, looking into her own hands. She held up the left, a simple gold band on her third finger. "Bound by a trick to help another. The ring she wears is her vow and her chain. This is why I have come to you. You see her as a beast to be hunted. But if she still lives, you must help free her."

"Ana," Gregor began, his eyes trapped in the old woman's worried gaze.

"Thank you, Amelia." Ana kissed Amelia's hand, then her cheek.

"You cannot kill her," Amelia tried again.

Ana shook her head. "There will be no repercussions for what you have told me. Now go back to your home and family. You must leave this to us."

Ana showed them to the door. Amelia held back at the end,

fussing with her blankets. While Ana reassured the others, Amelia sidled in close to Gregor.

"You're not as tough as you let on, are you?" She squinted at him.

Most mortals would have flinched away from the sight of his teeth. Amelia held her ground. She reached out a hand and he gave her his, surprised by the strength of the grasp that yanked him to her level.

"She needs you now."

"She doesn't want my protection," Gregor said.

"It doesn't matter, because you need hers too," Amelia said. "Be well, Sticks."

The laugh rose before he could check it. She pressed her cheek to his and breathed in deep before letting him go. A traditional farewell?

"He smells good too," Amelia informed Ana with a pleased little cackle. "Make sure you try before you buy though, you hear?"

Ana shook her head, laughing, but a pale shade of pink dusted her cheeks when she said her farewell. When Ana turned to him, she could not meet his eyes. "I see what you mean about meddle-some old people."

He almost smiled, but instead went to retrieve his bags. "I'll meet you in the car, Auntie."

* * *

"Does Raymond track lesser necromancers?" Gregor asked without taking his eyes off the road as Ana hung up from her latest attempt to reach Raymond.

She plugged the phone in to recharge and leaned back against the headrest, closing her eyes against the weary frustration of always being too late.

"He eliminated most before the twentieth century," she said. "The traveling circus was a convenient cover to hunt the last of them down. They swore fealty or he destroyed them. It's how he grew powerful enough to ascend. And just in time. When the Allegiance formed, he was ready. We keep records of anyone who's entered since the godswar but Huxley, wasn't even a blip on my radar. How did he hook up with our Laughing Girl, and why now?"

"Maybe we have it backward," he said. "Maybe she made the time now. Everyone has a blind spot. She's Raymond's."

"What makes him think he's strong enough to take on an Allegiance-level necromancer?"

"What makes you think he's not?" Gregor had programmed the tracker satellite information into the onboard navigation so they could get real-time updates on the dash screen.

It pinged and she opened her eyes. "Tell me."

He frowned. So it wasn't going to be something she liked then.

"I'm a big girl," she said. "And an old one. I can take it."

"Raymond skimped on his gift to the first of his Aegis. That means one of two things. He doesn't have the power to give anything more. Or he held out on you because he is conserving his strength. Either way, he's not as powerful as I expected. Maybe Barnabas knows it."

His voice held a curious mix of frustration, regret, and concern. She saw no lie in him. He believed it.

"Raymond's held the North American territory without challenge since the godswar ended," she said, unable to keep all the defensiveness out of her voice.

"Which means nothing," he said. "Except that no one has challenged him. He does put on a good show."

She wanted to argue, but he had a point. Good stories didn't just overlook the truth, they hid truths as well.

"So Barnabas Huxley stumbles on Laughing Girl," Ana said. "She can't come out of the sea. How would he even know?"

"He's a water." Gregor drummed his fingertips on the steering wheel. "The affinity always manifests with awareness of the creatures within. Maybe he lured her into a parlay and a bargain."

"And talked the wolves into teaming up to take Raymond down."

"Alliances are powerful things," Gregor said. "But the wolves are out now. You took care of that."

Was that admiration in his voice?

"And she is no longer a mystery," Gregor finished. "If she ever was."

Ana ignored the dig in his words. The case he built against Raymond was his own. He had no idea what life had been like in the first years after the godswar with Raymond drained from doing his part to form the barrier that kept the powerful entities known as gods from interfering in human affairs And now this upstart necromancer thought to swoop in and take what she and Raymond had fought tooth and nail for.

"He'll make his move soon then," Ana said. "One way or another, this ends."

Gregor shook his head, frowning. "This feels... incomplete. And Amelia's story?"

"That she's bound?"

"Laughing Girl loved Raymond. Why this desire to take him down?"

She scoffed. "He turned her into a monster. She's not strong enough on her own. She needs this alliance as much as Barnabas."

"And if she's being forced to work against Raymond? If we could free her, maybe we'd have an ally—"

Ana shook her head, furious. "She's cast her lot with that opportunist scum. Nothing else matters."

The rage burned clean through on a fuel she recognized well. Vengeance had a familiar taste in her mouth, the need for a wrong to be righted, a stain to be erased. Whoever this necromancer thought he was, she'd do everything in her power to help Raymond stop him from taking what wasn't his.

Gregor settled back in his seat, shooting a sideways glance her direction before his gaze returned to the road. His jaw worked, but he kept silent, as if sensing the chasm growing as the thing he could never understand wedged between them and drove deep.

Hard to believe just a few hours ago they had been wrapped up in blankets, skin to skin. But if she focused on it, the tenuous connection stretched between them.

Get a grip. She snapped herself back to the matter at hand. What happened in Seattle lay behind them. And all the better. She had a monster to kill and a rival necromancer to put down.

"Ana Gozen." The way Gregor said her name called her out of her thoughts and sent her sprawling into memory. "Onna Bugeisha."

The morning after she had taken her vow to Raymond, she watched the dawn from their river camp as the wondrous new powers surged through her body, repairing old injuries and imbuing her with strength and surety. She'd felt reborn.

He settled beside her on the rock overlooking the spill of water around the bend in the river. *"It's not my name—Raymond Night-feather."*

There was a new understanding between them now. They could communicate without speaking a word out loud. It was part of the thing binding them. He met her eyes briefly. *"My teacher said it's bad luck to go into a new life with an old name."*

The faintest traces of gray marked his temples, his skin no longer soft with the wear of age. She thought of the men they'd tracked, the ones he'd faced, frozen in a state he called In Between. Every time, he emerged younger, stronger, and his adversaries had fallen. Some of that power now ran through her veins.

For a moment they watched the trout break the still eddy, taking advantage of the waking insects daring the water surface as the light went from a pale blue to rose gold.

"Way I see it, this is a rebirth." He rose to go down to the water to fish with the long sharpened stick he favored. *"Best pick the name that suits you now and leave that girl behind."*

She took the title she could never have. Made it a name.

"My Lady Samurai." Raymond's back shook with laughter as he rose, a glistening trout writhing on the end of his stick as its gills opened and closed desperately. He cast a glance back over his shoulder at her. *"Suits you. Ana Gozen it is."*

It had taken Gregor long enough to see it, and for a moment she wished she had not tried to be so clever when she named herself. She closed her eyes against the swell of memories that rose and left anger in their wake.

"Who are you really?"

CHAPTER TWENTY-FIVE

"**G**ozen is a title," Gregor went on when she remained silent, watching her in sideways glances. "Something like lady, right? And Ana sounds close enough to an Anglicized version of Onna."

She hadn't responded to him, but she hadn't run him through either. He wanted to admire her loyalty, her selflessness. He'd tried to give Azrael as much in two hundred years, until the Vogels had come back into his life. The first time Azrael spoke her name—the dancer foisted on him by the Allegiance to help track a killer—his loyalty began to splinter. And when it became clear he could not scare or threaten Isela enough to make her fail in the job she had been hired for, the splinter became a chasm in his vow. Did he have any right to question Ana now?

"I thought it had a kind of symmetry." In the brief flash of hawk gold, he knew it didn't matter.

"Who are you, really?"

Her brows lowered in question, and her eyes darted to him.

"The name Ana Gozen," he said. "It's just a mask. One you've been using to hide yourself."

"Think having my real name will give you some power over me?" Ana laughed. "Make you feel better?"

"What would make me feel better," he said, keeping his voice steady, "is knowing you understand the disadvantage at which you've been placed and start responding with an ounce of self-preservation. Start with your real name and keep going until you stop wanting to die in the cage you've built for yourself."

"The cage…"

He recognized the look on her face, but he'd let her run him through a thousand times if it meant she heard him. "Azrael has never sent me to die to clean up his mess."

"Azrael inherited a territory so bowed into submission by the previous necromancer that the populace welcomed him with open arms," she snarled. "I saw the news feeds. A ticker tape parade for the benevolent Azrael."

Gregor stilled, unprepared for the raw fury in her voice.

"*These* fucking mortals. Raymond gave them everything Azrael did, and they still hate and fear him and revolt every chance they get."

The surprise must have shown on his face, because she loosed a hard laugh, shaking her head. "Let me tell you what we inherited after the godswar. Raymond has twice the geographic territory of your beloved Azrael and a more divided population in every way. They were tearing each other apart long before the rest of the world came at them. Floods and earthquakes and tornadoes and wildfires. Plague."

Her breath shuddered, and a note of horror edged her words. "The Eastern Seaboard wasn't destroyed by weapons. They ravaged each other with a contagion that makes the worst zombie look like relief. And there's no cure. He's maintaining the spell to keep it contained until the necromancers working on it can unravel the magic."

She took a hard breath, her jaw locked for a moment before she could speak again. "So no, he doesn't have any extra to spare for me. And why should he? I can put down most everything that comes my way with a single sword. He didn't offer and I didn't ask."

She shook her head, glaring out the window again. Her fists

clenched on her thighs, the knuckles white. On impulse he settled a hand over hers. She snatched hers away.

"Ana, I didn't—"

Her voice wavered. The fire of her words had burned out, leaving a weary rasp. "I don't know the content of your vow to Azrael, Mr. Schwarz—"

"One hundred years of service," he said.

She needed to know the truth of their different lives, even if she hated him for it after. He stated the terms. "I protect Azrael's life, enforce his codes. In his territory, I am his eyes and his ears—anything I see, he sees, same as hearing. He can control my body from afar—in his territory. In exchange, I got the sword, as you know, and the speed, agility—I can climb like a monkey, which comes in handy more than you'd think—and I can survive most anything except beheading or being cut into tiny pieces. And most importantly: choice. Whatever he sends me into on his behalf, he grants me access to all the information he has. I decide to go. He's given me his trust. At the end of the first hundred years, I chose to renew my vow. And I will continue to serve."

The silence stretched miles unbroken.

"There is too much hidden between necromancers," he said with a sigh. "I would not have it be so between us. I may have assumed too much, but Ana, being his enforcer puts a target on your back bigger than any of the other Aegis. You deserve more."

Her voice went cold. "Do you know what became of the men who killed my sister? I slaughtered them. I cut them to pieces. I may have avenged Takami's death, but I could never remove the stain of losing her in the first place. Nothing remained for me in any life. Raymond gave me a reason to keep going. Purpose. I wouldn't be here if not for him. Don't tell me what I deserve."

It was like trying to climb a talus slope—every grasp, every foothold, sent the surface sliding out from beneath him. Every step slid him farther away from her.

"We were opportunities," Gregor said. "You said it—we weren't normal, even before the gift. They plucked us from our darkest moments. They gave us this." His hand swept the car, taking in the swords and the powers and the whole damn world. "And we serve them in exchange. But it doesn't have to be blindly."

"It's my *duty*—"

Her phone rang. After a brief exchange she hung up, inputting an address into the navigation.

"Raymond's in San Francisco," she said. "Auger caught up with them. He and the boys are pursuing Barnabas Huxley's last-known whereabouts."

The navigation system chimed with a new arrival time and routing information. She swiped the tracking screen away and zoomed in on the city map.

"This is near the wharf," she said.

She brought the tracking screen back to the forefront. Laughing Girl was moving fast now. He laid down the accelerator, missing the roar of an engine in spite of the accompanying force pressing him into the seat.

"It's a trap," she muttered, reaching for her phone. "She's going to be waiting for him."

"Ana." He tried again.

"I've made my choice," she said before he could finish. "Raymond is my master. Ana Gozen is who I am now. And that's all that matters."

The Nightfeather's Talons. A single-minded hunting raptor. He wondered if Raymond had come up with it, with his badges and his comic books. Talons gripped and they held. The release took conscious effort, the desire to let go. Maybe the necromancer knew her better than Gregor ever could.

CHAPTER TWENTY-SIX

J ust after twilight, Gregor slid into a loading zone directly in front of the warehouse. "We should probably have a plan."

"Why start now?"

The car door slammed in her wake, leaving him in the insulated silence full of her scent. What were they if not weapons honed to a killing point to be wielded by necromancers? He'd made his vow. Whatever she walked into, they would do it together. He leaped out of the car.

The sword coalesced on his back as he closed the distance between them in a few leaps, strolling tourists screaming and scattering in his wake. He expected Ana to chide him, but the noises coming from inside the warehouse had her focus. The sound of a fight.

Ana went toward the chained double doors at the front of the building. Gregor didn't bother, scaling the outer walls hand over foot and leaping up onto the roof. Skylights ran down the center of the rectangular building. He picked the one closest to the noise, drawing his sword as he crashed through the window made opaque by frosted glass and sediment.

The darkness of the warehouse swallowed him. He landed in

the puddle of light created by the newly emptied window—arched black scimitar in one hand, the less beautiful but equally deadly semiautomatic in the other. Dust and broken glass glittered around him. He turned a slow circle, blade at guard as his eyes adjusted to the darkness. Grotesque, rippling shadows over-whelmed Auger and the giants.

Another clutch of demons.

Ana crashed through a side door, sliding to a stop with an expression of disgust. He wasn't sure if she was irritated with the appearance of demons or of the failure of her subordinates to do their jobs. He almost laughed.

"Just in time," Gregor said.

A misshapen canid waved a barbed tail in Gregor's direction and lowered its head. Gregor tipped the blade in invitation. The moment of reprieve broke in a cacophony of inhuman growls and shrieks. Gregor stepped into the fray, clearing a path for Ana.

"Where is he?" Ana snapped, freeing Auger up from the double-headed snake.

"Docks."

Ana hesitated. Raymond's guard was no match for the remaining demons. Gregor jerked his head. "Go."

Ana turned, and a bullish grotesque leaped into her path, lowering a leonine head with slavering jaws. She went at it running, flinging her body to the ground at the last minute and sliding past. Her blades flashed before they gored the clinging shadow, and the demon collapsed in her wake. Four legs skittered out around it. Severed, they began to melt into the nebulous gunk demons left behind. Gregor finished it with a bullet to the brain, sword ready in case that wasn't enough. Demon ichor splashed his pants, tearing holes in the fabric. He swore. He was out of suits.

He took down two more. Auger and the boys could handle themselves with the rest.

Like in the art studio, demons weren't the only defense the rogue necromancer had summoned. He recognized the clean slice of Ana's blades in the trail of undead body parts—no spare slashes or useless stabs. Each blow had struck precisely, severing a limb or a head, before she moved on.

Christ, this woman set him on fire.

Ahead, Ana yelled and something heavy slammed against wood and water. The building shuddered around them.

He crashed through the doors as the last of the creature disappeared under the dark, churning water of the empty boat launch. Ana flung herself out of a pile of splintered wood paneling and old fishing nets, racing down the dock in pursuit. "She has him."

"Not another fucking boat." Gregor shook his head as she leaped onto a boat tied at the end of the launch, working the ropes.

An armless undead rose from the netting with a snarl. He fired once without looking. It collapsed in a heap. He strode down the dock.

Ana brought the engine to life with a roar and tossed off the last of the ropes. It took him a moment too long to realize she intended to leave him.

Gregor bellowed her name, running. She cast a single glance over her shoulder as she opened the throttle and yanked the boat away from the dock.

He calculated the jump until he reached the end of the dock. Even with his abilities, he'd never make it. At a sound behind him, he spun, looking forward to slicing up whatever trailed him.

Auger drew up, palms splayed, the two giants behind him. They all looked worse for wear. What kind of Aegis was this? Infighting, lack of discipline, leaving their master to go off on his own, unattended. The only one of them worth the hide covering their useless flesh was Ana. And she was insane to think she could stop the thing that had Raymond and the necromancer waiting for it.

Repaying Azrael's debt and gaining intelligence wouldn't matter if Raymond fell tonight. Azrael would lose a potential ally. The North American territory, according to Ana, less stable than he'd assumed, would plunge into chaos.

A roar welled up deep inside him, sending the pigeons scattering from the rafters with cries of alarm. "Get me a fucking boat. Now."

* * *

GREGOR KEPT his eyes on the horizon. The dark-shuttered island grew larger as Auger pushed the boat faster over the choppy water. The speedboat surged and leaped at a bumpy patch, and Gregor's stomach engaged in the kind of acrobatics that would have threatened any recent meals. Chopper blades beat the growing dusk above them. Why hadn't he waited for the helicopter?

Ahead, two necromancers and a riddle of a sea monster waited, and gods only knew what else besides. He could not go in there on desperation and fury. As if reading his mind, Auger called over the sound of the engine, "Got a plan?"

Find Ana. Help Ana. Kill whatever it took to keep Ana alive.

Auger's loyalty to Ana might be more than the big men overhead: they hadn't shown even the slightest interest in getting in the boat, instead calling in the helicopter once Auger and Gregor were underway. Still, Gregor didn't trust any of them. He wanted them out of the way. Out of *his* way.

"You are Raymond's Aegis," he said, stifling the accusation in the words. "You get to your boss and do your job. I'll take care of the creature."

Auger cut the engine as the island loomed large. He navigated around the rocky base, searching the growing darkness for the shape of a dock.

Gregor pointed at the dock where Ana must have slowed her boat enough for a flying dismount. The craft drifted away from the rocky shore, its engine sputtering.

Auger drew in closer. "And Ana?"

Gregor stepped onto the bow, preparing himself for a leap. "Leave Ana to me."

A pack of undead in rotted prison gear staggered toward the shore, little more than senseless automatons. Auger joined him at the bow.

"Allow me to take out the trash," Auger said, surprising him.

Gregor acknowledged him with a nod. "Watch your right side."

Auger barked a laugh as Gregor leaped ashore, landing beside him in a crouch a moment later. He gave Gregor a salute. "Good hunting."

The street fighter stood, strolling toward the staggering mob with a thick metal-studded club in his left hand. The right uncoiled a chain and set it swinging with a dull *whomp, whomp.*

Whoever had created these undead had given them the typical drooling, savage-minded intent common to Hollywood zombies. These did the tradition proud, all bloody mouthed and wild-eyed. Auger skipped the last few steps into the fray, whistling.

The helicopter circled overhead, searching for a place to land.

Gregor skirted the mob, trailed by the meaty thumps of a club working its way through skulls. Lights flickered as he crossed the main road and started up the slope to the looming cell block in the center of the island. The electricity was on the fritz, spun into chaos by the necromancers drawing power. Energy crackled in the air, stinging his skin like miniature lightning strikes. Two powerful necromancers in the same place always had that effect.

It drew him like a beacon. He checked his ammunition, loaded a fresh magazine, and slid the blade from between his shoulders.

CHAPTER TWENTY-SEVEN

Ana watched the creature drag Raymond toward the cell-block building, bound from head to toe in the thick, muscular bonds of her tentacles. Not a creature. Laughing Girl. Ana's gift blurred her vision, and she blinked hard to clear it. Something else rose underneath, an image little more than a ghost but enough to screw up her sight. She focused on Raymond instead, picking out a geas for submission binding him as tightly as the tentacles.

The electricity had already been weakened by the proximity of a necromancer, but Raymond's presence sent it haywire. Transformers exploded all over the island, casting the dim structure in a shuddering darkness. Emergency lighting, the bare bones needed to maintain the island, flickered on in irregular bursts. The wind battered her, whipping her hair and clothes, and she recognized Raymond calling on his element and gathering strength. She stalked them, waiting for her moment.

The creature went through the open cell-block doors. Ana kept to the abundant shadows inside the building as Laughing Girl dragged Raymond down the aisle. On the overhead catwalk, a figure crouched, his cloak whipping in the growing wind. He leaped to the floor. The wind whipped his hood from his face, revealing the rival necromancer for the first time. Barnabas Huxley looked younger than the images Auger had sent. As he leapt to the floor to meet his prize, the grey streaked brown hair whipped around his face, and his skin was firmer and more vital. Necromancers stopped aging and sometimes even appeared younger as they grew more powerful. This was a bad sign.

Raymond, waterlogged and battered, didn't even struggle when Laughing Girl shook him loose from her tentacles. The creature kept him restrained, arms to chest and ankles bound, just out of Barnabas's reach.

Ana calculated her odds. If Gregor were here, they would have had a *plan,* even if it was mostly improvised. Having someone at her back had been a luxury she had never known until him. Fighting beside him felt natural. But Gregor had made clear in the car what he thought about her duty and loyalty to Raymond.

She glanced at her swords, a gift from her master when she'd been taken from her training. Even without Gregor, she was never alone.

"Old swords," the woman said, dismissing them as she placed them before the small roll of Ana's belongings. The mountings were old, the saya faded and cracked.

Ana tucked her chin to hide her shame that she was only worthy of such disused equipment.

"Too small for any respectable warrior," she went on, loud enough for the servants she knew had clustered down the hall, eavesdropping. *"But enough, perhaps, for someone not meant for daishō."*

Her face burned. Her master leaned into the space between them, lowering her voice. *"Enough, perhaps, for one who has earned the right anyway."*

Surprise at the curious softness made her brave, made her look into her master's weathered, inscrutable face. Yes, Ana thought centuries later, she had smiled. It wasn't until she'd unpacked her belongings in her new home that she'd understood the gift had been part of the lesson she'd tried to impart to her. *"Let them underestimate you. It will be their last mistake."* She studied the distinct waved pattern of the steel blade in awe, traced her thumb along the razor edge at the hilt and gloried in the flash of pain and bead of blood that emerged from the callused skin.

Centuries and wealth had seen mounts more fitting, and the fragile saya that housed her swords at her sides had been often been replaced. But the blades remained the same.

Late one summer night, when the heat made sleep impossible, Takami rolled off her sleeping mat and joined Ana on the floor. The girl had seen through the ruse of Ana being a country cousin long ago, though among the adults she was wise enough to pretend it still held. Shoulder to shoulder they peered at the blades revealed beneath the burlap where Ana kept them hidden.

Takami always begged to see them, and Ana—sleepless and irritable—had complied. *"What are they called?"*

Ana frowned. *"Called?"*

The younger girl bumped her shoulder. *"They all have names in the stories, the samurai."*

"I am not samurai. And these are just swords."

Takami rolled her eyes. *"Fine. I will name them for you."*

Her slim fingers hovered over the larger of the two, still small as katana went. Ana expected something fanciful and fearsome, something out of the old tales Takami snuck from her father's library. Takami smiled. *"Onee-san."*

Amused at the simplicity, Ana nodded. *"And the other?"*

Takami's brow furrowed, and Ana recognized her expression from their hours with the English language tutor. She formed the words carefully as she looked into Ana's eyes. *"Little Sister."*

Ana broke their stare first. *Imouto.* She often wondered how much Takami suspected of the truth of their relationship. She knew her mother's terrible barbarian features dulled any resemblance to their father. And yet. Takami had always seen true. They had that in common.

The names had stuck. Ana trusted no weapons more than these. Gregor could keep his soul steel. She had her swords, a century of skill, and death on her side.

After all these years, everything came down to this. If she put herself between necromancers, she would fall. Live to die, wasn't that the way of the samurai. True, she might not have been born one, but she couldn't lie that part of her had longed to be judged worthy. And now the moment of truth. The specter of death, the best gift that could be given, waited for deliverance.

She should act soon or lose her advantage.

The look on Gregor's face when she'd left him on the docks carved a hollow inside of her rib cage.

"You promised me," the creature grated out. Her voice reminded Ana of breaking surf on cliffs, just as uneven. "I give him to you, you release me. You end this life."

"Would you abandon your new promised one, lady?" Barnabas bowed, arms wide. Whatever color his eyes had been, a red, iridescent glow glazed them. He had not ascended as other necromancers had. Something was wrong with the power that clung to him. She narrowed her eyes, trying to refine her sight. "I have need of you yet."

Raymond's head lolled on his shoulders. With their connection Ana sensed his consciousness returning, but too slowly.

"You will be rewarded. A place of honor in my new house."

"I don't want your honor," Laughing Girl screamed. "I want my freedom. I want the death I was promised."

The words rocked through Ana. The bargain, the betrayal. She blinked again hard, and now the second image was clear. The woman beneath the monster, worn down with grief and age. The lines in a face once beautiful, the haggard slump of her shoulders.

"And you shall have it," Barnabas admitted. "But not today."

Laughing Girl shrieked and her tentacles tightened as fury got the best of her. Raymond groaned.

Ana attacked.

Severing tentacles had failed on the boat, so she drove Imouto down into the thinnest part of Laughing Girl's body, locking it into the floor. Laughing Girl screamed. Ana dodged, dancing closer to slice the two meaty ropes holding Raymond. Ana shoved him aside as the tentacles wrapped around her ankles, slamming her to the floor and the wall before she could cut herself free.

Gasping as pain rocked up her side, she staggered back, putting herself between Laughing Girl and Raymond. Laughing Girl managed to dislodge the blade and swung her bulk between Ana and Barnabas. Behind her, Barnabas's eyes flashed with rage.

Ana curled both hands around the hilt of Onee-san, preparing for the fight of her life.

"Missing something?" Gregor skidded to Ana's side. He kept his attention on the creature, but he offered Imouto, hilt first, over his forearm.

Giddy relief swept through her. The euphoric joy of feeling him in place beside her. Where he belonged. Ana closed her fingers over the hilt.

He flipped his wrist and the black blade appeared—smoke made solid by magic. "Soul steel not such a bad idea now."

She snorted. "You still seem to think I require steel."

"I'm beginning to understand what you're capable of, Ms. Gozen." Gregor winked.

At least she'd face death with a smile on her face. Raymond rose to his hands and knees, groaning.

Barnabas straightened, his gaze sweeping them. He didn't seem to want to issue a challenge that would send him and Raymond into the In Between to battle for supremacy, according to the necromancer code. He had no Aegis either. What had his plan been?

"Hold them," he shouted.

Ana dropped her shoulder, ready for a fight.

He ran. Laughing Girl maneuvered between them and the open doors through which Barnabas fled. Her tentacles slapped the cement floor, the metal-bound one ringing. But Ana only saw the woman within.

Gregor exhaled. Their eyes met, brows lifted in unison.

Ana almost laughed. Instead, she stood up and sheathed her blades. "Now we make an ally."

* * *

AN ALLY. Gregor should have been happy, but he didn't relax his grip on his sword. He didn't like that Barnabas hadn't challenged Raymond. Necromancers challenged for dominance and fought to the death. They absorbed one another's powers in victory. Barnabas, it seemed, had something else in mind.

Ana took two cautious strides toward the creature, her hands empty. The creature hissed and Ana stopped. Neither backed down.

Ana called back to him, "Sheathe your sword."

"Not until an accord is struck." He might be crazy, but he wasn't stupid. Those tentacles had crushed a ferry.

Ana frowned but turned her face back to the creature. "I can help you. *We* can help you."

The creature recoiled, hissed, and surged toward Ana. Gregor lifted his blade. Ana held up a hand. He waited.

The first tentacle closed around her legs, slamming her to the floor. She still didn't reach for her blades. To hell with this.

Gregor charged. Another arm slapped him aside. He rolled to his feet, reaching for the semiautomatic under his coat.

"Gregor, stop." Ana's voice, clear and calm, rang through the vast space. "Laughing Girl, I won't fight you."

He froze. The creature's movement slowed.

"I know who you are," Ana said. "I see you."

The creature rose, tentacles unfurling and sliding aside like hair as it revealed the face at the heart of them, twisted with rage. Metal clanked against the concrete floor, and Gregor's eyes found the rusted iron. An old manacle. The same kind that had once bound him in the hold of a ship.

"You are his," the creature said, looking at Raymond, still wavering in the pile of severed tentacles. "Same as I must serve the other. You must try to kill me if he gives the word."

"You haven't tried to kill us," Gregor said, sliding his blade home. He let the gun settle back in the holster and held up his palms. "Why is that?"

"Barnabas is sloppy," the creature said, slinking back. "Words are power. He should know better. 'Hold them' is not 'kill them.'"

Gregor started for Ana. "Let her go, and let us talk. Raymond can help you."

The creature's laughter became hoarse. "Help. The word means nothing to me now. Your Raymond promised to help me long ago and *this* is what came of it."

Gregor snuck a glimpse at Ana's face. Shock and recognition snarled in her eyes. They shone.

"I can end this, light of my heart." They all looked up at Raymond's words.

Raymond struggled to his feet. Barefoot and muddy, his jeans torn and his hair a tangled mess, only the shine of his eyes betrayed any remaining power. Even that flickered.

When the creature's attention shifted to Raymond, Gregor made his move. He grabbed Ana by the shoulders, lifting her out of the slack tentacle around her legs and drawing her backward.

"Are you out of your mind," he hissed, running his hands up and down her arms.

She knocked his hand away. "I'm fine. What are you doing?"

Gregor caught himself, fingers stilling. "I thought you were going to let her…"

"Suicide by cephalopod?" she whispered, brow raised. "I am stubborn, Sticks. Not an idiot. And maybe I have something worth living for."

Her eyes slid away from his face. He caught her chin and brought them back, the kind of relief he barely acknowledged possessing sweeping him. "Good."

She tilted her head. "You were right."

He followed her gaze. Raymond had gone down to one knee before the creature, one of the gnarled, sea-roughened hands in his own. They spoke in hushed tones.

"Do you understand what they're saying?"

"Pieces," Ana said. "He's apologizing for abandoning her. For sending us. She's afraid of something. Something Barnabas has… or controls. I don't understand."

From the mass of tentacles, a great knobby rope of muscle rose and settled in Raymond's hands, sliding until the manacle rested on his palm. Now that they weren't all attempting to kill him, Gregor noted it looked withered compared to the others. Raymond bowed his head over the metal.

"It binds her to Barnabas. He says this is his fault for leaving her vulnerable. He's going to try to break it."

Gregor winced at the sizzle and stench of burned flesh. A distant pain in his own hand made him look down. Ana gripped his fingers. He shifted their grip, lacing fingers together.

Ana let go when Raymond rose, the burn fading from his forehead. He strode toward them, his back to the creature who had settled, weeping, in his wake. Raymond took them in but seemed to be looking elsewhere.

"I cannot break it," he said. "I suspect killing Barnabas is the only way."

"Of *course* it is," Gregor snapped. "Or you need his power to do it."

Raymond's eyes flashed with a hint of his old capricious fury. Gregor rose to his full height.

Ana stepped between them. "It doesn't matter. Barnabas can't be allowed to live after what he's done. This ends one way."

"She knows where his aedis is," Raymond said, looking back at the creature. His eyes couldn't stay on her long, and his anger withered to something internally focused. "He meant to strip me of power and keep me under his control… as she is."

Gregor had never heard of such a thing. To sidestep the risk to himself and keep Raymond alive was a coward's trick.

"She'll help us stop him," Raymond said. "And I will free her."

Gregor shook his head. "Even if she wants to, she's bound to obey his command. This stinks of a trap."

Both Ana and Raymond stared at him. The hint of a smile played at one corner of Ana's mouth. Raymond turned a glower on her.

She shrugged. "He doesn't trust anyone. It's served him well thus far."

Raymond sighed. "It's a chance we have to take. We go after him now, before he can regroup."

Gregor opened his mouth to argue, but Raymond beat him.

"Your duty has been fulfilled here," Raymond said, lifting his hand to sketch a symbol in the air. "I release you from my service."

No. Not now. Not yet.

Raymond's finger left a trail of ochre sparkling in its wake. Released from the binding of his vow of service, Gregor staggered back a step, relieved of a sudden weight. He should have been elated. Instead, a spiraling sense of despair rose in its wake. Without the bond to Raymond, Gregor had no legitimate way to help Ana.

Auger and the giants slowed to a walk in the doorway, taking in the sight of the enormous creature with awed breaths. Raymond started toward them, pausing when he noticed Ana hadn't moved.

"Ana," Raymond called.

Her eyes settled on Gregor, cool and dark. She turned her back and rejoined her master.

Gregor didn't miss the victorious expression on Raymond's face.

The giants smirked. Gregor gave them the finger. They closed ranks around Ana and Raymond, the creature trailing, and Gregor let the sinking in his stomach hit bottom. His liberty tasted sour in his mouth. Something tugged in him, a thin strand of something—a promise unspoken.

It grew tight as Ana walked away, leaving a painful wringing in his chest. She'd made her choice.

Best to get back to Prague before he had to fight his way out of the nightmare this territory would become in the transition of power. Barnabas had gotten the upper hand thus far because he'd managed to find a weakness of Raymond's to exploit, and if one of the Allegiance didn't take him down sooner, another younger necromancer craving power would later. Gus, the Suramérican necromancer, would have to be warned in her seat in Mal País. She would bear the most strain if the North American territory plunged into chaos. Ito would need time to gather intelligence and help Azrael prepare his strategy.

Gregor started for the courtyard in time to watch the helicopter swing away from the island.

Super.

Another interminable boat ride later, he ignored law enforcement and gawkers to reclaim his car. One dared to approach and he let out a savage roar, sending the crowd screaming and tumbling over itself to get away.

He slammed the car door hard enough to rock the vehicle and pounded his hands on the dash. It took the remaining scraps of his control not to rip the interior apart with his bare hands. Helplessness shook him by the throat, left him raging at his own inability to see a way through this situation.

In the artificial silence of the automobile, his hand stilled on the wheel.

Ana hadn't chosen. She'd followed because her vow had demanded it. There had been no choice at all.

He would not abandon her now.

Certainty calmed him—the certainty of what he must do overriding the magnitude of what must be done. Even then, on the first day he'd known it: he'd follow her into hell.

He should have fought harder to stay with Raymond. He had no idea where Laughing Girl would lead them. He scrabbled for his phone, dialing as he started the car. Free of his vow, he was no longer risking eternal damnation asking for help.

Gregor couldn't remember ever hearing the phone ring so many times before being greeted by Ito's cheerful bark. "*Moshi, Moshi.*"

Azrael's head of intelligence sounded like he was running from something. "I need a track. Cell phone?"

"Difficult. Not impossible." Ito sucked his teeth and went into an explanation of satellites and piggybacking off signals that lost Gregor almost immediately. "Please hold…"

Running, yes, and fighting something based on the sound of body strikes and soft gusts of air forcefully liberated from the body in the background. Ito's voice returned. "So you and Ana Gozen, huh? I've got a bet she runs you through at least once before this is over. A moment—"

As the dashboard navigation initialized, a familiar ping sounded. He paused, considering the map of the coastline and the moving arrow. Laughing Girl's tracker.

"Never mind, I've got them," he said, grinning as he put the car in gear. "And Ito-san, *ki o tsukete*."

Ito laughed, and it sounded like he crashed through glass. "*Sei vorsichtig*, man."

"That's no fun." Gregor stared at the phone for a moment after the call disconnected. What the hell trouble had Ito gotten himself into now?

Then he turned his attention to the road and flung the car into traffic. Horns blared and tires shrieked around him as he avoided a pileup. Whatever geas Raymond had put on the car to help clear the road must have been released with his vow.

Good. He dodged cars and pushed the Audi to speed. It was much more fun this way.

CHAPTER TWENTY-EIGHT

A na scanned ahead as the helicopter closed in on their destination. Another island. A tactical advantage for a necromancer who controlled water. They pulled strength from the energy of their elements.

On the small rocky island half a mile from the mainland, the Año Nuevo lighthouse station had long been abandoned by human inhabitants. Seabirds and elephant seals held court now, using it as a nesting ground and sanctuary. The original structures remained—foghorn station, keeper's house, shed, storage—all beaten by the elements and slowly surrendering to decay.

Her preternaturally sharp eyes picked up no human movement among the swarming birds and protesting seals. No light or curling flashes of power indicating the presence of another necromancer. Beside her, Raymond tracked the water beneath them, relentless in his search. He also benefited from being this close to the ocean. The wind buffeted the craft, and his color and vitality had returned as the last of the geas wore off. He almost looked like his old self.

Seeing Laughing Girl again had done something to him. As if talking to her, touching her, had broken something in him he'd restrained for all the years Ana had known him, and probably longer. Without thinking, Ana laid a hand on his shoulder. She knew regret firsthand. She'd left Gregor without an explanation, an apology, or even a goodbye. He had come for her and she had walked away with barely a glance.

Obsidian eyes and their unearthly metallic sheen rose, his gaze fixing on her with the inhuman consideration she knew all too well. The cold light offered no familiarity, no comfort given or received. She withdrew her fingers, settling her palm on the hull of the rocking helicopter as it circled for a landing. Whatever the reappearance of his former lover had brought out in him, it did not extend to her.

"No sign of Huxley," Auger confirmed from the copilot seat.

Raymond pointed toward the flat area on the north end of the island, close to the channel dividing it from the mainland. The light swept the ground, wind buffeting the banking helicopter and making the landing difficult. Raymond needed to get control of himself, or they would crash before they ever made it to the island.

Ana gripped the handhold, bracing her legs. The helicopter swung around and then came to a shuddering stop in midair. She knew that scent—cephalopod and seawater—and the curling tendril of a tentacle circling the helicopter's chassis slapped against the window.

Each sucker was like a living, moving thing, gripping against the chassis as the whole muscle tightened. Metal screamed, and the instrument panel began to buzz in warning. She glanced out, expecting to see Laughing Girl.

But the thing pulling itself out of the surf along the jagged black reef below them resembled a humanoid in the most vague sense—shoulders, neck, and head. But instead of a face with a nose and mouth, a mass of writhing tentacles slashed the air below a single, solid black eye. The wet, sucker-lined ropes continued down what should have been a chest and throat, disappearing into the surf. The tentacle around the helicopter was attached to a barnacle-crusted hand. The second hand braced on the rock below.

Ana scanned it with her sight but found no sign of Laughing

Girl's familiar shape in the beast. Beneath the surface was only a sucking darkness she could not stare into long without feeling herself drawn into it. Dread expanded in her chest, pressing against her rib cage.

The tentacle yanked and the helicopter plummeted toward the monstrosity. Horror shocked her into motion. Ana kicked open the opposite door.

"Petr, Mitko, you're up," she shouted. "Catch."

The giants moved fast, diving out the open door.

Ana caught Auger's eye. "Get clear."

She grabbed Raymond and pitched him out of the helicopter. Auger kicked out the front window and dove. She wasn't going to be able to stop this thing on her own, but she could buy them some time. Helicopters didn't usually explode on impact, but anything was possible with the right help.

Ana unsheathed her short blade. The instrument panel gave beneath sufficient pounding, sending sparks flying. She caught a flare and gripped it in her teeth. The helicopter dove and she lost her footing, turning her fall into a roll. She slammed off the back wall, slid out the open door, and caught a hand on the runner.

Using the momentum of her fall, she swung back up the belly of the copter, encased in tentacle from midpoint all the way to the tail. She used the turgid skin for handholds as she worked her way to the fuel tanks. She buried her short blade in the metal skin until fuel leaked. Clinging to the hilt, she rocked back and forth, using her body weight to increase the opening. With a grunt, she pounded a flare on her thigh, jammed it into the opening, and flung herself free.

The heat of the explosion washed over her as she fell. She tucked, landing in a roll, certain she'd broken a few ribs on impact. On her feet again, she took in Raymond and the rest of the Aegis, staring up the monstrosity illuminated in the glow. She glared at them all. What good was a godsdamned diversion if they weren't going to use it?

"Move," she barked. "Get to the house."

It wasn't going to provide them much cover, but better than

being out in the open. On the ground, the stench of guano and marine mammals crowded her nostrils mixing, with burned kelp and meat.

Auger broke first, running point as she'd trained him. His catlike reflexes and preternaturally sharp hearing would catch anything ahead. Mitko grabbed Raymond, ready to lift him off his feet if needed and fight with one massive arm. Petr brought up the rear, all brawn.

Ana put herself between the monstrosity and their escape, Onee-san bared. A flash of silver caught her eye, and she looked up with a little grin. Her hand snaked out and snatched the smoldering hilt of the short blade from the air as it fell.

She flipped it, blade out and flexed her knees. "Nice timing, Little Sister."

The monstrosity shook itself free of the broken, burning wreckage, showering her in flame and twisted metal. Scorched, flopping tentacles hung amid the rest of the writhing mass. Unlike Laughing Girl, who seemed to generate two new arms for every one disabled, this creature seemed to have a finite number. It was still three times Laughing Girl's size.

Dragging itself on its arms, it rose out of the surf, crushing or knocking aside the churning mass of elephant seals that did not flee fast enough. It swung a massive lumpy head to sight Raymond in its single lidless eye and then paused at the sight of her. It crouched on its arms, preparing to pounce. The tentacled maw opened, revealing rows and rows of sharklike teeth leading into an infinite darkness.

Blades bared, she showed the monster her own teeth.

It lunged. Instead of fleeing, Ana ran straight for it, dodging and slicing through tentacles whipping into her path. If she could get to the throat or whatever served for a solar plexus, maybe she had a chance. Hell, she'd even settle for that big lidless eye.

Before she could reach it, the monster screamed, arching as a black harpoon erupted from just below its collarbone, punching through the tough hide. The harpoon claws opened like a flower, digging into the surrounding skin. The beast flopped backward with a roar, collapsing against the cliffside. Dark liquid rushed from the gaping hole in its chest as the harpoon dissolved into smoke. Groaning, the monster sank into the sea.

A motorboat beached on the east side of the island, and as she jogged down the sandy shale path, Gregor appeared over the side of the cliff. He fell in step with her.

"Another advantage of soul steel," he mused. "A little creativity goes a long way."

"Handy." She settled Onee-san in its sheath. "What are you doing here?"

"I didn't make my vow to Raymond, and we're not done…"

The whitecaps churned, and a set of barnacle-crusted knuckles appeared over the top of the cliff. Ana sighed. "Hold that thought."

Gregor lifted his hand and the black blade appeared in its more familiar form.

She grabbed his arm, pulling him away from the cliff. "Let's go. We need a plan."

He laughed. "Now you want to plan?"

"Better late than never," she muttered. "Come on. We're safer in the interior."

The monstrosity rose, the hole in its chest still oozing. The wound slowed its movements, but it didn't stop until its chest was out of the waves. It went no farther.

"How…," Gregor began.

It roared and Ana jerked her chin. "It can't leave the water yet. If Barnabas summoned it, it may not be at full power. Maybe he's counting on using whatever power he gets defeating Raymond. Something's not right with that guy, haven't you noticed?"

He nodded. It trailed them along the edge of the cliff the entire way. They met Raymond and the others, and she herded them all as far inland as possible. Ana sent Auger to scout the buildings for a refuge. The creature circled the island but couldn't get close enough to do more than flail nasty tentacles and roar at them. Raymond took in Gregor's presence with dispassionate consideration.

"You've been released." Raymond lifted his chin. "Waste my time at your peril, *Jäger*."

Ana had never heard of a sworn Aegis volunteering without some sort of contract or exchange. Gregor straightened his tattered lapels, his face as cool and expressionless as ever. Only she recognized the light in his eyes. The blue, still vivid as glacier ice, now burned.

"You could use another set of hands."

Raymond inclined his head. "Yours?"

"Azrael would not be pleased if I sent an ally into a trap without at least offering my service." He even managed to look inconvenienced.

Raymond's mouth canted, but his eyes did not lighten. He scanned Ana, but she had centuries of practice at keeping her heart rate smooth and her expression even.

"Suit yourself."

* * *

"Who invited Cthulhu?" Ana asked as they mounted the porch behind the others, sweeping the darkness with her gaze.

Gregor paused, confused. "Khul—"

Ana squinted at him. "Dreaded dark lord? Great old ones? Elder gods?"

He blinked. "Is this a Morodor thing?"

"Mordor." She shook her head but seems to be losing the battle with a smile. "And no. Unrelated. No time for twentieth-century genre fiction, eh?"

He spread his hands to take in their current situation. "I'll keep to the stock market, thank you."

Ana looked dangerously close to laughter, and the sight of it did him more good than he wanted to admit. The tension in him eased the moment he was by her side, softened under the bright glare of her gaze. He wanted to assess the burns on the back of her neck, check to see how much of the blood on her was her own. He kept his hands to himself.

He turned his attention to the churning dark, full of the bellowing monster and panicked seal cries. Raymond seemed to accept his presence, but he had no doubt he would be the first the necromancer sacrificed if need be. He didn't care.

Raymond joined them, searching the waves. "I've heard of such an entity. A beast so terrible humans worshipped it as a god and sent their children for its feast before a coven banished it to the valleys of the sea."

"And Laughing Girl…"

"No sign of her," Ana said.

"She feared it," Raymond murmured. "That thing. Barnabas lured her with the promise of vengeance and bound her. Then he used her as an offering to the beast. The manacle binds her to obey Barnabas, but that thing kept her in line." His voice rose with rage.

"And it helped in the attacks," Ana finished. "Not just the rogue pack. It can't leave the sea, but she can. It used her to drive the mortals to him."

"Do you think that thing—"

Raymond shook his head. "I would have felt it."

"She's out there." Gregor sighed, and Ana found his eyes in the near darkness, an exchange of suspicion. *And whose side is she on?*

"And where is the master of ceremonies?"

Barnabas rose from the sea, arms wide like a victorious conqueror.

"Be careful what you ask for," Gregor muttered as he and Ana stepped in front of Raymond, blades ready.

"The Black Blade of Azrael," Barnabas said, walking the worn trail toward the house, oblivious to the mud and the cold. Beneath his cape, the ill-fitting gray suit looked like something out of a film noir detective movie. "Freed from your leash."

He stopped twenty paces from the porch steps. The beast sank into the waves, its lidless eye fixed on Barnabas as if waiting for command.

The necromancer settled his hands on his hips with a smug grin. He cocked his head, scanning in that way Gregor associated with Ana using her sight. "No vow binds you here. Not of ours at least."

He didn't like the way Barnabas's eyes skimmed Ana. So far the necromancer had been adept at manipulating connections to his advantage—first Laughing Girl and Raymond, the wolves, and now he seemed to sense the thing growing between him and Ana. Something even Gregor himself hadn't yet named. Barnabas seemed to like feeling as if he pulled the strings behind the scenes. That he had the upper hand.

"Perhaps you would consider mine?" Barnabas said. "Join with me now and I will spare her when this is over. The others will not be so lucky."

Behind Gregor, Raymond swore. Gregor had to agree with the sentiment.

He's sloppy, Laughing Girl's words. And if he was sloppy with his words, what else might he be lax about? Azrael once told him power was easy to gain, the challenge was in the control. It was one reason emotion could be so dangerous. That was where most necromancers failed. Losing control could unleash their powers in unpredictable ways, was a weakness that could do as much damage to themselves as others.

Gregor took a chance, vanishing his sword. Ana sucked in a breath beside him. He didn't dare look at her. *Come on, Ana. I need you now.*

He stepped down off the porch, and Barnabas's smug expression blossomed into a grin. But instead of joining him, Gregor slipped his hands into his pockets and frowned. "That's interesting. Before tonight, no one seemed to know you existed. Ana?" He glanced over his shoulder.

Her eyes darted from him to Barnabas. Then she smiled. "Not even a blip. And I know all the necromancers worth anything on this continent."

Barnabas flushed a deep red and his grin faltered. "That won't be a problem after tonight."

"Perhaps," Gregor said. The waves battered the seaward side of the island, and even the beast stirred uneasily. "Think he's got it in him?"

Ana sheathed her sword, cocking her head with an assessing glare. "He's not much to look at, is he?"

Gregor tsked. "That's unkind. But I have seen more flattering suits."

"Maybe give him the number for your tailor."

Barnabas's face grew increasingly red and blustery. Power crackled around him, red flares snapping off the rocks and singeing the edges of his cape. "You dare mock me on the night your master falls, bitch?"

"That's optimistic of you." Ana raised her brows at Gregor in disbelief.

Gregor shrugged. "No deal."

Barnabas's composure began to slide. "You'd have these animals over me? You stupid fool. This territory will be mine and you will die."

"I have known a great many necromancers in my years, but you are the most repugnant." Gregor turned his back to Barnabas as the necromancer surrendered into a howling rage.

Gregor kept his pace steady and his gaze on Ana's face, as though he didn't consider Huxley enough threat to worry. Her gaze never left the necromancer, and though her expression remained impassive, he counted on the first hint of an attack from Huxley coming from her face.

"You're insane, Sticks," she hissed when he joined her. Even Raymond's eyes settled on him with new regard.

"It seems likely," Gregor breathed as the sweat cooled on his back. "But if his ego is that fragile, it won't take more to pushpin him past control. Raymond—"

"You're lucky to have him." Barnabas's voice cut through his warning. Gregor turned to see Barnabas watching Ana, a little smile playing over his face. "Not everyone here honors their word."

Beside him Ana stiffened and sucked in a hard breath. She

muttered something to Auger, and the other members of Raymond's Aegis closed ranks.

A moment later, Laughing Girl emerged from the waves, staggering to Barnabas's feet. Her head bowed, the mighty tentacles limp around her. The monster on the cliff howled and she shuddered.

"Go to your mate," Barnabas commanded.

Gregor met Ana's eyes and drew his sword. He read his thoughts in her face and they went something like, *Oh, fuck.*

Raymond broke ranks with a terrible roar, his hands in fists at his side and the swirling ochre sparks of his power clustering around him. "I challenge you, Barnabas Huxley, usurper."

CHAPTER TWENTY-NINE

"Your soul or mine," Raymond roared, striding down the path as the wind whipped anything not nailed down into the air around him. "One leaves tonight."

Ana's chest clenched.

"Accepted, Raymond Nightfeather." Barnabas smiled. "This territory is mine after tonight."

Barnabas dropped into the In Between and Raymond followed, their bodies frozen in place. Their battle would be fought on the plane between life and death, where power flowed free of physical constraints.

"Plan?" Auger shouted, sharpening her focus.

The giants waited instruction. Whatever animosity they held, when they fought for Raymond, they fought together. They couldn't interfere in the challenge once issued and accepted. It bound the combatants until one emerged victorious. They could do nothing for Raymond now.

But, like a demon, the monster had been summoned, which meant it in some part relied on the necromancer for power.

"We weaken the thing, we weaken him," Ana said. "Give Raymond better odds."

"And Laughing Girl?" Gregor said.

Ana frowned. Laughing Girl was trapped in this. More than any of them, she needed Raymond to succeed.

"We focus on the demon for now," she said. "That ought to free her up as well."

Auger grunted assent. He and the giants charged toward the monster, fanning out to divide its focus.

Gregor tipped an imaginary cap. "After you."

In spite of everything, Ana wanted to laugh. They charged into the fray together. Even if Raymond fell tonight, she would be glad they had this battle. She made a silent vow of her own.

You'll survive this, Gregor Schwarz. I promise you. She was no necromancer—there was no power in the words but her will.

Gregor hadn't lied about making himself useful. He took hits they wouldn't have recovered from, and so he dared more direct attacks. As she watched him scale the monster for the third time, severing the tendons at the shoulder and leaving one arm limp and useless, she admired Azrael's strategy for his Aegis more than ever.

Petr and Mitko proved creative and destructive, tearing off tentacles and using them to beat the monster back. Until the demon got ahold of Petr and shoved him in its massive tooth-lined maw.

She would hear the screams the man made as he was mashed and shredded until the day she died. Blood darkened the ropes of flesh on the demon's chest and neck. Reinvigorated, it made a grab for Auger. The street fighter managed to keep his arms free, and he ripped fingers off the demon's remaining hand before he was flung away. Auger crashed through the south wall of the old keeper's house, disappearing in a shower of broken wood and dust. He didn't rise.

Ana regrouped beside Gregor, her breath coming hard. He looked as cool as ever, but the slight downward twist of his mouth betrayed his concern.

Raymond sank to one knee, groaning. Wounds appeared all over his body at once, damage inflicted in the In Between catching up to the physical plane. His hand clutched his throat as dark lines poured from between his fingers, almost black in the failing light. His eyes fluttered open. Why hadn't Barnabas finished him?

"Nəmá sk"áči." He staggered toward Laughing Girl, his heart on his face.

The monster came first, lunging even farther from the water than ever before. Its waist disappeared into slim hips and a scaled tail lined with curved spines. A horizontal slit below its sternum gaped, exposing vulnerable flesh. Gills?

It stretched out its remaining fingers, grasping for Raymond.

Laughing Girl reached it first. With more strength than Ana anticipated, Laughing Girl flung herself at the demon, her tentacles grasping and clawing at his, intertwining. The monster ripped them away, one by one, but they returned, tearing at its face.

Raymond dropped to one knee, howling at the sight of her being decimated before him. Her hands plunged toward its eye, and the sharp, wicked fingers found their mark. Lidless, the giant eye had no protection from her talons. It roared in pain and snatched her away, flinging her to the ground. She lay still.

Behind Raymond, Barnabas staggered from the In Between, crippled with injury but his eyes on the other necromancer. *Get up,* Ana willed Raymond. *Fight, godsdamn you.*

Gregor spoke, breaking Ana's focus from the horror of the scene. "The opening under the breastbone, into the heart, if that thing has one."

"I'll distract it," Ana said, leaving Raymond to his fate. She had no idea what would become of her if he fell, but it would do no good to fear that now. "Make that sword into something capable of doing some damage."

Gregor flashed his teeth. When she charged, he moved as an extension of her body. She grabbed a dagger from the small of her back, Imouto still in hand.

She whistled three sharp blasts for Mitko and prayed he remembered the signal from the circus days. He glanced over his shoulder with a nod, dropping to one knee. He laced his fingers to form a stirrup, hunching his shoulders in anticipation. She tucked her blades against her chest and planted one foot in his cupped palms. He launched her through the air like a missile.

She twisted as she flew and landed somewhere around the beast's neck, forced to cling to slippery tentacles.

Even without the eye, the beast had some sense of the attack. It careened around, and she caught a glimpse of Gregor racing toward the thing with a long blade that looked to be out of a medieval handbook of war. She'd seen his speed before, but never like this—he blurred in her sight, vaulting over fallen tentacles and skating across the rocky ground as surefooted and indefatigable as a hunting animal. He didn't bother to hide his charge, or dissemble, cutting a path directly for the glistening line of vulnerable flesh they had spotted from below. His faith in her ability to distract it seemed to be absolute.

Time to go to work.

Ana clambered up its face, so close the meat-and-seawater reek of its churning maw made her gag. She caught hold of a barnacle's edge and kicked away from the offal and brine, letting momentum carry her to the side of its head. The rough edge of the barnacle shell opened the skin of her palm, but she ignored the pain. She plunged Imouto into the dark hole she hoped was an ear.

The beast roared, forgetting Gregor to swing its hand up against its head. She let go of Imouto to avoid being crushed, and lost her footing. The surf crashed on the rock-strewn beach below her as she tumbled loose, and she had a glimpse of herself shattered on the rocks below, battered by the tide and dragged out to sea. No coming back from that. But she wasn't ready to die. She twisted in the air, digging the dagger into the flesh of the beast's shoulder as her other hand sought out the short knives at the small of her back. Momentum dragged her down until she buried the second blade in flesh. Her grip on the dagger slipped. She gave it up in favor of freeing the short blade holstered at her thigh and burying it deep. The beast howled and arched away, but one knife, then another, snagged on the clumps of barnacle, stopping her fall.

She clung to the rough surface for a long moment, amazed

that she wasn't dashed on the rocks, that one breath still followed another. The razor-sharp shells sliced her clothes and skin as viscous blood poured over her. She didn't notice. She'd seized her own life back from death.

The demon shrieked and its entire body shuddered. A grin stretched her face, savage and victorious. Alive.

A rope of muscle snatched her away, suckers like needles along her skin. Ana struck out with a dagger, and another thick rope of muscle closed on her wrist, holding her fast. The blade tumbled free. The last exhale left her straining for air but she could not open her ribs to draw a breath.

The tentacle on her wrist snapped tight as the first wrapped around her body from shoulders to knees. The tension yanked her shoulder out of the socket. The bones began to snap beneath her skin, one at a time and then in chorus. She would have screamed if there had been air left in her lungs.

Agony rose in a tide, dragging her beyond consciousness. And then, nothing.

* * *

GREGOR MADE his charge as soon as Ana was airborne, summoning a glaive like ones favored against cavalry and armored infantry alike centuries ago. Perhaps more polearm than sword, it was bladed in any case, so it fell under his command according to his bargain with Azrael. The glittering black blade solidified as he ran, the razor edge curving toward a wicked point, a second edge curving away from the spine so it would do as much damage going as coming. A little creativity went a long way.

Dim awareness of Raymond rising to face Barnabas for one final confrontation reached him. If Barnabas won, the vows between Raymond and his Aegis would shatter. Barnabas had no Aegis of his own—perhaps the others would bend to him as their new master if offered the chance. Not Ana. And if she refused to serve, he doubted Barnabas would let her live—with her skill, she would make a powerful undead servant.

Gregor had been careful not to damage the boat when he'd landed on the island. He'd left the Audi charging at the dock. If he could end the creature and get to Ana before Barnabas turned his attention to them, they might have a chance to escape. If they could make it to the southern border, the Suramérican necromancer would grant them sanctuary. Gus owed him that much. Boat. Car. Border. It was a good plan.

But first, to kill a monster.

The massive torso rose above him, showering him in icy seawater and slicking the path before him. The glistening inner edge of the long gill below its sternum made a target only a fool could miss. Gregor summoned all his strength and leaped, driving the blade up and into the beast's rib cage.

Dark, viscus liquid rushed over him. Heart blood. He let go with one hand to grip the beast's open gills, using what little leverage he had to drive the weapon home. The apex of the heart surrendered, and the blade tip appeared through its ribs, an obsidian black gleam amid raw flesh. A heart blow might not kill it, but it would at least slow it down.

A tentacle whipped around his arms. It slammed him into packed earth once, then swung him skyward with dizzying speed. A flash of swords tangled up in another tentacle caught his attention. He summoned the sword again, this time between his feet. When the demon spun him again, he jackknifed his body, kicking the blade through the tentacle and freeing himself.

He hit the ground hard, rolling free. He called the glaive to his hand again as he got his feet underneath him.

The sound the beast made battered his eardrums. It sank to the ground. The battle was done, but not over. There was one way he knew to make certain a grace-blooded creature was dead.

Gregor ran forward and the glaive became a battle-axe. The beast flopped and shuddered on the rocky ground. Gregor found the neck and started at the spine. Three swings, powered by all the strength of his gift, and the head rolled free. The body went slack, sliding backward over the cliff.

He'd lost sight of Ana. The memory of dim light of swords

gripped him. Was she tangled up in the beast? He had to get to her before she was dragged into the sea.

He hacked at tentacles, kicking them aside and calling her name.

A blast of energy behind him knocked him forward. He didn't look over his shoulder, didn't want to see Barnabas coming for him, empowered by Raymond's destruction. He kept hacking, calling her name. There were too many tentacles, all clutching and still tight.

Ana. Boat. Car. Border.

Raymond's voice rose over his head, a command and a release. The last of the strength went out of the beast in one great exhalation of power, and all the remaining tentacles softened at once. The paired swords glittered in the moonlight. Ana. He lurched to his feet.

She lay bleeding in a puddle of seawater and beast ichor. Her breath rattled in her chest, catching and hesitating before catching again. Too weak to cough up the liquid collecting in her throat, she gagged. Gregor dropped to her side, weighing the damage moving her might do before shifting her so the blood trickled out of her mouth instead of choking her.

"Stay alive, Ana Gozen," he commanded. "You'll be working off my dry cleaning bill for the next hundred years."

A sound from deep within her chest—a laugh? He thought more likely it was a groan, but he would take whatever he could get. If she could hear him, understand him, she couldn't be too far gone. He glanced back. Raymond bent over the crumpled form of Laughing Girl. She had shrunken, pebbled skin going gray. His hands on her glowed, the words a litany of undoing.

Ana breathed as much of his name as she could manage. "Send Ray your fucking bill."

The tightness in his chest cracked, spilling terror through him.

"You don't get to die here," he snarled. "I forbid it. Do you understand?"

Ana's gift was not strong enough to save her. Not against this.

Ana and Laughing Girl stopped breathing at the same time.

Gregor closed his eyes. He focused on every bit of magic Azrael had ever granted him, scraping the edges for anything he could use to help her. He wrapped it around her and dragged her back from the edge. Her will knit to his effort. He gasped when he opened his eyes, rocking backward. He understood the expression to feel one's age. Ana's chest rose and fell again in irregular rhythm.

He looked up. "Nightfeather!"

Raymond looked more vital than ever, his skin alight with Barnabas's power as the wind whipped his hair into a frenzy of black strands. The necromancer laid a hand on Ana's forehead, sweeping away hair matted with blood. He met Gregor's eyes as he crouched beside them, lowering his mouth to her ear. He whispered and her eyelids fluttered.

"Death claims her." Raymond nodded once. "She is not long for this world."

The sound tearing from Gregor's chest was a beast of its own —grief. It shredded him from the inside out, leaving him a husk. "You'll let her die here."

"I would have let her die five minutes ago," Raymond said. "As a *mercy*."

"There is no mercy in this," Gregor screamed. "What life did she have before you sent her to die for you?"

Raymond's eyes narrowed, and Gregor prepared himself to die with Ana. The calm settled over him. So be it. He held the necromancer's gaze. But dying wouldn't save her. He lowered his eyes. "Please."

Raymond's gaze held the weight of consideration. With the pad of one thumb he traced a geas on her skin, leaving a fading trail of ochre sheen as he went. He ended with a single stroke between her eyebrows, leaning over her again to exhale a single breath into her nostrils.

Ana inhaled. The bleeding stopped.

"She needs more than I can give." Raymond sank back on his heels, his elbow braced on his knee. "She has a few hours. Maybe less. Maybe enough to make the journey." He reached forward and

Gregor tensed. The necromancer's smile held no humor. "Come now. It's too late to fear me, you crazy son of a bitch."

Raymond's thumb sketched a figure over his brow and cheeks, then dusted his eyelids. The power itched. Not a binding. Something else. "There is one thing that may stop this. The gift your master sent. I must stay and finish this. But the geas will allow you to enter my aedis unmolested and find the ambrosia. Touch nothing else or the consequences will be dire. One drop. Better less than more. There is no telling what too much will do to her in this state. When this geas wears off, if you are still inside, you will die."

New plan.

Boat. Car. Aedis.

Raymond's gaze returned to the lifeless form of the unnatural thing he'd created out of love and the destruction it had wrought. In one hand he held the rusted manacle inscribed with symbols that had bound her. Without looking back at them, he gave a final command. "Go."

Gregor slid his arms behind Ana's knees and under her shoulders. He scooped up her swords in one hand, and the blades sliced into his palms and rivulets of blood ran down, mixing with hers on the shale and wet sand. He felt nothing but the ticking of a clock inside him, marking her last breaths. Her head lolled at an unnatural angle.

Boat. Car. Aedis. It was all he had left.

"Stay with me, Ana. I need you."

CHAPTER THIRTY

Gregor gave more weight to speed over caution, hoping Raymond's charm would be enough to hold her together as they bounced over the waves. He wrapped her in an old blanket reeking of oil and the ocean for the trip to the car and carried her up the silent dock. The small community he'd procured the boat from was quiet, but he could feel the eyes following them from the windows of the buildings nearby. A curtain stirred, faces appearing silhouetted by light, then drawing away. What did they feel—fear, hatred?

The camaraderie of Azrael's Aegis was its strength. They moved as a single mind, recognized all over the territory as the hand of the necromancer, and he stood at their head. The stirrings of human dissatisfaction cropping up in Prague had seemed like fleas on a giant's back. What must it have been like for Ana, alone with a necromancer she could barely trust and a cohort nipping at her heels?

A ragged sound escaped her as he settled her in the passenger seat. He pushed the car to speed, grateful for the clear road in the predawn hours. Sluggish but steady, her pulse beat under his fingertips. Impossible considering how much blood she must have lost.

"You almost had me convinced," she said between gasping breaths. "After the trick with the harpoon. To renegotiate my contract."

"That was pretty clever, wasn't it?"

She sucked her teeth. "But if *this* is what it feels like to draw your sword, you can keep your soul steel."

He laughed in spite of himself. Her eyes slid shut. He counted every hitching breath. Immortality did funny things to the ability to reckon time with any reliability. Once, in London, Azrael had gone into a library for "a moment" and disappeared for a week. Lysippe had laughed at Gregor's concern, taken rooms at a local luxury spa, and proceeded to sample the menu of treatments. *"You'll learn to enjoy it. A few days for yourself here and there is a good trade-off for letting him drag you around the world for the rest of time."*

He found it even less amusing now. A few hours could be two or ten at a necromancer's pace.

A little moan escaped her. When he peered into her eyes, it was clear Raymond's magic kept her alive but did nothing to dull the pain.

"You were right," he said, hoping to distract her. "I misjudged. Raymond, the territory. I was arrogant and made assumptions I should not have. I only saw you. And I wanted..."

"To rub in how good a deal you have with Azrael."

You to be safe. Aloud, he muttered, "I *am* good with negotiations."

She snorted. "You accepted Raymond's oath, no questions asked."

"I knew what I was getting into when Azrael sent me." He bit his tongue on the rest. *I knew I would walk through hell with you the moment you told me to mind my business in the hall.*

Her eyes found his in the dark. "Why are you doing this?"

Because waking up in a world without you, you and your terrible food and your inability to plan and your wonder—at whales and trees and people who love you—is no longer an option. The words stuck in his throat. "It seemed to irritate Raymond."

"I don't think anyone's yelled at him like that in a few hundred years." Amusement quaked in her voice. "I was pretty sure he was going to end you."

After a moment he laughed too. It felt good, this aching deep in his chest. "So was I."

"Death comes to us all at some time or another," she said. "You owe me nothing."

I owe you everything.

On the night he'd taken his vow, when the words had been exchanged but the gift not yet given, he'd stopped Azrael. "*One more thing. I want—I need to keep this.*"

His hand settled over the scar on his chest. Curiosity quirked Azrael's lips in an amused smile. They'd been in close enough quarters that Gregor had seen Azrael's scars a time or two. He wondered that the necromancer who could have made himself unblemished had kept them and knew they must convey some meaning.

"*A memento?*"

Gregor did not answer.

Azrael's eyes darkened, but he nodded. After the exchange, Gregor drew the sword for the first time. When Gregor regained consciousness, the necromancer's power racing through his body, he studied himself in the warped mirror. Subtle changes marked his physique—increased strength, the sloughing of damage from sun and wind, the disappearance of signs of age. The scar remained, unchanged. A reminder of what a foolish master emotion is.

In the car he touched his chest where the uneven jagged line ran, surprised to find the well of memories clambering to the surface. He'd spent hundreds of years building a barrier so they could not remind him of what it was to be human: to hope, to fear, to love. He'd thought himself better without them. Cold calculation, willing to make sacrifices.

"*The only things worth fighting for are the things you believe in. The things you love,*" Lark had chided him. He'd buried that truth away with the rest of the memories.

This was what Azrael had seen when he'd chosen Isela. What she'd embraced when she knit herself to the necromancer. Fighting together made them stronger; fighting for one another made it matter. There was no serving one without the other.

Ana had given this truth back to him. Truths hurt. Maybe a story was good for relieving that pain too.

Gregor cleared his throat. "How about a story?"

Ana's smile filled him with relief. "Going to tell me about your not-a-demon?"

"We have some time to kill."

She grunted, and her gaze skated over the dashboard screen before her eyes closed. The memories crowded his chest and his throat until if he inhaled deep enough, he could smell the pine and bayberry.

"My commanding officer sent me on a reconnaissance mission with two in my unit who had no love for me. I was not supposed to return. I managed to get the best of them, but not before one left me bleeding out from this." He touched the line on his chest. "I should have died."

He spoke of Haven, and Heinrich and Iain and Talking House. And Lark, putting him back together with herbs and her voice. Of the years he'd become something more than a foolish, brokenhearted boy to earn the heart of a woman who shouldered the burdens of the world.

"Lark would do anything to protect her folk. And they followed her without question. She also could outshoot me with my own rifle. I was determined to be worthy of her. I failed, often and spectacularly for years before I figured out how. Still, she chose me anyway." He paused with wonder in that. Her patience. Her forgiveness. Her strength. "We were married by an old Quaker. A common law marriage. For outlaws. Still, I used to dream of a gravestone in my family's crypt with her name on it beside mine. Ridiculous, no? To have been willing to give up all this for love?"

Ana's eyes stayed on him. "Not at all."

After the war, as colonies became states and new laws were

drafted, they fought attempts to overrun the settlement by militia and scavengers alike. He grew weary of fighting as Lark grew more patriotic, more determined to carve a life out of the land of her birth.

It was one of many little ways they began to fracture. Moments of silence between them became vast crevices.

Gregor broached the subject on the next hunting trip with Titus. The former slave served in the Continental Army during the war, where his ability to read and write and knowledge of military strategy gleaned from listening in on conversations had made him a favorite of his commanding officer. When the war ended, his owner reneged on the agreement to free him, so Titus ran. Lark's brother had helped to hide him until they could bring him to the relative safety of Haven.

"*Should go before we can't.*" Titus stared into the fire. "*Declaration of Independence wasn't for us. They say that new gin will increase production of cotton and the need for bodies to grow and harvest it. If that time comes, papers won't matter when they come with the chains.*"

Gregor wrote his father, and on the next supply run received a letter welcoming him back with open arms. His commander had entered him as missing and presumed dead in official documents. Apparently reporting desertions was bad for the man's own record. After years of mourning him, his family was ecstatic.

"*There's a ship leaving, from Philadelphia,*" Gregor told Lark over dinner. "*Perhaps it's time we took a honeymoon.*"

She saw right through him. As always. "*You mean not to come back.*"

He showed her the letters, waiting impatiently as she read each word. When she finally looked up again, he was on his feet, pacing the cabin. "*They've settled a sum on us. A belated wedding present.*"

"*A sum.*" She echoed the words.

He tried to lighten the moment with humor. "*Princeling, remember.*"

Silence greeted him.

"*Little bird. Say something.*"

"*Your little adventure in the wilderness is done. Time to run home. Did you enjoy playing frontier man?*"

"*I've never—*"

"*How can you think of leaving now? These people need us.*" Haven didn't need Lark anymore. But he did. Now he just had to make her see it.

"*Look around, Lark. Haven is finished. Most of the cabins are empty. Talking House says they will join up with the Catawba or Cherokee. Titus is taking a group up to Ohio when the weather turns. I spoke with your brother—he won't feel safe until they make Toronto. We need to go.*" Titus's words haunted him. "*Now, before we can't.*"

"*We,*" she echoed.

The calm steadiness in her voice confused him. Where was his fiery wife, the one who shouted down men who towered over her, including him? "*You are my wife.*"

"*Your property? You decide to turn tail and run, and I am just baggage to be loaded on your wagon.*"

"*You're being absurd.*"

"*Am I?*" She rocked back in her chair, contemplating him.

"*I vowed to protect you—and I am afraid I won't be able to do that here.*" He took a deep breath to steady himself. "*And there is so much more out there to see Lark, so much more than just—*"

"*This backwater?*" Her voice lowered, the silky purr lulling him into thinking she was beginning to come around. "*This falling-down cabin in a gully so high in the mountains even the bears won't come here?*"

He nodded.

"*More than this rabble of runaway slaves and Indians without a place to go? A castle to escape to?*"

He froze. She'd trapped him again, led him into a briar of words in which every turn cut like thorns. She rose from their dinner table, collected the plates and slapped them into the slop bucket.

"*Someone has to fight for the future of this country and all the people in it."* She refused to look at him. *"There's talk of a route to get slaves to freedom. I want to help."*

"You'll get yourself killed. Or worse."

Lark's eyes fixed on him, solemn and unflinching. *"The only things worth fighting for are the things you believe in. The things you love."*

They argued bitterly. He booked them passage on a ship bound for the continent. She refused to discuss the trip. The last morning in the mountains she rose early, her belongings packed by the time he woke. He pressed the jäger rifle into her grip. She kissed him goodbye. *"Go home, soldier."*

She joined Iain and Talking House outside, hunting packs loaded and a single mule. Gregor watched, mute with anger. He wanted to turn away first. At the tree line, Lark waved the others on and the forest swallowed the two men and the mule. She cast a single glance over her shoulder, full of acceptance. Then she too, vanished.

He needed one last glimpse of dark braids, riotous curls at her temples springing free.

Still he remained. Dawn came through the turning branches.

"Soldier." Lark's voice rang through the trees. *"Husband."*

He squinted at the sight of her on the ridge, the jäger strapped to her back. It comforted him, knowing she would carry some part of him with her even as she left him behind.

"I will love you every day of my life." Her voice broke. Something in her was dying, same as him.

He did smile then, though it cracked his resolve. *"We're outlaws. Don't you know better than to go whooping and hollering?"*

She laughed, the whiskey-rasp sound echoing.

"I love you," he managed before his throat closed.

He stayed at the cabin. She was being stubborn. She would change her mind. A week passed. Two. He walked out of the wilderness alone. Days later in a hotel room in Charleston preparing to scrub off years of mountain living and return to civilization he'd once abhorred, he discovered the last bar of her soap in his bag and wept over the scent of her—pine and bayberry.

In modern days, couples used the term "breaking up" for the dissolution of a relationship. Like a ship crashing on rocks, its many pieces once operating in concert now cast into an immovable, unfeeling obstacle and dashed to bits. Occasionally a salvager could come up with some useful piece, but the whole was never the same again.

By the time he finally returned home, he'd served Azrael for twenty years. Tucked into the pages of his father's old journals, letters in a familiar scrawling script caught his eye. The first had been addressed to him.

Lark read enough to manage wanted posters and news dispatches, and wrote infrequent, often illegible notes scratched out on scraps of paper to her brother with shipments of pelts. He saw the labor she had put into this letter. Each word carefully formed, each sentence full of emotion. Her joy, her fear, her worry, her hope. She wished only for a chance to share this news with him, with no expectation. The letter was kept with the one Gregor had written a year before, announcing their intention to return before his ship was lost to pirates and he was counted dead again. His father recorded his reply in his journal—news of Gregor's death and her lack of claim to the title or privileges. But her letter must have moved him, because there was also a sum recorded.

Gregor sighed and pushed the car out of a curve, gaining speed. "I was always close to my father, and he was generous with his grandchildren."

"Your child," Ana breathed.

"They corresponded for years," he said. "He liked her candor, as I knew he would. Lark's brother convinced her to settle in Toronto, and Rose—our daughter—was raised among her cousins. My father became a silent benefactor of sorts. Rose was educated in the best schools, had a family of her own. Lark married again, and well. They had no other children.

"I was bound to Azrael by then, and perhaps he would have released me, but I told myself I didn't want to upset the peace they'd found by showing up like an old ghost." His voice strained under the weight of the truth. "I was a coward for leaving her to fight alone, and I was afraid. I couldn't see how she would ever forgive me for not moving heaven and earth to get back to them.

He reached up at the sight of wetness at the corners of Ana's lashes, thumbed away a tear. "It's been centuries since I boarded that ship, and every step since then has brought me to you. I walked away once. I won't do it again. So that is the tragic story of Gregor Alexander Leopold Von Schwarzberg."

He'd done away with much of it over time. He liked the way Gregor Schwarz sounded. Like the honed edge of the blade he had become. He didn't judge Ana for giving herself the name that fit best. Hadn't they all remade themselves with the help of necromancers?

Ana closed her eyes. Panic gripped him. She'd seemed alert while he spoke. In the silence her breath seemed more labored. He checked her pulse.

"I'm not finished," he said, loud enough to startle her eyes open. "This is the most important part of the story. The part... the part that you need to know."

Her eyes widened. "There's more?"

"Well, there were no threats of seppuku," he drawled.

Ana coughed, the ghost of a laugh, and the dullness in her eyes frightened him.

Gregor had spent days in the dusty reading chair in his father's long-closed-up study, amidst the stack of letters as he'd tried to figure out the best course. Even new to serving a necromancer he had seen how dangerous his connection to Azrael could endanger Lark and Rose. But he couldn't abandon them to time, either. At last, he had swept it all into the fireplace—journals and letters— and struck a match. No one must know. It was the only way to keep them safe. But...

He cleared his throat. "I've kept watch on Lark's line ever since. Protected them, when I could. There has always been a daughter who manifested signs of the blood. A few generations passed uneventfully. The godswar broke out, and I lost them in the chaos. That was the most difficult time. Not knowing. And maybe relief, that it was finally over. When I found them again, the witch had met and married a man with a recessive wolf gene. I orchestrated a way for the family to immigrate to Prague so I could continue to watch over them. They had three boys who can change shape at will and a daughter who became a dancer. It wasn't the witch's power that activated the wolf gene in her sons but her own blood. The Schwarzbergs and the Vogels had a family line in common in the old days."

"Vogel," Ana breathed. "Isela is your great-great…"

"One more 'great,' I think."

"Does she know?"

"They were never to know. I expected the line would die out. I hadn't counted on the fecundity of witches and wolves."

"Does Azrael know?"

"I told him I owed their family a great debt, from the war. He didn't ask for specifics and I didn't offer. But it appears—because of what she has become—I may never be free of my vow to keep Lark's daughters safe."

"Good," she whispered, fierce.

Surprise wrinkled his brow.

"I'd hate to think of a world like this without you in it."

His nostrils flared as the words broke the ache in his chest open wide. When he finally got control, she'd turned her gaze to the distant dawn creeping outside the window.

He touched her hair. "I cannot ask of you what I cannot offer myself. Trouble comes to Azrael's door, and I am more than just honor bound to him. He is my friend, and where he commands, I go willingly. His consort is my blood, and I must protect her in this world as best I can. But if you would have it, all of me that is not theirs would belong to you. For whatever it's worth, that includes my heart."

Her voice shook. "I'm afraid. I don't want to die."

"You're not going to."

"Because you forbid it?"

"Exactly."

"Gregor Schwarz, has anyone ever told you how stubborn you can be?"

"Lately?"

The gate at the top of the horseshoe drive opened as he approached. He slid to a stop in front of the palatial compound.

Ana stopped breathing.

CHAPTER THIRTY-ONE

When Raymond approached, the chair Gregor had commandeered outside Ana's quarters stood empty. A closed book beside a cooling cup of coffee indicated a recent occupation. Raymond nudged the book with one finger to view the title. *The Necromancer, or a Tale of the Black Forest.* He'd managed to find a copy in the original German.

Gregor's value had been proven the night of the challenge, as had his innate ability to be an irritating son of a bitch. He didn't know when to be afraid, to back down. Or when to quit, even against impossible odds. He had no respect for power. Maybe there was truth to the Black Blade of Azrael being a little mad. And if not for him, Raymond might have lost two of his Aegis that night. Raymond found it difficult to dislike this enforcer of Azrael's.

The sound of Ana laughing made it a little easier. Had Ana ever laughed like that in the years they'd walked together? Strange, longing for something he hadn't known possible before this moment.

"I may have broken every bone in my body," she said, gasping for breath. "But I do not have a cold."

"Mein Gott, frau." The responding snarl brought the hair up on the back of Raymond's neck. *"Isst die suppe."*

Raymond turned off her awareness of him so he could observe in peace and entered silently. The bonesetter's progress reports indicated the ambrosia successfully anchored her long enough for her gift to mend her body. Over the weeks, he'd registered her pain through their connection. Perhaps he might have sped up the healing, but years of conserving, measuring his power for the tasks at hand made him cautious about expending any of it. She would either emerge stronger or not at all.

Now the worst was done, and he wanted to see what was left of her. He needed the old Ana back. His talons. For the past 120 years he'd relied on her, more than he should have perhaps, but she had never flinched or failed him.

She had never laughed like this.

Raymond gathered the shadows in the doorway, creating a visual redirect that kept him from sight. Ana might have seen him if she focused, but with the bed angled toward the window, her gaze was directed away from the door. Gregor perched on the edge of the bed, the trolley containing lunch within easy reach.

"Bitte. Isst die suppe. Jezt."

"Since you asked nicely."

Silence, punctuated by soft slurping.

"Was that so hard?" Gregor muttered with a little sigh.

"I hate soup."

Gregor returned the empty spoon to the bowl, and they both looked out for a moment. At the center of her garden, the still darkness of the pond reflected the little bridge, forming an unbroken oval. A frown creased his mouth. Her fingertips settled on his thigh.

Gregor returned his attention to the soup, swallowed a spoonful, and shrugged. "Chicken soup. It's good for the constitution."

"Butternut, potato leek, roasted red pepper, curry lentil, now chicken." Ana grumbled. "If it's to be a liquid diet, I'd rather have a beer."

Gregor's mouth quirked. "Ordinarily I would approve," he

said, cradling his hand below the soup spoon on its path from bowl to patient. "But until you can manage solids, the soup, yes?"

Slurping. "The kitchen has been on the same boring-ass menu since we moved in. Did you just march in and demand chicken soup?"

A telling silence followed as he contemplated the bowl in his hands. "I said please."

More of her churlish wheeze followed by slurping.

If Raymond stepped into the room now, it would destroy this little tableau. It would serve them both right. Remind them who she belonged to and what Gregor's place in this house was. And this laughing, teasing Ana would vanish. He remained in the shadows.

Ana coughed around a mouthful of soup. "Sure you're not trying to drown me?"

"I am not a nursemaid." Gregor muttered something uncharitable.

Ana's hand reached up from his leg. Scabbed-over knuckles and bruised fingers settled on the hand holding the spoon. Her fingers couldn't close, twitched with the effort. Gregor set down the bowl and placed his free hand over Ana's broken one. Turning put him in profile, revealing new lines bracketing his mouth and threads of silver racing through the dark hair. He had given up something of himself that night to keep her alive.

"You're doing a damn fine job." Ana's voice, trembling with unspoken feeling, froze Raymond's feet in place. "If my face wasn't broken in a thousand pieces, I'd kiss you."

This time Gregor did smile. The light and the relief made his face unrecognizable. "If you would permit me?"

As he leaned over the bed, Raymond left without a sound. He turned his connection to Ana back on in time to feel the burst of emotion. Joy. It exploded behind his eyes and he stopped, bracing a hand against the wall until his vision returned. He shut it off again, breathing hard. Power surged in him, restless with his own unease. He retreated to his office and the balcony overlooking the distant ocean.

Barnabas had been more powerful than Raymond expected, and it had almost cost him the challenge. But Barnabas collected people, not power. He wanted to control Raymond as he had the beast and Laughing Girl. He'd pulled back at the last, hoping he'd weakened Raymond enough to force his submission. Raymond had lived too long, survived too much to submit. He held no fear of death. In the end, Barnabas begged for his life, promised his service and his debt with the kind of terror reserved for mortals. Afraid to let go. Raymond hadn't hesitated to end him. And he had no regrets.

Save one. Laughing Girl. Didn't matter that love created her. He'd made something monstrous out of love. Out of being afraid to let go.

Mastering this new power would take time and effort. He had to do something with what built in him, give it some avenue. Let go.

He wanted to feel the ocean, taste the salt in the breeze. A flick of the wrist swept the air around him into a whirlwind, spreading his fingers widened it, drawing other funnels and sending currents dancing. The air pressure changed as the storm built, moisture beaded on his skin, clouds traveling fast over the water and headed inland. He turned his face to the sky and breathed the first drops of rain. Letting go.

CHAPTER THIRTY-TWO

Gregor's lips settled over hers. Warm, dry. Chaste. The kind of kiss exchanged at the close of dime novels when all ended well. The exquisite pressure brought sensation singing to her body that for the first time in weeks was not pain. Salt stung her eyes on the heels of a bursting warmth in her chest like a summer day on the beach. This was what it was to be alive, and this was why it was worth it.

He settled back in his chair and the smile softened, the lines on his face easing, the blue of his eyes brighter than before.

"Is Raymond gone?"

His brows dipped. "How did you know?"

"He relies so much on our bond; he forgets everything else." She sighed. "I know his footsteps, saw his reflection in the window before he hid himself."

Raymond's face, without the usual studied blankness or watchful guardedness, had startled her. Raw and vulnerable, full of a pain that had nothing to do with broken bones. She wasn't surprised when the wind picked up and rain began. It stirred the turning leaves on the trees, darkening the ground in patches and then collecting in puddles.

Gregor frowned as raindrops streaked over the window and

the daylight dimmed under clouds. The sky had been clear for days. "Is this normal for this time of year?"

"No."

Once, she would have gone to Raymond when he called a storm like this. She'd find some excuse—a report to make, an update to give—just to be there in his presence in case that would be the day he opened up to let her see more of him than the controlled exterior. He'd never acknowledged her presence in those instances, not once.

She found glacier-blue eyes waiting for her.

They'd been the first thing she was aware of when she woke up in Raymond's aedis after a vanishingly sweet, sticky taste on her lips and power surging through her, lighting up the deadened connections in her body. Her bleary eyes marked the unkempt black hair, the hollows worry carved in his features. The hand cradled her cheek, warm and rough. Calling her name. Calling her back.

Each time she woke, he came. Consciousness immersed her in a symphony of pain, each tone ringing against another in miserable chorus. Pain did funny things to her brain. An animal noise of anguish reached her at a distance. She struggled to recognize the voice. Her own voice.

She lost track of time as pain stretched hours into days. Then her body crested a wave. Committed to living, it knit itself through fevers and held off infection until she woke clear and calm in the middle of the night. She yawned so hard her jaw popped.

Footsteps from the other room signaled his return.

Welcome back. The soft glow from the nightstand lamp pooled his face. He settled into the chair beside the bed. Exhaustion drew his features gaunt, cheeks hollow, and smudged darkness beneath his eyes. He looked older, or was it just the light falling irregularly on him?

A week later she knew it hadn't been her imagination. The sight of crow's feet and the lines around his mouth deepening startled her as much as the easy smile.

"Can you open the window?" she said, taking in the changes in his face. "I just want to smell the rain."

He stood for a long moment at the window, his back to her as he watched the leaves darken with rain. His shoulders rose and fell. Her hand slid over the blankets beside her. "Get up here."

There had been moments in the worst of the darkness when any touch had been too much to bear. The Aegis metabolized human painkillers too fast for them to be of use for long. When she screamed and begged for release, he brought water and cool cloths. When she cursed him for his helplessness, for refusing to end her suffering, he sat in silence. She'd been awful, said unforgivable things. He'd remained. *I'm afraid there's nothing to do but endure. You won't do it alone. I promise you that.*

He hesitated, and a shadow of doubt crossed his face. "Are you sure?"

The worst had passed, leaving her mind clearer than it had been in days. "I want more of those kisses. And I don't want you to get a crick in your neck giving them to me."

The bed was too small for two, but they made the best of it. It took a bit of wriggling and a few spikes of discomfort to get settled side by side amid sheets and blankets. Unable to resist, she brought her fingertips to the black sweater he wore over a T-shirt and jogging pants. The sweater was even softer than it looked.

"I can't believe you went shopping without me."

"I ran out of suits." His laugh warmed her mouth. "It was a torment for all involved."

She'd never understood kissing. The wetness and the closeness made her anxious. The pressure and invasion of tongue and teeth set her on edge. But when his mouth brushed hers in slow, closed sweeps, she thought she might be on her way to figuring out the appeal. He rolled onto his back, making space for her beneath his arm.

"Are you going to tell me why it took so long," he asked as she settled her head below his collarbones and closed her eyes, savoring.

"Does it matter?"

He exhaled. Fingertips traced her hairline, sliding through the strands. "No."

"Then no."

She heard the smile in his voice. "Will you tell me if you're ever ready for more?"

"I will."

"Good." He stretched his free arm over his head and extended his legs before him with a yawn. His bare feet, long and pale as the rest of him, dangled over the edge of the bed, crossed at the ankles. "Should I read?"

She remembered his voice, an anchor in the tormented sea of healing. His chest shifted beneath her cheek as he searched the nightstand for a book.

She shook her head. "Let's just watch the rain for a while."

Outside, daylight dimmed to a steady gray as the storm intensified. Distant thunder echoed through the hills, and she counted the long seconds until the crackling flash of lightning. The wind whipped the first of the changing leaves loose from the branches and sent them dancing. They skittered on the surface of the water, sending ripples that collided with drops of rain. The scent of fresh rain on dry soil and the tang of ozone blended with the woodsy suggestion of his aftershave.

She missed the sound of his voice but accepted it as fair trade for his heartbeat and the rise and fall of breath so close she could touch them. And she did, ignoring the discomfort in her trembling hands to splay her palm over the center of his chest. His hand slid over hers, stilling the trembling.

She breathed him in, wanting this moment locked in her memory in all its dimensions for the entirety of her long-lived life. It would have to be enough. After a while, she slept.

* * *

"A REAL SHOWER." Ana sighed, leaning back into the towel Gregor wrapped around her chest and tucked under her arms.

Even with the ambrosia, standing took a week, and another before she could walk on her own into the shower.

"It is the simple things that make life a pleasure."

Like a glimpse in the mirror at the naked man behind her, skin beaded in water and hair slicked back on his head. Now *that* was a sight worth living for.

She watched his back in the mirror as he retrieved his own towel. When she wobbled, he handed her a cane and went to the sink.

Without much conversation, his belongings had appeared in her suite. She'd lived alone for a hundred years, and as roommates went, he was fastidious. She liked how his small toiletry kit looked beside her sink, implements laid out on the hand towel. She liked his insistence on remaining clean-shaven. As much as she liked that he'd let his hair get a little longer in the past few weeks, it confirmed the presence of new silver streaks at his temples and through the dark length. The sight of him shaving and grooming in her bathroom was becoming familiar. Welcome even.

In defeating Barnabas, Raymond solidified his hold on North America. Her duties had been assigned to Auger. The packs were being hunted from Alaska to Seattle. She would be amazed if a single wolf survived on the North American continent by the time Raymond finished. Raymond's preference for vengeance ran deep as well as wide. But she thought of Fred, and the Vogels, and an aching despair filled her. She hoped he was safe. This was the world she'd chosen.

Gregor belonged elsewhere. Watching over his descendants, wolf and witch, protecting his master. His friend.

Yet he stayed.

For her. His words in the car came back to her from memory. *If you would have it, all of me that is not theirs would belong to you.*

And what would that look like, with them oceans apart? This was dangerous. She could not afford this—attachment dividing her attention, splitting her focus. She had made a vow and owed her life to it. That duty had sustained her for centuries when she would have chosen surrender to the blade.

And yet.

"I will dress now," he said, standing before her and smelling of shaving cream and soap. "You will…"

Two perfect creases on either side of the base of his abdomen and the long line of downy soft hair south of his navel disappeared into the crisp white towel wrapped around his hips. She was starting to feel better. She wanted to taste him.

She gripped the cane with one hand to keep her fingers from trembling. "I'll be out in a minute."

His mouth formed a grim line. "If you need me?"

"My windpipe is healed," she said wryly. "I'll shout."

He did not laugh. "If you crack your head open on the floor—"

"O ye of little faith," she said, crossing the bathroom to the counter in careful steps. "Better go sharpen your sword while you're at it. I'll be back in the sparring room in no time."

The ache in her hips had dulled under hot water, but now it crawled back up her spine to her shoulder blades. Soon her head would hurt enough to force her to draw the curtains and lie down. But she refused to allow herself to surrender to it. To give up one moment of standing like this, with him.

She wanted to retreat under the scrutiny of his gaze. He saw her, clearer than anyone had since she was mortal. Still he nodded, accepting her effort, and showed his teeth again. "That's the advantage of soul steel: it never dulls. But it is missing its sheath."

The man could light a fire with those ice-blue eyes.

When the door closed behind him, she sank into a seat on the bench meant for storing towels. She pinched her mouth shut to avoid gasping and pressed the heels of her hands into her eye sockets and tried to pretend the tears were only from the pain.

CHAPTER THIRTY-THREE

In the dark, Gregor navigated the suite by memory. He'd been gone most of the day. It had taken all his willpower to leave her alone. But after three weeks she hardly needed the cane, and she could use it as a bokken when needed. In a few days, she would no longer need that. Her blades lay on the kitchen table on their cushion of silk, the whetting stone close by. She was preparing herself.

As he knew he should be.

Instead, he slipped into the bathroom and closed the door before turning on the light, then shucking off sweat pants and the soaked T-shirt. She'd had a shower before bed; he could smell the lilac-and-honey scent of her shampoo, and the tiles were damp with her presence. He stepped under the hot water, feeling hours of sweat shed from his skin.

Delaying his departure to help Raymond maintain stability during the cleanup had been reason enough for Azrael. And Gregor *had* taken on security detail and enforcement work until Ana's recovery was certain. But Ana had already begun to take briefings from her staff. He would be redundant, and necromancers never tolerated those not avowed to them in their service for long. Taking Raymond's vow again was out of the question.

Gregor gave Ana his heart, in no uncertain terms, but with so many conditions, he didn't fault her lack of reply. He wanted to say *Come with me. Stay by my side and we'll carve a space for us in all this madness, or at least if we fall we'll be together.*

But no matter what he felt for her, she chose to serve Raymond. The necromancer had saved her life, given her purpose. Gregor envied her conviction, her loyalty, even as he must leave her behind. And one day, whether a year from now or five hundred, she would be cast as a die by her master, and she would fall. The ache in his chest made breathing difficult when he focused on it for too long.

He pounded his chest with one fist, distracting himself with the physical pain of a rib splitting under the force. He bowed his head and willed himself back to the cold calculation that had guided him for so long. Like an old suit, it no longer fit. His heart strained for the freedom it had discovered. There was so much more to living now. He found himself ravening for it all.

She stirred when he slid in beside her, molding herself to him. Her toes tickled his shins. "You smell like lilacs."

"I've run out of shampoo," he said. "Rest now."

She squirmed. "I've had nothing but rest for weeks. I'm going to go insane if you tell me to rest one more time."

Unable to resist, he grinned in the darkness. "You should—"

Her hand slapped over his mouth. The contact was electric. He parted his lips, tasting the skin before his teeth closed on the fleshy pad of her palm. The shiver running through her brought her skin into more intimate contact with him. His body responded, as it always did, but he released her hand and stroked the back of one shoulder blade with his fingertips.

For three weeks she had allowed him to deny her advances. This time she turned to him, forcing him onto his back. When her thigh slid over his hips, wet heat against him, he bit his mouth and groaned.

He gripped her hips in restraint.

She pressed her lips over his. "Stop blocking me, Sticks, or I swear to the gods I will brain you with my cane."

* * *

Despite threats of violence, they joined in incremental slowness.

He was right. She was probably not ready for this. But now that they'd embarked, he refused to rush and she refused to turn back. She let herself go in his hands. The long sweep of pleasure and release robbed her of everything but breath for a few moments of eternity.

Sated, she rested her head on his chest, listening to the racing thump of his heart. She smiled, enjoying her effect on him. He settled her against him, soothing the skin along her spine with his fingertips.

His voice drifted in the darkness, so quiet she went still in an effort to hear him better. "I will come for you, Ana. Whenever you need me. No matter what it means to Raymond or Azrael. I swear it."

It took me too long to understand the mistake I'd made, trying to force her to leave her home.

Ana's breath stopped, trapped in her throat. She propped herself up on one elbow. In the darkness she saw him in a way she thought no one had in a long time. The long, stern lines of his refined face and eyes the color of a battlefield sky. Swirling curls of emerald over the glowing light of his soul.

A soul bound to a necromancer in service didn't leave the body. Rather, the power of the necromancer they'd chosen encircled them, like an ethereal armor. Through the sparkling emerald, his life force shone through, as wild and bright and fierce as the eyes that did not look away from her face, even in the darkness.

Cradled in his gaze, she felt parts of her long dormant stirring. Fetters she'd believed tied fast shook off their knots and unfurled hope like a vast sail.

The fingers of her free hand slid into the wild black and silver of his hair, and she lowered her lips to his. For all the heat between them, the kiss was a tender benediction. When the soft searing pull of his mouth released, she spoke into the darkness between them, her hand settling over the beat of his heart. "I see you, Gregor Schwarz."

"I trust that you do," he said, "Ana Gozen."

He kissed her again, a longer, lingering, more thorough exploration of what moved between them. When her breath left her in a soft sigh, he pulled her head back to his chest.

"You know, in the old days, before politics and alliances," she murmured, "when a man and a woman took to bed, after three nights they were considered married."

His laugh sent tremors through his rib cage below her ear.

"I'm not sure the first time counts."

"Technically," she asked, earning another laugh. "And I'm not sure how to account for the time we lost in Seattle."

His arms tightened around her, sending waves of delicious pressure from skin to skin. "By my count, this is night three."

Against expectation, when she closed her eyes, she slept.

CHAPTER THIRTY-FOUR

My name is Ana Gozen, and that is no longer the lie. It
never had been.

Ana's cane tapped out a rhythm on the polished
floors. It should have been comforting, regular as a metronome.
But the closer she got to Raymond, the more it reminded her of
the countdown on a bomb.

Emotion battered her like surf on a rocky shore, leaving her
belly a churning mass of foam-capped confusion. She could no
more slow the hammering of her heart than speed her healing.

When Gregor had asked, on rising, what her day held, she had
been proud of the ease in the way the words left her throat.

"Catching up on reports." She'd leaned into the curve of his
palm on her cheek. "Physical therapy. A nap. You?"

"Raymond asked me to look in on a group of moirai in the
fashion district," he said. "He'd like to relocate them if possible.
Too many humans who buy from them have been dying."

Her brows rose. A simple cleanup job, something hardly
worthy of the attention of a hunter like Gregor. But it would keep
him busy most of the day. Which gave her the time she needed.

She waited until the guardhouse confirmed the Audi had left

the compound before making a call to Raymond. "I need to see you."

His answer had been immediate. "I'm available for you anytime, Ana. You know that."

For a moment she wondered at the outcome of this meeting. Perhaps she should have waited for Gregor. But this was between her and Raymond. At least this way Gregor would never know she'd tried. He wouldn't ask her to come with him and she wouldn't offer to leave. He wouldn't risk himself in a battle he didn't know she'd lost.

"Please have a seat," Raymond said as the doors closed behind them with the same tug of his power that had opened them.

"I'll stand," she said but rested her cane on a chair before his desk and set her fingers on the chairback.

Raymond nodded, leaning on the edge of his desk. Five feet divided them, but it felt like an ocean.

He had never been the most powerful of the Allegiance, and he had fought his way to ascendance with as much cunning as claw. He held his hand close and moved when he bore the least possible risk. Only those driven foolish with pride would begrudge a scavenger. Apex predators went extinct all the time. Scavengers survived. They had that in common at least.

As a child, the way had been impressed on her as a path to a life beyond what birth would have allowed—into the life of a warrior whose greatest gift was the death he could give to his master. In the most ancient times, a samurai earned rank and title through proving themselves. In a child's mind, she'd equated that as blind obedience. Loyalty first and always. Order. Duty. Respect.

But beneath the code and the duty lay an instinct to survive. It had always been in her; it was what her teacher had seen long ago when she'd taken Ana under her tutelage. She learned and conditioned her body and mind to the path before her.

Let them underestimate you. It will be their last mistake.

Standing before Raymond now, knowledge knit together in her bones and her fear fell away. To follow the way was to understand the only thing under her control was effort, to give up concern for outcome. It was not the same as being willing to surrender her life to another's whim.

The lie she had mistaken for her identity fell away. She wanted to live. Not just survive. And if she could not do that, then she would not do either. Whether he accepted or denied her request, she would never belong to him again.

Raymond watched her, his inscrutable obsidian eyes on her with all the focus of a raven examining a puzzle it hadn't yet solved.

"You came to see me," she said, watching the flash of surprise disappear under his mask of implacable calm. "Why didn't you stay?"

"I had no reason to," he said, angling his body away from her to look out the window. "Your progress exceeded the healer's expectations. I confirmed it. That seemed enough."

A part of her that sometimes believed Raymond cared about her well-being or her happiness drew up at the confirmation otherwise. She remembered laughing around campfires at getting the upper hand on a group of arrogant outlaws who assumed an old man and a girl would be easy pickings. Later, standing at his back as he assumed his place in the Allegiance and took over his section of the world, she had felt a measure of pride and accomplishment.

She had seen him take and discard more lovers than she could count. She'd vowed she would never be among them. But they might have been friends, comrades, if only... She folded her hands on the back of her chair and met his gaze.

"I have served you for one hundred and twenty years," she began without tremor or rancor. "I am grateful for the gifts you have given. But now I must request release. My contract—"

"Your contract has been fulfilled a dozen times." Raymond turned his back to her. "You were indispensable on the island. But I am strong enough to withstand challengers now. You are free to go."

A wave of anger crested over all the other emotion unleashed in the past weeks. She took a breath, then another. She had gotten what she wanted. The prudent thing to do would be to go. But the part of her content with survival had vanished. The warrior in her spoke instead.

"I'll have your vow that Gregor and I will be free to leave without molestation from your house," she said. "Magical or otherwise."

Raymond half turned, revealing a three-quarters profile of his face. He smiled in the knife-edge sort of way that presaged danger for anyone on the receiving end. "So you have chosen Mr. Schwarz."

"If that's what you think this is about, you don't understand me at all." Ana shook her head with a little huff. "I will have your word that Amelia and the Kwih-dich-chuh-ahtx will bear no retribution for their part in this."

His brows rose. "I always suspected Amelia Gray would not be so biddable. She grew up in your shadow."

She almost smiled. "You should see them more. They miss you."

His face shuttered.

"In exchange," Raymond began.

Her heart stuttered. Would he remove her gift now, leave her in this half-healed state, or mortal? She hadn't considered what he would take in exchange.

"Your gifts, such as they have been given, are yours to keep. Death has forgotten your name, but be careful, you will no longer draw from me for healing. And you will keep the secrets of my past. As long as you live."

"Agreed," Ana said, proud that her voice did not shake.

Raymond nodded, looking back over his ocean.

"Your vow, Lord Nightfeather."

"You have it," he said after a moment, sealing the split between them once and for all.

The connection loosened in her chest, sliding away. She hadn't realized how heavy his constant contact had been. Freed, she turned away, gathered her cane, and prepared to leave.

His words stopped her at the door. "I never imagined love would undo you, Ana."

"It hasn't," she replied. "It pieced me back together."

CHAPTER THIRTY-FIVE

"**A**re you sure you're ready for this?" Gregor said, circling her with his guard up.

She raised a brow. "Are you afraid of me, Sticks?"

Today she carried the naganata like an extension of her arm, the only concession to her still less than optimal strength and speed. He kept his distance from the wide sweep of the bladed staff. He slipped forward, light strikes before sliding back out again, unscathed. Barely.

Her brow slid higher. "Testing me?"

She struck and he moved sideways, losing a swatch of his shirt over his rib cage to the edge of her wicked blade.

"You were right," she said, and for a moment the distraction of her words stilled him.

He waited to see where she would take them.

"In the car," she elaborated. "About being blinded by duty."

She feinted, and he met the real blow that followed. This time she withdrew.

"Dual forces are always pulling on us," she said. "Order and chaos. Duty and desire."

His blood was up, his nostrils flaring and heart pounding with the promise of crossing blades with her. He enjoyed it marginally less than sharing her bed.

"*The way* makes much of duty. It gives a code of values: the debt of obligation one can never hope to repay. It is a way back to humanity for those of us who have had to step onto the path of war. The value of all over self."

Sweat beaded on her hairline and cheeks from exertion.

"But we also have desires that must be defended, protected, fought for, even when they conflict with duty. The right wrong."

He grunted, fending off a surprisingly strong attack.

She had him on the defense. "Do you still offer your heart?"

She must have read the answer in his face. Her eyes lit and a little smile softened the hard line of her mouth.

"My obligation to Raymond has been fulfilled," she said. "It's time I see to my own desire. My duty to self."

She disarmed him, pinning him to the floor with the blade against his throat. She withdrew, blade up.

"That's twice, you know," she said, scowling at him as she leaned on the staff, panting a little.

Gregor kicked the staff out from under her, sweeping the blade free as he rolled. He cradled her landing with his body, drawing her to the floor beneath him. He couldn't stop sweeping her face with his gaze, searching for confirmation.

"I spoke to Azrael," she said and returned his glare. "Don't look at me that way. You earned it for going to Raymond behind my back."

Gregor waited, hope beating its wings hard against his rib cage. "What did he say?"

"That Gregor's mate would always be welcome," she said and gave a little laugh. "He seemed to indicate there might be a role for me there."

Gregor rested his head against her collarbones. He suddenly understood the human urge to thank an unseen god for an uncounted-upon favor.

"I have a few things to see to here," she said, hesitating. "And a stop to make on the way, but I hoped…"

He could not speak. He knew he must, and soon, but for the moment his voice had abandoned him.

"Shirokane," she said. "You asked me... well, my family name was Shirokane, once."

He slid his fingertips along her jawline, and when his mouth met hers, he tried to pour all his relief into her. Her response was fierce and hot, her fingers knotting in his hair and driving him to a frenzy. They broke apart, laughing at the clash of lips. He tasted iron. Even love would be a battle between them. One he looked forward to winning and losing.

She dabbed at his split lip. "First blood."

CHAPTER THIRTY-SIX

Isela looked up from the witch's grimoire balanced on her knees at the scent of agar and toasted cinnamon. The distant squeak of the front door opening and the energetic ripple of the valet's mental greeting reached her. Elmo woofed at the foot of the bed, her plumed tail thumping the coverlet.

"You'd better be on the floor before he gets here," Isela told the dog.

Elmo whined a long yawn, then slunk off the bed, mincing her way to the palatial cushion near the hearth. She cast one long, pitiful glance back at Isela before circling and flopping into place.

"One of us has to follow the rules." Isela grinned.

He took his time coming to bed. She fidgeted, torn between demonstrating her dedication as a student by focused study on her book and letting her eagerness to see him show. The dog had no such conflicts. She rose again as his footsteps came down the hall, stretching her upper body long and low as she yawned a welcome. Before the door opened, she was dancing on her forepaws. Her great plumed tail swung back and forth.

He'd showered, which explained the delay and meant he'd been summoning. He knew she could smell the dead on him afterward, and this was his way of not bringing his work home.

She appreciated the gesture even if it gave away the scent he meant to remove.

"I spoke with Gregor." He greeted her with a brush of lips against her temple before bending to the dog. "He's coming home soon."

Isela's brows slid northward. "I thought they'd wrapped up that thing weeks ago. I wondered if he'd gone rogue."

"Miss him?" Azrael slipped into bed beside her. Damp skin, warmer to the touch than a mortal's, slid against hers. His teeth grazed at the skin of her neck.

Isela shivered and fixed him with a long look. "We need him here. The Allegiance—"

"The Allegiance will hold," Azrael said, careful to avoid the book in her lap even as he teased her earlobe with his lips. "He asked for a few more weeks. It seemed a small request for what I put him through."

Isela obeyed his unspoken request and closed the grimoire, sliding it onto her nightstand. At the coven's insistence, she'd begun studying witch spells as well as those of necromancers. She had a temple thumper of a headache. Fingers crossed her sister-in-law, the coven scholar, Bebe would be able to explain what she'd read. Every spell she'd tried to cast so far had been a miserable failure.

The book crackled with protest. Her mother warned her it hadn't been opened recently and might make a nuisance of itself. Unused grimoires tended to accumulate excess energy.

A low rumble from deep in Azrael's chest sent the hair on her arms and neck standing on end and heat pooling in her belly. She surrendered her mouth for his kiss.

"Shit," Isela said, remembering too late as she elbowed Azrael aside to lift the book again.

He leaned back, amused. "Another one?"

She slid the sleek black rectangle out from beneath the book. The screen stayed dark. "My phone. I forgot—"

"That's the fourth one in as many weeks," he said, plucking the dead thing from her hand.

"Can't you…" She waved her hand, biting the inside of her cheek to keep from smiling. "Do something."

"I am a necromancer, Isela."

"It's dead."

Azrael tried not to laugh. He lay back on his pillows and examined the useless bit of electronics before setting it on his side of the bed. "Tyler will bring you a new one in the morning."

Isela glared at him. "I can take care of my own—"

"Sending you inside a store full of these things with a grimoire in your purse is going to cost me a fortune."

"I don't carry a purse," she grumbled. "And it's my fortune. I'm not a kept woman, you know."

"You are witch blood and wolf hearted. It's not so much a matter of keeping you as enticing you to remain."

She laid a series of wet, noisy kisses down his bare chest to the blankets at his ribs. When she looked up, his eyes lit expectantly as if to say *go on*. She slid the blanket down, happy to oblige. His skin tasted fresh and damp. It took a moment before her exaggerated kisses turned into real, heated ones. By the time she reached the thin line of dark hair below his belly button, steam rose from his chest and his eyes hooded, smoldering. She sent her hand ahead of her, and his eyes closed.

Something niggled at her. "I don't question his needing time off."

"Are we still talking about Gregor?" Azrael slapped his hand over his eyes with a snarl.

Undaunted, Isela stacked her palms on the rigid plane of his belly and rested her chin. "He's earned it. I just wonder what's got his attention. Gregor doesn't seem like an LA kind of guy."

"I don't think it's the city that's holding him," Azrael growled.

"You think he and Ana worked it out?"

"He hasn't been run through, yet. I'd have felt it."

"Gods' tears," Isela muttered. "Thinking of the two of them together gives me nightmares."

Azrael lifted his hand, opening one eye to study her. "It's best you get used to waking up in a sweat then. I get the impression Gregor is not coming home alone."

Isela's smile faded.

Azrael laughed. "My consort, speechless?"

"He's bringing *her* here?"

Azrael's chin tilted, and his gaze fell heavy on her skin. "That bothers you?"

"Yes!" Isela yelped before she got ahold of herself. "No. I mean, no. Just, I thought she served Raymond."

"If she completed the terms of her service to Raymond or they came to an agreement by which he released her, then she is free to go as she is," Azrael said. "It happens rarely, but it's not unheard of. Ito—"

"But what will she do here?" Isela said weakly. "I can't imagine her playing happy hausfrau while Gregor runs around all day killing things for you to summon up later."

"Is that how we operate?" Azrael pinched her chin before sighing. "That's up to her now. Her soul is her own again—unless she chooses to serve another."

Isela turned her eyes on him and for the first time wondered at his expression. "You?"

"I doubt it." Azrael shrugged. "But you might consider adding an actual warrior to your council."

"What, a phoenix, a scientist, and a spider aren't enough?" She grinned.

Azrael drawled, "You are awash in academics and librarians."

She paused, torn between continuing their playful banter and responding to the darkness behind his gaze. A new thing, but worrying. Best to confront it head-on.

"Azrael, you didn't think I objected to Gregor bringing her here for any other reason, did you?"

He went still, and the darkness flared once behind his eyes then receded.

"That I was… jealous?"

His eyes again filled with the bright, affectionate glow she was still getting used to. "Gregor is connected to your family in ways I still do not fully understand," Azrael said, running his fingers along her hairline. "Which I suppose he will reveal to us both in his time. But no, I do not fear it."

Isela frowned at his calm, even tone. She could not forget the darkness now that she had seen it. She thought of his new power and the fractious effect a change in abilities had on necromancers.

"Good." Isela made herself grin, refusing to worry about something in the distance. Correction: something *else*. For tonight they had one another and all the time in the world. She pressed her mouth to the furred skin below his navel. "Now then, where were we, *my lord*?"

"Master?" Azrael teased.

"Keep dreaming, death dealer."

If you enjoyed The Talon & the Blade, check out the rest of the Grace Bloods series at www.jasminesilvera.com/books

GLOSSARY

Aedis—Secret room used by witches and necromancers to cast spells and protect magical objects.

Aegis—The warriors designated by a necromancer to provide protection and loyalty in exchange for immortality.

Allegiance of Necromancers—The eight most powerful necromancers in the world divided the world into territories and rule each.

Geas—Spell or compulsion used by necromancers/witches.

Gods—Powerful entities that evolved out of their physical forms and began to interfere with the humans, mistaken for human deities. In mixing with humans they gave birth to necromancers and witches.

Godswar—Conflict brought by humans who learned to manipulate the power of gods through dance. Ended by the Allegiance of Necromancers.

Godsdancers—Humans trained to dance in specific choreography to manipulate the power of gods for human benefit/gain. Regulated closely by the Allegiance following the godswar.

Grace bloods (grace blooded)—All supernatural creatures descended from the gods intermingling with the mortal world. Necromancers and witches are their direct descendants.

Necromancers—Offspring of gods and humans, capable of raising, commanding, and communicating with the dead. Each identifies with a specific classical element (fire, water, air, earth) and have unique abilities.

Praha Dance Academy (the Academy)—A necromancer-sanctioned school for teaching humans how to dance for gods.

Prague coven—First openly practicing witch coven in the post-godswar world.

Undead—The formal name for humans turned into servants for necromancers in exchange for extended lifespans. Turning can also be used as punishment for crimes committed. Derogatorily referred to as zombies.

Wards—Spells for protection placed on objects or persons used by necromancers/witches. These can be used to keep energy in or out.

Witches—Offspring of gods and humans, capable of raising, commanding, and communicating with the energies of living things.

Vogel pack—Markus, Tobias, and Christof Vogel in their wolf forms.

Zombies—see undead

ACKNOWLEDGMENTS

I've decided that whenever I need reassurance that we live in a kind universe conspiring to help us achieve our goals, I'll set out to write another book. The usual suspects were out in force for this one, along with a series of fortuitous coincidences, connections, and the incredible staff of the Seattle Public Library, who are a godsend to an author who turned up repeatedly with big ideas, rudimentary research acumen, and a very busy four-year-old in tow.

I am extraordinarily grateful to Bethany Robinson, who saw clear to the heart of the story I was trying to tell and left an impeccable (and occasionally hilarious) trail of comments to help me find my way there. To Beth Green, Eva Moore, Neile Graham, Esha, Oliver, and Mama Silvera for being in the inner circle of cheerleaders, drill sergeants, and fairy godparents. To Eilis Flynn for consulting on Japanese language used in the book—any remaining errors are mine. To Jo Bryant for spiriting me away to Lopez Island to help me find the focus needed make it to the finish line. To my fellow members of GSRWA who patiently listened to my ranting over titles and offered helpful suggestions, and Clarion West for ongoing support of their volunteers and alumni. As always, gratitude to Damonza, Victory Editing, and Vellum for making the book in your hands so beautiful.

Finally, this book wouldn't be what it is without the readers of *Death's Dancer* and *Dancer's Flame*, who confirmed enthusiastically that finding out what makes Gregor tick was a story worth reading. This is for you.

ABOUT THE AUTHOR

Jasmine Silvera spent her impressionable years sneaking "kissing books" between comics and fantasy movies. She's been mixing them up in her writing ever since. A semi-retired yoga teacher and amateur dancer, she lives in the Pacific Northwest with her partner-in-crime and their small, opinionated, human charge.

Connect with Jasmine at www.JasmineSilvera.com or on Facebook at www.facebook.com/JasSilvera/

THANKS FOR READING

Reviews help other readers find their next favorite book. Please consider leaving a review on Amazon, Goodreads or your favorite source for book recommendations.

* * *

Interested in more Grace Bloods? Be the first to find out about new releases by subscribing to the mailing list at www. jasminesilvera.com where you can also find deleted scenes, extras, and other goodies!

CPSIA information can be obtained
at www.ICGtesting.com
Printed in the USA
LVHW111738011019
632855LV00003B/584/P